The Failover File

The
Failover
File

Al Haggerty

Uncial Press
Aloha, Oregon
2017

This is a work of fiction. Names, characters, places and events described herein are products of the author's imagination or are used fictitiously and are not to be construed as real. Any resemblance to actual events, locations, organizations, or persons, living or dead, is entirely coincidental.

The Failover File
Copyright © 2017 by Alan E. Haggerty

Published by Uncial Press, an imprint of GCT, Inc.
Visit us at http://www.uncialpress.com

ISBN-13: 978-0-692-83877-8

Book Production by Flying Pig Media with ProEbookFormatting

For Patricia

prologue

It started in the dark.

The controller on duty saw the jet's lights at the end of the runway and keyed his microphone. "November two-one-five echo sierra, Peterson Tower, cleared for takeoff, runway one-seven left."

The pilot acknowledged the clearance, took one last look around the cockpit and smoothly advanced the thrust levers to takeoff power. The aircraft surged down the runway in the darkness, splashing sheets of water off the rain-soaked concrete as it gathered speed.

The pilot smiled to himself, delighted with the power of the pristine new business jet. The ship had been in service less than one hundred flight hours since leaving the factory. It was gloriously modern, with every safety feature and performance to spare. And it still smelled like a new car.

The twin fanjet engines at the rear of the fuselage gave a muted roar under precise computer control while the nose wheel tracked the runway centerline perfectly, the plane's course held by inputs from the automated flight management system in the ship's tail section.

The young copilot called out rapidly increasing speeds while lightning flashed in the distance. A thunderstorm had passed to the south of the field fifteen minutes before, but a climbing left turn would clear the storm easily. The pilot felt a gust of wind rock the wings as the plane accelerated through a hundred knots but a light touch on a rudder pedal held the ship on the runway centerline.

The copilot called out liftoff speed and the pilot eased the control yoke backward slightly. The long, pointed nose of the business jet lifted, rotating the racing aircraft back on its main landing gear. Lift swelled beneath the long, sharply swept wings. The pilot grinned to himself again as that magic moment came when the wheels grew light on the runway and the airplane gathered itself to fly.

A second after the wheels broke free of the ground the pilot knew something was not right. The aircraft's nose continued to rise rapidly past the pitch angle the pilot had commanded, and he pressed forward on the yoke to counteract the motion. Turbulence, he thought.

But the nose kept rising toward the dark clouds that hovered just above the ground, and the air was smooth.

The pilot shifted his vision from the outside world to the instrument panel, scanning the electronic flight control screens as the glow of the runway and city lights faded to cloudy blackness. A glance at the attitude indicator confirmed that the nose was continuing to rise dangerously. He increased his forward pressure on the control yoke, the first tinges of fear beginning to enter his consciousness. He knew this could not be happening, but it was.

The nose continued up through fifty degrees from the horizontal, and the pilot saw that the plane had ceased to accelerate. It hung briefly at a safe speed before beginning to slow because of the extreme nose-up attitude. He was now pushing so hard on the yoke that his hands were white. His breathing labored from the strain, but there was still no decrease in the aircraft's uncontrolled rise.

The copilot stirred in his seat, watching the instrument displays in confusion. "What the hell?"

"I know, dammit. I'm pushing." The pilot now felt an icy wave of terror wash over him. This would not end well.

They watched helplessly, nearly lying on their backs in their seats now while the plane's nose pitched past seventy degrees above the horizon and the airspeed dropped below eighty knots. The yoke pulsated in the pilot's hands as the stick-shaker warned him of an impending stall.

Years of experience and flight training told him not to give up. He turned the control yoke hard left. If he worked fast enough, the unwanted pitching might be converted into a turn, and the high climb angle could be wrestled down with rudder control.

But the pilot could tell from the aircraft's drunken response that he was too late. The aircraft was unable to continue its steep climb as gravity won out over lift and engine thrust. It gave a hard shake and rolled drunkenly to the right. The nose began to fall now, the wings fully stalled, lift gone.

He felt a sickening sensation of falling and spinning in the pit of his stomach as the aircraft tumbled out of control. Dirt rose up from the carpet and into his eyes.

The copilot grabbed instinctively at his shoulder straps. He had to swat with one hand at a ballpoint pen as it rose off the center console and attacked his face like a hornet.

Both men struggled to bring the aircraft back under control, but it was no use. The uncontrollable motions continued, and the pilot watched in horror as the plane spun completely inverted and beyond.

"Shit," the pilot shouted. "Oh, no."

In the rear cabin, the lone passenger grabbed at his laptop as it tried to rise off the solid walnut table in front of him. He ducked as a crystal tumbler of excellent scotch flew past his head, spewing the thirty-year-old liquid and a few ice cubes as it passed. The heavy glass rolled for a second on the ceiling, and then made a second pass at his head on its way to the floor. He felt himself surge upward against his seat belt. Fear and his abused sense of balance sent a blast of nausea through him.

J. Wesley Corso, Captain of Industry, Arbitrageur, Magnate, did not expect such gyrations from his private jets. His surprise and fear were overruled by anger at such unacceptable behavior from his hired help. He was reaching for the intercom handset to call the cockpit when the lights of the airport came into view again through the cabin window at his side, whirling crazily past the airplane's wing tip.

Corso did not have time to react to the sight of the airport's blue and white lights as they raced up to meet him. He did, however, briefly recognize the fact that he was going to die. The beginnings of a scream formed in his throat.

An instant later, the hurtling jet smashed into the ground belly-first near the airport perimeter and was engulfed in a mass of flames.

chapter

1

My name is Michael Francis O'Hara. I am an engineer.

I read a poem once, in high school. It was written by a dead Englishman sometime before the invention of the integrated circuit, and it went on at length about a small piece of pottery. The poet said that in beauty one could find truth, and in truth, beauty.

I didn't get much out of this. Truth is not an absolute, at least not in Washington DC. I work in my nation's capital, and in DC the truth is often adjusted or recalibrated to fit a situation.

You can't adjust physics for your own convenience, though. An engineer tries to build a perfect system, to achieve a sort of truth or beauty in perfection: Perfect reliability, or perfect safety, or whatever.

Of course, engineers work in the physical world, and our products are never really perfect. The reliability or safety of a machine made by human hands is always finite, no matter how much time or money is spent on its creation. When the limits of safety or reliability are exceeded, society demands to learn causes and place blame.

I work for the National Transportation Safety Board, and my job is to do those things.

I did nine years out of college on active duty as an officer in the Navy. I signed up for Navy flight school because I thought women would be impressed. It turned out they weren't, or at least not that I noticed.

The Navy gave me two tests when I got to flight school, one for technical aptitude and one for vision. I got the highest score ever recorded in the technical test, but my right eye was 20/35. They had plenty of pilots at the time, so instead of being a Naval Aviator I was designated a Naval Flight Officer, or navigator. I was sent to radar intercept control school and into the back of a Hawkeye airborne radar plane. The pilots in the front seats looked out large windows and got the glory while I chased green dots around a radar screen in a dark cabin and told people in other planes where to go. That's life, I guess. My life.

As a part of my regular squadron duties I was sent to crash investigator training. After a full tour on sea duty I was assigned to the Navy's postgraduate school, where I took a master's degree in engineering physics. People were impressed, but it seemed pretty easy to me. I graduated summa cum laude and gained eight pounds.

A guy I knew a couple of classes ahead of me was selected by NASA to be an astronaut and said I should give it a try. To my surprise I got picked up for that, too, but after my second week in Houston the head of the astronaut office took me aside. There had been a massive budget cut and I should not expect to fly in space for the next century. So much for NASA. Things happen, I guess.

I saw an opening for an investigator advertised at the National Transportation Safety Board and applied, showing them my degree and background. It turned out the NTSB knew who I was and after a day of interviews I was offered a position. I left the astronaut office the next month. To my slightly guilty satisfaction none of the others in my astronaut class at NASA had flown in space the last time I checked.

I have not led a completely blameless life. I was ticketed for stopping my car on the Memorial Bridge leaving DC one hot July midnight, and I received a traffic conviction from the State of Virginia for reckless driving.

I'd had been forced to stop there so I could throw an unneeded engagement ring in the Potomac River and the police had taken exception. I pled nolo contendere. It screwed up my car insurance for a while, but it was worth it.

I had been with the NTSB for six years when I flew south to Colorado Springs. My aptitude for technical things was a blessing and a curse. I had an interesting job with steady pay. But I was on the road all the time, living out of a suitcase, smelling like burned jet fuel and unable to keep a relationship or a goldfish alive. I had gone through life like an electron in a wire, following the path of least resistance and repelling others. I was thirty-five years old, and all my close friends were machines.

"It's not damaged too bad but it's totally burned out. They must have stalled and spun in." The pilot had turned to talk to me as I sat alone in the rear passenger cabin. The landscape reflected in his mirror-finish sunglasses while he pointed out Peterson Field in the distance. We were beginning a descent into the airport, still a few miles away but easily visible in the impossibly clear western air that had followed the previous night's cold front.

I nodded and yawned as Colorado slid past the window of the Cessna. I was alone in the back of a Caravan turboprop that belonged to the Colorado state government. I'd scammed a ride down from Denver

International Airport to Petersen Field in Colorado Springs and had almost an hour to sleep, but the bright sun and low-altitude turbulence kept me awake. I looked at my shoes six feet away and moved them in a circle to keep blood flowing.

It was noon on a bright day in late September. I stretched again in my seat, fighting the fatigue that had been hammering at my forehead since my phone had rung two time zones in the past.

The call had startled me awake in my bachelor apartment in suburban Virginia, just outside the Washington beltway. My boss, the head of the NTSB's aviation incident response unit, or Go-Team, was calling from New Orleans, where he was investigating the spectacular failure of a huge natural gas pipeline where it crossed the Mississippi River. He had worked a pipeline job somewhere in the past, and was on loan for that investigation.

"Get out there as fast as you can," he'd said. "I'll be stuck here for three or four more days at least. A business jet crashed on the airport at Colorado Springs. Three fatalities. You handle the show, Mike. You're in charge. You've got enough experience now. It'll be a good one for you to go solo on."

I took notes as he rapped out instructions. Five hours later I boarded a United 787 at Dulles International Airport for the flight to Denver. The heavy jet was climbing through choppy turbulence over southern Ohio before I realized that I had just been promoted to a higher level of responsibility. But not pay.

The Cessna's pilot had been cleared by Peterson Field's controller for a pass over the crash impact zone in the airport's far-southeast corner. We descended to eight hundred feet above the ground and flew the length of the runway so I could get a clear look at the wreckage from the air. I snapped several pictures with my phone, and then took the last few seconds before we entered the normal landing pattern to memorize the local terrain and the layout of the wreckage.

What was left of the Aries GlobalMax business jet sat in the dirt just off the end of runway one-seven left. It was two hundred yards past the end of the pavement and to the right of the centerline of the two-mile-long runway. A wide skid mark slashed through the dry native grass for fifty yards, leading from an area of disturbed earth and small bits of wreckage where the initial impact had probably occurred, pointing to the wreckage itself like a big arrow stamped in the scrub.

The wreckage was still obviously the remains of an airplane, burned and broken but nearly intact, and the tail assembly stood tall above the rest of the wreckage. The inner two-thirds of the wings and much of the fuselage were burned black and a rough area of blackened vegetation surrounded the wreck.

The cockpit area had smashed into a small outbuilding of some sort as the plane slid across the ground. The nose section was crushed back to the first row of cabin windows. The pilots had died quickly, I thought to myself.

We circled back to land in the same direction as the GlobalMax's fatal takeoff. The pilot turned off the runway at its end and onto a taxiway that led near the wreckage. He braked to a stop and slowed the engine to idle.

"Close as I can take you," he called back over his shoulder.

I grabbed my bag of gear, opened the cabin door and jumped down into the prop wash, noise and cool mountain air. As soon as I was clear, the Cessna taxied away, and I had to shield my eyes from the dust blown up by the prop wash. I stood there holding my bag beside the taxiway like a hitchhiker dropped off on a lonely roadside.

The scene was less crowded than the aftermath of an airliner crash would be. An airliner meant more bodies, more grieving loved ones, more lawyers, more press.

A hundred yards away I could see a gray airport sedan, a state police car with its roof lights flashing blue and white, and a large white van. All three were parked at random angles, arrayed around the wreckage at a respectful distance from the wreckage. Two people were speaking to each other while other individuals poked at the remains of the plane.

I skirted the impact area I had seen from the air and followed the skid path toward the wreck. A heavy vehicle of some sort, probably a fire truck, had driven over the path more than once sometime during the night.

The impact area and skid path told me things as I walked past. Impact had left an oval depression about five by twenty feet, oriented along the same direction as the skid. Farther on, flanking the skid mark about twenty-five feet on either side, were two deep scars. Just past the two marks, the main path became indistinct for twenty yards.

A picture of the impact began form in my mind like an incomplete puzzle. I had seen a lot of pictures like this, and I knew when enough puzzle pieces showed up, they would snap together in my head to let me imagine what the crash looked like as it happened.

From what I saw, impact must have been very hard and at a low forward speed. As the investigation shaped up, my team would have to analyze the geometry of the marks on the ground to determine exactly how the GlobalMax hit the ground, but dirt didn't lie. For now, I needed more pieces.

I snapped another picture and dropped my gear next to the airport sedan as I walked toward the two men I had seen when I arrived. One man, a tall, trim figure in a state police uniform, held back slightly. The other, a civilian in a short-sleeved white shirt, held out a hand as he eyed my NTSB ball cap.

He looked me up and down with a quizzical expression. "Are you Lew Hills?"

"Ah, no," I answered. My boss was a legend in the crash investigation business, known by aviation authorities from Afghanistan to El Paso County, Colorado. "I'm Mike O'Hara from the DC office. Lew's in New Orleans on another job. I'll be handling this one."

He shrugged, containing his disappointment. He introduced himself as Joe Gilles from Colorado Transportation, and pointed to the wreckage. "One of your guys is already here."

I had seen one figure in the distance with a ball cap like the one I wore, and guessed he was from the Denver field office.

"There'll be one more guy coming in from Washington," I said. "Not sure who. I haven't been in the office for three weeks, so I don't know who's on call. I'd like to get a look at the wreckage myself. What do we know about the accident?" I pulled a notebook and mechanical pencil from my pocket. I am mostly old school and have not fully mind-melded with digital equipment.

"The wreckage is cool," he said. "There was a hell of a fire, but the fire department guys had it out in about five minutes."

"Who'd the plane belong to?"

"A company called ZYCO. Z-Y-C-O. They're a big employer in this area. Big money, too. Something high tech. Software, I think. Their world headquarters is here in town. We think the passenger was the CEO of the firm. His name was on the passenger manifest. A couple of ZYCO guys were here at about dawn and then left."

I excused myself and walked to the remains of the business jet. A heavy smell of kerosene, scorched earth and a touch of burned flesh filled the still air.

Ten yards from the wreckage I stopped and surveyed the scene, trying to take it all in at once. The small orange-and-white sheet-metal outbuilding it had hit was destroyed, wrapped around the mangled nose.

I read what the crushed metal of the wreckage looked like. All the plane's Plexiglas windows had melted in the fire, leaving gaping holes on both sides of what remained of the cabin, but the gracefully pointed tube of the fuselage was mostly intact. The nose was deformed a little by impact with the building, but of the rest, only the bottom of the tube was crushed and deformed by impact. There were deep dented scrapes on the bottoms of the wingtips. The impact had smashed the wheel struts upward into the tops of the wings leaving large irregular bulges.

I stood for a second to let the puzzle click together. The shape of the scrapes and length of the pattern on the ground confirmed that the plane had dropped steeply to Earth at low forward speed, probably less than 75 knots. It was nearly level when it hit. The nose was not smashed by ground impact, judging by the angle of crushing I could see. It hit hard enough that the wings flexed down, and their tips had gouged the ground alongside the skid mark from the fuselage. The wheels were still down at impact. It had all happened so quickly that the pilots hadn't had time to retract them after takeoff.

The puzzle formed itself into a picture in my head with an almost-audible click. A normal takeoff, followed immediately by something that made the plane go out of control. Next came impact, leaving a smear of gouged ground and scattered bits of airplane junk. Then fire and death. I could visualize the plane dropping out of the clouds and sliding to a stop in front of me. We would squeeze more details out of the rest of the data, but that was the picture the dirt gave me. My goal from that point on was the find out why, to fit any other parts of the puzzle we found into the picture.

Three figures came around the smashed nose section, one in a blue NTSB cap like the one I wore, the others dressed in paramedics' uniforms. The medics headed for the white van, and the third man walked to meet me, wiping his hands on a rag.

The NTSB man pulled down his surgical mask

and removed his rubber gloves, jamming them in his belt. I recognized him as Steve Penney, a GS-12 from Denver. I knew Penney vaguely from other jobs, but I couldn't remember which one. He was usually on call for the Western region.

"Where's Big Lew?" he asked as we shook hands. I mumbled another explanation about the boss's absence and introduced myself. He looked disappointed, too, and not too happy to have a guy from DC looking over his shoulder.

I looked into his eyes and saw heavy fatigue. "Been here all night?"

"Most of it. I drove down from Denver and got here at 3:00 a.m." He yawned and stretched. "I photographed the site after dawn." His speech was the typical short staccato of an official in charge, tired, puzzled and trying to get the effort organized and moving. "I was just helping the medical examiner's people get the passenger's body ready to move." He looked at me. "You're going to run the show?"

"Yes, Lew put me in charge. I'll handle the accident file."

He inhaled heavily, crossed his arms across his chest and looked at the ground. "What do you know so far?"

"What the State Department of Transportation guy told me." I summarized briefly.

"You have that much about right. They were cleared for takeoff at twenty-two-eighteen hours local, on an instrument flight plan, non-stop to Paris."

"France or Texas?"

Penney gave a thin smile. "France. They rolled normally, and lifted off about where they should have according to the witnesses. Observers said they climbed pretty fast into the overcast. Ceiling was measured about three hundred feet, and these things climb like crazy, even here." He motioned toward the plane. "The next thing anybody saw was the aircraft's lights coming back out of the clouds a few seconds later, with the nose about level in pitch. I expect the wings were fully stalled. The left wing was a little low, rolling right and descending almost vertically."

"Hmm. Any reports of unusual engine noises, or compressor stalls, that sort of thing?" A malfunctioning jet engine could emit loud bangs that could be heard from a long distance.

Penney shook his head. "No. The pilot waiting to take off said he heard the ship's engines above his own. He said the jet sounded normal, right up to impact. I haven't heard anybody report anything else, either."

I considered the information for a second. "Doesn't seem too likely to me that the crew would just screw up a takeoff that badly."

"We'll have to check out their qualifications, but

yeah, you're right." He hesitated. "There's one other thing. I know I may have been jumping the gun, but I called Aries, in France--the company that builds these things. I met their chief engineer a couple months ago at a conference in Washington. He went crazy when I told him about the crash. He yelled at me in French for about thirty seconds, and then he said this really weird thing."

Penney's eyes narrowed, and his voice became quiet, almost a whisper. "He said, 'That is not possible.' He was absolutely freaked out, almost panicked. At first he just denied that it happened. Then he calmed down and said that Aries had designed the flight control system to not allow the airplane to act like that, and ZYCO must have made a mistake on the control software."

I looked at him with a question.

"Yeah, the plane's owner, ZYCO, built the flight control software."

I nodded in understanding. "Nice. We haven't found the problem yet and they are already trying to finger the other guys." I ran the scenario again in my mind. "Maybe the witnesses are wrong about the engines."

"No. The engines look like they were running OK at impact. They sucked in lots of dirt and brush when the plane hit the ground, and the brush in the combustors is burned. I reached in and got some." Penny pointed to grime on a sweatshirt sleeve. "You'd need to be at full power to get that kind of scorching." I agreed with him.

"Um, how about thrust reversers? Maybe they opened them accidentally."

"No. No, that's the whole point. The chief engineer said it couldn't happen. I asked about that. He said that the flight control system watches everything-- control inputs, engine conditions, air data, speed, altitude, everything. The computers are in charge and they won't allow the pilot to do anything to put the airplane in danger. Even if the engines quit cold or went into reverse, the airplane would level itself out and just glide down. This thing looks like it was totally outside the controlled flight envelope. They shouldn't have been able to screw things up that badly. He called it 'pilot proof.'"

I frowned. "'Pilot proof.' Interesting choice of words."

"Yeah." He didn't sound amused. "He said the only way to crash this airplane is to run it into terrain, and even that can be programmed out of the autopilot." He stopped and squinted into the sun, stretching his back, fighting fatigue. "These airplanes are getting too damned complicated. You have to be smarter than the equipment to be safe. That's what I always thought."

I heard a car approach. I turned and saw a block-long Mercedes-Benz sedan slowing to a halt just a few feet from the wreckage, straddling the skid path. I swore under my breath for not getting the area cordoned off and waved the police officer over. He walked past the Mercedes and I spoke as soon as he was in earshot.

"Sergeant, could you get some crime scene tape or something up around the wreckage to keep everybody out? Right away, please." He nodded and headed for his car. "And keep everybody off the big skid mark in the dirt until we can examine it," I shouted after him. He waved over his shoulder as he left.

The driver-side door of the Mercedes opened and a silver-haired man stepped out, looking around importantly. He was athletically slim, a little taller than me, had a hundred dollar haircut, and wore Italian-looking shoes that must have cost five hundred bucks. He looked like he had paid so much for his suit they could have hired a new Brooks Brother. Mr. Big, I guessed, come to kick butt and get results.

I was suddenly very aware that I had dressed before waking fully, and that my cotton trousers probably should have been laundered before being worn again.

I was put back at ease by the figure that got out of the passenger side of the Merc. He was younger than the driver, of medium height, painfully thin through the shoulders and running to fat elsewhere. His cotton pants looked worse than mine and his dress shirt was open at the collar. A thick brush of dirty-brown hair hung over his forehead, and he wore thick glasses and a vaguely distracted expression. His face was familiar, like I had seen him before, but I couldn't place him. He stood beside the car and looked the wreckage over, showing no sign of a reaction to the destruction.

The Brooks Brothers suit walked toward me, glancing at the medics as they carried equipment past us to the plane.

"Are you in charge here?" He fixed me with an Ivy League stare.

I stared back. "Yes." A weak breeze stirred the scrub brush around us while I silently looked up the car's path and then back at the Brooks Brother. "You just drove your car through my evidence field." It wasn't an attack, just a fact and a mild assertion of authority.

It worked. He immediately backed down a step and made a perfunctory apology.

"You'll need to back out and try not to go over anything."

"Certainly. Of course." He paused and then spoke, more politely this time. "May I ask your name?"

"My name is O'Hara. I just got in from NTSB headquarters in Washington." I pointed at Steve Penney. "That is Mr. Penney from our Denver field office, who has been working the case before my arrival. May I have your name please?"

He cleared his throat. "Harrison Randall. I'm chief financial officer of ZYCO. I take it you don't know what caused the crash yet." He looked over at the crash.

"No. Right now we're getting the bodies out of the plane."

Randall's face changed a little, moving from tension and anger to something else that I couldn't read. "I'm sorry. Of course, I'm sure you're doing everything you can. Mr. Corso was a friend, you see. This is all a terrible shock."

"Sure, I can imagine. Corso was the passenger?"

"Oh, yes. He was going to Paris to consult on future business with Aries--the company that built the airplane--as a matter of fact. Terrible..." He shook his head, and allowed himself to look a little less in control. It made him seem slightly more human to me, and he was obviously disturbed by the death so close to him. People usually were, even kings of the world. Different people had different ways of handling such things, and I'd seen them all.

"We'll do our best to find the cause, and you'll be informed about what we find." I cleared my throat. "Could I ask you to move your car now?"

He was in the process of apologizing again when his casually dressed companion called to me. "Do you have his body?"

Where had I seen him? "The passenger?"

"Wes Corso's, I mean." Mr. Casual pointed to the M.E. van.

"The body from the passenger cabin is being

removed now," I said. "The medical examiner will have to identify it."

His face showed an odd mixture of sorrow and impatience. "OK, OK." He shifted his attention to Randall. "C'mon, Harry. Let's get out of here and let them work." He turned back to me. "Sorry to interrupt you."

He abruptly opened the car door and got back into the Mercedes without waiting for an answer. Randall turned back to me and reached into a pocket of his perfectly cut suit jacket, pulling out a business card. "My personal numbers are on this. Please let me know how it's going, if you can. The company is ready to help you, of course. If you need any assistance at all, please call me direct. Twenty-four hours a day."

Before I could answer, he turned and walked briskly back to the car, entering and closing the door in one quick movement. Randall backed the Mercedes slowly several yards away from the wreckage before turning around and driving back onto the taxiway. The state trooper saluted the car as it passed.

I slipped the business card in my pocket, noticing the heavy embossed paper's satin smooth finish.

As the car departed Steve Penney walked up behind me. "Wow. Royalty."

"Who? Them?"

"Yeah," Penney said. "That was the Boss."

I felt for the card in my pocket. "He said his name was Randall."

"No, the other guy. That was Eric Zygler. One of the richest men on Earth. Top hundred anyway. He used to own ZYCO, before they went public. I think he's their Chairman of the Board or something now."

That was it. I'd seen him online and on magazine covers, including that morning while walking past a newsstand in the Denver airport terminal. He was famous all over the world for being the smartest, nerdiest--and richest--of all technology entrepreneurs. He was the personification of the modern geek/billionaire/celebrity.

I watched the limo disappear in the distance.

2

The paramedics entered the cabin and removed the passenger's body while we watched. They had to wrestle their stretcher on its side through the cabin door, and both swore loudly as they maneuvered the load back out, a plastic body bag strapped in with nylon bungees. The passenger's body was the easy one. The EMTs wanted to get the pilots' bodies out of the cockpit and turned over to the medical examiner for autopsy as fast as possible--the day was getting hot fast--without damaging any evidence.

I had been deliberately avoiding looking at the cockpit where the pilot's bodies were mixed forcibly into smashed metal and other airplane bits. Memories of my first investigation came to my mind. Pulling the burned corpses of my commanding officer and my best friend from a crashed Hawkeye radar plane were still fresh. When the dead were strangers it eased the strain a little, but not enough. Seeing the bodies would add nothing to my investigation, anyway. That's what I told myself.

Penney was in the van, working over a notebook computer. He waved me over and I left the wreckage, trying not to look relieved.

"Stuff's starting to come in," he said. "I got some information for you'll want to see from the FAA. Big files. And there's a long email you'll want to see, too. I just forwarded everything. I had to stop and file stuff to keep my inbox working." He sounded annoyed.

I asked him to forward anything else he got.

Penney hit send again, before walking back to the wreckage to survey progress while I retrieved my computer and booted up.

What started arriving in my inbox was the first of hundreds of megabytes of licenses, data, reports, documentation, and what seemed like a million other possibly useless bits of information. It would all have to be read, digested, vetted, filed, cross-referenced, passed up and down the chain of command, and somehow woven into the investigation. By me. This was the biggest pain-in-the-butt part of the business, but it had to be done. I took a deep breath, prepared myself and dove in.

The first files in the folder were summaries of the two pilots' backgrounds. The pilot, John Fleet, age thirty-six and married, ex-Air Force officer. His training records were in order and he ticked all the boxes for experience and ability. The copilot's name was William Berry and his paperwork all checked out, too. He was younger than Fleet and a bachelor. No military time. Both pilots had perfect flying records and held appropriate medical certificates. In fact, there was nothing remarkable about the reports on either.

Behind the pilot biographies was one on Corso, with a ZYCO logo at the top.

Mr. J. Wesley Corso was fifty-one years of age at the time of his death. He had been CEO of ZYCO for thirty-five months, starting a year before the company went public, and he had worked for three different commercial money-moving firms since graduating from Harvard Business School in his twenties.

His photograph was included in the file, and I clicked it open. It was taken while he was standing at a lectern somewhere. I always felt a little weird barging into people's lives like this after they were dead, but not weird enough to stop.

Corso was tall and health-club muscular. He looked damned near perfect, with no double chins, eye bags or receding hairline. Cosmetic surgery was pretty common in big-buck executives. He had sandy hair and a perfect tan. He had probably driven women crazy all his life.

A few delicious seconds passed while I hated J. Wesley Corso.

The next files were copies of computer-prepared forms documenting the way the aircraft had been prepared for its flight. All the dispatch paperwork showed that the aircraft was completely prepared to fly the planned mission. The GlobalMax had been filled with just over twenty-thousand pounds of jet fuel. Weight and balance looked OK at takeoff and fuel samples were checked and good. There should have been no problems.

I sat for a moment in the front seat of the van, staring at the horizon. What would Big Lew do next?

Lew Hills was in Louisiana, mucking with backhoes and mud-caked boots, messing with a gas pipeline. Check that, he was probably at a bar, glass of beer in one hand and cigar in the other, preparing to write a report while ogling the waitresses in whatever steak house where he had set up shop. Although over sixty and due for retirement, Lew knew how to live on the road. "A man, a mission and a per diem check, Bubba," he had told me on our first job together. "That's how to get the job done."

The next files were scanned hard copies from Washington, with NTSB headers on the printed sheets.

There was a note attached that said: "Please pass to Mr. O'Hara, NTSB, ASAP. FYI, SM." I didn't know who SM was.

At the front of the folder were scans of the crashed airplane's registration and other official information. There were copies of articles from Aviation Week and other trade publications about the development of the new aircraft. The GMax, as the aviation press referred to it, was the first of a new wave of ultra-long range business jets, meant to meet the needs of top executives of multinational corporations. The plane was built to fly non-stop from New York to Johannesburg, and everything about the new ship was superlative: Structure the strongest and lightest, flight controls the most advanced, price the most stratospheric. Gold plumbing fixtures were an option.

The flight control system got a special write-up in Aerospace America Magazine, hitting the big time for gear nerds. I gathered that there was some controversy about the basic design philosophy, although my postgraduate degree was getting old and withered from lack of use. I had a hard time following some of the details.

The GMax was not the first airplane to be certified with a fly-by-wire control system, I read, but the overall level of automation was unprecedented. Fly-by-wire meant that there was no mechanical connection between the pilots' controls and the airplane's control surfaces or systems. This method saved enormously on weight, allowing a plane to carry extra fuel for long flights. All pilot inputs went directly to computers, which in turn would evaluate the inputs and set controls appropriately. Control surfaces, like ailerons, elevators and rudders, were positioned with electric motors or servos. The computers were also supposed to watch over the pilots and keep them safe. Who watched over the computers? They watched over each other.

All this was normal, state-of-the-practice. But the GMax's French designers wanted to go even further, and to try to assure that a two-pilot crew could fly for ten or twelve hours and arrive safely at a strange airport, landing without the crew's fatigue hurting their performance. Aries was planning to totally computerize control of every system, from primary flight surfaces to engines to air conditioning. Even the flushing system in the john was controlled by a computer. The GMax was designed to fly its missions almost hands-off, to minimize the workload for the crew. The only manual piloting required would be on takeoff and landing. It was basically a cruise missile with leather seats.

The next step would be no crew at all, I thought.

The article ended by saying that Aries had contracted with no less that Eric Zygler, the American king of embedded software systems, to create the software for all those computers. Zygler was fresh from triumphant efforts building control software for Boeing's latest airliner, and for General Electric's newest dishwasher. Zygler and ZYCO would get the project done right. The article noted that both Aries's and ZYCO's stock had gone up on the announcement of the agreement. At the date of the article, there were over 300 GMaxes on order and the planes were selling fast. A note attached to the file said that there were more than forty airplanes actually in service.

Thirty-nine now.

Aries kept the first airplane for company use, and ZYCO got the next two, serial numbers 002--the burned out hulk a few steps away--and 003.

I started to put the laptop in my bag, but spotted a new email. I didn't recognize the sender's name. The message read: "I am bringing FBI Special Agent George Tidings along at the request of the Chairman and L. Hills. Will arrive with the gear and a car about three PM." It was signed "Sally."

I wondered who Sally was. I knew that Lew had been interviewing applicants for over a year to fill a GS-11/12 investigator opening on the team as my assistant. He'd said he was being extra careful, taking his time to avoid making the same colossal screw-up he'd made when he hired me. He made that point loudly to me whenever anyone else was in earshot. I assumed he had hired someone in the last three weeks, while I had been in Alaska, crawling in cold mud under defective school buses, helping out the board's ground transportation office.

Sally. She would turn out to be an ex-Marine women's hand-to-hand combat instructor, I was sure. I hoped I wouldn't have to explain too much.

I looked up the number where Lew was staying and punched in his number. After three rings, he answered.

"Hey, Bubba. Where the hell are you?" He sounded cheerful but tired.

"Colorado Springs, boss. We're just getting things going here."

"Got everything you need?"

"Not yet. Steve Penney is here from Denver."

"He knows his stuff." His voice faded a little, and I couldn't tell whether it was him or the phone.

"Another staffer is coming from Washington," I said. "She'll be here this afternoon. I guess you hired her while I was out."

Lew gave a little laugh. "Yeah. Sally Montez. Great application. Gave a good interview. Ex-Air Force. Experienced as hell. I decided to make the offer on the spot. I've been looking long enough. Oh, and I didn't get a chance to tell you, The FBI is sending George Tidings out. Gotta make the Bureau feel important."

"I heard. He'll be here today." Tidings was the FBI's designated hitter for crash investigations, and I'd worked with him several times on other cases. I knew him well enough to gather that this wasn't a plum assignment for an agent. No shootouts or car chases, and most of our investigations didn't have a criminal angle. The FBI didn't always send somebody, but they had the option to show up when they wanted. Like most agents, Tidings lived in a world built around the Bureau. His thought processes ran to legalities and kicking in doors with guns drawn instead of physics or technical matters. Sometimes it was good to have him there and sometimes it wasn't.

I told Lew that Steve Penney had called France, and described the chief engineer's extreme reaction. "Engineers always freak out when they discover their products can kill people," he said. "Watch that angle, but work the wreckage." Lew coughed a wet-sounding spasm into the phone.

"Uh, boss, are you going to come out here after you wrap up that job?"

He wheezed in my ear. "Nah, I don't think so. You can handle it OK, Mike. Just use your instincts. If you get hung up, remember that once you eliminate all the bullshit, you have to fit what's left together. That will give you an answer, even if it looks wrong. You have to answer all the questions in your mind, not just the easy ones. Call me or the Chairman if you need anything." He coughed again. "I'm feeling a little under the weather. Gonna head home and get some rest."

"Hung over?"

"Must be. So, what do you have?"

I briefed him on all I knew. He listened silently, and I had to pause several times, waiting for a response to be sure he was still there.

Finally, he responded. "Bet that's an interesting one, Bubba. What's your plan?"

I hated oral exams but I had been preparing for this one. "Aside from the fire damage, the wreckage is pretty good shape. I'll want to do as much mechanical examination as I can without moving anything. The weather's good and there's not too much press interest yet."

"The sharks will be there, don't worry." Lew said grimly.

"I'll look for mechanical failures, engines, that sort of thing, but the way it came down, I'd say they had to be loaded wrong, or something. Even though the dispatch information says it was OK, there had to have been some problem like that."

Lew wheezed again. "You won't find a broken whatever or something obvious to cause things. The paperwork is probably right. I bet some digit-head got a bit jammed in sideways in that super-whammodyne control system. Call for help if you need it. The chairman can get you experts if you ask for 'em."

He sighed. "This shit's getting too complicated

for me, Mike." He sounded very tired, now. I could hear a long, hard drag on a cigar, followed by another cough. "Keep the chairman informed, Ace. Gonna be lots of outside interest on the case, because of this guy Corso. ZYCO's a big deal in the aerospace industry. Cars, everything else, too. Don't let the boss get blindsided."

I thanked Lew and he clicked off.

Penney and the firefighters had used a set of hydraulic jaws to bend the crumpled nose section off the cockpit, revealing the bodies of the two pilots. Both were burned heavily except for their legs below the knees. Lower trouser legs were untouched, contrasting sharply with the charred fabric above. Fleet had worn expensive-looking boots.

"Their legs were trapped under the control panel when it collapsed," Penney remarked. "The fire department got the fire out so fast it didn't spread down there."

I found a reason to go aft, to look in the electronics compartment I remembered was located under the tail between the engines. The bodies didn't really bother me, of course. It was just that I was more of a technology guy. I could contribute to the effort more this way.

Before ducking under the tail cone, I gave the right engine pylon a hard shove, to check for structural damage. I didn't want the back half of the airplane falling on me while I poked around in the rear bay. The structure still seemed solid enough.

I dropped to my hands and knees and crawled under the tail cone. I had to lie on my back to get close enough to reach the access door. The door responded easily to a borrowed screwdriver and fell open to reveal the darkened cavity behind it. I flicked on my flashlight to check for head knockers, and then pulled myself up into a seated position with my head in the space.

Wire bundles all looked undamaged, and snaked into three large flight control computers mounted on the front bulkhead. In the rear corners of the space were the cockpit voice and flight data recorders--the black boxes. Recorders didn't always give you the whole answer, but they would be crucial to the investigation.

I looked around for a few more minutes, searching for burns, loose wires or other obvious signs of trouble. Obvious things killed you just as dead as deep mysteries. There was nothing--the space looked new.

Penney and the medical examiner's men were putting the second pilot's body into the white van when I got back out into the sunshine.

I walked around the right wing to meet him as he returned to the wreckage. "How long until we the medical examiner's report?"

"They said tomorrow for preliminary causes of death. Longer for toxicology. Three, maybe four days."

"Not sure what to expect, but I bet they don't find much," I said.

Penney looked back at me like I was supposed to say more.

I stuck my hands in my pockets. "I'm going to go for a preliminary look at the skid path. Want to come?"

He looked at the wreckage field, shrugged, and matched my hands-in-the pockets stance. "Sure."

We walked to the tail cone and turned our backs to the ship, facing the runway. I pulled a note pad and pencil out of my pocket, and I noticed that Penney had opened up his pad device thing. We walked and both took pictures of anything interesting as we went.

After fifty yards I stopped and took pictures of a landing gear door, bent and dirty with a broken push-rod hanging from one side. I shot another picture and went on. We walked another hundred yards, finding and noting other metal pieces all of which I photographed. When more people arrived I would get the entire area surveyed, but for now our notes would do.

My phone buzzed in my pocket and I took four buzzes to get it out and on.

A feminine and very formal voice came on the line. "Mr. O'Hara, this is Ann in the chairman's office. Please hold for the chairman."

Before I could answer, the formidable Ann put me on hold. I swore again under my breath, wishing I could have called first to make a report. I sighed as I waited.

I didn't know F. Brooks McCall, Chairman of the NTSB, very well. He had been named to head the board only three months before, replacing Jack Strauss, who had held the job for many years.

Chairman McCall had not had an easy time with his congressional confirmation. The President had made a couple of appointments in the Defense Department and at Treasury that had not held up well under pressure, and McCall was perceived as being too close to the President. The two were roommates in college and they had been close friends since. The appointment was denounced as cronyism by the press, and McCall had been questioned for three days in what should have been a routine appointment.

On paper, McCall looked like a good choice. He had been an Air Force fighter pilot, decorated for valor in one war or another. He had left the service and joined a major Texas aerospace firm as a test pilot. He'd eventually become the company's CEO. After being shuffled into early retirement in a merger, McCall had been tapped by the President for the NTSB job. He was not well liked by the career civil servants at the board, mostly since he was replacing Strauss, who had risen up through the ranks. He seemed to handle the load of the job well enough, at least from my worm's eye view. In my limited dealings with him, I had found him tough but smart. He knew how to give direction and make decisions, two talents that not all presidential appointees seemed to have.

The phone clicked. "Mike, Brooks McCall. How's it going, son? Do you have a handle on things?"

"Well, sir, we just got the bodies out of the wreckage. The rest of my team should be arriving in the next hour or so."

"Yep, right. Montez and the FBI's guy. I'm gonna have to keep you pretty thin out there, Mike. We're right at the end of the fiscal year, as you know. Worst possible time, of course, and we've got Lew and that team down in Louisiana, burning operating budget at ten-thousand dollars a day. The comptroller's crawling up my ass back here. He seems to think that I personally crashed all those airplanes this year. I need you to keep a lid on your costs, son. Run it lean and get it done."

There was a short pause, and Penney walked into my field of view, a questioning look on his face. I mouthed the word "Chairman," and he nodded, staying close to pick up intelligence.

"I need to tell you, Mike," McCall went on, "I've gotten calls about this case already. The FBI has some information for you. I think it's crap, but Agent Tidings will fill you in." He paused for a second. "I know you've worked with the Bureau before, but remember that agent and you are there for different reasons. You are trying to figure out what happened and keep it from happening again. He's there to arrest somebody and make a case stick. The difference is that we know there was a crash, but we don't know if there was a crime or not. That's why this is your investigation until you decide they should take it over, OK?"

I assured him I was on it and understood, but wasn't sure how things were going to go with my FBI brother.

The Chairman continued. "The French are very spun up. Their ambassador called me this morning, right after the news about the crash came out. They're worried about their foreign trade numbers and all that, and these airplanes are selling like hotcakes. Or crepes, I guess. Anyway, they want a quick answer. I have never talked to an ambassador when I wasn't half crocked at an embassy party or something. Made me want to wash my ear out after I listened to him. Just be prepared for lots of attention. Aries is sending help. Try not to talk to the press if you can help it, but don't be impolite, either. They home in on things like that. Stay on the line for a second." I was put on hold again, and I turned to see a green minivan pull up to the edge of the taxiway.

Penney walked to meet the van as the chairman came back on the line. "Sorry. Now, Mike, Lew Hills says you can handle that job just fine, and I trust Lew." He paused dramatically. "But son, the mark of a good leader is to know when to call for help. You keep my number handy and use it whenever you need to, got it?"

I just had time to answer before the phone went dead.

I clicked the phone off and dropped it in my pocket, just as the front doors of the van opened and two figures stepped out. Penney spoke to the new arrivals, and pointed to me as I began to walk toward them.

As we neared each other, I stopped.

In front of me was the prettiest woman I had ever seen. She was tiny and Hispanic. Her skin was like porcelain, her shoulder-length hair full and richly textured in a way no beauty salon could ever make it. Even in her bulky work clothes and sweater she was a traffic stopper. I was taken back to my first parachute jump for a second, remembering the feeling when I let go of the wing strut and fell into space. How was it? Breathtaking. Whatever she wanted, I was hers.

She walked toward me, her face bright but serious. She spoke to me. "Mister O'Hara?"

"I, uh, yes. Mike. I'm Mike O'Hara." The sun suddenly seemed hot, like a nova. I could hear Roy Orbison singing somewhere in the distance.

She held her hand out to shake, and I took it. She smiled professionally, her eyes cool.

"I'm Sally Montez. Lew said to come straight to you. I'm your new assistant."

chapter

3

I shook her hand and tried to smile back. "Lew didn't say...uh...um." I stopped and forced myself back into normal consciousness. "Welcome aboard."

She smiled again, professionally, and thanked me.

My mind went completely blank. Why was I reacting like this? So, she was a beautiful woman. So what? I knew lots of gorgeous women, didn't I?

No, definitely not. Her attractiveness seemed to reshape space in ways Einstein hadn't predicted. I sensed that I could feel local distortions in time and gravity that pulsed and flowed around her, and I liked it.

I gradually became aware of the other figure standing beside her. The man next to her cleared his throat and held a hand out.

"Hi, Mike. Good to see you again. Special Agent George Tidings, FBI."

I turned to him with a start. "Oh, hi, George." I paused, trying to drop back into work mode. "Good to see you again." We shook hands, Tidings winning the usual FBI manhood rite to see who had the stronger grip. Tidings was tall, muscular and slim, the way all FBI agents seemed to be, and carried a blue FBI windbreaker over one arm.

"I just talked to the chairman," I said as we dropped hands. "I understand you have some information for me."

"Yes." The FBI man looked furtively at the others. "I'd like to speak to you in private about it."

I looked around, hesitating. "Well, I guess Steve could go give Ms. Montez an orientation to the crash site while we talk."

Penney's eyes brightened immediately. "Sure," he said with a smile. "I could do that." He held out a hand toward the wreckage and ushered her away.

As they left, I called out, "Ms. Montez, we can go over your assignments when I'm done here."

She looked back over her shoulder. "Call me Sally."

I tried not to stare as she walked away. When I looked back at Special Agent Tidings, he was just dragging his eyes away from her. When he noticed that I had caught him, he cleared his throat again and reached a hand up to straighten a necktie he wasn't wearing.

"My new assistant," I said.

Tidings and I walked over to the rented van and leaned against the grille.

I opened the conversation. "George, I really appreciate the Bureau's help, but why are you here? I know you can pick and choose what you work on."

He leaned in conspiratorially. "I don't know how much you know about the Bureau's financial crimes group," he began.

I shook my head.

"I didn't know much before this business, either," he went on. "The Bureau, the IRS and the Securities and Exchange Commission have a small standing team that monitors major financial dealings, mostly through open sources like trade magazines and such, plus the normal channels at IRS and SEC."

"I'm not surprised. I'd hope someone is watching things like that."

"Yeah, well, not everybody in the financial industry is real happy about it. The group stays under wraps most of the time." He leaned back on the van's hood and crossed his arms. "I don't know if you follow the markets, but Aries, the French aerospace concern, is working on buying a controlling share in ZYCO. We think they want an in-house software outfit. They've been buying shares on the open market for a while, and they have about ten percent of the company."

"So, is ZYCO going to fight 'em?"

Tidings shrugged. "I'm not sure we care. Nothing about that part is illegal."

"OK, that's is all interesting but this is a plane crash, not a stock market crash. What's so hot about this one that you are out here getting burned jet fuel on your shoes?"

He looked down at his polished Wingtips. "ZYCO's stock price. The SEC says it's been going up and down sharply for the last few months for no apparent reason--no news or anything. There's an appearance of illegal manipulation. Someone may have been manipulating the price to keep the French out. Or maybe to make more money for the French on the stock that they hold. We can't tell."

I stuck my hands in my pockets. "How do you manipulate stock prices?"

"Lots of ways. It doesn't take much. ZYCO is the sort of small, rich company that attracts speculators, and speculators are easy to panic. Could be something like off-the-record calls to analysts or the press with insider information. That would be illegal and we're looking into it. It's something we keep a close eye on."

"OK, what does it have to do with this accident?"

He took off his sunglasses and rubbed the bridge of his nose. "This morning, the SEC called us about Corso. They've been watching everything about ZYCO very closely--that's a part of their investigation protocol. When they got word of the crash out here they called the Bureau. The Director decided that the accident should be checked out, and here I am. My brief on this one is to cooperate and assist the NTSB, and keep my eyes open. I'm not interested in taking your investigation over. There may not even be a crime here."

I kept my hands in my pockets and inhaled deeply, thinking over what he'd said. The FBI had a natural tendency to run roughshod over any investigation they were involved in, Tidings' statement notwithstanding. He seemed friendly enough, but I could have done without the FBI's brand of help.

"Well," I said finally, "what are we looking for? Any ideas?"

"I have no information on that. Wish I did." He looked around again, scanning the horizon for unknown threats before going on. "I'm not exactly undercover here, but I'd rather not announce my presence any more than necessary."

I stood there with my hands in my pockets for a few seconds, staring at the ground and moving a pebble in a circle with the toe of my shoe, pondering what he'd said.

Finally I looked up, and squinted into the sun. "I guess we just go to it. I was planning to have you work with Steve Penney on the mechanical checks. You'll be able to get familiar with the wreckage that way." He agreed and we began to walk toward the GMax's remains. "If you think of anything I should be looking for in the paperwork, let me know."

We found Penney and Sally Montez at the plane's nose. She was examining the smashed nose area and the remains of the crushed FAA outbuilding under it as we walked up.

"Too bad about the building being here," Sally said. "They might have survived if they hadn't hit it."

Penney shook his head. "I doubt that. They hit hard, and the passenger in the aft cabin was burned pretty badly."

"The medical examiners will tell us soon enough," I said. "How beat up is the wiring in the nose section? Did the crushing of the structure crimp anything that you saw? See any shorts or breaks?"

Penney thought for a second, staring in the smashed cockpit windows. "No. I wasn't really looking for anything like that, but as I recall, things were scorched but not destroyed. The main displays on the control panel are shot. I could check the rest of it out if you want."

"Have you looked at the flight control computers

yet?" Sally interjected, glancing at me. I nodded.

"I did," I said. "They looked new, no crash damage. Both of the black boxes too." I paused and thought about a hundred different aspects of the crash scene: hardware, software, weather, people. Normally, we would have been preoccupied with recovering and reassembling the wreckage in order to search for damaged parts that might hold clues about why the airplane crashed. In this case, the ship was in such good shape that I was playing it by ear. "What would you all think if we got a ground power cart out here and tried to start the system up? I know it's a little unusual."

Penney and Tidings looked doubtful, but Sally had a far-off look in her eyes, and a little smile.

She nodded, her expression serious now. "That's not what they teach in the Air Force. But we could try the control surfaces and whatever systems were still operational."

"Right. And if there were any kind of readout in the equipment bay, we could do a self test." I turned to Penney. "Get back with your chief engineer friend in France tomorrow morning and see if he has any ideas about how to proceed. Maybe he'll have a suggestion or two about what to look for."

Penney still looked doubtful. "Shouldn't you check with Lew Hills?"

"Lew put me in charge."

He frowned but agreed to make the call.

I asked Sally if she could build a test plan for the power-on system check. I was worried for a second that I might have embarrassed her with too much for her first day on the job.

Instead, she looked very serious for a few seconds. "OK, I'll try it."

"Nothing formal, just get me your ideas and we can figure out a plan together."

She nodded and made a note.

We decided to work until sunset at the wreckage, and then push on with paperwork. The rest of the evening could be spent beginning the task of building the bureaucratic monster that was the NTSB Form 6120, also called the accident file. It would be the first of a lot of late evenings.

We decided to split up and work on several tasks at once. I borrowed a flashlight and tools, trying to guess at proper bolt sizes for removing the boxes, and then grabbed an adjustable wrench and a pair of pliers for good measure. There wouldn't be any professional mechanics watching.

I found my way back into the avionics bay, swearing as my head collided with the corner of a computer box, and placed the flashlight in a forward corner for illumination while I worked.

All the wiring looked OK and came loose easily,

but the mounts were not as simple. A skilled mechanic would have done the job in a few minutes, but I used up half an hour, most of the skin on my knuckles and my full supply of four-letter words before the first recorder was loose. The second box was easier, since I had seen the first one's tricks, and I was soon crawling back out into the sunlight, pushing the two boxes ahead of me. Once clear, I carried them to the van.

I looked around for Sally and Tidings, expecting to see them working with surveyor's equipment to map the skid path. Instead, Tidings was out walking the area alone, stopping to call comments out to Sally while she consulted an instrument in her hand and punched a note into a pad. I walked toward them, the beginnings of annoyance entering my thoughts.

She smiled as I approached. "Hi. Any trouble with the recorders?"

"No, all done. How's it going?" I said, expecting a mumbled or embarrassed reply. "No survey?"

She looked up again from her pad. "Sure." She held up a phone she had been consulting. "I'm building a site map with differential GPS." She held up the phone and I looked at the screen.

"There's an app for that?"

"Yep. I have George out finding scraps, and the app notes the locations and stores pictures. I used one of these on my last job in the Air Force. When I saw the theodolite and tape measures and other junk in the office, I talked Lew into buying us one." She made another note.

I was pleasantly surprised. "Good thinking." I knew Big Lew. He was lucky she hadn't asked for a remodeled office or a new Corvette.

"We put a new total station surveying system on order, but it's not in yet." She handed me the DGPS receiver and I studied it for a few seconds. "Really speeds things up. We should be done this afternoon. I'll build a database and get a grid map punched in tonight."

Lew did have legitimate reasons for hiring her after all, I thought. Impressed and a little intimidated, I shoved my hands into my pockets and walked back to the wreckage.

Penney was on his knees in the front of the passenger cabin, up to his elbows in burned upholstery. I spent the rest of the afternoon helping him check wiring, and the control system looked OK. The next morning we would begin dissecting the crushed cockpit, and I would have to sell the test plan to Lew and the chairman, but the day had gone well enough. So far, so good.

We found the workroom in the state office building across the field and unloaded everything we wouldn't need at the site. Sally had the recorders in large boxes for shipment by the time we were done. The recordings would be deciphered in the Board's lab in Washington. Penney called the Denver office and arranged for the boxes to be picked up there in the morning and flown east the next day. We would have transcripts and data files from the lab within forty-eight hours or so, barring technical difficulties.

We gathered for a conference just after seven that evening. I laid out ground rules for the team: 6:00 a.m. staff meetings every day, send me notes before the end of every day, even if it was midnight, and call for help if you need it. Eyes rolled all around the table. I then turned to Steve Penney.

"Steve, I want you to finish the checkout of the controls and let me know about anything you find. I want to get on with a powered-up system check as soon as possible."

He shook his head, and clasped his hands in front of him on the table. "Not sure I agree with the test at the scene. I'd rather reassemble the whole plane in a hangar somewhere, just to get more controlled conditions."

"Understood, but we might damage something or lose some information in the move. I want to try it before we go anywhere."

His shrug was eloquent. "Whatever." He was reacting to having an asshole from headquarters show up and take over his job.

I sympathized, but he was going to have to adjust

or find a job at the General Services Administration. I looked across at him and invited more.

He studied the table in front of him. "I'll get up early and call the Aries guy again before we meet tomorrow morning."

"Good. And I'll pass your opinions on to the chairman in my report tonight," I said.

I'd wanted to sound reassuring and evenhanded, but Penney seemed to take it as a threat. "Fine, go ahead," he said, his voice tinged with belligerence. He stared at the table in front of him, tapping his fingers. "I need manuals."

I grimaced. "They haven't come in yet. The ship is too new, and they are holding them close." I paused for a moment, thinking. "You know, that bigwig from ZYCO who came out said he'd help if we needed it."

"Their flight department must have a set," Penney said.

I made a note.

Looking around the table, I saw a group of people who had been in the sun too long and seen too much destruction in one day. It was normal to get worn down and depressed working on a crash site. I slouched back in my chair and adjourned the meeting for the night.

Penney headed immediately for his car. He would carry the recorders to the Denver office that night and return the next day with a full suitcase.

We stopped at the first hotel we came to and, after extracting the cheapest government rates we could screw out of the night manager, we checked in. I suggested dinner. Tidings begged off and headed for his room, saying he wanted a workout before sleeping.

Sally and I dropped our bags in our rooms and then met back at the van. From the driver's seat I looked both ways up and down the street.

I sighed. Junk food everywhere. I asked her what she wanted.

"Find something with lots of salt and fat. I'm tired and hungry."

I steered left and pulled into a burger place a block down the road.

The dining room was nearly empty at that hour. After buying enough cholesterol and salt to kill a crowd, we took a booth next to a window.

"So, anyway, I didn't know I had an assistant until you got here," I said as I squeezed ketchup onto my fries. "I never got a look at your Form One-Seventy-One but you sure seem to know your way around."

She smiled.

"You were in the Air Force?"

"Six years. I was in Europe, mostly. My degree is in computer science, actually. I ran the line operation at our base at Aviano, Italy, for a while and did staff work at NATO headquarters in Brussels."

I was impressed. Logistics for a front-line NATO outfit, with staff work at the head office. "You did investigations at the NATO staff?"

She inhaled some of her Pepsi through a straw and unwrapped a chicken sandwich. "It was a collateral duty, but I worked several big jobs. I was on that one three years ago where we found cracks in C-5 wings. I got half the Air Mobility Command grounded for a month." She smiled at me conspiratorially, and the smile made me warm like the sun. "I wasn't very popular for a while."

I choked back a comment that I doubted that, but then stopped, remembering something.

"Um, stress corrosion cracking in major structures? I remember that paper. You wrote that?"

She beamed over her dinner. "Yes, but it was a big team. I got lots of help."

I agreed. "If I know work like that, you had more help than you wanted."

She made a face. "You got that right. Anyway, when I got out of the Air Force, I went to work as a beltway bandit in Washington. But my father told me I should get into the civil service if I could. Job security."

"I know, I got the same lecture from my parents."

She gave me an understanding smile. "When I saw the job opening on the civil service web page I applied, and here I am."

"We'd been advertising the position for months. I

was surprised when Lew finally filled it as fast as he did, but I can see why."

She smiled politely. Gorgeous women are usually good at accepting complements, and she was no exception.

"Why'd you decide to get out of the Air Force?" I said.

Her face darkened a little, and I realized I should have skipped the question.

She tilted her head to one side and pushed a hand through her hair. "Fighter pilots."

"Umm, I..."

She took a french fry in her hand and waved it in a little circle, staring at the ketchup-smeared end as she spoke.

"Married twice, divorced twice."

I tried to think of a way to change the subject, but she sighed and went on.

"The second one is final in three months." She took a deep breath. "All my friends were getting married. And I had this gorgeous dress, you know? I bought it in London."

My mind reeled for a second, thinking of how she would look in a wedding gown.

She went on. "Fighter jocks make great dates, but they're lousy husbands. And they're like potato chips. Once I got started on them it was hard to stop. I kept expecting them to get better, but they didn't." Her voice grew harder, and she shook her head a little as she spoke. "I just got tired of the atmosphere. All that testosterone in the air, like cheap cigar smoke." She looked into her drink, and then looked out the window. "It was less than a tragedy and more than a pain in the ass. I wanted to get away, and now I'm away."

"Well, you've got taste, anyway."

She looked at me coolly, through half-closed eyes. "I do now."

I concentrated on my cheeseburger for a while.

She finished her sandwich and sat back. "Lew said you were an astronaut. Was he serious?"

I laughed self-consciously. "Sort of. Lew exaggerates." I told her the story of my short adventure in Houston.

She looked at me incredulously. "That's awful. You must have been devastated."

I shrugged. "I don't do devastated. I've worked a lot of good investigations since then. It puts things in perspective. Life isn't fair and doesn't always make sense. You just have to get over it and keep on."

She stared at me again for a few seconds like she was looking for something, and then looked back at her fries.

"You were in the Navy. Fighter jock, I suppose." She arched her eyebrows.

I shook my head. "Nope. Navigator. Radar controller. Airborne Early Warning. Dull stuff. It got pretty old. I have a civilian pilot's license but I don't get a chance to use it much. The Navy offered to take me back after I left NASA, but I didn't go. I don't know why not. Guess I just wanted to try something else."

She slurped the last of her Pepsi. "You joined the Board right after you left Houston?"

"Yes. I investigated the crash of my squadron commanding officer's plane just before I left to join NASA. The crash killed him. It was hard to take, but once I got through it, I knew the business."

She looked at the floor for a second, as if thinking. "Was that in San Diego? I remember it because I'm from San Diego"

"Yes, Miramar Air Station."

"I read that report. Crew coordination, fatigue and end-of-tour psychology. I made it required safety reading at NATO."

I basked a little at the recognition. "I got lots of help, too." I let the sentence trail off.

After a few seconds, she said, "Married?"

I shook my head and smiled sheepishly. "My parents are always trying to fix me up."

She laughed. "My mother, too. I think that's why I don't go back to San Diego much."

I laughed then.

On the short drive back to the hotel, she was quiet. I parked near the lobby, and as we walked in through the rapidly cooling evening air, she spoke again. "I was kind of nervous, coming out here."

"You don't seem very nervous to me. New job, and all?"

"Partly." She walked a few more steps. "Lew said you were his star. A rising talent."

I guffawed, and stuck my hands in my pockets, "Lew is about ninety percent full of it."

"No, the Chairman said the same thing. I'm really looking forward to working with you."

I blushed again in the darkness, and we said good night, agreeing to meet at five-thirty in the morning.

I walked to my room, pondering the universe. Not only was Sally out of my class, but since I was her nominal supervisor she was protected by all the federal sexual harassment laws on the books, plus about half of the Civil Service personnel manual. I had finally met and was even making friends with a fabulous woman, and she might as well have been my sister.

Unbelievable. Just great.

When I got back to my room I checked my answering phone for calls from anyone who might have missed me after my quick departure. The machine held four messages, but two were hang-ups, and one was a marketing call offering yet another credit card, this one platinum. I punched the erase code for the first three recordings.

The last call was from my mother. "Hello, dear. I got your message about being gone again. Doesn't your office understand how much you travel now?"

Yes, mom, they knew.

"Well, we'll miss you, but maybe you'll meet someone nice in Colorado. I just worry about you getting old and not having anyone, Michael. I think it's that job. All those dead bodies, and the terrible hours. It's just not very attractive, dear. You know I think you should have stayed in the Navy. The uniforms look so distinguished. Did I mention that I talked to your Uncle Mike yesterday?"

Uncle Mike worked for one of the major aerospace contractors.

"I know they're laying off, but I'm sure he could find you a position in St. Louis if you'd just ask."

There were new sounds in the background. "I hear your father, so I'd better go, dear. Take care of yourself, and let us know when you're coming home."

The phone beeped in my hand indicating there were no more calls, and I hit the erase code reflexively.

chapter

4

I used to try to find good restaurants and explore local eateries when I'm on the road, but after a day or two of recovering bodies and sifting through wreckage, I'm usually ready to just grab whatever won't cause bodily harm near-term.

Sally turned out to be a fellow traveler, ordering french fries for breakfast at a quarter to six the next morning, on the way to the airport. Tidings sat in the front seat of the van, surprisingly sleep-wasted for a physical fitness type, while Sally curled up on the rear bench, eating fries and drinking orange juice through a straw. She wolfed down her fries and was ready for the day.

We knocked out the first morning meeting quickly, and by seven Tidings and Sally headed to the wreckage. I stayed behind to use the phone and make plans, expecting to snag a lift from Penney when he came in.

After scratching out a plan for the day, I dialed Lew Hills' number in New Orleans. There was no answer. Probably up to his armpits in Mississippi mud, I thought. I would have to brief Lew later. I took a deep breath and dialed Chairman McCall's number in Washington. His admin answered immediately, and after a two-minute hold, McCall came on the line.

"Mike, got it wrapped up out there yet?" McCall said in a cheery shout. He had me on a speakerphone, and his voice sounded like he was talking through a long pipe.

"Not quite, sir. But I've got George Tidings from the FBI here now, and Sally Montez."

"What do you think of Montez?"
"I, uh, well, she looks great. Her resume looks great." I could hear McCall snicker. "She's already contributed on the scene, just in her first day. Seems to be a good hire."

"Good." He waited for me to continue.

I scanned my notes, cradling the phone on a shoulder and shuffled through the two-page message as I summarized the information as best I could.

"You gonna start disassembly pretty soon? Remember, I need you to move along out there as fast as you can. Keep your costs down, son. We're runnin' on fumes back here."

I caught myself nodding into the phone. "I remember, yes sir. We...that is...I have something I want to try before we tear it down."

"Mmmmmm?" McCall sounded like he was doing something else while he was listening. "What'd you have in mind?"

I took another deep breath and pressed on, describing my plans and reasons.

"Did you tell Lew about this plan?" he said.

I sat back in my chair. "I tried to call Lew but I got no answer. I'll try him again later. I bounced the idea off Montez, and she thought it was worth a try. Steve Penney's not real happy, and there are some risks, of course."

"Like you could light the wreck back on fire, for instance."

I bounced a pencil on the desk in front of me. He was right. "Yes, sure, but we're doing a careful examination of the wiring before the test, and I'll have the fire department standing by."

"What do you think you're going to accomplish?" He didn't sound as if he was annoyed, but wanted more information before he endorsed the idea.

"A self-test of the flight control computers, for one thing. Steve Penney has talked with the chief engineer at Aries already, and we'll coordinate with him before starting any tests. We can look for software glitches, sneak circuits, that sort of thing."

"Pretty unconventional, Mike." McCall sounded doubtful.

I fired my big gun. "I might be able to eliminate dead ends this way, boss. Save some time and effort out here."

McCall hesitated for another second, but he knew how to make a decision. "OK, get Lew's concurrence on what tests to run, and talk to that Aries engineer before you go. What else you got?"

I turned to my next page of notes. "The chief financial officer of ZYCO has offered us any assistance we want." I laid out what I wanted. "I'm not sure what the legalities are about accepting assistance, and I'm very sensitive about keeping the investigation independent, so I'll have to be careful."

McCall chuckled. "Don't let ZYCO charge you for anything." His voice became stronger and more serious. "Make damned sure you keep a complete record of all your actions. Keep a clear paper trail in case we get audited or sued."

McCall hung up before I could cover the other items on my list, but they could wait. The first rule of conduct when briefing a senior is once he's agreed with you: Shut up.

I was writing up a note of what to ask the ZYCO CFO Harrison Randall for when my phone buzzed in my pocket. It was Steve Penney.

"McCall says we can go ahead with the power-up check." I said. "Did you talk to the chief engineer at Aries yet?"

"Yeah, I got hold of him. Marcel Covert." Penney spelled the name for me, pronouncing it cov-air. "He wants to do the check, too, but he wants us to wait for him to get there. I guess he wants to show us something about the control system. He asked to talk to the FBI, too. He's leaving with their test pilot in the company prototype in a couple of hours. They're going to stop in Minneapolis to clear customs. They'll be here this evening."

I looked at my watch. "Any specifics? I need to brief Lew and the chairman if we're going to use their inputs."

"I got some. He said he didn't want anybody to talk about it on the phone. Pretty weird if you ask me. Not really up our alley. Look, I'm just leaving the Denver office now. I'll be there in before noon and I can lay out what I have for you."

I agreed and asked Penney what other support I should try to get from ZYCO. He gave me a half-page list off the top of his head and we signed off after I told him to meet us at the site. I would have to steal a ride out to the wreckage from the police.

I next dialed Harrison Randall's number. The call was answered on the first ring. After a polite "Whom shall I say is calling?" and a ten second wait, Randall came on the line.

"Mr. O'Hara, Harry Randall. How can I help you?" Randall's voice was serious and strong, and had the texture of white-chocolate fudge from an expensive candy shop.

"Good morning, Mr. Randall," I said. "I'm reaching a point in the investigation where I could use some support, equipment, that sort of thing."

"Of course. Eric gave me explicit instructions that any support that you might need be furnished immediately. And without cost, of course. I quite understand about the end of the fiscal year. When I was at Treasury we used to tear our hair out around this time." Chairman McCall would love this guy.

I thanked him and explained what we had planned.

"Of course. We at ZYCO are vitally interested in the safety of the GlobalMax jet. Not only do we own two... Well, one now, but we also were responsible for the software. Eric was quite involved in that project himself, you know."

"Really?" I had assumed that Zygler would be absorbed in running his newly created corporate empire.

"Oh, yes, Eric likes to keep his hand in. He says it helps him keep abreast of state-of-the-art. Things change so quickly in this business, you know." He paused. "I'm more of a spreadsheets and strategy man myself. So much of what we do seems like, well, I don't know."

"Magic?" I said.

"Yes, exactly. It is such powerful stuff, and so few people in the world actually know how it all works." He hesitated for a few seconds. "I'm sorry to ramble like this. I was a very close friend of Wes's, if he had any friends. I'm afraid the impact of the crash is just sinking in."

I assured him that it was no problem, and that people need to talk about things after a loss. I actually would have been happier if all contact with bereaved survivors, friends and, lawyers were prohibited by law, but I wanted to keep the channel open.

Randall didn't sound at all like the smooth Ivy-Leaguer that he had seemed like the day before. I listened as he spoke for a few minutes about how long he and Corso had worked together, and of how frightened he was of flying. I took a few notes as he went on, and eventually he stopped reminiscing, and asked for detailed list of what we would need for support.

I laid out what we thought we would need in the near term, in hardware, manuals, hangar space and people. It was a long shopping list and we needed it all.

He made understanding noises as I spoke. "I'll tell you what. I'll put you in direct touch with our transportation department, and they'll give you anything you need." He rattled off a name and number.

I scribbled them into my notebook.

"Give me a half hour to call ahead, and then feel free to contact them direct. As I said, ZYCO has a strong interest in this case and we'll help in any way you need." Randall was all business again, in charge of his destiny.

I thanked him and clicked off.

I found a local airport administrator at his desk and talked him into giving me a ride to the scene. After a call to the tower we headed out. It always felt strange to me to drive a car across an airport. The wide-open spaces of the airfield felt foreign in a car, like driving on Mars. We carried a radio to help stay clear of airplanes, and the tower guys used a colored spotlight to clear us across the runways as we went.

Sally and Tidings had removed every access panel and door that could be unbolted, screwed out or pried open. The once-proud business jet lay on its belly on the dirt like a rich man lying in the gutter after a mugging. The only other vehicle in attendance was a state police car, complete with resting officer. Any novelty the assignment might have held for the police had clearly worn off for this guy. He looked pretty comfortable.

Sally and Tidings were inside the cabin, and had unbolted all the cabin furniture, leaving a small pile of charred leather armchairs and heavily distressed mahogany outside the entrance door.

I ducked my head into the cabin and saw Tidings on his back, head and shoulders shoved through an access panel leading through the bulkhead into the cockpit. Sally sat on the floor in the rear of the cabin, writing notes.

"Making any progress?" I said.

I heard Tidings say "some" as Sally looked up, looking busy and gorgeous, even sitting on the floor with her knees pulled up and leaning against the scorched wall coverings.

"George has almost all of the mechanical inspection finished, and I'm about half done with electrical checks. We're making good progress." She used her pencil to move a stray strand of hair away from her face, and showed me her notes.

"Good," I said. "I should have some electronic manuals this morning, and we can check them out to see if we missed anything."

Tidings' voice came through the bulkhead, muffled by the small opening and sound-deadening insulation. "Where'd you get manuals? I can sure use 'em."

I answered with a description of my call to Randall, and the FBI agent suggested additional tools that might be handy. As I talked, Tidings extricated himself from the bulkhead and sat on the floor opposite Sally.

"Steve Penney is on his way down from Denver. He talked to the chief engineer from Aries again this morning, Marcel Covert. Covert is on the way here from France in the factory prototype, and Steve said he has some information about the accident that sounds like it might play into your ideas."

Tidings glanced at Sally quickly, and then back at me. "Did you tell him about the matter we discussed?"

"No, and he didn't tell me what the deal with the Aries people was, either."

He glanced at Sally again. "I'd like to talk to you alone."

Sally began to get up to leave, but I motioned her to stay.

"Look, Agent Tidings--"

"Call me George."

"OK, George, look. Sally is a federal employee, ex-Air Force, and she's part of my team. She can keep a secret as well as anybody. Why don't we just drop the cloak-and-dagger stuff with her, and with Steve Penney. They might be able to help."

Tidings thought for a moment, and then shrugged. "OK, I can do it your way. I didn't have any specific instructions, anyway."

He related his information about the financial

investigations and I explained about Penney's call and the information that he was holding so close. As we talked, Sally sat and listened without showing any reaction.

Finally, she took a deep breath. "So, could we be looking at a crime, then? Sabotage? Or murder?"

"Maybe," I said. "We haven't heard what the French have to say, yet. There are plenty of other things that might explain what we're seeing. And coincidences do happen. We need to treat murder or sabotage of the airplane as a possibility. But just a possibility. I certainly haven't seen any trace of a bomb or anything."

She nodded in agreement. "So, I guess it's back to work for us, then."

"Right. Push on regardless." I stepped back out of the cabin, blinking in the harsh Colorado sunlight, pulled out my phone and punched in the number Randall had given me. I asked for the director of flight operations.

A voice answered, alert, cooperative and professional. Very few corporations had a full-time position like flight ops director, and Penney had mentioned that ZYCO had a reputation for paying well. The voice on the other end of the line made it very clear that all the assets, as well as the hearts and minds, of ZYCO's flight department were ours for the asking, and that no request was too great.

Roger that.

I laid out our needs in detail, and he offered to

send technicians out to operate gear and assist with the wreckage recovery. I accepted one man and a vehicle for the time being, and was assured that more later would be no problem, no sir. Delivery of the requested items and help was promised by 1:00 p.m.

I tried Lew's number again but got no answer. I called his hotel and left a message, since I needed his OK before we went much further. That done, I returned to the cabin where I got on with helping Sally and Tidings with their tasks, inspecting cable runs and mechanical systems for signs of failure or damage.

I lost track of time, for some reason finding that looking at runs of wire bundles was highly entertaining while working next to Sally. In addition to everything else, her Air Force training was damned good and she had obviously paid attention. She also had a sort of fearlessness that let her learn new things and then immediately start using them. She was going to be very, very effective.

After what seemed like a short time she asked if I wanted to break for lunch. I looked at my watch. It was nearly noon.

"I wonder where the hell Penney is," I said. "He said he was headed straight here. He should have been here two hours ago."

She looked at her watch. "Hmmm. Maybe he had a flat tire or something. Could you call him?"

I didn't want him to think I was a hard-ass from DC harassing him. "I'll wait 'til after lunch before I try him." That decided, I invited George to go to lunch, but he--happily--refused, and I promised to bring him a bag of something later.

Sally and I headed for the far side of the airport around the perimeter road, staying clear of taxiways. The drive was a little longer, but I didn't mind. I tried to relax and pulled my phone out of my pocket, tossing it on the dash. We made small talk, discussing our work progress and what to plan for the live power test. Pulling out onto the main road, I drove toward town, and Sally picked a place with salad bar. I was stopped in the left turn lane in the center of the road when the telephone beeped for attention.

Sally answered while I drove on. "Montez, NTSB." She listened. "Yes, who's calling, please? Yes." She was silent again, and I stole a glance at her. Her face was serious and her eyes worried as I parked the van in the restaurant lot.

"Yes, he's right here. Just a minute." She handed me the phone and said quietly, "It's the head of the Denver office. Steve's been in an accident."

I shut the engine down and took the phone. "O'Hara."

"Mike, this is Harold Keats." Keats was a GS-15 in his mid-fifties, a contemporary of Lew's.

"Ms. Montez says that Steve Penney's been in an accident. Is that right?"

Keats exhaled heavily before answering. "Afraid so. He left the office early this morning, headed back down to see you. The state police say he went off the freeway at high speed about thirty miles south of Denver. He's in critical condition at the hospital at Castle Rock, and he's about to be airlifted to University Hospital in Denver. Should be there in about an hour."

I scribbled down the information. "Where's the accident scene?"

"Southbound side of Twenty-Five, just past exit One-Sixty-Seven. The state police are still there."

I relayed the news to Sally. She mouthed the word "family." I nodded. "Have you called his family yet?"

Keats sighed. "Yes, I called Mrs. Penney myself, and I'm going to meet her at the hospital. We've got an emergency plan here, and I've got folks from the office assigned to take care of her."

"Have you called Washington? The Chairman will want to know."

"I'll call right now. I'll, uh, I'll have to get someone else down to help you out tomorrow." Keats sounded tired.

"Don't worry about that. I'm getting some local help, and the French have got some people coming in tonight." I shook my head as I absorbed the bad news.

I got directions to the hospital from Keats and said I would come by later in the afternoon. I started the van again and headed back to the airport, while filling Sally in on what I'd heard.

"I'll have to rent another car," I said. "I'll go check on the accident scene and then head up to the hospital in Denver to see how he is. I'll be back by six or so to meet the Aries guys."

Sally sat with her arms crossed in front of herself.

"George and I can go on with the checks, I guess. I'll meet the ZYCO people this afternoon and get a look at the manuals. I'll try to have a test plan together by this evening for you and the French to go over." She looked at the floor for a second. "God, this is awful. I hope he's all right."

"They always say 'critical condition' when an accident victim first comes in," I said, not even convincing myself. I pulled into the shiny new airline terminal to shop for a rental car and stopped in the loading zone.

"Call Ann in Chairman McCall's office and let her know what's going on. If McCall calls you, let him know I'm en route and tell him about any test ideas you have."

I stepped out and she climbed across into the driver's seat. As she adjusted the seat forward, she said, "Should I call Lew?"

I'd forgotten about Big Lew. "Yeah, try him again if you don't mind. I haven't been able to get him since yesterday, so fill him in on the whole picture. McCall wants him to concur on the test plan before we go."

She nodded as I closed the door and waved goodbye.

A major rental firm had a government rate, and I rolled out of the lot onto Fountain Boulevard in the sort of nondescript mid-size domestic sedan that seemed to be made only for rental fleets. I was on I-25 headed north ten minutes later. The cruise control held my speed precisely, and I thought the case over as I drove.

A new, freshly certified airplane, operated properly, with a well-trained and professional crew. Nothing overtly wrong with the airplane that we could see. Check that. We would find out shortly about the flight control system. The weather hadn't been perfect, but not particularly challenging either. There was even a possibility of some kind of sabotage, but where was the bomb damage, or the contaminated fuel, or whatever? This case was supposed to have been an easy one for me to break in on, but it was getting complicated fast, and now part of my team was in the hospital.

I groaned inwardly when I thought of how the press would react when they heard a member of the NTSB had been in a one-car accident. I hoped they would be dispassionate and circumspect, having a reasonable regard for the feelings of the family during this trying time. Fat chance of that. Maybe the police hadn't released any information about the victim.

A half hour later I passed Exit 161, and I began looking for the scene on the opposite side of the road. Five minutes later, two state police cruisers came into view. They were parked together, lights flashing, and a smashed car was visible far off the right-of-way in the scrub. Noting the odometer reading, I pressed north to the next turn off, reversing course and heading back. I searched the road for the last mile before the accident scene for skid marks or other telltale evidence, but saw none.

I steered onto the road shoulder and parked behind the rear cruiser, pulling as far off the road as I could without worrying about getting stuck or dragging something. Rumble strips on the shoulder buzzed loudly under the wheels and vibrated the steering wheel in my hands.

There was an officer in the front car, and I walked to the passenger side window, noting that he watched me carefully in his mirror as I approached.

I flashed my NTSB ID in the window and leaned my head in. The officer was filling out part of the mountain of paperwork that went with any investigation.

I introduced myself, holding the ID card for him to study. He looked it over, comparing my face to the picture before responding to me directly, his eyes narrowing.

"Can I help you?" His voice was flat. He was black and seemed very young, but had the look of a veteran's wariness in his eyes. His name tag said "Maxwell."

"The victim of this accident is an employee of the NTSB. We were working an investigation together down in Colorado Springs, and he was on official business at the time of the accident. I was wondering if I could get a little information for the Denver office before you wrap up here."

The officer thought it over for a few seconds. I was federal, and this was not a federal matter. Technically, the NTSB didn't have any direct jurisdiction. But after a few seconds, he nodded his head. "OK. Sure." He got out of the car, and we walked together off the roadbed and out the sixty yards to Penney's car.

As we walked, I noticed that the ruts left by the car's passage didn't start until nearly twenty yards off the road. Maxwell saw me looking for marks.

"He must have really been hauling ass when he went off the road," the officer said. "I'd bet ninety or more. Maybe a lot more. The car flew sixty-three feet before touching down the first time. Bounced twice and rolled over. He's lucky he survived."

I winced at the thought of the impact. "Did you

see any skid marks, or anything in the road?"

He shook his head. "Nothing. He must have gone to sleep or something."

"Any witnesses?"

"Not yet. Traffic is usually moderate along here that time of day, so somebody should have seen something. A witness called it in, but we didn't get a name."

The area where the car hit first was marked by deep gouges left by the front wheels. I stopped and stared into the ruts for a second. Something was not quite right. It took me a few more seconds before I realized what the problem was. There was a reasonably clear tread pattern in the moist, sandy soil at the bottoms of the holes. "Did you notice these tread marks in the bottoms of the ruts, Officer?"

He looked. "Uh, no. Is that significant?"

I looked longer. "Well, maybe, or maybe not. I've seen a couple of jumps like this in the past, but usually when you go off the road, the first thing you do is panic and stomp on the brakes. The wheels stop while you're in the air, or at least slow down. It leaves a smear in the bottom of the rut when you land. His front wheels must have been turning close to the speed of the car when it hit." I crouched down to look closer. "Kind of interesting." I took a picture on my phone.

Maxwell stared a second longer. "I'll put it in my

report." We walked on toward the car. Another officer stood next to the car, taking pictures of the passenger cabin.

Two more areas of disturbed earth lead up to the car, which was sitting on its side, smashed nearly beyond recognition. Steve really was lucky to be alive.

It was, or had been, a late model domestic sedan, the same make as my rental. Both sides and the roof were heavily damaged, and the front end had been smashed in during the final impact against the sandy berm where the car rested. Every window in the car was shattered, the smashed safety glass filling the car's interior with clear pellets.

Both front seat airbags had gone off and hung limp from their mountings. The engine had smashed through the firewall, occupying most of the front passenger seat, and much of the driver's side foot well. Penney's injuries would be to internal organs, and to his legs, arms and back. The airbags probably saved him from massive head or facial damage, if he was lucky. He would likely be temporarily deaf from the air bag's deployment charge.

There were marks on the doorframe where a Jaws-of-Life had been applied, and the driver's side door had been roughly pried open. I noted the positions of switches--lights off, keys in the ignition, heater to vent, nothing unusual.

There was a lot of blood spattered in the car's interior.

I stood back to look the wreckage over, trying to spot anything out of place, but aside from the grotesque damage, nothing seemed wrong.

I turned to Officer Maxwell. "I guess I'll head north. Could you forward a copy of your reports to the Denver NTSB office for me?"

He nodded, and I gave him Keats' voice and fax numbers at the Denver federal center.

As I walked back to my rental car alone I considered what I had seen. Steve had run off the road at high speed, and even if he had gone to sleep at the wheel, he should have been awakened by the rumble strips on the side of the road in time to save it. Anti-lock might have explained the absence of skid marks, but the whole scene didn't seem right. Sober, middle-aged guys in domestic sedans driving in broad daylight didn't have accidents like this one.

The crash ran through my mind over and over on the drive to Denver. I would call Big Lew, and he would know what to do.

chapter

5

The trip to Denver took me until three. I turned off I-25 onto Colorado Boulevard, heading north in stop-and-go traffic to the hospital. I checked in at the emergency room admissions desk and found my way to intensive care. Outside Penney's room were two people sitting in plastic hospital chairs. The furniture was the sort favored by hospital administrators, uncomfortable to sit in but easy to clean.

One figure, a young, slightly overweight woman, sat hunched over a large purse, crying quietly. The other, an older man, tall and patrician in a sport coat, tried clumsily to offer her comfort. I walked within whispered earshot and cleared my throat.

"Mr. Keats?" I said quietly. The man looked up, showing no sign of recognition. "Mike O'Hara."

He nodded and excused himself from Mrs. Penney's side, walking a few steps away, relief at the interruption showing in his face. We shook hands and made an awkward hash of introducing ourselves.

"I stopped at the accident scene on the way up," I said.

He glanced at Penney's wife to make sure she was out of earshot and spoke quietly. "Pretty bad?"

"The passenger space stayed almost intact, but the car's totaled. The airbags worked. How's Steve?"

He exhaled and crossed his arms. "The doctor says he's going to survive. No major head or internal injuries that they can see. They have him in an induced coma because of brain injuries they might not have spotted, but he should recover. The neurologist said the next few days are critical. He's in stable condition right now, which is better than I had expected after hearing about the accident. I'm afraid he's going to lose a leg."

"The right one, I bet" I said. I grimaced, remembering the engine intruding on the driver's foot room in Steve's car.

"Yes. Just below the knee, they said." We both stared at the floor for a second. "He'll be a while recovering." But would he ever have a full recovery?

"Did you get a chance to talk to him?" I said, trying not to be too pushy.

"No, he was sedated when I got here and they put him in the coma right away. The nurse said he said 'accident' several times, and he shouted 'no' over and over."

I couldn't find anything to do with my hands, and ended up sticking them in my pockets. "Did the police tell you much about the wreck?"

"No. Just that he went off the road at high speed."

I took two minutes to describe what I'd seen, and my impressions. He listened intently, professionally, asking for details as I went. Finally, I said, "Does Steve have a bad driving record? Any moving violations that you know about? Is he a chronic speeder, or anything?"

Keats shook his head again. "Not that I know of. But, you know, we all drive pretty fast out here in the Wild West."

I had to smile. I had grown up in rural Oregon, and had found the terminal velocity of my father's small Japanese sedan before my seventeenth birthday.

"A one-car accident on a clear interstate, in broad daylight, with a good driver. The whole thing just doesn't make a lot of sense," I said.

"Maybe Steve will be able to tell you himself in a few days ." Keats sounded hopeful.

I told him to expect a report from the state patrol, and promised to keep in touch about the main investigation. He briefly introduced me to Mrs. Penney, whose eyes were red and swollen from crying. I offered the sympathies of Chairman McCall and tried to make reassuring conversation, talking up the benefits of modern cars and modern medicine.

Broken hearts and shattered lives are not my area, and viewing them at close range robs me of my few social skills. After a short, uncomfortable stay, I made my apologies and headed south again just before five.

Twenty miles south of Denver, traffic was light and flowing above seventy-five miles per hour. As the rest area north of Steve's accident site rolled past, I was sucking the last of a warm Coke I'd picked up on the way. I pulled into the right lane and slowed to the speed limit-- which drew honks and annoyed stares from passing drivers--in an effort to avoid having my view of the road blocked by any truck or van too close to my line of vision.

I scanned the roadbed intently, searching again for a mark or skid mark or any other sign of a flat tire or some other malfunction that might explain Steve's plunge into the Colorado countryside. The milepost that marked the accident site went by with no sign of Steve's detour. Looking off to the right, I could see that the car was gone, towed away since I had inspected it with Officer Maxwell. In the flat afternoon sunlight, the ruts left in the native soil by the impact of Steve's car were barely visible from the road.

So much for that.

The rest of the trip back to Peterson Field passed in slow motion for me, as my mind raced back and forth between the smashed business jet and Penney's destroyed car. Why was there no easy explanation for either? What would cause two trained and qualified pilots to crash a plane like that? How the hell could Penney end up in the weeds next to an interstate with a totaled sedan and minus a leg?

Of course, I thought to myself, if everything about accidents were self-evident, I wouldn't have a job.

The last rays of daylight were cutting across the Rampart Range of the Rockies to the west as I arrived back at Peterson Field, purple twilight spreading into the foothills below. Pike's Peak was still brightly illuminated in the distance, like a huge lighthouse in the mountains.

I followed the access road around the field to the wreck again. A dark brown van with the ZYCO logo on its doors was parked next to the wreck, and Sally and Tidings were conferring with two men in neat white shirts and black pants: ZYCO maintenance men, as promised by Randall, one more than I had asked for.

I pulled up to the tape and walked to the van, arriving unnoticed. One of the ZYCO techs was sitting in the open van door with a large manual in a notebook and a laptop open on an empty seat. Tidings was standing next to the door, looking over the tech's shoulder and writing notes, and Sally and the other were conversing. She looked up as I approached, and a concerned expression crossed her face.

"How is Steve?" she asked. The others turned to me, the two ZYCO men drawing back respectfully. They had been briefed by their boss, I guessed.

"He's going to live." I gave her a rundown.

Sally bit a fingernail, her worried look deepening. "Was his family there?"

"His wife. She wasn't taking it real well. Keats is handling things."

Tidings said, "Did you see the car?"

"Yeah." I leaned against the van. "I'm surprised he survived. The police think he went off the road going over ninety."

Tidings harrumphed. "Miss a turn or something?"

I couldn't keep a tone of exasperation out of my voice. "No, the road was straight. There were no good witnesses. Keats said he had a good driving record." I let the thought hang in the air for a second. "Any sign of the French?"

Tidings looked at his watch. "They should be in any time now. They haven't called or anything."

"We've been working on a test plan," Sally said. "We've got things pretty well ready." She held up her notebook, and the two ZYCO technicians showed signs of motion.

I introduced myself to the two techs, Mac and Sam, who wore name tags on their shirts. Mac was tall and thin, and looked like he had gotten his avionics training in the Marines. Sam was a short, middle-aged man with long, scraggly red hair and the look of an incompletely reformed flower child about him. Both spoke in reverential tones and called me "sir," knowing that their jobs might be on the line.

The group had made fast progress while I was gone. The cockpit controls had been damaged too severely to be used in tests, but Mac and Tidings had rigged special gear into the equipment bay to check the computers. They had used electronic test gear that ZYCO had furnished to test all wiring in the controls electronically and everything was OK. Despite the fact that the plane had hit the ground hard enough to leave a twenty-foot gouge, the damage that hadn't happened in the fire looked pretty minor.

We went over the test plan in depth, Sally presenting, with Mac backing her up using quotations from the aircraft maintenance manuals. Tidings sat back with his arms crossed, not listening closely, his face a blank and his mind somewhere else. Not much for computer science, I supposed.

At one point I tried to delete several tests to save

time. Sally argued expertly that each test was necessary. She had built a plan that progressed logically through each control system capability, eliminating major red herrings early in the plan while giving us the pieces of a puzzle about how it all worked. The entire interlocking scheme unfolded like a good novel. She expected it to take about five hours altogether.

I was extremely impressed, and I told her so. She beamed in return, and Mac stood back with an awed expression.

I eyed the area around us as the taxiway and runway lights began to illuminate the scene. The sun had gone down a good forty-five minutes before. The field was enveloped in full darkness, and we had to read our notes by flashlight.

I squinted at my watch. "Let's see. It's past nine in DC, and eight in New Orleans." I turned to Sally. "Did you get hold of Lew or McCall?"

Sally shook her head. "No answer at Lew's, and the chairman left early today." She hesitated for a second, and I heard her say "oh shit" under her breath. "I forgot. McCall called just after you left. I meant to text you. He wanted to talk to you, and wouldn't leave a message." A sound of nervous fear crept into her voice, afraid that she had wiped out all the good she had done on the second day of field work in her new job.

"No problem," I said reassuringly. "If it had been

important, I'm sure he would have called again."

She relaxed partially, clearly relieved at my calm reaction.

"Well," I said, "we aren't going to get any more done today. Let's go back to the office and consolidate our notes for tomorrow. Sally, why don't you and I plan on being back at the DOT building about five-thirty tomorrow morning? We can get hold of Lew and brief him, and then call the chairman for his chop before we go."

I asked for the two ZYCO men to return the next morning at eight with a ground power cart. They agreed, and headed for their van.

As we adjourned to our vehicles, I heard Mac say, "Man, she's smart."

Sam replied quietly, "Yeah, and real decorative, too."

Tidings refused to eat dinner with us again, even more standoff-ish and "Mr. Big Deal FBI Agent" than before. I gave him the van to drive back to the hotel. He seemed tight-lipped as he left. Sally said she was starving, and after a few minutes at the office in the DOT building preparing for the next day, I drove her to dinner.

We splurged, stopping at a pizza place this time instead of the usual burger-joint. Salads, pitcher of Coke, large thick-crust pepperoni. She didn't like black olives, and I am not partial to mushrooms or onions. These are among the perks of official government travel.

Sally sat through the meal quietly, listening to me talk about the condition of Penney's car and tell tales from the Legend of Lew Hills. She smiled pleasantly, and chuckled in all the right places, but she seemed a little more distant than the night before.

Her eyes had a luminous quality that was especially enchanting at night. As I sat there, all the girls who had ever refused me for dates and all the missed proms of my life came flooding back to me. She was a different person that evening, though. Something had changed, and she didn't want to say whatever it was for some reason.

"So, did something happen while I was gone?" I said, finally.

She sat silently for a few seconds, and looked away, out a darkened window. "What do you mean?"

"I just noticed that George Tidings was pretty tight this evening, and you seem kind of preoccupied, or... I don't know. Annoyed. Did you two have an argument? Are you mad at me, or anything?" I tried not to let my voice squeak.

She leaned on an elbow, and twirled a finger through her hair, looking around the room. "Oh, no, it's nothing, really."

I looked at her until she looked back, and smiled. "Can I help with anything? I am your supervisor, remember. I'm supposed to be interested in any problems."

She looked at me, eyes half closed, appearing a little disgusted and a little tired.

Finally, she sighed. "Let's just say that you're the only federal employee on the job here that hasn't made a pass at me today."

I sat back in the booth, embarrassed, and she smiled again, more broadly. "And thank you for restraining yourself, by the way," she added with a twinkle in her eye.

I was mute. Say something witty, quickly.

"Gee." I tried to sound innocent. "There goes another cherished dream."

She laughed, louder than she intended, and drew stares from the other patrons, which made her laugh more. She covered her mouth with her hands, and I laughed along.

After we quieted down, I cleared my throat. "Um, I'll say something to him tomorrow."

"No, no, no, it's all right." She shook her head, smiling a little now.

"But you shouldn't have to put up with that sort of thing if you don't want it." I began to get annoyed, thinking of her being bothered by strange men all the time, some stranger than others. I cleared my throat. "Look, the civil service has got really strong instructions on sexual harassment and workplace environments, things like that. I want you to feel OK about the job, and I promise I'll handle any issues you have."

She looked like she wanted to laugh. "I wasn't calling for help or anything. It's going to go fine."

I shook my head. "No, I'm serious," I said. "I'm your supervisor and it's a part of my job."

She continued to look amused and doubtful at the same time. "Good grief, you really are serious."

I sat back and felt like I was turning an odd color. It seemed like she had that sort of effect. "Yes, I am. There are rules to protect you from the sort of things you talked about and I am supposed to make sure it all works. It's my responsibility."

I was sure my nerd score was shooting up fast, so I shut up. She stared at me for a few seconds like she was having a hard time not laughing at me. She held her hands up in front of herself, still smiling but serious again. "Don't worry, Mike. I'm a big girl, and I can handle it."

"But--"

"It's OK." She hesitated. "I really appreciate it. But I'm a big girl, like I said. I've been through it before." She seemed like she wanted to say more now, and I leaned forward, waiting. "I really appreciated the way you listened to me about the test plan for tomorrow. I've had trouble in the past, in the Air Force, getting people to listen to my ideas."

"I couldn't have written a test plan that good," I

answered, truthfully. I was very impressed with her work.

She sighed, and frowned again while twisting her hair into a spiral. "Well, sometimes it's hard to be taken seriously when every guy you meet thinks you're a Mexican Barbie doll."

This time I laughed, and drew stares. I shut up as best I could, and she went on, wagging a finger at me. "Don't get me wrong. I've had a lot of fun. I don't want to gain weight and get my nose broken, or anything." She looked down at the junk food feast and shrugged. "Anyway, this crap will probably hit me all at once pretty soon and I'll wake up one morning blown up like a life raft."

We laughed and talked some more, and finally walked out into the night. We stood, staring up into the clear Colorado sky, marveling for a few seconds at the stars. As I unlocked the car, I realized that I had forgotten something. "Hey, I wonder if the French have landed yet. I expected them to call."

We slid into our seats and buckled up. Sally called the number for the airport control tower as I backed out of my slot and headed for our hotel three blocks down the road.

I waited while she listened to the ringing.

After several seconds she began to talk, out of the personal voice she had used in the restaurant and back into professional-speak. "Hello, Sally Montez, NTSB.

Yes. I was wondering if a GlobalMax jet on a flight plan from Minneapolis has landed in the last hour or so? ...Did you have a flight plan? ...No, I don't know a side number, but it was registered in France. It was an Aries GlobalMax. Yes, like the one that crashed."

She listened for a few seconds as I pulled up to a red light. She began to look perplexed. "Closed? But you had one, right?"

She listened for a few more seconds, and then put a hand over the phone, turning to me. "They say there was one due in this evening, but the flight plan was closed five hours ago."

I raised an eyebrow. "Well, they were stopping in Minneapolis for customs. Maybe they had to hold there, or something." A horn honked behind me, and I looked up to see a green light. Driving on, I said, "Ask 'em to call Minneapolis and see when they got off from Paris."

She nodded to me and made the request. A few seconds later she said "Thank you," gave the number to the phone and punched offline. "They're going to call back. It will take a couple of minutes."

I drove the rest of the way to the hotel, and parked in front. We climbed out, Sally with the phone still in her hand. I locked the car, and we began to walk into the lobby when her phone chirped.

"NTSB, Montez," she answered. She listened for a few seconds, her eyes growing wide. She nodded. "Ten hours ago? ...Goose Bay. OK. OK ...Uh, not right now, but my boss may get back to you. Thank you." She punched off the phone again, and took a deep breath preparing her report like a cadet spewing memorized gouge to an upperclassman at Officer Training School.

"They were lost off Canadian controller's radar about a hundred miles out from Goose Bay, Labrador, over the Atlantic Ocean. No distress calls or other warnings. They took off from Paris about ten hours ago, great circle route to here with a stop in Minneapolis, like you said. Four on board. The Canadian Defense Forces base at Goose Bay is sending an Aurora patrol plane out to search. They have no reports of emergency locator transmitters or anything."

"Shit," I said. "This can't be a coincidence."

I stood for a moment in the darkness. Dammit, Lew, what do I do now? There was no checklist for this situation.

"OK, get hold of Tidings," I said, but then reconsidered. "No, I'll call him."

"That's all right, I can handle him." Her voice was determined, and all business. She pulled a pad and pencil from her purse. "Are you going to call the Chairman?"

"Yes, and then I'm going to the office at the airport. You two meet me there as fast as you can. This is bullshit, and we're going to get to the bottom of it."

"Right."

I turned and walked away without thinking, and then caught myself, and turned to see Sally still there, looking back.

"I'm sure glad you're here, sister. This could get more exciting than we bargained for." I jumped into the car and broke the speed limit back to the airport. I called Lew's hotel in New Orleans first, asking for his room by number. After three rings, a groggy voice answered--not Lew's--and swore at me before hanging up.

Dialing the number again, I asked for Lew by name this time.

"I'm sorry," the switchboard operator said. "Mr. Hills checked out this morning."

Checked out? Lew had told me he would be in New Orleans for several more days. He must have moved to a hotel with a better bar.

I didn't want to bother his wife at home, especially at that hour, but the matter was important and I was feeling distinctly lonesome, riding herd on what was quickly becoming a major investigation. I dialed his home number in Maryland and waited while the phone rang. No answer there, either. I left a message and stopped to collect my thoughts.

I sat for a second, staring at the phone. The Chairman had said to keep Lew informed, and to get his chop on my plans. But Lew was doing his best to hide from me, and I had a big development to report. I didn't want the boss to find out about the second GMax crash from his morning Washington Post.

I wrote down what I wanted to tell McCall, took a deep breath, and dialed his home number. It was just after eleven in Washington, and a slightly groggy voice came on the line quickly.

"McCall." He cleared his throat.

I apologized for waking him.

He cleared his throat again. "It's OK. What do you need?"

"I've tried to get hold of Lew Hills, but no luck, and I have a couple of major developments that I think are pretty time critical."

"You haven't heard about Lew?" he said, his voice clear now.

"I, uh, no sir."

"OK, Mike, hold the line for a second." I could hear rustling in the background as McCall moved to a different phone. I heard him say quietly, "business, honey," before he came back on line. "Mike, I'm afraid Lew's in the hospital. He had a heart attack. He was out on the job when it happened."

"Is he going to be all right?"

"Could be, hope so. Too many cigars and steaks, I think. When you get to be as old as Lew and I are, you've got to be careful." McCall didn't smoke, and played racquetball like an assassin. I'd played him once, and his serves left little round bruises all over my ankles.

I was silent for a few seconds, at a loss. Finally, I said, "Where is he now?"

"He was flown to Baltimore today. Johns Hopkins. You couldn't do better for a hospital. He'll be out of action for a long time. Weeks, at least. Maybe months. It looks like you and I are on our own." He waited for a few seconds, while I digested the news. "So, anyway, what do you have?"

I cleared my throat and consulted the notes in front of me.

"Sir, I have just gotten news that another GlobalMax aircraft has crashed. It was on its way here carrying the chief engineer for Aries to help with the investigation."

"Holy shit. Where?" McCall sounded incredulous, and there were scratching sounds like he was taking notes.

"North Atlantic, near Goose Bay, in Canada. There's a search going on by Canadian Forces now."

"They won't find anybody in the water," he said firmly. "I flew out of Iceland for a while when I was on active duty. Even if anybody survived the landing, the water's so damned cold up there that you freeze in a minute or so. Maybe some wreckage."

"Yes sir," I said. "Obviously, it's very likely that the two accidents are related."

"Damned straight they are."

"Montez and a couple of technicians from ZYCO that I borrowed have worked out a good test plan, based on their maintenance procedures. I didn't get a chance to clear it with Lew, but we're ready to go ahead tomorrow morning with testing."

"Good," McCall said. "Press on with that test as soon as you can. I bet you don't find anything, but at least you can eliminate the obvious stuff. Let the locals go on with disassembly after that. When do you get flight data back?"

I looked at the ceiling, trying to remember what day it was. "We should get data back tomorrow, and autopsy results soon, too."

"OK. Now, look. I got a chance to talk to Lew before he went down. He doesn't trust that flight control system as far as he can spit. You're not going to find anything big. You are probably going to have to get into some serious simulations over the full system to get any answers. How cooperative has ZYCO been?" His Texas accent became thicker when annoyed, or tired, and it was dense now.

"Very cooperative, anything I have asked for. And I've got more help coming in."

"You bet they're being cooperative," McCall said forcefully. "They've never had one of their products bite 'em in the butt like this before. If they're payin' attention at all they're scared to death. Most of Zygler's money is tied up in ZYCO stock."

McCall paused, and I could imagine him staring at the ceiling, or scratching his head. "Now, let's see. Get with your pals at ZYCO tomorrow, after the testing, and tell 'em you are going to need simulation support. I'll have the office here get with Aries and get an early read on the crash in Canada. Call me with your results by close of business, latest. OK? Whatever you've got." Without waiting for me to answer, he went on. "Did you get to see Penney?"

"I missed him. He was just going into surgery when I got there. I gave Mrs. Penney your regards. I checked out the wreck. It was pretty bad. A total."

McCall growled. "Piss-poor timing. Press is going to have a field day. How'd it happen?"

"Can't say, sir," I answered. "The road was straight, and he must have been really moving. No witnesses, of course."

He was silent for a second, and sounded resigned when he spoke again. "Well, shit. You didn't get an easy one, did you?"

McCall signaled that he had heard enough, and I signed off with another promise to keep him informed of my progress. That would entail making some.

Sally and Tidings walked in as I hung up.

"Lew Hills had a heart attack," I said.

Sally sat across the table from me and covered her mouth, the way actresses do in the movies. "Oh, what else? Is he..."

"He's alive," I said. "He's at Johns Hopkins, going to have surgery. McCall says we should press on with the tests."

Tidings sat down heavily at the end of the table.

"Sorry to disturb your evening, George," I said.

Tidings shrugged. "I was watching an old movie." He seemed a little more relaxed now.

I sat back in my chair and put my feet up on the table. "George, you're a detective. If we assume that some kind of illegal crap was going on here, what would you do? How would you proceed?"

He leaned forward on his elbows and interlaced his fingers, staring at a class ring he wore. Now he was getting interested. This was good police stuff, his stuff. "It depends. You suspect something criminal now?"

I closed my eyes for a second, beginning to feel seriously tired. "I don't really know. Could be something like covering up a known defect, or just errors. Or something else. Lew and McCall think the control systems might be at fault. It could be the airframe, or engines, or anything else. I am just getting a weird feeling that we're missing something big. But if this all caused by an intentional act or acts then there were three murders before, and there are seven now."

Tidings smiled and shook his head. I had heard his lecture on the superiority of the Bureau and its unending quest for justice before and it was starting again. "Are you finally ready to get serious? It's about time."

I held up a hand. "George, could we stick to my question for now?"

He interrupted. "The Bureau doesn't have time for all the Fun with Science experiments you want."

"I understand that you need to arrest somebody."

"And get a conviction."

I tried not to sound angry but my voice started to rise. "I know, and you won't make Special-Agent-In-Charge if you can't march somebody out in leg irons and handcuffs. But if we lock in on police activity too soon we'll miss technical details and maybe the real cause. I have to deal with your Bureau, and the FAA, and the Department of Transportation, and everybody else. The Board is in charge of this investigation, at least for now."

I forced myself to calm down. "Look, I need a technical solution as bad as you need a conviction. If there is something wrong with the technology, it might be a problem for a lot of other planes, maybe airliners or whatever." I paused for a little dramatic effect. "Besides, if we have every question about what happened answered you'll have more evidence. Now, can you help us?"

Tidings stared at me for a few seconds and then

stood up, walking slowly to a white board that hung on a wall opposite the door. He picked up a marker pen and began to write, but the pen was dry. He pitched it into a wastebasket and grabbed up another, facing the board as he wrote.

"What we would usually do is to list every fact that we know about the case, categorize them, and then stand back and look for a pattern. The pattern will show us where to look for more information. When you get enough info, you can build a credible case and make an arrest." He turned back to face me. "I am going to need a lot of other data to throw into the process. Things that may not be connected to your investigation, but we won't know until we sort it all out. Personal stuff, business stuff, the works. Think you can get it from ZYCO?"

I considered the problem for a second. If I threw him a bone at this stage it might help later. "I might have to tell them I'm asking for you and not the Board."

"If you have to, OK. Just don't volunteer that information if you can help it. I might not be able to use it as evidence, but we need something to get us going."

"I'm not sure how I'll do it, but I'll give it a shot. Give me a list of what you need."

He took a note and leaned against the board. "So, what do we know?"

I crossed my arms behind my head. "Well, we know there are two crashes."

"Three," Sally said.

Tidings stared at her, not overtly hostile, but not friendly, either. "Three?"

"Three. Steve's wreck makes three."

Tidings looked doubtful, but I nodded. "OK. Three crashes until we can prove otherwise. It's probably a long shot, but what the hell, it's only ink."

Tidings drew three columns on the board, and we began to fill them in with what we knew. As the exercise continued, it became apparent that we didn't know much. The two aircraft crashes had happened in different phases of flight, with different crews, different loads, in different weather. Steve's accident was completely separate, except that he was associated with the investigation, and was carrying important information--he said--down from Denver.

We all stared at the board, willing a pattern to appear, but none came. We gave up at midnight and went back to our rooms for a few hours of rest.

I spent part of the night staring at the ceiling, thinking about Lew. Along with my worry for my old friend's health, I was angry with him for leaving me alone with this mess.

chapter

6

Mac and Sam's boss, the guy I'd spoken to the day before in the flight department, turned out to be an earnest young management major in a gray pinstriped suit. He showed up with the two mechanics the next morning, looking out of place in the mechanic's van, riding in the back seat between piles of reference manuals and toolboxes. The ZYCO vehicle towed a small ground power unit behind it.

Sally met them at the crime scene tape perimeter at 8:00 a.m., precisely on time. She waited while Johnny Pinstripes got out of the van, and then directed the two techs to drive behind the aircraft's tail. As they parked and began setting up for the morning's tests, he walked up to me.

"Mr. O'Hara?" He extended a hand. "Clinton Harding, from ZYCO Transportation." He was short, thin and bird-like, seeming even more earnest at close range. After we shook hands, we both turned to watch the action at the wreckage. "I got a call about this matter from Mr. Zygler himself," he said, sounding terribly impressed.

"Telephone or burning bush?" I said as he looked away, toward the work in progress. I guessed it was the first time he had ever talked to the great man.

He turned back like a startled wren. "I beg your pardon?"

I waved the question off, and he went on. "Mr. Zygler wants to accommodate you completely. The assets of the entire corporation are at your disposal, and I am to keep him fully informed. Fully informed."

"Well, I appreciate that." I scanned the skies above the Rockies in the distance, seeing a high thin layer of clouds, the precursors of an approaching weather system. "When we're done here, I'd like to begin moving the wreckage indoors, out of the weather. You have a hangar on the field, don't you?"

He nodded. "Oh, yes. Thirty-thousand square feet. Heated and air conditioned, of course."

"This wreckage is still ZYCO's property," I said, "and if we could use the space it would help. Could you arrange for a flatbed truck and a crane? By noon, say?"

Harding pulled a phone from a jacket pocket and began calling for help. I walked to join Sally and Tidings, who had just arrived. They were watching the two techs plug the external power cords into a connection at the aircraft's tail.

By eight-fifteen, a foam pumper truck and three firefighters were standing by. Sally pronounced herself satisfied, and I gave permission to power up the control system.

After all the preparations, the actual event was an anticlimax. When Sam applied power, one small short appeared in a cable bundle under floorboards at the smashed pilot's station, but Mac quickly patched around the damage and the three went to work on the test plan. The fire fighters and the lone police officer on duty watched for a few minutes, and then lost interest.

Sally had set up a laptop computer in the ZYCO van, with wires running to the on-board computers. While Sam sat with his head and shoulders in the equipment bay, Sally and Mac ran through a series of diagnostic checks of the flight control system, with columns of data scrolling across the screen as the testing proceeded. Sally sat engrossed in the data, seldom looking up from her work, communicating only with Mac, and then only in short bursts of computer jargon. Tidings watched over Sally's shoulder, taking notes in silence. I hung out, working on my laptop and appreciating a few quiet minutes.

After a half hour of preliminaries, control surfaces began to move at random intervals, sometimes moving to their full lock positions, sometimes quivering rapidly. At one point, the wing flaps lowered to a ten-degree setting, but a shout from Mac stopped the movement before the surfaces contacted the ground. I watched for a few minutes while things moved randomly and Sally took notes. As the testing went on, the main sound to be heard was the clicking of keyboards.

An hour later I was getting as bored as the firefighters. I had begun to fidget and wander around the GMax when my phone beeped for attention. The call was from Keats in Denver.

"I thought you'd like an update on Steve," he said cheerily. The tone of his voice was enough for me to know that things were going well. "He seems to be doing better, and the doctors are very optimistic. They got a top orthopedic man in to look at his leg, and managed to save most of it. He will have a much easier time walking than we thought when you were here."

"That's great news," I said with real relief. "Have you been able to talk to him yet?" I continued to walk around the aircraft, stopping our conversation to watch as a 737 lifted off and roared overhead into the now-cloudy sky.

"I'm afraid not," Keats said. "They still have him in the coma, and the neurologist said not to be surprised if he doesn't remember much. They're concentrating on getting him functioning again."

I stopped, looking at the ground for a second. "I was hoping he could tell us more about the phone call from the Aries engineer."

"Nothing is sure until they bring him out." Changing subjects, Keats went on. "I want to have some help down there for you this afternoon. A senior technician."

"Thanks. I can use him."

I explained my short-term plans, and he offered more assistance if I needed it. After agreeing to report anything interesting from the morning's tests, I hung up.

The phone almost immediately beeped again. It was the medical examiner's office, inquiring if I could come to a preliminary brief. I looked back at Sally, engrossed in her testing, and offered to come any time. He gave me a time and sent instructions on how to find the office in town.

Sally looked up from her work long enough to give a quick thumbs-up evaluation of her progress. Tidings accepted an invitation to come with me to the M.E.'s office, and we took my car, winding slowly around the perimeter road until we came to the airport exit.

I followed Fountain Boulevard into town, and Tidings rode quietly. After ten blocks, I saw him cross his arms and shake his head.

"So, what's on your mind?" I said.

Tidings hesitated. "Sally's really some girl."

Bastard.

My anger at Tidings from the night before began to creep back into my consciousness, but I suppressed it.

"Yeah, I guess so. A good job of hiring. She's really sharp on the technical side of things." I kept an even tone in my voice, but I could feel a vein bulge on my forehead.

He was silent again for a few seconds. "Got a kind of an attitude, though. Seems to think she's smarter than everybody."

Asshole.

I didn't speak for three breaths, and then let a note of irritation creep into my voice. "Could be she is, George. Maybe she's tired of being chased all the time, too. Did you think of that?"

He looked across at me, his face blank.

I smiled at him. "So, have you talked to your wife lately?"

He looked away, and mumbled. "Kid's sick. She says it's raining."

We didn't talk again for three blocks.

"Do you think we'll hear anything surprising from the medical examiner?" I said, to break the icy silence.

"No," he answered quietly. "If there was a bomb or anything, we'd have seen evidence in the wreckage. And I don't think either crewman was a drunk or a doper."

It took another twenty minutes to reach Memorial Hospital where the M.E.'s office was located, and I managed to miss the turn north onto Hancock. I had to circle through back streets to pick up the main drag. We searched for a parking place for ten minutes more before heading to the basement of the building.

The room number I'd been given turned out to mark a large conference room, with freshly plastered walls and new carpet. A large table ringed with office chairs nearly filled the room, and several people were there ahead of us.

A reporter who identified herself as Liz Fowler from the local newspaper wrote down my name when I mentioned the NTSB.

"Have you figured out what caused the crash yet?" She pulled a small tape recorder from her purse. She was tall, and not terrible looking, and I wondered if Tidings was going to hit on her, too.

I assembled several standard phrases from NTSB crash-language. "Not at this time. We are still in the very early phases of a systematic investigation. I don't want to speculate at this stage. It sometimes takes a year or more to find a probable cause." The public affairs office would love it.

"Do you have any opinion about the crash of the other Aries jet?" she asked, holding the recorder in front of my face annoyingly. She had done her homework.

I shook my head. "The Canadians are following up on that. We'll share any information we have with them, of course."

She nodded, the way they teach in journalism school. "Does Aries or ZYCO have any ideas?"

"You'd have to ask them," I said with as pleasant a smile as I could manage.

"Have you asked them?"

I answered with a broader smile, feeling more irritation. She turned her recorder off as two official-looking figures entered the room and walked to the head of the table.

After taking seats, the medical examiner and his assistant, both middle-aged men, introduced themselves, and asked who we all were. The others were from the FAA, state police and insurance companies. I introduced myself as the investigator in charge from NTSB headquarters and Tidings as "also from Washington."

The medical examiner sat back and let his assistant brief their results. "Let me say up front that there isn't much surprising here. All the victims were in reasonably good health, and there are no signs of drug or alcohol use. Injuries and causes of death are all consistent with what we would expect in this situation."

He consulted notes that he had spread out in front of himself. He began by reading ages and general information about all victims, and then gave details for each.

"The pilot, Mr. Fleet, was apparently flying the aircraft. Both thumbs were broken and torn off on impact by the control wheel, and he was probably pushing hard on a pedal, since the left ankle was broken. Mr. Fleet's cause of death was massive injuries to the head and abdomen, plus severe spinal injuries suffered on impact. Death was nearly instantaneous, and injuries from the post-crash fire were not a factor." I took notes for the 6120 file, to supplement the official reports. Nearly everyone around the table was scribbling into notebooks as the assistant spoke.

He shifted to another sheaf of papers before proceeding.

"The copilot, Mr. Berry, was also apparently assisting Mr. Fleet on the controls at the time of impact, as all the fingers of the right hand were broken."

The reporter raised a hand. "How do you know that he was helping on the controls? Couldn't that injury be from something else?"

The assistant looked at her over his glasses. "There

was a distinct imprint of the Aries company logo on the tips of the victim's fingers, which matches the logo on the copilot's control wheel." He looked down at his pile of papers and resumed. "Mr. Berry also died of massive injuries consistent with impact and collapse of the cockpit structure."

He shifted to the third set of papers and resumed. "The passenger, Mr. Corso, was severely injured in the impact, suffering a catastrophic failure of the spinal body in the vicinity of the third and fourth lumbar vertebrae, as well as a fractured right wrist consistent with whip-lash type action, and several severe object impact injuries." The assistant looked up from his notes, and spoke conversationally. "It looks like he was hit in the nose and forehead by a laptop computer during the crash, and he suffered severe damage to the facial structure. He died of smoke inhalation and burns caused by the post-crash fire."

The Liz Fowler raised a hand again. "Was he conscious?"

The briefer nodded. "Yes. There are injuries on the left hand--uh, torn fingernails--that suggest he was trying to unfasten the seat belt after the impact. Of course, he was paralyzed from the waist down by the spinal injuries. With that and the broken wrist, I doubt he could have gotten out of the cabin anyway."

I looked around the room. Most of us were

unsettled by the information, and were at least attempting to remain impassive. The reporter was nodding vigorously, a slight smile curling her lips, and scribbling vigorously on a note pad.

Mild disgust rose in me. I had worked investigations for many years, and had attended dozens of sessions like this. There was no information here that would benefit the public, but broad dissemination would almost certainly disturb or cause anguish for friends or loved ones left behind by the wreck. The reporter was onto a juicy story, however, and might even rate a headline on the front page. Gore sells.

She looked up from her notes. "How long did he live?"

"He was probably conscious about twenty seconds after smoke entered the cabin. He lived about a minute after that."

I raised a hand. "So, you found no evidence at all of explosion, fire before impact, or anything else suspicious?"

The briefer shook his head. "Nothing."

The reporter looked at me. "Do you suspect an explosion?"

"No," I said. "This just helps confirm things. It's a routine question, that's all."

She wrote another note, and the medical examiner asked for other questions. The insurance agency representatives asked for more information on toxicology, probably for their reports, and the meeting was done.

I took copies of the formal reports from the medical examiner for the accident file and walked to the door, with Tidings close behind. Before we could escape, the reporter caught me and pressed a card into my hand.

"Liz Fowler, Rocky Mountain Times. What do you think about him getting caught by his seat belt?"

"What do you mean?" I asked, but I knew what she wanted to write already.

"Well, he couldn't get the seat belt unbuckled, and he couldn't get out." Her eyes were bright, lit up by an ironic headline dancing in her mind.

"That's not what the medical examiner said, Ms. Fowler," I interjected. "Read your notes. The only reason he survived the impact was that he was wearing his seat belt. If he hadn't worn it, he would have flown around the cabin and gotten smashed into strawberry jam, OK?" I felt my skin getting hot, and calmed down again, going on in a quieter tone. "Please don't write a story that says he was killed by his belt. First, you would be wrong, which God knows you don't want to be, and second, one of your readers might decide to not wear the belt in his car because of your story and get killed in the next minor accident he gets into."

"How can I get more information?"

I resumed my walk out the door. "There is an

NTSB field office in Denver, and they would be happy to answer any questions you have."

"Do you have a number?" She called down the hall after me.

I looked back over my shoulder. "It's in the book. U.S. Government. You're a reporter. Find out."

We headed back toward the airport. Tidings made tsk-tsk noises.

"You should be nicer to the press than that, Mike. They can cause you trouble." He shook his head in disapproval.

"I know." I grimaced mentally at the tone of voice I had used on Liz Fowler. "I've seen too many reporters jump to conclusions and cause pressure to find someone to blame when there isn't anybody." I lapsed into silence, and we returned to Peterson Field.

I would have to call Ms. Fowler later. Lew would.

Sally was just finishing her tests when Tidings and I got back to the scene. She sat in the open side door of the van with a laptop balanced on her knees. The two technicians were huddled next to the ZYCO van, deep in consultation when we pulled up, while the manager, Harding, hovered around the edges. Sally and Mac were shaking their heads as we got out of the car.

"Anything?" I said.

She looked at me blankly for a second, as if she didn't recognize me. Finally, her eyes refocused and she tilted her head toward me. "We're done with the tests." She sounded frustrated.

I leaned against the van next to her and waited. "Find anything odd?"

She hesitated again. "Yes and no. Everything checked out. All the tests were OK. And we added a couple of other things that we thought of at the last minute. All the controls responded exactly as they should have, with no problems." She stopped and looked at the computer again.

"That's the no," I said. "What's the yes?"

She pursed her lips. "There's an anomaly in the RAM loading in one of the computers."

I mentally pleaded for her to go on so I wouldn't have to admit I didn't understand what she'd said.

"It's kind of geeky. The flight software is held in flash random access memory in each computer, and it's completely redundant across all three. In fact, according to the manuals, it's supposed to be absolutely identical." She stopped, and looked at the computer again.

"And it's not?"

"Yes." She shook her head in annoyance, still preoccupied by the problem. "I mean no. It's not. After we'd been running for an hour or so, Sam noticed that the RAM readout at the computers was giving a different answer for one computer than the other two."

I crossed my arms. "So, what was the flash-RAM

loading before you started? Were they the same then?"

She winced, and closed her eyes. Quietly, she said, "I don't know. I didn't think to check before we started." She looked up, still wincing.

I smiled and shrugged. "Hey, that's OK. I didn't think of it either. Neither did McCall."

She relaxed a little. "Um. Anyway, we couldn't think of a reason why the B computer--they're marked A, B and C--we couldn't think of a reason why B should be different. It's not discussed anywhere in the manuals. I wish we could get the Aries guys here. Maybe they could explain the blank space."

"Blank space?" I asked, trying to keep up.

She nodded into the computer. "The B computer has less code than the others. Not much, but it's supposed to be exactly the same. I asked the machines to show how the code is distributed in the RAM. It's supposed to follow a protocol that's listed in the service manual, but the B system has a large section the size of the missing code that doesn't seem to follow the rules. Pretty weird."

I agreed. "What's missing? Can you tell?"

"I think so. We tried it on each computer. It seems to be a driver for a control surface. The elevator, I think."

She added apologetically, "I was hoping I'd found a smoking gun, but I think it's going to be more complicated than that."

I thought for a moment. The elevators control how high an aircraft's nose rose above the horizon. This airplane appeared to have stalled, possibly because the pilots let the nose get too high on takeoff. "There might be a connection in there somewhere," I said to encourage her. "So, where do we go from here? Do you have any ideas about how to proceed?"

She pecked at the keyboard, saving data to a file. "I guess we talk to ZYCO. They must have an explanation. It's their software."

"We'll do that, of course, but think about a third party." I said. "If there's a problem or an error, ZYCO would be opening themselves up to a bunch of lawsuits if they admit it. We need to think of someone else to ask. Chairman McCall might know somebody."

She nodded and went back to her keyboard, and then swore to herself again. She looked up sheepishly. "I'm sorry. I forgot again. Chairman McCall called while you were gone."

I laughed. "You have a mental block about McCall?"

"He was a general, and I was a second lieutenant, I guess."

"He'd tell you that he was a second lieutenant once, too. Anyway, you're civil service now, so you can relax. What did he want?"

"He sounded annoyed that you haven't been

answering your phone," Sally said, smiling nervously.

"He always sounds annoyed. It's his natural state."

I have a mental block about answering cell phones--I never seem to get good news when I do--and I keep the ringer off. It drove people nuts. Chairman McCall in turn hated leaving voice messages, so it worked out.

She leaned back and stretched her arms, and I realized that she had probably been sitting there hunched over the keyboard the whole morning. "He wanted a dump on the tests, and I gave him one. We hadn't hit the anomaly yet. And he said the voice and data readouts from the recorders will emailed to us today. They should be here this afternoon."

"Maybe the readouts will help your RAM anomaly make sense," I said. "We can go over it all tonight. If you're done here, let's go give McCall a ring."

We left Tidings and the ZYCO men to break the test rig down while Sally and I headed for our office.

I called the chairman. After waiting on hold for three minutes, I heard McCall come on the line with his usual expansive Texas greeting.

He listened quietly while I outlined the results of Sally's testing and the medical examiner's findings. As I finished my discussion of the autopsies and toxicology reports, Sally walked in with her computer under her arm. I clicked on the speakerphone and helped her unload.

"Ms. Montez is here, sir," I said as she sat. "She did have one interesting finding this morning, and I wanted to cover it with her present."

"OK, shoot, and hello, Sally." McCall was still cheerful after a long day in his Washington office.

I motioned for her to talk, and she smiled at the phone. "Hello, sir. Our testing did find that all the controls worked as expected, but we did find one item that wasn't according to Hoyle." She spent a minute going over the anomaly in less detail than she had with me.

After listening to Sally's description, McCall commented, "Damn. Whatever happened to pulleys and cables and bell cranks? I know I am an old guy, but we seem to be awfully dependent on computers. Sally, what chance do you think there is that this problem could be a causative factor?"

Sally frowned and said, "I'm not sure I can say. I really need some expert help. Somebody with some serious experience with fly-by-wire control systems. Do we have anybody on staff that could help?"

I broke in. "This could definitely be a causative factor, and Sally found it on her first pass through the system. Really good work." She looked embarrassed. "We could use some advice, but I think we need to keep it separate from ZYCO."

McCall was silent for a few seconds, and then

answered, "Not sure, folks, but I'll see who I can find. If not in-house, I'll find somebody in the industry, or maybe the Defense Department. Why don't you give the Bird a call down in the lab and talk to him while I'm looking, and I'll get back to you."

McCall began to sign off, and then caught himself. "And hey, Lew's going in for surgery tomorrow morning in Baltimore. I'll let you know how things go there." He gave me a phone number to call, and we thanked him for his time before clicking the phone off.

Sally booted up her laptop while I dialed the NTSB technical branch in Washington.

Dr. Thomas Schmidt, head of the technical branch, answered the phone himself. I knew that Schmidt had lettered in football at Holy Cross, but his high-pitched voice and odd mannerisms had earned him the nickname "The Bird" at headquarters. He was very tall and profoundly bald, and he reminded me of a huge stork with a PhD.

I told him the chairman wanted me to give him a call. He asked me how the investigation was going and I gave him a rundown, and then introduced Sally.

"Ms. Montez, you'll have to drop by the lab if they ever let you come home. I'd love to show you around and talk about how we can support you in the field. I understand you're a computer scientist by training."

She smiled into the phone. "It was my degree

field, but I'm very interested in aerospace technology in general. Engines, structures, materials, everything."

I waved my hands and tried to stop her before she mentioned materials, but it was too late.

"Materials! How wonderful. I'm a metallurgist, actually. We have several studies started on failure modes on hybrid structures of carbon composites and aluminum. I'll have to show you our new electron microscope." Before I could cut in, Schmidt started into an eight-minute discussion of metallurgy and his latest work on ductile-to-brittle transition in non-ferrous metals. Sally asked polite questions. I managed to slip in a few specifics about support we needed, and he promised to work on it. Eventually we wound up the call. She swore to make an appointment to see Schmidt as soon as possible and we rang off.

Sally smiled and rolled her eyes. "He seems to love his work."

I had to smile myself. "Pretty common on the board staff. He's OK, actually. His staff loves him, and he is a recognized expert in the whole business of the board. Damned near as smart as you, in fact." She laughed a little and shook her head.

By the time we got the voice transcript, data and audio files from the voice recorder in and opened up, we had a pile of laptops open, each with a charger and other electronic garbage. The place looked like a used computer store. We opened the transcript on one laptop and the data on another, trying to match the data readout to it page for page, but the acres of numbers from the flight data recorder that stretched down the pages in endless columns were too much to compare. I gave up and sat down to read the transcript as Sally loaded up the CVR audio file.

I followed the recording by reading the transcript, and we played the sounds of the crash back several times to make sure that we understood all of Schmidt's marginal notes.

The transcript didn't really tell us much. The start up and checks were routine. Taxi was normal, with the pilots engaging in small talk about the weather and other more personal matters.

At one point, the pilot asked the copilot if he was ready for the stop in Paris. "We have 20 hours for I and I."

The copilot asked, "What's I and I?"

The pilot replied, "The French version of R and R. Intercourse and intoxication."

Laughter. "I'm too broke for that. Did you see the stock price? My 401K is tits up in the fish tank."

"I couldn't look. Didn't have a barf bag with me."

There was a pause and a short radio discussion between the pilot and Peterson Field ground control, and then he took the subject back up.

"I bet Corso's going to try to talk the French into something on this trip. I'm surprised Randall isn't going. Money, money, money. Don't sell out your company stock yet."

"I hope it works. Zygler's head will blow off again."

"Nah, he'll blow off theirs."

The copilot responded quietly. "He's going to be too busy to care."

The pilot agreed. "The shit's really hitting the fan."

Sally looked across the table at me with a disgusted expression. "They aren't following sterile cockpit procedures. And by the way, men are pigs."

"Thank you. Sorry. Nobody ever plans to have their last words recorded for posterity." I shrugged.

The engines sounded like they had accelerated normally, and the copilot's speed callouts sounded right. Liftoff sounded smooth. At that point in the transcript, everything sounded good. Shortly after takeoff, a rasping sound appeared on the tape, and Schmidt had identified it as "labored breathing, probably pilot" in his notes. Fleet was working hard at something, and scared.

Five seconds later, and less than ten seconds after liftoff, the copilot could be heard to say "What the hell?" The pilot's response was immediate: "I know, dammit. I'm pushing." At that point, Schmidt had made a note that both engines' fan speeds had begun to decay slightly, indicating that the aircraft's speed was decreasing despite the thrust of both engines at full power. He had noted the decay on the data recorder, and confirmed it by graphic analysis of the background noise on the voice tape. A few seconds later the engines began to labor, the stall warning stick shaker began to vibrate the pilots' control yokes, indicating that a stall was imminent. The stick shaker made a loud, rapid clicking sound that continued to the end of the tape. Shortly after the clicking began, I could hear a low-pitched rumble.

Sally said, "What is that sound?"

"Stall buffet. The airflow over the wings has separated because of too low a speed and too high an angle. The flow becomes turbulent and the wings lose lift. It shakes the whole airplane like a wet dog. You can't miss it."

She nodded, and we listened to the rest of the CVR file in silence. The last voice heard before the ground interrupted the recorder's power supply was Fleet's. "Shit," followed by "Oh no" were his final words. Pilots in crashes often died with words like that.

Three seconds later, a crunching sound ended the audio file, followed by a beep, inserted by Schmidt to mark the impact for his analysis instruments.

After the fifth time through the audio we had heard enough, and I closed the file.

c h a p t e r

7

The flight data described the deaths of three men and the destruction of the fabulous new airplane in excruciating detail. Sally and I began deciphering the readouts, file after file, separated by phases of the aircraft's movement.

The flight data recorder was a new type that I had read about but had not seen before. It recorded sixty different lines of data, including everything about controls, engines and just about anything else we would need to know. The information was recorded at half-second intervals whenever electrical power was on in the airplane. The columns of data flowed down the computer screen like a waterfall. This mass of information was presented in columns spreading across the screen of Sally's extra wide machine. The font was small to allow showing the whole thing across the screen, and my eyes ached in minutes.

Sally wasn't doing any better than me. "Do we really have to read all this?"

I sighed in agreement. I opened the files that came up first after engine start. "Let's go through the pre-flight stuff and see if we can eliminate some of it."

The technical staff would give us a video portrayal of the aircraft's attitude and motions, but it would take days to get it in. We began reading and making notes just after three. Within three hours, I had formed a clear picture of the GMax's flight path from takeoff to impact and I started summarizing my findings in an outline while Sally researched a question for me in an Aries maintenance manual.

Tidings walked in, followed by another figure in an NTSB vest. He closed the door behind himself and the new arrival. "Mike, we knocked off for the night. And we got some help. This is Leland Wang from the Denver office."

I stood and shook his hand. Wang was nearly as small as Sally, and as we went through polite welcoming pleasantries, his speech was nearly inaudible, and his face was fixed in a polite new-guy smile. He was ex-Navy like me. We'd traded calls and email over another case in the past.

I glanced sideways at Tidings. "So George, does Lee know about your, um, status?"

"You, mean that I'm FBI? I told him."

Wang said, "George says you may have sabotage here."

"It's a possibility," I said.

Tidings sat and leaned his elbows on the table. "You found something else?"

I sat back from the paperwork and rubbed the bridge of my nose, fighting a headache. "It's what we're not finding that is bugging me." I swept an arm out above the papers. "There's nothing here to explain what happened. There ought to be, and there isn't. The airplane didn't act right for the way they tried to fly it or the way it was loaded."

"Oh, yeah," Tidings interjected. "We pulled an access cover off the main fuselage fuel tank, and it was filled just like the loading diagram said. It was the only tank that didn't rupture on impact or the fire would have been a lot worse. And we got the door open to the aft baggage compartment. It was the only door on the whole airplane too sprung to open easily."

Wang nodded again. "We had to drill out the hinges from the outside to get it off."

"And there was nothing inside?"

"Nothing," said Tidings, and he was echoed by Wang.

I shook my head in disgust and crossed my arms. "It would've had to be filled with lead bars to make the plane act the way it did, anyway."

Wang indicated the data sheets. "What do you have?"

I sighed, and scanned across the screens. "Loading was OK, flight planning and preparation appear to be good, as required by federal regulations and by Aries procedures. Engine start sounded normal, and taxi to the runway was about what you'd expect. They were cleared for takeoff, and rolled normally. The nose then rose fast, and stayed way too high, over sixty-five degrees. They climbed to roughly one thousand feet above ground level, and then the airplane stalled." I consulted the pages of data again. "It looks like he tried to roll the airplane to the left just before the stall occurred. If he thought he'd lost pitch control, I'm thinking he might have tried a vertical recovery maneuver. He'd try to roll into a steep turn, and then kick the pitch out with rudder. They teach that in Air Force pilot training, and Fleet was ex-Air Force."

"The Navy teaches that, too. It's pretty standard."

I held out a hand and simulated the aircraft's gyrations in the classic hangar flying style. "It looks like the right wing stalled first, maybe due to turbulence, or maybe because of Fleet's control inputs. Hard to call." I summarized what we knew about the plane's flight. "The airplane hit the ground ten degrees left wing low, with about a flat pitch attitude. They hit, slid into the equipment shed off the side of the runway and burned." I folded my hands on the table. "That's it. Total fight time thirty-one seconds."

Tidings sat silently, and pursed his lips.

"It looks like they did everything right," Sally said. She highlighted several columns on one section of data in red on her screen turned the computer to show us. Wang read over her shoulder. "The autopilot and flight control system were set up for departure. Fleet held the yoke forward during the takeoff run, as the Aries procedures require. That's to help with nose wheel steering effective on the ground. As he got to takeoff speed, he pulled back slightly, as you'd expect."

She spaced down through the data she had marked and pointed to data on control position. "You can see here, he didn't pull back too far on the controls. And here--" She pointed to the top of the circled columns. "--you can see that he started pushing hard forward again almost as soon as the nose started to rise."

"He knew something was screwed up right away," I said.

Sally marked another set of figures. "Here he has the yoke all the way forward, commanding a full nose-down pushover, like going over the top on a roller coaster. It corresponds to the time on the voice recorder where Fleet says he's pushing."

I looked at Wang. "Lee, you're a pilot, right?"

He looked up from the data. "Sure, in the Navy."

"When was the last time you pushed a stick all the way forward in flight?"

He shook his head. "Never. Doesn't happen, unless you're doing aerobatics or something. All the way back, maybe, but even then just when you're landing."

"So Fleet knew things were bad." Sally said.

"Panicky move. Reflexive," Wang said.

There was silence, while we all digested the information.

Finally, I spoke. "We need to dig into the code, but all this was tested extensively in development, both in the lab and in flight tests with production aircraft." I looked at Wing and Sally. "Could this be some accidental assembly of air data and control inputs that caused this strange action? Something that wasn't designed or predicted?"

Sally shook her head vigorously. "No way. There are cross-checks on top of cross-checks on every move. Can't happen accidentally. Not a chance."

I looked back at the data. "I agree. All this brings me back to the idea of murder or sabotage. It's all a damn sight more likely now than it was yesterday."

"You mean somebody murdered Wesley Corso," Tidings said, "and the weapon was a hundred-million dollar jet airplane?"

I looked across the room at the notes we had made on the board the previous night. "So, where do we go from here, George? Do you want to start questioning people?"

Tidings slouched back in his chair and stuck his hands in his pockets. "Well, this is a federal matter now, of course." He looked at the ceiling. "Aircraft are registered and certified by the FAA, and interference with flight operations is a federal offense. But I'd probably be obligated to inform the El Paso county sheriff and maybe the Colorado Springs city police."

"And you'd rather stay out of the spotlight," I said.

"For now," he said, smiling. "It's not exactly the Bureau's approved procedure, but if I start asking a lot of questions I have to identify myself as an agent. Maybe you could nose around a little, before I come out in the open. You might be able to find out things in the normal course of your investigation that I couldn't."

I thought the proposition over. It wasn't exactly NTSB procedure, either. What would McCall think about it? I'd have to call him with a progress report in the morning anyway.

I had turned my cell phone on in case McCall

called again and it buzzed in my jacket pocket. It was Keats, calling from Denver again.

"Mike, Steve is doing a little better," Keats said. "They brought him out of the coma for about a half hour. He has a lot of pain, and they didn't keep him awake long." Keats sounded exhausted.

"Good news," I passed the news on to the others. "Has he said anything else about his accident?"

"No. He wasn't very lucid. The doctors are going to bring him out again tomorrow afternoon and he may be better. Can you break loose down there long enough to come up?"

"I can come up tomorrow. When are visiting hours?"

I noticed Tidings get up from his chair and walk to the board.

"Nine to five," Keats said.

I wrote a note. "Are you free after that? I want to bounce a couple of ideas off you while I'm in Denver."

He agreed, and we made an appointment for five-fifteen. I put down the phone, and looked at the board where Tidings was working.

The FBI agent turned his back to the board, and slouched against the wall, flipping a felt-tip pen with one hand.

"Here's what we have." He pointed to the left end of the board. "One. A wrecked GlobalMax, three dead.

Aside from being a burned-out hulk, the only squawk on the airplane is a minor gap in the program of one of three computers. Someone may have been angry at Mr. Corso for stock manipulation. Or maybe not."

He moved to the center of the board, and Sally turned in her chair to follow. "Two. Another GMax has crashed, on the way here. Four dead, cause unknown, and connection to our crash unknown. Marcel Covert, the chief engineer at Aries died onboard, and he may have had some ideas about what was going on here but didn't tell anybody except Steve Penney."

"And Covert wanted to talk to you," I added.

"Right." Tidings nodded and wrote another line on the board. He moved again, and I swiveled to follow.

He pointed to the board casually with the pen he held. "Which brings us to three. Steve Penney does a demolition derby off the interstate on the way here from Denver, after telling you about the aforementioned French guy. He may have been run off the road, but there is no evidence of any foul play, and Mr. Penney isn't talking much. Maybe there's more information coming. He had put in a lot of long hours, and may have gone to sleep at the wheel with the cruise control on."

Tidings put his pen down and wiped his hands. "There's not much in common there, not much to go on."

I sat and stared at the board. It was nearly seven,

and the long days were beginning to wear. Breathing deep to try to drive the fuzzy edges of fatigue out of my mind, I leaned forward with my elbows on the table. "I guess you could say that the second two events were related to the first one. I mean, the Frogs wouldn't have been flying if the first wreck hadn't occurred."

Tidings shrugged. "Yeah? So? Doesn't prove anything."

Sally had kicked off her shoes, and sat curled up in her chair. She held a finger in front of her lips, like a librarian in full cry. "I know something all three of those things have in common."

Tidings turned to her with an expectant look. "Tell us, please."

She nodded to herself as she spoke slowly and clearly. "The one thing they all really have in common is embedded software."

The light came on over my head as soon as she said it. "The plane had all its control surfaces directly operated by computers," I said. "No cables or anything they could use to override. If the software was messed up, the computers could go nuts and the pilots couldn't stop them."

Tidings looked at her quizzically. "But, Penney..."

Sally held up a hand to silence him, speaking louder and faster now. "Steve was driving a mid-sized domestic sedan. All three major Detroit automakers use processors that run all the systems in the car: engines, transmissions, anti-lock brakes, the whole thing. Computer code is in everything. The typical car has fifty or so microprocessors in it, and all the major systems are linked together."

She looked at me, and then at Tidings. "Embedded software is like mildew. It's everywhere, even when you can't see it."

I sat back and contemplated the board, while ruminating over Sally's conclusions. There was silence around the table.

"OK," I said after taking a moment to organize my thoughts. "I'm going to do a dump of our progress today to McCall. I'll include this in my report tonight and call him in the morning to let him know that I am burning the book in my first job going solo." Everyone smiled except me. "George, you and Wang continue on with disassembly. I want you to come up with a list of questions I should be asking, and things to be looking for. Let's work on it tonight."

Tidings nodded and began making notes. "No evidence about who did it or motive, but it'll do for a start."

I thought for a moment longer. "Can you get hold of your financial crimes group in Washington? See if you can get any more information on what they think we're up against."

Tidings agreed.

"Sally, I want you to get on the horn first thing tomorrow morning to Transport Canada in Ottawa and maybe at Goose Bay if you can get hold of them, and find out what they know. Tell them what we've found so far, just the physical stuff, and see what they'll tell you. After that, start working on getting some major help with the computers. I'll let you know what McCall says about that."

I sat back. "I'm going to go see young Mr. Harding at ZYCO transportation and find out everything I can about their work with the GMax and Aries. And then I go see Harrison Randall. I bet he has a lot to tell me."

Despite the late hour, I was able to make appointments to see Harding and Randall. Sally and Wang made a hamburger run while Tidings and I worked on a list of information we would need and who to get it from. After a feeding frenzy that left french-fry grease and ketchup smears on our official paperwork, we went over our next day's tasks and filled the now-huge 6120 accident file with more files, notes and forms. We agreed on a time to meet the next morning, and I spent a half hour in my hotel room, writing and sending a long memo to the chairman before knocking off.

Just as I hit send my phone rang. It was Sally. She apologized for the late hour and I castigated her for working too late. She laughed while I wondered for a second if she was in bed.

Whoa. Hold it, stop, back to work.

"Thanks for taking my input seriously today."

"It was the insight I was looking for. Thanks for letting me steal it." I paused. "Look, we're going to have to keep a close watch on the FBI."

She asked what I meant.

"I threw them a bone and they have something to play with now. But all they care about is arrests and putting bad guys in jail. We have to make them keep their brains open and not focus in on one cause too fast. If we give them a bad guy and bogus code, they'll grab the baddie and forget the code and all the rest. If there is some kind of a problem in the system, we're the ones that have to find it. It's not their job."

She said she knew I could handle it and she was having a great time working for me, which made me unreasonably happy. We said good night and hung up.

Before crapping out completely, I took a look at the email of information Tidings wanted. There was a long list of items like personal schedules and contacts for Corso and the others, etc., and I scratched my head about how to get it. I finally decided to try the ZYCO transportation department. I sent it off to Clinton Harding and said it was all stuff to support the investigation. I crossed my fingers and hit send, and then set up a wake-up call for 5:00 a.m. and went to bed. Alone, as always.

McCall's voice boomed loudly in my ear the next morning in his cheerfully-in-charge tone. I sat on the too-soft hotel bed with my feet up and notes from the day before spread out around me. I had CNN on the television out of habit, with the sound off. At 6:00 a.m. local, it was still dark outside.

"Got your email this morning, Mike. Not sure I can go along with you running traps for that FBI agent out there. Don't let him pressure you into anything. Are you sure that approach is necessary, son?"

I caught myself nodding into the phone. "I think so. I don't plan on doing anything underhanded. I really think I will get better results from going out alone than having Tidings run things. I plan on asking questions and looking into matters that are within our charter. I'm just not planning on hanging a 'federal agent' sign around my neck when I approach people, and I'll tell Tidings about anything interesting I hear. That's as far as I plan on going, and I'll keep you informed, of course."

McCall sounded mollified, with his Texas accent thinning noticeably. "OK, Mike, use your judgment, and try not to get in over your head. Or mine, either."

"Yes, sir." I consulted a note on the bed next to

me. "Did you have a chance to find any technical support for our computer questions? I think that angle is going to be important."

I could hear the Chairman drink from a coffee cup, and my question caught him in mid-swallow. "Mmm, yes. I went through my old contacts at DoD, but nobody thought they'd be able to help. I did find somebody interested in the case, though. You need to call this number--" He quoted a number with a Maryland area code. "--and ask for Dr. Anders. He's expecting your call, and you might want to catch him this morning. It's government, and all paid for, so use him all you want."

"Yes sir, can do. I'll let you go." I made sounds to end the conversation, but McCall spoke again.

"Oh, hey, I heard from Lew's wife last night. He's through the operation all right, and he's cranky as hell."

"Sounds like a good sign."

McCall chuckled. "I think so. I'll let you know if I hear anything else."

I thanked him for the help, hung up, and dialed the new number immediately. My call was answered after two rings, but I could hear no background noise on the other end.

"Extension seven-oh-nine-oh." A click at the end of the answer told me that the phone on the other end was fitted with a push-to-talk switch. Probably a high security telephone with a noise canceller so you couldn't hear what was happening in the background. The kind of phone you had if you worked on top secret, burn-before-reading things in a cleared-for-weird office. The CIA? No, the number was in Maryland, not Virginia.

I had called the National Security Agency.

"Uh, Dr. Anders, please."

There was another click, and the line went silent again. I waited nearly a minute, and began to wonder if I had been cut off. Finally, the phone clicked again "Anders."

I introduced myself we and exchanged pleasantries, but the clicks and lack of sounds coming back made normal conversation difficult.

"General McCall tells me that you have an interesting problem with a computer," Anders said. Click, silence. Hearing Anders call the chairman "general" gave me a good idea how they knew each other.

"Yes. I have a blank section of flash-RAM in a flight system computer from a crashed airplane. The ship's maintenance manuals say it shouldn't be there, and we're trying to find out where the blank came from. Was there ever anything there, or has it always been blank, whatever else you can come up with."

Click. "And if there was something there, what was it? That sort of thing?" Click.

"Yes, exactly." The security measures on the phone were just enough to break up the normal rhythm of conversation, and I was beginning to get annoyed. "Can you help us?"

There was a delay, and I was about to ask again when the phone gave another click. "That isn't our normal line of work, but I may be able to help. I'll need the computers. Can you ship them here? And there is more information I'll need."

I sat up and swung my feet to the floor. "I have a computer engineering expert on my staff here," I said, puffing my position up just lightly. "I'll have her contact you this morning for shipping data, and she can fill you in on some of the details."

Anders agreed and clicked off, leaving me with a dead phone in my hand. I called Sally in her room and she answered after five rings. She apologized for taking so long to answer, saying that I had caught her in the shower. It took me several seconds to get over the mental picture from that. I stammered through the next few sentences. She suggested we meet for breakfast in the hotel coffee shop.

I gave her a few minutes to get dressed--more acrobatic gestalt therapy there--and went down to the restaurant. She was sitting in a booth, reading a USA Today.

Her face lit up like the sunrise as I sat down, and I contemplated the idea that maybe she didn't really understand the way she affected men. I hoped she didn't know how she affected me. That could be embarrassing.

"I hate this paper." She held up the colorful front page. "There's nothing here, like somebody already read all the words off of it. I usually just get news off the net, but this was free."

I laughed. "I usually try to read the local papers when I'm on the road. I like to compare them to the Post and the Times. It's interesting to read editorials from outside the Beltway."

She nodded her understanding, and I added, "There are also funnies and horoscopes."

She smiled again over a cup of tea. "I'll try it," she said, and put the paper aside. "Did you talk to McCall?"

"I did. He said Lew is doing fine. He came out of the operation OK."

We made small talk before ordering breakfast She maintained her figure by ordering a slice of dry toast and fresh fruit, and I maintained mine with scrambled eggs and a sweet roll. I gave her the information on Anders, and she wrote the number down on a napkin, promising to call first thing from the office. We discussed what we might find, and the quality of Colorado eggs before we finished. She sneaked a couple of bites and seemed to love the sensation of cheating a little. I was getting used to meals with her and gladly would have made the arrangement permanent right there.

As we walked out, I said, "I'm sorry to be leaving

you with Tidings. I hope he hasn't bothered you again."

"It's OK, he's been a regular guy lately." We stopped at the door. "Did you say something to him?"

"Not really. Well, just in general terms." We walked out into the morning air, swept clean by a fast overnight rainstorm. "Actually, I guess I did. If you have any more trouble you'll tell me, right?"

"I promise. And thank you." She walked back toward her van as I peeled off to go to my car.

She called after me, "I've never had a big brother before. It's kind of nice." She smiled, waved and disappeared in an entry door.

I unlocked the car and flopped into the driver's seat, feeling as though the Earth's gravity had suddenly increased in El Paso county. The reflection in the rearview mirror held the truth: A few new wrinkles, a slowly expanding double chin and the first gray hairs, which had appeared the previous month. And that was all on a face that hadn't been a prizewinner to begin with. I was now relegated to being a big brother.

"Shit," I said to the face in the mirror.

I started the car and drove off to my first appointment.

Clinton Harding met me at the front desk of the flight operations suite, which adjoined ZYCO's massive corporate hangar on the west side of Peterson field. From his demeanor, I guessed that he had been waiting there patiently for me all night.

"Welcome to ZYCO Transportation," he said earnestly. As he led me down a hall he assured me he had received my email asking for Tidings' information and asked for a day to gather it all. He seemed relieved when I said no. "Can I show you around before we begin?" he said, as we walked through a spotless, brightly lit hall, over a carpet that must have been an inch thick, to an entrance door and into the hangar itself.

"Sure, fine," I answered as we walked. "I have a few specific items to get from you, but mostly I'd-- Wow!"

I was struck dumb as we entered the massive enclosure. The building was famous in the aviation community, larger even than the hangar built by RJR Nabisco in Atlanta in the go-go nineteen-eighties. But the magazine articles hadn't done it justice. The square footage numbers that I had heard did not come close to conveying the size or opulence of the building. The ceiling towered over us seventy-five feet or more, and the total effect was like an indoor stadium.

"Geez," I gasped. "It's like the Grand Canyon upside down."

He laughed proudly. "You could almost play a regulation game of baseball in here. If the roof was a little higher, maybe we could handle some football too."

I gaped like a fish in brackish water. The space was a huge sheet steel and beam structure, with translucent plastic panels inserted into the roof for natural light. The size of the room was accentuated by the white paint on all the walls and the ceiling. The light gray floor was spotless and was buffed to a blinding shine.

In the far corner sat a beautiful Learjet 55 and two rakish Cessna Citation Xs, with parking spots for several more of each type visible, spaced around the floor. The center-rear of the cavern/room was a large empty space surrounded by temporary dividers. "We've reserved that spot for you to work on the crashed GMax." Harding swept an arm theatrically. "Our other GMax is here."

I turned farther to the left, and saw the familiar outline of a GlobalMax, wheels chocked, with flaps lowered and boarding stairs down. An engine nacelle was opened for maintenance, and a technician in spotless orange coveralls stood on a ladder, head inside the opened engine. "After the crash in Canada, Aries has asked us and all other operators to ground the aircraft, pending the outcome of your investigation," Harding said. His tone was clipped and precise, as though he had memorized the speech.

"Why is the place so big?" I asked, looking around in awe one more time.

"Mr. Zygler wanted to be able to house all our

aircraft at one time, plus have room for visitors. He had the CEOs of GM and Ford in for the Super Bowl in Denver last year." He tittered decorously. "He actually got the two into the same skybox. Mr. Zygler is a brilliant businessman, and a real people person," Harding said as we walked toward the GMax. "And he loves to fly."

Ten paces short of the jet, I stopped in my tracks. Behind the French plane, nearly hidden behind it, was an instantly recognizable form, one so sensual and intentionally aggressive that it could only be one thing.

"Ah, I see you've spotted Mr. Zygler's Mustang."

I walked around the GMax to the WW II P-51 fighter, stopping to run a hand over a wing tip in admiration. It was no reproduction but the genuine article, ready to fly to hell and back on a mixture of high-octane gasoline, testosterone and money. It was a spectacularly successful engineering design, cruelly effective and yet strangely beautiful. The few remaining examples were highly sought-after flying antiques and fun-bomb toys for rich-guy pilots. It also had a reputation for being a challenging plane to fly, an evil-handling bitch as well as a beauty that occasionally killed an airshow pilot or wealthy owner.

What did a toy like this cost? A million dollars? Two million? Was something like this worth the expense, and the danger?

Yes.

I slowly ran over a list of body parts I would trade for this four-hundred-mile-per-hour monster.

Two mechanics polished exhaust stains off the plane's sides while a third had an access panel off the engine and was removing one of the engine's 24 spark plugs. The airplane sparkled like a new quarter.

"Zygler flies this?" I asked. I was quickly developing more respect for the slightly comical figure I had met briefly at the crash site on my arrival. Zygler lived the way I would, given unlimited money, which of course he had and I didn't.

"He's taking lessons, although I'm afraid the insurance people will never let him fly it solo. He's too important to the company, of course." Harding shook his head sadly. "It has a second set of controls in the back seat. The chief pilot, Mr. Grimsby, flies with him. Which reminds me," he said, looking at his watch, "Mr. Grimsby is back from Mexico City. He's set his morning aside for you."

Harding pulled politely at my elbow, not wanting to keep the head pilot waiting, but I stood there, transfixed. He could wait.

"I didn't know Zygler was into war birds," I said.

"Mr. Corso convinced the Board of Directors to give him one as a, well, a sort of a gift to celebrate their success when the company went public." Harding's tone was positively reverent, now.

"The two were close, I understand."

I stood in silence for a few more seconds, vowing to return, to crawl all over it and memorize every detail. As we walked back to the management suite, I thought to myself that there must be more to Eric Zygler than his public reputation allowed. A machine like a Mustang was so dangerous to fly and so much trouble to own that it could only be needed to answer a driving passion, a fire in the heart of a pilot. A very wealthy pilot.

Zygler was known in the business world as a cool calculator and a meticulous technician, not given to rash actions. His success in business stemmed from his ability to produce perfection in incomprehensible packages of computer code.

The P-51 didn't fit in that picture. The Mustang was a piece of art, beautiful metal work and mechanical perfection, welded into a highly efficient killing machine, the perfect tool for sanctioned killing. A possession like that spoke to something like an obsession. With what? Power? History? Leaded gasoline?

Who the hell was Eric Zygler?

chapter

8

The chief pilot was waiting for us in a large conference room that was lined around its walls with computer workstations. He sat at one end of a large polished wood conference table next to one computer.

He stood as I entered. "Mr. O'Hara, David Grimsby." He gave me a businesslike smile. We shook hands and he motioned me into a chair across a table corner from his.

I sank into the chair and wondered how anyone stayed awake while sitting in it.

Grimsby looked like a pilot, tall and slim, face lined and well-tanned from hours at high altitude. He had the characteristic pilot's tan lines around his eyes from wearing sunglasses constantly. He talked and carried himself with the kind of authoritative nonchalance that senior pilots always seemed to have.

"Thanks for seeing me today," I said. He really didn't have much choice, but it never hurt to be polite, at least at first.

"Not at all." Harding hovered by my elbow until Grimsby asked for coffee. "I'm sorry I couldn't get here sooner. I was on a round-robin trip through South and Central America. We have a team out working with local authorities in Latin America on public transportation issues. I flew them in from Mexico City last night in the Lear you saw." He fixed me in a searching gaze. "I, uh, I don't suppose you have any ideas on a cause yet? For the, uh..."

I shook my head. "Nothing. This case has been a frustration so far. That's why I'm here. The obvious things haven't panned out, and I'm looking for the less obvious ones now."

He clenched a fist. "Mr. Zygler has left orders for me and Clint..." Harding didn't seem like a "Clint" to me, but I didn't interrupt. "You're our top priority, and anything you need is yours for the asking. This might end up reflecting on the company's products, and well, I'm a stockholder, too. Most of us are, so it's personal."

Harding returned with three Styrofoam cups and a small tray of condiments. He sat across the table from us and pulled out a notebook and pen.

I stirred sugar and latex creamer into my drink to make it palatable before opening my note pad and looking the scribbles over. "Hmm, where to start? Could you tell me in general about the ZYCO corporate operation? Normal usage, that sort of thing?"

Grimsby nodded. "We have eight airplanes... Well, seven now. We just replaced our two Gulfstream Fives with the GMaxes. We now have the one GMax, two Lear Fifty-Fives and three Cessna Citation X's, plus the toy in the back of the hangar." He smiled reverently.

"I saw the Mustang. Beautiful."

"It's a great machine. Awesome to fly. Maybe we can get you a ride."

I know my face brightened.

Harding made a note.

Grimsby's face grew serious again. "We operate strictly within the requirements of Part 135 of the Federal Aviation Regulations. Maintenance, crew training, everything. Actually, we go quite a way beyond those requirements. Mr. Zygler insists that we cut no corners and operate a perfectly safe operation. The loss of the GMax the other night was the first time we have ever hurt a passenger, or so much as scratched an airplane."

Grimsby leaned forward, spoke more intensely and poked the tabletop with a finger. "We've never even dented a wing tip on a hangar door, until now. I've been with ZYCO for five years. I quit a job as a captain in heavy jets for a major airline to take this position." He relaxed in his seat and looked at the wall behind me, clearly taking the crash hard.

I wrote a note and went on. "I've seen all your records. Could you tell me about how the company uses the airplanes? Travel patterns, and so on."

He settled back, taking a drink of coffee before answering. "First of all, these airplanes are not toys. They are vital to the way ZYCO does business. The planes let us avoid delays at terminals and keep teams of technical types together, arriving when needed, staying as long as necessary, and getting back as soon as possible. This is a fast-moving business, and we can't have our top people tied to airline schedules. It may sound like pampering, but Eric Zygler is very positive about keeping his software engineers comfortable and happy. Says it makes a big difference in the company's performance."

"So, the actual business usage is pretty high? Not too many runs to Monterey for golf?"

"Very high. Overall, the strictly business use is about ninety percent by flying hour across the fleet." He turned in his chair, and worked at the keyboard of one of the computers nearby. "Personal use of the jets by top corporate officers is authorized by the board, and I have to report to them at every meeting about how much we fly, and what for."

He found the display he wanted and read from the screen. "The two GMaxes have been in the fleet about a month. I just got back from Paris myself, getting checked out at the factory." He held a finger to the data he wanted. "Yes, two-one-five echo sierra, the ship that crashed, had made one trip to Paris the week before, and one to Moscow. There were two trips to Palm Springs mixed in. I think Mrs. Zygler takes tennis lessons at a club there. A total of about a hundred flight hours for us. The other GMax has a bit less on it. The other ships fly about one hundred to a hundred fifty hours a month, so we keep busy."

"How many crews do you have rated in the GlobalMax?"

"Three, counting John and Bill. More in training." Grimsby took another swallow of coffee. "They were the first to check out. We all went through the full training pipeline at Paris."

"Did Fleet and Berry fly the earlier trips in two-one-five echo sierra?"

He peered at the screen again. "Yes." He looked across the table at Harding. "You need to get this thing caught up, Clint." He turned back to me. "The plane was going back to Palm Springs again the morning after it crashed, but Corso's trip to Paris took priority at the last minute."

"How much warning did you have that Corso wanted to go to Paris?" I said.

He thought for a second. "Let's see. I wasn't here." He looked at Harding.

"Um, about four hours." Harding squirmed in his seat. "I took the call from Mr. Corso myself. I was in the operations center, and he called about five-thirty. The regular dispatcher had already left."

"And he gave you a departure time?" I said.

Harding shook his head. "He said he wanted to go as quickly as possible. He came here and waited for almost two hours before takeoff."

I looked at Harding. "What kind of state was he in? Angry? Happy? Did he make a lot of phone calls, or anything?"

"Well..." Harding squirmed again. "He was, um...how do I put it? He was his normal self. Uh, he could be quite demanding."

Grimsby cut in. "He was a pain in the ass. Treated the hired hands pretty rough. Didn't care much about anybody. I think they teach 'em that at Harvard. Not like Eric, er, Mr. Zygler."

I wrote that down, and then changed the subject. "Do you have any comment about the quality of the checkout?"

He looked at the ceiling. "Only that it was the best training I've ever had in an airplane."

I made another note. "Want to say anything about the two crew members? Anything at all?"

"They were both outstanding, or they wouldn't have been hired. John Fleet came over with me from the airline, back when we were first setting up the department. He was a superior airman. I cannot believe that this could happen." He spoke more to himself than to me, and he shook his head slowly, in disbelief.

We were all silent for a few seconds.

"Tell me about the Mustang," I said.

"Nice ship. The boss loves it. A wonderful toy, and he doesn't have very many things to amuse him anymore."

"How did you come to have it?"

Grimsby smiled to himself and shook his head. "It's an interesting story. You know, the boss's grandfather was a big time flying ace in World War Two and Korea. I guess Mr. Zygler looked like he was going to be a big disappointment to Granddad, being a computer nerd and all."

"And Corso bought it for him?"

He paused and chuckled. He looked around furtively, like he knew he shouldn't be talking out of school. "Mr. Zygler really built this company from scratch. He literally started it in his parent's basement. He was critical to the initial public offering--the IPO--that's the first time the company sells stock on a public exchange. He did almost all of the calls on major investors himself. It raised billions more than they expected. He made all the corporate leadership really, really rich. The story is that he and Corso got drunk the night before the initial stock offering went out. Zygler made a bet with Corso that the stock would go up fast and they would double the estimates in a week. If he won, the company would buy Mr. Zygler a fully-restored P-51. They apparently signed a contract on a bar napkin."

"I've been drinking in the wrong bars," I said.

He laughed and went on. "Anyway, after they had made nine billion dollars in one day on the IPO, Corso told the CFO about the bet. I guess there was a major flap with the Securities and Exchange Commission. I actually heard that Zygler threatened to quit over it, and things were really tense for a while. Corso took a lot of hits. But the board okayed it eventually."

"So Corso got him the plane." I began. "They must have been friends."

"I guess. I'm not sure these high-end types really have friends. They worked together closely. A good team. Corso really tried to teach Zygler how to live. Took him out partying. Introduced him to his wife. Have you met her?"

I shook my head.

"You'd remember her if you had," Grimsby said.

Harding rolled his eyes.

"Anyway, they seemed to mesh OK," Grimsby continued. "It was surprising, because they're so different, but the two of them really tried to get along. I've heard the boss is taking it hard. He doesn't show things, but I think it hurt him pretty bad."

We spent another hour going over training and maintenance records. It was apparent that ZYCO's flight operation was as top-drawer as Grimsby had said. It takes more than large amounts of money to make a flying organization safe, and the right habits and audits and attitude were all there.

Grimsby and Harding promised to send copies of documents that I had requested to our office on the other side of the field by later that day, and I thanked them both for their time. Harding dropped me in the opulent building's lobby, where I stopped to call Sally at the office before my appointment with Randall across town at ZYCO headquarters.

I sat in a wonderful leather armchair in the lobby while I dialed.

Sally answered on the first ring. "Mike, I just got off the line with Goose Bay."

"What do they have? Any wreckage?"

I could hear her rustle notes. "The aerial search found an oil slick and some small debris on the water near the coast. They couldn't positively identify anything, but a Canadian minesweeper is on the way to the area with a special sonar system to look for the plane. It's pretty cold to use divers, but they have some kind of underwater robot."

"I know the kind. They have a remote-piloted submersible with a television camera, for mine hunting." I moved in the chair, and the leather made a loud fart-noise that drew a look from the cute receptionist behind the front desk.

"That's the thing," she said. "They said it would take a day or so for a thorough search."

"They'll call us if they find anything?"

"I gave them my number. I'll call them if I don't hear anything." She paused, and I heard more notes being shuffled. "I called Anders, and he has an idea about how to find the missing data. He didn't make any guarantees, but it sounds good to me."

"Are you ready to ship the computers?"

"Working on it. I'm going to try to catch FedEx this morning." She sounded a little harried.

"Could you call McCall for me?" I asked. I could hear her give a little sigh. "It's OK, he won't bite you. You're a civilian now, remember?"

"Oh, all right," she said, in a resigned tone.

"Tell him what you told me, and let him know I talked to their flight department this morning. I'm going to talk to some corporate types now, and then I'm heading up to see Steve and Keats in Denver. And," I said mischievously, "tell him ZYCO has a P-51, and I'm trying to scam a ride in it."

She said she would comply, but still didn't sound happy when I hung up.

The drive across town went slowly in stop-and-go-traffic, and it was nearly ten before I had found my way into the western hills above the city. ZYCO headquarters was located on a beautiful, rolling campus, complete with a lake, jogging trails and verges of manicured lawn among hundreds acres of carefully-tended native vegetation. It looked like a huge private golf course with an office building in the middle and nobody around in loud polyester clothes. The building was only four stories high but must have covered ten acres, and the overall ambiance said tasteful and understated, but rich.

The visitor's parking lot was crowded, and I was about to pull out and take my chances in the employees' lot when I spotted a space next to the front entrance, marked with a sign that said "Mr. O'Hara, NTSB." I left the rental car in the spot, parked next to the huge Mercedes that I recognized from the crash scene on my first day there.

My canvas brief case had swallowed my

government ID, and I was fishing in the bottom as I walked up to the receptionist's desk. The search was interrupted by a sweet but business-like voice, and I looked up. The receptionist was very young and very pretty.

"Mr. O'Hara?" she asked, with just the right smile. I nodded. "Mr. Randall is expecting you." I drew envious stares from three pinstriped-suit-types who were waiting in the lobby for clearance. She pointed to the bank of elevators on the far side of a security desk and handed me a typed ZYCO badge. "Fourth floor. Look to your left and go in the glass doors." She pressed a buzzer as I thanked her. The Muzak on the elevator ride up was Bach.

The carpet on the fourth floor was even deeper than the stuff in the pilot's offices had been, and I found the glass doors into the inner sanctum as directed.

Inside the doors, the carpet was deeper still, and I actually stumbled on the thick wool as I walked through the heavy glass portals. The outer inner sanctum was all pastel wall coverings, indirect lighting and tasteful objects d'art. The reception area alone had probably cost as much as my entire apartment building and I doubted that any of the paintings or sculptures were copies.

The receptionist here was a bit older, still attractive but in a more substantial way, and I wondered if she had a pistol tucked into her desk to handle the riffraff. She was cool, collected and probably really efficient.

"Mr. O'Hara?" she said coolly.

I nodded and gave a smile that was not returned.

"Mr. Randall is expecting you. He is in conference with Mr. Zygler right now, but he wondered if you would wait in his office?"

"Fine. Thank you." Another smile produced a hint of a response, and I gathered that this person was "she-who-controlled," resenting anyone who dared to enter her range or interrupt her routine. McCall's secretary, Ann, was like that, and he claimed she increased his ability to work by fifty percent. She never interfered, but she filtered the noise out of the boss's contact with the outside world.

Randall's office faced south, with a breathtaking view of both Pike's Peak and the city spread out below. A small Matisse original in a large mat and frame hung on one wall. His desk was a sheet of glass supported by two marble pillars. A top-of-the-line laptop was tossed casually to one side of a leather blotter, and I could see no sign of drawers, paper or pencils anywhere. There were two large leather armchairs set at angles to the desk, and I sat in one, passing ten minutes thinking about how I could never get any work done with a view like that.

While I had a second I checked my phone. I spotted nothing of interest and turned it to Do Not Disturb before slipping it back in my pocket.

Randall walked in followed by a familiar figure: Eric Zygler.

The great man held out a hand. "Hi, I'm Eric." His voice was nasal, and a little higher than I had heard at the airport.

"Mike O'Hara, Mr. Zygler." We shook hands. His grip was surprisingly strong, not quite FBI-Agent meaty but up there, tough and manly.

He smiled charmingly, and motioned for me to sit. "I wish you'd call me Eric. Nobody wants to anymore." He said the last words absently as Randall took his seat behind his desk, enveloped in the huge guy-in-charge leather recliner.

Zygler sat in the other seat, curling one leg up under the other. "I'm sorry we kept you waiting, but we were on a conference call with the French minister of transportation and the CEO of Aries. We are all very...um, perplexed over the problems with the GlobalMax. As I'm sure you can imagine, the loss of Wes has had a pretty severe impact on us all, professionally and personally." His speech was formal and stilted, but it didn't seem that he had memorized anything. "When Harry told me you were coming to see him today, I decided I wanted to horn in on the meeting. I hope you don't mind."

He smiled again, a deep, genuine smile, and I saw his eyes through his thick glasses. They were bright blue and intense like lasers, but were surrounded by wrinkles and worry lines. I noticed gray hair mixed in with the brown. He was older than he appeared on television, beginning to show the effects of a life of stress and work. Kind of like me.

"Of course. I really appreciate you taking your time."

He waved a hand. "No, I'm glad you're here to help us." He sighed and looked at the floor. "We have a problem, I think. I have never had anything like a fatal error slip through our process in one of our products before, and it will affect the company if we don't root it out."

"Sir--"

"Eric, please."

"Eric," I said, "I haven't zeroed in on your software. There could have been aerodynamics or a hundred other systems-related problems."

"You have to keep your options open, of course." He nodded vigorously. "I'm operating under the assumption that it is our code that's at fault. I think we have to."

Randall cleared his throat. "We have the stock price to think about, and the French are worried about their certification agreements with the FAA. That was what our call was about just now. We were about to go out with a stock offering. Today, in fact. I had to call

New York this morning and shut it off until this matter is behind us. Could cost us millions. Hundreds of millions."

"That's not the point, Harry." Zygler raised his voice a little. "The point is, we have a product with an error. We don't do that, Harry. There is more to it than money. Screw the stock price. Those hash houses out in California can slap code together for half our price, but they make errors. Perfection is what we do." He spoke quietly. This wasn't an argument to him, just a statement of facts.

Randall held out a placating hand. "Eric, you can't take personal responsibility for everything. The effort is too big now." It sounded like it wasn't the first time they had discussed the subject.

Zygler sat for a moment, and then looked back at me. "Mr. O'Hara..."

"I'm Mike, please."

He chuckled. "Mike, sorry. You're an engineer, right?"

"Engineering physics. Aero, mostly. I did most of my work in engine theory."

"Ouch. Thermodynamics." He almost smiled. "That stuff is hard. I got C's in Thermo." He scratched his chin, was thoughtful for a moment, and then spoke quietly. "You know, Mike, the civil engineers have been building roads and forts and things for a long time. Thousands of years. The Pyramids, and all that."

"Caesar's roads, that sort of thing."

"Right," Zygler's eyes flashed. "And we know how to do that. If you want a road built, you look it up in a book, or call somebody that built the last one, and find out. Mechanical systems are the same thing. Newcommen built the first steam engine in the seventeen hundreds, and now we have fan jets that can shove a plane around the world, no problem. We know how to do that, too."

He gripped the arms of the chair and leaned forward. "I'm not saying that those things are easy, no way. The design of a bridge, say, is a very complicated thing. But basically, those kinds of physical things are a matter of doing known trade-offs differently, or changing the values of coefficients in a linear equation. But software is different. You can't stand back a little and look at it to see if you are doing it right."

He took a deep breath. "Writing software, especially embedded software, has always been very creative. Artwork. More like writing a play than building an engine. To take our place as an engineering discipline, we've had to invent a process to follow, to make sure that the products are right the first time. It will take centuries to really get it right. The software community is a few decades into it."

He wagged a warning finger at me. "You can't test quality into a software package. Too complicated. There are hundreds of millions of logic paths through a typical software system. Quality, even perfection, can and has to be built in from the very beginning. The problem," he said, and held another finger up for emphasis, "is that the kind of people you get in the software creation business are not very disciplined, by their natures." He laughed without humor.

"We're all a bunch of dorks. Look Geek up in the dictionary. My picture is there." More laughter, and then he got quieter, Olivier doing Shakespeare, working a crowd.

"What I have done, more than anything, is to create a team of disciplined engineers who adhere to a process. But they still have a rage in them to make a perfect product." He face was red now, and his eyes flashed. Little bits of passion leaked out when he when he talked. "Our success is not inevitable. Our stuff is superior because we make it superior. It doesn't just happen."

He looked over at Randall. "That is what I can't get across to you guys. It's creation. Disciplined creation!"

He caught himself, and looked embarrassed. "I'm boring you, aren't I, Mike? I do that a lot."

I laughed, louder than I intended, and Zygler laughed back. "No, Eric. Actually, I don't get a chance to do real engineering very often."

"Well," Zygler sat back and continued seriously, "I'm sure you can imagine how the crash has affected my team. The confidence of the marketplace has been shattered, and our own confidence has taken a hit, too."

"The French--" Randall said, quietly.

Zygler gave a quick jerk of his chin. "The French are appalled. They went through a hellish negotiation over certification of the GlobalMax in the U.S. It took almost two years to work out an agreement so that the American authorities would accept the French certification process. And of course, the American market is the most important because of its scale--bigger than the rest of the world put together. Problems with the GlobalMax could affect France's national economy if they don't sell as many airplanes as projected."

Zygler waved a hand derisively. "To hell with all that shit. To hell with the money. I don't care, and in the long run, the markets won't either. But I'll guarantee you something. If we find the problem, root it out and fix it, the market will be back in a big way."

Zygler got up and walked to the window. We were all quiet for a few seconds. Randall and I waited for the great man to speak.

Zygler clasped his hands behind his back, and faced the window. "Where do you stand, Mike? Where are you in the investigation? Can we ask that?"

I thought for a moment. "The airplane shouldn't have crashed. We've been through it all end-to-end and it should have flown safely."

Zygler was impassive. I laid out the testing for them. "Everything worked as designed. The systems all tested out well. Your flight operations department here looks good, as far as I can see. The airplane shouldn't have crashed."

Zygler continued to look out the window, and he mumbled to himself. "To err is human. To really screw things up takes a computer."

"I beg your pardon, Eric?" Randall said.

"It's a software problem, Harry. We'll find it and fix it, get it right and on the first try, in public, with everybody watching. I'm telling you, we can turn this into a good thing."

The two ZYCO men looked at each other, and then at me.

Randall said, "Where do you want to go from here? How can we help? Is Harding taking good care of you?"

"Yes, I've got plenty of help. I talked with your chief pilot this morning. And your technicians have been great."

I slouched back in my seat, and crossed my hands in front of me, noticing for the first time the dirt under my fingernails. It had to be burned, oil-soaked dirt from under the crashed plane.

"I don't want you to take the questions I have personally," I said, "but if you do, so be it." I looked up, and could see that I had their attention. "Are your products really as good as you say? Or is there a certain amount of marketing bullshit involved?"

Randall looked shocked, terrified that I would challenge the great one so directly.

Zygler's eyes were serious behind the thick lenses. "The package we wrote for the last build of the control system for Boeing had over a million lines of code, exclusive of documentation," he said, quietly, and with pride. "We had it verified and validated by two independent organizations, one picked by me, and one by Boeing. And then Boeing did another audit, in-house. The error rate was zero." He paused.

"Zero. We really are that good. There really is a reason why our stock got so high."

"Well, here's another one," I said. "There have been reports of possible manipulation of ZYCO's stock price. What was Corso going to Paris in such a hurry for? Did it have to do with that?"

Randall leaned his elbows on his desk. "We discovered a case of insider trading in the firm in Kansas City that works our stock for us on the exchange. We stopped it, and we wanted Aries to hear about it from us and not from the SEC or the Wall Street Journal. Wes decided to take the meeting himself. I was going to go, but he thought it would be best to handle it alone. It was just a reasonable courtesy to a major stockholder."

Randall looked shaken, as if reflecting on a brush with death.

I continued to study my hands. "OK, I'll buy that. Here's my next question, then. If you're so great at this stuff, how is it possible that your code is killing people?"

Zygler's face turned red.

Randall said, "Mr. O'Hara, really. How can you ask that?"

Zygler waved a hand. "It's OK, Harry. This is good."

I looked Zygler in the eye. "The next logical step is to assume that your process has broken down somewhere. If we assume that the process you have set up here is so good at detecting and preventing accidental errors, then the next step is to look for intentional interference."

"You want to look for sabotage," Zygler said.

I nodded. "I'm not an FBI agent or anything, so if you want to call me bad names, go ahead." I put my notes down, and made eye contact with Randall. "Off the record, now. Do you know, or can you think of anybody who might have a reason to murder Corso?"

Randall stared at his shoes.

Zygler looked at the floor, and then at me. "There are a few," he said quietly. "He, uh, treated several people pretty badly when we were going public. It could have been handled more gently. I didn't know any better."

Randall cleared his throat. "Eric, I don't think we should be discussing this."

"He asked, Harry." Zygler went back to looking out the window.

Randall cleared his throat again. "Before we went public, Wes and I went over the legal status of Eric's finances. We determined that three engineers who had worked for Eric might have a reasonable claim to partial ownership of the company."

"They lent me money in the early days," Zygler said, just above a whisper. "They skipped a lot of paydays, along with me. I kept track, and I promised to pay them back."

"When we got close to the IPO date," Randall went on, "Wes decided that we should close out their ownership. We put together what appeared at the time to be very generous offers, and all three agreed willingly."

"How much?" I said.

"Several million dollars apiece," Randall answered. "We did not accurately forecast the way the stock would behave. It ended up setting a new record for initial public offerings. We didn't actually make nine billion dollars in one day, as you may have heard. It took several weeks. But the men who were cut out felt understandably, well, cheated. Their millions should have been hundreds of millions."

I thought of my checkbook with five hundred some-odd dollars in it. And my car needed new tires.

"They blamed Corso?" I said.

"And me," Zygler said, sounding stressed. I looked closely, and thought I could see a tear forming in the corner of his eye.

"Would any of them, or anyone else I should be interested in, have the ability to make the kind of changes in flight software it would take to kill an airplane, and get it inserted? Who would have been able to do such a thing?"

Zygler looked at me. "You mean, aside from me?"

Randall regarded him, annoyed, tense.

"Three might," Zygler said, his voice shaky. "One is dead. Drank himself to death. Died last year. The family sued, but they withdrew the suit before it went anywhere. One took his money and bought a boat. He was in Australia the last I heard. He sounds OK. Sends me Christmas cards, in fact."

"And the third?" I pressed.

"He works downstairs." Zygler went back to the window and looked out again, staring at Pike's Peak in the mid-day sun. After a few seconds, he walked to Randall's desk, and picked up the telephone.

After dialing three digits, he said, quietly, "Diane, cancel all my appointments for the next week. Yes, I know. Thank you."

9

Zygler rapped out a series of orders and Randall made hurried notes on his computer. Randall was to issue a press release canceling the planned stock offering, and explain in a supporting release that no financial actions would be taken until the potential of problems with ZYCO software was eliminated.

Randall looked horrified. "Eric, we can't say that."

"We have to say that." Zygler was starting to look angry, with a vein bulging in a bald spot on his head. He glared at the suave executive through his thick glasses, and spoke quietly. "Harry, get ahead of the situation right now. Remember how the markets treated MicroPod when they had that problem with their new chip? It was a really minor glitch, but they tried to stonewall the public, and they managed to turn it into a disaster."

Randall began to light up himself but kept a coating of respect in his face. "I remember."

"Take decisive action, now. And let's have people see us taking decisive action." He smiled, like a wolf this time. "Like I said, we can turn this into a positive if we work fast."

When Zygler turned to me his expression had changed in an instant, all smiles again. It was a little confusing, and I had a fleeting thought that he could do this on purpose, as a control tactic. If that was right it was a pretty damned good one. "Mike, do you have a few more minutes for me? I need some help, some of your advice."

He led me out of Randall's office and down a busy, carpeted hall. Men all but bowed and women nearly curtsied as we passed, murmuring greetings to Zygler. Everyone called him by his first name, and everyone eyed me with a mixture of awe and suspicion. A picture of pre-revolutionary France came into my mind as we swept into an even plusher office complex.

Zygler strode past a receptionist, another no-nonsense type, and into a brightly lit room. Light flooded in through the panoramic windows, the noontime sun reflecting from the Rockies in the distance. There was no desk, but the room was furnished lavishly with leather covered sofas and armchairs. There was a large coffee table in front of one couch, forming a barely recognizable but very comfortable work area.

Zygler flopped down at one end of the sofa, with a laptop and a phone on the table in front of him, and waved a hand for me to sit at the other end. He slouched into the furniture and put his feet up on the table, pulling the laptop onto the arm of the couch, instantly beginning to fiddle with it. "Email, texts, ugh. Direct mind injection is next" he said absently. "Can't keep up. Just be a second."

I waited, and after a few seconds I noticed how comfortable the sofa was. It held me firmly, the stout but supple cushions reminding me of the seats in a Porsche. Zygler must have had a bad back like mine, I decided. I had to get a couch like this one. I would sleep on it every night.

After cursing under his breath a few times, and writing one quick note, Zygler looked up, closing the computer's lid. "Sorry. I get two hundred or so messages a day. Can't afford to fall behind."

He spread his arms out across the back of the sofa. "What do you think I need to do next? Any suggestions?" He arched his eyebrows above his glasses.

I turned toward him across the eight-foot expanse

of leather. "I suppose you should tell me more about the man you have here."

"Tom. Tom Sutton. Yes." He studied the floor for a moment, gathering his thoughts. "I feel a little guilty even talking about Tom like this. He's really a good man. I just don't think he should be judged by the way he's been recently. I can't believe he would be capable of the kind of things we suspect."

My ears pricked up. "You said 'recently'. What's he been doing recently?"

He sighed. "He'd been doing well, for a long time. He seemed to accept the situation better than the other two. As I explained, he was money ahead, and for a long time things were good. Tom and I had been very close friends for some time. I had hoped that he would stay on. After the first stock sales, when the prices had gone so high, he had some trouble."

He hesitated again. "Depression, and so on. We got him to the best doctors. They recommended work, so I offered him a position as technical manager for our commercial systems department. He's been going at it hard for over a year now."

Zygler had begun to ramble, and I tried to lead him back onto the track. "But lately? Has he changed?"

Zygler nodded absently. "I-- Well, he's been late quite a bit recently. Or out sick. I'm afraid he's been drinking heavily. At least he has all the signs."

I wrote a note on my old-fashioned paper pad. "And he would be able to cause a problem like this?"

"Oh, yes. It wouldn't be all that hard. He has the experience and skills. A lot of people do, actually. I wasn't entirely joking about me, either. Although, my skills have been deteriorating pretty badly from disuse lately. But nothing is hard when you know how to do it." Zygler shook his head, and stared at the carpet. "He's done flight control system work before and I think he could do it again."

I pursed my lips. "I have someone on my team who would need to talk to him."

"Tidings? The FBI agent?"

I know I let my surprise show before I could catch it. "How did you know he was FBI?"

Zygler looked sheepish. "I guess I wasn't supposed to know that." He pointed to his computer. "I have every database in the world, and a couple from elsewhere. All right here. I had Harding get me your names, and I looked you all up in the Washington area telephone directory. When I didn't find him under the NTSB or FAA, I looked around a little more and found him in the FBI listings. It took about three minutes."

I tried not to be unnerved and decided to change the subject. I suggested we talk technicalities, which he quickly agreed to.

"How do you load software into the plane itself?

If somebody wanted to load bad software, how would they do it?"

"For our two planes and the Aries factory plane you can get the code to the field by telephone." Zygler crossed his arms, and looked back at me. "And a technician can load the software with a regular device like a thumb drive. It goes in a port in the aft equipment bay."

"Yes, I've been in it."

"The normal certified configuration for the aircraft has the flight control system code carried in read-only memory," he went on. "If you want to change the code, a mechanic would have to do a minor software change and then reboot the system. But for our planes we wanted to be able to connect up anywhere, in case a change had to be tested quickly, or if we were doing research."

I took notes quickly while Zygler talked. "We have special permission from the FAA for our two planes, and the French operate under a special waiver from the French government. We can do that since none of our planes carry passengers for hire. The code on our ships and the French plane can be erased or changed just like a disk in your personal computer. The code is loaded up from memory whenever the aircraft is powered up, or as commanded. The processors in the aft equipment bay have a connection, a port. You just have to hook a computer up in the bay, with the right software, and run a phone wire to it. You just send the code from the lab to the plane."

"Could you use Wi-Fi?" I said.

He scratched his chin. "Sure. But land lines are faster and usually have a lower error rate."

I tapped my lips with the end of my pencil. "So, you'd have to get a laptop computer into the equipment bay of the plane?"

"No. Our two planes have been kind of trial horses for us. They're set up with some special hardware that lets us install software remotely to test changes. Minor stuff mostly, to make sure changes run ok. We've been doing tests almost continuously."

"What about the one in France? Didn't Aries keep one plane?" I said. "Was it used that way?"

"I expect so. We asked Aries to double-check our work. It's all pretty routine," he said with a shrug. "This kind of activity will drop off after the planes have been in service for a while."

"Does the FAA have control over your activities? Or the French? Can you just change the systems whenever you like?"

Zygler shrugged again, as though the question weren't important. "The FAA... Let's see, I don't want this to sound patronizing." He paused. "The FAA doesn't really have the expertise to rule over our designs. We self-certify, and they have the right to go back and check up on us. All the major manufacturers have the same sort of arrangement, although our special trial-horse hardware configuration is a first, as far as I know."

I frowned again, and studied my note pad for a second. "So all you'd need would be a laptop."

"It's not quite that simple. Everything's password protected, and encrypted, and the code is held very tightly by the people I have working on it."

"So, a hacker couldn't get in?"

He shook his head and pushed his glasses up on his nose. "No. We thought about an additional encryption scheme for a while on top of what we already had, but it just didn't seem necessary. On top of that, this is a really specialized area. I just don't think a propeller-head on a toy computer could do it, even if he had access."

"Couldn't this be spurious data somewhere? Corrupted code? You send stuff by phone everywhere. Couldn't that cause a bit here or there to be screwed up?"

"No, no. We thought of that. The data is sent over in small packets, and each packet is received and checked out automatically," Zygler explained patiently. "The processors on board the plane pass the new programs around, compare them to each other, and then send the results back to the sender for comparison. Some of our approach is old fashioned, but like I said, it works. We invented the technique.

"Boeing loves it," he said. "Everybody loves it."

I wrote more notes while Zygler got up and moved to another seat, a large leather chair. I wrote myself a large note at the top of the page that said "Boeing issues?" and circled it.

"You're helping me, Mike. What else can we do to help you?"

I was about to answer when the phone on the desk beeped quietly. While Zygler walked to the table to answer I checked my cell. Four missed calls from Sally.

"This is Eric... Sure, he's here. Hang on." He held out the phone. "It's for you."

I excused myself and took the handset, surprised that anyone could find me. "O'Hara."

It was Sally. "Hi, it's me."

"How the hell did you find me?"

"I just Googled the ZYCO number, and they knew right where you were."

I glanced at Zygler, and he smiled back.

"Listen, I thought you ought to know, the Canadians found the French wreckage. They've got pictures from the little submarine, and you can really see the damage." Sally was talking quickly, and she sounded excited.

"What kind? From impact?" I kept my voice as patient as possible.

She slowed noticeably. "There was a lot of impact

damage around the nose and the wings are nearly destroyed, but the tail is the interesting part. The whole vertical assembly was pretty much intact. The horizontal stabilizer and elevator are torn off. One side is completely gone, and the other is hanging by shards of metal." She sounded excited again.

"Which way did it fail? Up or down?" I was getting excited, too.

"Down, I think. Not back. It definitely failed in the air, and not on impact. They sent us pictures, and I think I can make out dents in the sides of the rudder. The elevator must have made the dents when it failed."

"OK. Are you at the office?"

"Yes."

"Call the Chairman and let him know. I'm heading up to see Steve in a few minutes. I'll be back from Denver about seven-thirty. I'll swing by to look at the pictures and we can talk it over during dinner."

"Oh, we get time to eat?" Definite sarcasm was in her tone.

"If you're good. Is Tidings there?"

"He's at the wreckage."

"I'll call him, and then I have to head north. I'm here with Eric Zygler right now."

"The Eric Zygler?" Her voice became a squeal, like a teenager swooning over a heartthrob rock idol.

I looked up at Zygler and he smiled.

"Yes, the Eric Zygler. You just talked to him on the phone. Goodbye, Sally."

Zygler laughed as I put down the handset.

"My new number two. She's a computer science major. She should probably be here instead of me."

"Nice voice. I'd like to meet her," he said.

"I think you would, yes." More seriously, I said, "If my FBI agent wants to question Mr. Sutton, when would be convenient?"

"I can have him here any time. In the morning? Say, Nine?"

"Good." I picked up the phone.

"Would it be OK to give Tom some warning? He might want to have an attorney or something," Zygler said.

"I'll ask George," I answered as I punched in the number. The phone beeped three times before Tidings answered. I explained the situation to him, and told him about my discussions so far.

"OK, nine is good," Tidings said. "Tell him it's strictly preliminary and voluntary, but if he wants a lawyer, it's his call. Where do I meet him?"

I asked for directions, and Zygler took the phone. "Hi, this is Eric. Yes, hello. Just come to the front lobby, and they'll tell you where to go." Pause. "I'm looking forward to meeting you, too. Sure. And, by the way, if I don't get a chance to talk to you before the questioning, please be easy with him. He's an old friend of mine, and I'd hate... Yes, I'm sure you understand. Thanks very much, Agent Tidings. Tomorrow, then."

He put down the phone slowly. "I'll have to tell Tom, I guess. I wouldn't want Harry to do it. Tom doesn't trust the money types." He looked as if he dreaded the task. "What else? Do you need any specific support?"

I thought for a second. "Simulations. I need to know what control inputs could make the plane behave the way it did. If any." I described the GMax's fatal gyrations as best I could remember, and gave him the office phone number to call Sally for more details.

"And I need to know from the Aries engineers and your team what kind of control movements it would take to tear the tail off the way the Canadian ship failed. Nothing fancy, just a basic picture." I described the damage that Sally had told me about.

"I'll get on that right away." He opened his computer and began to type furiously. "We'll use the full hardware-in-the-loop test suite, and I'll coordinate with Marc Van Damme in Paris. He'll be their new chief engineer, I think. I'll use the other jet, the one in the hangar, if we need it." He stopped. "I'll have you an answer by tomorrow morning."

He stopped to rub his eyes under his glasses, pushing them up on his forehead, and sighed heavily. "I suppose I should go tell Tom right now. I'm not looking forward to this, Mike."

He was the richest man I'd ever met, but he didn't want to turn over a dirty job to his hired hand.

I nodded my understanding. "I'll go with you, Eric."

He closed his laptop and thanked me.

Tom Sutton turned out to be a classic computer geek, even more prototypical than Zygler. He looked like he hadn't moved anything bigger than a mouse for years, and his skin had a sallow color that ruled out any recent history of contact with sunlight. He also looked haunted, with deep pockets under his eyes from lack of sleep.

Sutton sat in a windowless interior office, at a desk overflowing with papers. His sleeves were rolled up raggedly to his elbows, and he wore his dark hair in the standard bizarre turbine-like pattern of a man going badly bald, and trying to make the last few precious hairs cover his entire scalp in a swirl. If Dairy Queen sold licorice ice cream, a soft cone would have looked like Sutton's head.

"Randall said you were coming," he said in a squeaky voice from behind his papers. He hunkered down like a soldier under assault, behind protective sandbags. He saw me. "Who the hell is this?"

Zygler answered patiently, and soothingly. "This is Mike O'Hara, from the NTSB."

I held out my hand to shake, but Sutton shrunk

back. The silence was brief. I pulled my hand back.

After a few awkward seconds, Zygler went on. "Mike and an FBI agent will need to talk to you tomorrow, at nine."

"About the wreck?" Sutton spat out the words.

"Yes, Tom." Zygler remained cool, but sympathetic. "You may want to have your attorney come, too. I would."

"You're going to blame this shit on me, now. That's the plan, isn't it, Eric? Fine." His head jerked as he spoke the words. "Fine. Nine tomorrow morning. Here, or in the Sistine Chapel?"

Zygler smiled in a friendly fashion. "We can do it in my office, if you want. We'll be comfortable there."

As we turned to walk out, Sutton sank lower in his chair and held his head in his hands. "I didn't do it," he whimpered.

"I know, Tom," Zygler said.

Out in the hall, I aimed at the elevators. I held out my hand to shake. I was drained from the encounter.

Zygler's grip was weaker this time, like he was exhausted. He slumped against the wall.

"Thanks for all your help, Eric. Do you think he'll be all right until tomorrow?"

He put his hands in his pockets as we got to the elevator. "He doesn't have any family here. His wife left him recently. I think it's what started the drinking again."

The elevator arrived, and I got on.

He called through the closing door, "I'll make sure he has someone with him."

I drove across town in heavy traffic, waiting in line at lights and thinking about Eric Zygler, and Tom Sutton, and the mess at ZYCO. Money was supposed to make people happy, wasn't it?

Zygler had surprised me. I had expected him to be a nerdy jerk with the social skills of a banana slug, and he had turned out to be personable and interesting. He appeared to care more about the people he had working for him and his firm's reputation with the public than he did about money. He sort of reminded me of me, only smarter, richer and successful.

I had been raised by schoolteachers, and worked for one government agency or another my entire adult life. I had even gone to a state university. The predisposition to dislike gigabuck captains of industry was ingrained deeply in me. And yet I found myself liking him. It was easy to see how he had molded a massive company from nothing, essentially inventing a new industry single-handed, and how important he was to the business.

Now that I had the help of the entire ZYCO organization, I was sure we would find the common thread that had caused the two air crashes. I was filled with optimism.

I pulled onto the freeway at 1:00 p.m., knowing that I would be a little early for hospital visiting hours, but I found myself driving faster than traffic anyway. Working back and forth between lanes, I passed trucks and old men in Buicks until I was five miles north of Colorado Springs, passing the Air Force Academy nestled in the foothills.

The traffic grew steadily lighter, and two miles farther along I reached for the cruise control button. I set the controller on seventy-five, fast enough to make me feel like I was making good time without attracting the attention of local law enforcement agencies.

As I released the control button on the steering wheel, I felt the accelerator pedal drop out from under my right foot. The sedan's V-6 engine wailed and thrust the speedometer needle to and past eighty before I realized anything was wrong.

This was the first time I had used the cruise control since renting the car. Traffic had been too heavy on my previous trip to Denver. The speed regulator circuit had to be out of adjustment. I would have to put together a juicy "up-yours" note on NTSB letterhead to the manufacturer. I began to absently compose the nasty communication as I tapped the brake pedal to disable the cruise control and take over all the driving tasks again manually. I'd have plenty to say in that memo.

The cruise control didn't disengage.

The throttle was still wide open, and the car's speed was over eighty-five and increasing. I was impressed at how fast this plain domestic sedan was, and the strength of the acceleration, even at this high speed. I stepped on the brake harder, intending to trip the micro-switch to cut off the control once and for all.

The throttle remained wide open. Speed was now over ninety.

I stepped on the brake pedal hard, now, not panicking, just being decisive.

A hard throbbing sensation pressed back at my foot, battering the sole of my shoe. The anti-lock brake system was working, sending impulses to the brake system hydraulics, backing the brake calipers off their discs to keep the wheels from locking up, and incidentally robbing me of most of my braking power. It wasn't supposed to work like that, but it did.

I flicked my thumbs onto the push buttons on the steering wheel hub, trying to shut off the cruise control at the main switch, but I couldn't remember which button was on/off, and which was resume/accelerate. A quick glance down to the wheel put me onto the right button, and I pushed it. The button had no effect, and I looked again to be sure I had the right one.

In my peripheral vision, a yellow form appeared.

A school bus, trying to pass a loaded semi, was blocking my lane less than a hundred yards ahead, and I was screaming up on it from behind at over a hundred miles per hour. I grabbed at the gear selector and tried to put it in neutral, but it was locked in place. I wrenched at the shifter until it bent and nearly broke. Nothing.

OK, decisiveness hadn't worked. Panic was now appropriate. I reached for a horn button and missed, while stabbing again at the brake pedal to no effect.

In desperation, I pulled onto the wide left shoulder, praying that there wasn't a narrow bridge or construction ahead.

The shoulder was barely wide enough, and I swept past the school bus traveling fifty miles per hour faster than it was cruising. One front wheel rumbled dangerously on the rumble strips carved into the edge of the pavement. The car tried to swerve off the road into the sandy brush-covered median strip, and I had to saw the wheel hard to the right to bring it back. I lunged across the road into the right lane and past it before regaining directional control.

My excursion had scrubbed off a little speed, but the car quickly raced through one hundred again and finally stabilized with the speedometer needle bouncing against the stop at one-fifteen. The broad freeway now seemed distinctly narrow, and I cringed as I saw another knot of traffic a half-mile ahead.

More stabs at the brakes and buttons failed to bring the car back under control, and I reached for the keys, to shut the engine off.

I hesitated. Didn't the keys engage an anti-theft steering lock when you shut them off? How far could I turn them? And would the power brakes or steering still have enough boost to be effective as I slowed?

The modern, computer controlled safety and convenience features of this fine American automobile were banding together to piss out the flame of my life.

As I hauled up on the next traffic, I saw with horror that a rental truck was pulling slowly into the left lane to pass a heavily loaded mini-van pulling a trailer. Is that tow within the vehicle's rated capacity, sir?

I thought not, and desperately wished for a chance to stop and write a quick report on the subject.

I would try the trick of passing on the shoulder again, and began to carefully pull out onto the left verge, while sounding long blasts on my horn. An overpass was coming up, with fearful looking bridge abutments narrowing the roadbed a few precious feet on either side. There would probably be enough room to pass by, I thought. Probably.

As we flashed under the overpass three abreast, I heard a loud crash from my door, and noticed that the side window next to my ear had cracked. Too close.

Out onto open road again, I could feel the

steering wheel shaking slightly in my hands. The scrape on the overpass support had knocked the front wheels out of alignment, and the car's speed had dropped to just below one-ten. The transmission was shifting up and down out of overdrive and back in, torque and power demands now out of its design envelope.

In the rear view mirror, a flashing blue light appeared. My speed and movements had attracted the attention of a state trooper, who was now blasting down the on-ramp in hot pursuit.

Well, fine, I thought. If I lived, I would have to talk my way out of a ticket, too.

Scanning forward and back for traffic, I saw that I would have a clear road for a few seconds, and decided it was time to try the last trick available. There was one system on board that still had no electronic doodads, no unseen electronic mind controlling its actions.

I pulled into the middle of the roadbed, straddling the center stripe, and pushed gently on the emergency brake. The carmaker had designed a mechanism that was set with a pedal. To release it, the pedal had to be pushed all the way to the floor before letting up. I was committed to stopping with the emergency brake, no matter what.

The brake pedal went down several clicks, with no discernable effect. Oh, swell. Had whoever it was that had screwed with the cruise control and brakes also done in this? Great.

I pushed harder, and began to feel a slight pull from the rear wheels. The speed fell to ninety-two. Bingo, this would work. Just a few more clicks would do the job.

One more push on the pedal and the rear wheels suddenly locked.

The car slewed hard to the right, diving toward the shoulder and a four-foot deep drainage ditch beyond. I swung the wheel hard left. The back end of the car began a slow, smoky slide to the right, trying like hell to pass the still charging front end, and I had to saw the wheel back right to halt the skid.

The car was now turned twenty degrees off the road, and I flew over the rumble strips, steering desperately left to keep the car on the pavement. The front wheels dipped off the road and into the gravelly sand, spraying a loud staccato of rocks onto the floorboards.

The front wheels, still under wide-open power, caught the bare ground and jerked the steering wheel out of my hands. The car lurched hard to the right, and went airborne.

For an absurd second I was flying, and the engine raced as the front wheels lost their burden of traction, spinning freely. The front wheels would slow to match the vehicle's speed at impact, I thought, and leave neat impressions of the tire's treads in the resulting ruts like Steve's had.

The car hit again and bounced in the dirt, still moving at over seventy, spraying gravel and sage. Crossing the near side of the drainage ditch at a shallow angle, the right side dipped, and the car was beginning a series of rolls as the nose smashed into the berm on the far side.

Slow motion, now.

I developed a new respect for the basic laws of the Newtonian universe as the car's structure collapsed around me.

Force does in fact equal mass times acceleration, and velocity really is the multiplicative product of acceleration and time.

The air bag in my steering wheel inflated, the explosive force of deployment seeming like the cool breath of a spring breeze. I read the supplier's logo off the front of the bag as my face flew through it like a hammer hitting a marshmallow.

As the engine compartment collapsed, the hood jackknifed in half, blocking my view of the world. How sad.

This was not what I wanted. I wanted to fly in space. I wanted to be envied by the entire world. I wanted to be obscenely rich, like Eric Zygler. I desperately wanted to take Sally Montez to a five-star resort in Hawaii and have endless sex with her as warm tropical airs blew over our hot, sweat-covered bodies.

None of this would ever happen now, because I

was about to be killed in the crash of this shitty rental car.

I could feel my brain sloshing forward in its cranial cavity, and wondered if they would use a saw or a hammer and chisel in the autopsy to peel back my skull so they could see what had happened to that ridiculous mass of pulp.

The sound was so loud that it was quiet, and the light was so bright that it was dark. Through it all, I remained conscious and cognizant of everything, but I couldn't imagine why.

I knew that I was in the process of being murdered, and I wondered how it was going to end.

Gradually, like the sun coming up on a winter day, I became aware that the car had stopped moving.

I was upside-down, and the locked inertia-reel shoulder strap held me in limbo, not tight enough to keep me in my seat, head off the ceiling. My arms hung limp over me, and my wrists rested against the headliner.

I shook my head to clear away the unfocused results of impact. It hurt, and I moaned.

I was immediately disturbed, because I couldn't hear myself moaning. Was I dead after all, and merely sentenced to a particularly uncomfortable hell? Inverted Hades? No, crashes were loud, and air bags could leave an accident victim temporarily deaf. A good trade for massive facial or head injuries, actually.

I saw movement out of the corner of my eye. Feet

appeared by the smashed roof, and a voice called out, but the reduced state of my hearing kept me from understanding.

I moaned again, louder.

Feet were replaced by knees, and a black face, tilted on its side. The voice came again, and I could make it out this time.

"OK, we're gonna get you out of there. Hang on." The voice was cool and calm, and so was I. I heard the voice say, "We'd better get him out. There's gas all over the place."

The feet walked around to the smashed-out rear window, and were joined by others. I felt hands on my shoulders, and someone unbuckled my belt. Despite the efforts of the rescuers, I fell on my head with a crash and cursed loudly. As my saviors pulled and tugged to move me across the ceiling, I noted with some satisfaction that I couldn't feel any broken bones grinding together, and didn't seem to be leaving a trail of blood. This was good, I was sure.

As I was dragged out, I began assembling my explanation. Why was I driving so fast? Had I been drinking?

The two men moved me clear of the car and laid me down on a soft patch of earth. One left to get help, and I opened my eyes to see his form disappearing toward the highway.

A vaguely familiar face looked at me from beneath his state police hat, his African features fixed in a scowl, and his head shaking slowly back and forth. "Damn, you federal types are sure a lot of trouble."

"Ah, Officer Maxwell. Long time no see."

I passed out.

chapter

10

After a while, I was flying.

I didn't hear the helicopter. I wasn't hearing anything yet, but I could tell by the wind from the rotor and the smell of engine exhaust that I was being flown somewhere.

To a hospital, I hoped.

I was very tired, but an excessively vigorous young woman shook my hands and patted my face, and would not let me go to sleep. Gradually, I got the idea that she was doing this on purpose, and that I shouldn't drift off.

My hearing improved slowly, and the rhythmic

whirring and rotor beat of the helicopter's flight began to pulse through into my brain. Although addled by G-forces and shock, the abused gray matter inside my head was beginning to work again, and little by little I began to think about the impact of my ride into the ditch beside the freeway.

What had Steve Penney said at the hospital? What did Keats say his words had been? "No" and "Accident."

No accident.

No shit.

I caught the flight nurse's hand and shouted over the din. "Cruise control."

She shook her head. "I don't understand."

I inhaled deeply, and shouted again. "Cruise control. Anti-lock brakes. Software. Tell the police to impound the car. Sabotaged." I was very tired now, and sagged back on the too-short stretcher and its lozenge-sized pillow. My head pounded, and the sky outside turned orange and purple. "Tell Maxwell to impound the car. Evidence."

She shook her head again. "It's OK. Don't exert yourself. Relax, now. Keep your eyes open, and look at me. Relax. We'll land in a few minutes." She held her arms on my shoulders for a few seconds, with the strength of a thousand Olympic weight lifters. I rested. Small animals danced and capered on the edges of my vision and the sky turned other colors in a paisley pattern.

The sounds changed and there was a thud that made it into my mind. I found myself being carried and wheeled out of the helicopter. Downwash from the rotor splashed over me again as we crossed the helipad and rolled through a door. After a short elevator ride, I was surrounded by people in green clothes who poked and prodded me and invaded my privacy in several ways.

Another woman put a plastic probe in my ear while an unseen helper slipped a blood-pressure cuff on one arm and inflated it. There was flurry of activity, and at one point she asked my name. "Mike," I said, as clearly as I could.

"I'm Dr. Pulaski. How do you feel, Mike? Do you hurt anywhere?" She looked into my eyes one at a time as she talked.

"My head hurts. My knees hurt." There was something I needed to say, but I was very tired. Maybe that was it. "I'm tired." No, that wasn't the thing. The room was rotating slowly counterclockwise, and the lights turned colors and became dimmer. There was a loud, pulsating hum.

"You're going to be fine, Mike. Stay awake for a while, if you can." She turned away to fiddle with a tray of instruments.

"I'm tired." What was I supposed to remember? "My car. The car I was in." That was it.

The doctor smiled, looking back into my eyes.

"You are going to be fine. Don't worry about your car," she said patiently.

"No, no--" I realized I was shouting, and quieted myself a little. The room's rotation slowed, and then reversed itself. I concentrated hard, and spoke clearly and slowly. "The car was sabotaged. Tell the investigating officer, Officer Maxwell, that he needs to impound the car, and protect the electronics under the hood." She stopped what she was doing, and looked at me as a complete being instead of one isolated body part or another.

"OK," she said. "How do you know that? What should I tell him?"

"Tell him to call the office in Denver he faxed the stuff to. NTSB." I felt myself moving into the air while rotating slowly head-over-heels, and I wondered how they did that.

"Relax, now. Rest. I'll call him." Her face looked like Sally's, except for her blond hair and blue eyes and everything else.

I faded to blackness.

When I woke up the next day, alone in a hospital room, my head felt better and the rest of me felt worse. My knees and shins had made contact with the bottom of the dash during my big off-road thrill ride. There were astonishing black and purple bruises from the top of my feet to my waist, and both knees had swollen to twice their normal size. Every muscle in my body had one complaint or another, and a quick look in a mirror during a stumbling trip to the john revealed two huge shiners on my face, plus bright orange hemorrhages splotching the whites of my eyes.

Early in the morning I spent ten minutes with a neurologist, who made me squeeze her hands and watch her fingers move. No, my stomach felt OK. Yes, I was a little irritable. Why the hell shouldn't I be? Dizzy, yes. Fatigue, yes.

She spoke briefly--very briefly--about the effects of concussion and the need for rest, and then departed quickly to see her next head case.

The good news was that I had no major internal injuries and no broken bones. The attending doctor announced that I should plan on staying in the hospital at least two more days before release--I had slept for almost twenty hours--but that I shouldn't suffer any permanent ill effects. My eyes would clear up quickly and the bruises would fade. I just felt like hell.

Despite my ravings and shouts, Dr. Pulaski had taken me seriously. Just after 10:00 a.m., Officer Maxwell arrived. He walked quietly to the bedside and stood with a note pad in his hands, his leather gun belt and freshly cleaned Beretta pistol incongruous in the medical venue.

The aroma of warm gun oil clashed with the antiseptic smell of the hospital like garlic in a chocolate shop.

I sat up in bed when he entered. "Thanks for pulling me out of the car."

He raised an eyebrow and smiled briefly. "No problem. It's my job. The doctor said I could talk for five minutes. I'm here because I'm curious about why two government crash investigators would have accidents so similar on the same stretch of road. My stretch of road. You said something about the car being sabotaged?"

I started to nod, and then instantly regretted the motion as I watched the room do barrel rolls for a few seconds. "Yes," I said as my eyes fluttered and spun like broken window shades. "I think the brakes were tampered with."

He looked doubtful. "We looked the car over, and tested the brakes."

I held my head against the pillow, to avoid shaking it and zooming off into the ozone again. "The anti-lock brake processor, I think. And the cruise control." I paused and rested for a second. "And maybe the engine control computer. The car ran away from me, and it was moving faster than it should have." I rested again.

"You think the other car was fooled with the same way?"

"Uh-hm," I said, without nodding.

"Your car is in a wrecker's lot. We were going to turn it over to the rental agency."

"You need to get it under control," I said, with all the force of an enraged kitten. "It needs to be in impound. It could be evidence." I was feeling tired suddenly, and my eyes tried to slam shut. "Call the NTSB office here in Denver... "

"I'll take care of it." He backed out of the room.

I slept.

By early afternoon it was clear that my aches and pains would keep me from sleeping any more, and so during a lull when there were no nurses in sight, I painfully edged to the side of my bed and pulled up a telephone. I dialed the number for Sally's cell.

After three rings, she answered. "NTSB. Montez."

"Sally, it's Mike." My voice croaked.

"Mike!" she shouted. "What are you doing on the phone?"

"Uh, it's easier than shouting that far." I chuckled at my own joke--somebody had to--and could hear her talking to someone in the background. "Hey, I need to tell you some stuff. Tell McCall--"

"Why don't you wait about half an hour and we'll be there. We're on the road now."

"You're coming here?"

"Yes," she said. "Everybody wants to talk to you."

"Well, don't use your cruise control. I think mine was messed with. So was Penney's."

"We're going to try to talk to Steve, too. Just wait a little while." She admonished me to rest and relax, and hung up, just as an avenging angel in scrubs and comfortable shoes walked in and took the phone away from me.

Twenty minutes later my door opened, and an entourage filed in like priests at a high mass. On the point was a medical type who turned out to be the head of the trauma department. Behind him were Sally, Eric Zygler, Keats of the Denver field office, and F. Brooks McCall, The Chairman himself. Sally and Zygler were dressed casually, and McCall and Keats wore gray suits and important-government-guy ties. The doctor's motions toward Zygler suggested deference bordering on worship.

Sally hung back, horrified for an instant by my bruises and hemorrhaged eyes and, perhaps, intimidated a little by the company. Zygler slouched against the far wall. He gave me a slight smile and a little wave but he seemed elsewhere. Keats and McCall came to the bedside.

McCall towered over the others, tall and still military in bearing despite his long years in industry and the government. He leaned over me and shook my weakened hand.

"Jesus, Mike," he said with a smile, his Texas

drawl thick. "You look like absolute hell. Feelin' pretty rough?"

I cleared my throat and spoke quietly. "Just a little banged up, boss. I'll be OK."

McCall smiled and looked to the doctor. "Will he be able to play well in the big NTSB golf tournament next spring?"

The doctor smiled. "Sure, definitely."

"Funny," McCall said, and gave me a wide country smile, "He never played well before." There were chuckles all around the room. McCall specialized in corny humor.

I groaned. "Please don't encourage him."

McCall' expression became serious. "Mike, between you and Lew Hills, I feel like I'm spendin' half my time in hospital rooms. Hospitals give me the willies. Don't like 'em." He paused. "What happened to you?"

"Somebody fixed my car," I said quietly. "I couldn't stop it."

"Steve Penney's car the same way?" McCall said.

"I think so."

His Texas accent thinned noticeably. "And you think this is related to the GMax crashes."

I looked at Sally, and she seemed nervous. "I'm not sure, boss. Nothing we could prove in court, at least not yet."

"Tell me about it," McCall said. He sat on the

edge of the bed and crossed his arms. "I already got a briefing from Sally, but I want you to lay your case out for me."

I took a deep breath. "I was driving normally."

"Too fast," McCall interjected with a hint of a smile.

I nodded. "Seventy-five or so. I hit a stretch of light traffic and put the cruise control on, and everything went to hell. The throttle went wide open; the anti-lock brakes activated and wouldn't give me any stopping power. The car ran off, and I tried to use the emergency brake to stop. It locked the rear wheels up, and here I am."

McCall was silent for a moment, studying his watch. "And you think Penney's car was screwed with the same way?"

"Same make and model," I said. "All the electronics are under the hood. Somebody with the right knowledge and the tools could have done something to the processors."

McCall glanced at Keats, who looked non-committal. "OK. If we accept all that, what's the connection to the airplane crashes? Lay it out for me."

I looked at Eric Zygler for a second, and I saw a slight nod, along with a sense of resignation. As I stared into his eyes, the nod grew stronger.

I took another deep breath. "Embedded software,

boss. Both the fly-by-wire control system and the code for the various processors under the hood of my car."

Zygler cleared his throat. "It's all ZYCO software, Mr. Chairman. My products, my team. The cars, too. I had to check with our contracts shop to be sure."

McCall looked around the room, settling his stare on Zygler. "Mr. Zygler, I spoke with the President this morning. He shares your concern for the good name of your company, and greatly values the support you have shown him."

Zygler waved a hand and shook his head. "I appreciate the President's words, of course, but he doesn't have to worry about me being embarrassed. My concern is for the integrity of my products. And the best way to keep that integrity intact is to get to the bottom of this business and stop whatever or whoever is doing it."

McCall smiled warmly. Zygler was a strong backer of the President, and the ZYCO political action committee had contributed both money and time to the President's campaign at a critical juncture in the previous election year's primary effort. Zygler could have demanded special favors and maybe have gotten them. This Harry Hairshirt act could have been for show.

"I certainly appreciate that, Mr. Zygler."

Zygler smiled shyly. "Eric, please. I'm working very closely with Mike and his team to figure the matter out. I'm just glad you have such terrific people working for you. I'm very impressed with their work."

McCall beamed. "I've always been lucky with people, Eric. I'll relay your thoughts to the President the next time I talk to him."

McCall turned back to me and stroked his chin. "Mike, tell me what you think the deal is, here. How do you think whoever it was did it?"

I was beginning to feel heavily fatigued, but I was determined to lay the case out. "I'm not sure I have it straight in my own mind, but here it is." I took another deep breath and closed my eyes for a second. "The ZYCO airplane was loaded right, and the pilots were qualified. The airplane took off, and seems to have pulled up into a full-power stall right after liftoff. The elevator had to have gone to full nose-up when the pilot rotated the nose up to fly."

McCall interrupted, staring at the floor. "Were you able to tell what the actual position of the elevator was when they hit?"

"No," I said, and shook my head. It was a mistake, and the room started to spin again.

I held my head against the pillow for a second before things began to stabilize. "There wasn't any visible damage to the hinges, or anything. If they had hit harder there would have been, but there wasn't." I started to sit up, and turned to Sally. "Maybe a metallurgical check would tell us if the hinges were overstressed. We might be able to tell what direction they were pointed in, if they were. Call the lab--"

Sally began to reach for the electronic toy in her purse to take notes, but McCall waved her off. "Relax. We'll check out the hinges for you. Go on, tell me your idea."

I slumped against the pillow again, and gathered my thoughts. "OK, here's where the logic gets shaky, but I can't find any other explanation. If the elevator were full up, the airplane would have acted the way it did. Now, Sally found a glitch in one section of computer driver code for a control surface appears to be missing. If that computer had an instruction to drive the elevator full up and then erase itself, that would fit what we saw. Could be hacking."

"Hacking?" McCall looked at me with a doubtful expression. "Mike, there have to be other explanations. Hell, you got a good check of the control systems."

Sally broke in. "Sir, I was using what was left of the system, and it acted normally. But the three computers were redundant. Any one of them could do the job. If the bad command was planned to erase itself, things could end up the way they did. The NSA might tell us."

"NSA?" Zygler said, sounding surprised.

"They're checking the hardware for us," Sally said.

McCall broke in. "I'm not sure Eric is cleared for

that information, Sally." She leaned back in surprise then covered her mouth in embarrassment and started to apologize.

"It's OK, no harm done," McCall said. He smiled, and she relaxed a little. "Eric, we're getting some technical help to see if we can read the parts of that memory that are erased. That's all. Don't know if it will work or not."

Zygler said, "Sure, I'm familiar with the technique."

"I bet you invented it." McCall chuckled and turned back to me. "Go on, Mike. You think maybe the elevator was stuck full-up, and the software erased itself. What else?"

"The Canadian crash." I was tiring rapidly. "Sally got pictures in from the robot sub they searched for it with. The horizontal tail failed downward. The rudder was beat to hell. If the elevator went full-up at the GMax's cruising speed, it would overstress the airplane right away. The tail would fail downward if it went..."

"The wing would fold up, I'd think." McCall made a broken airplane with his hands. He shrugged. "At least, it could go either way."

"I'd bet on the tail in this one," I said. "In a pitch-up this fast, the elevator would be fighting the inertia of the fuselage rotation, in addition to the air loads. If they find the data recorders we might be able to confirm it."

McCall stroked his chin again and nodded. "We'll have to check with the Aries engineering staff on that one."

Zygler said, "I'll talk to them in the morning. Mike has me setting up some simulations, and I'll throw that scenario in."

McCall pulled a knee up and held it with interlaced fingers. "OK, so you're saying that both airplanes were wrecked the same way, presumably by the same problem or person. What about the cars?"

"The cars were essentially identical to each other," Zygler said. "You could install new control chips in each car that would cause the problems we saw." He sounded pained. "There isn't a lot of control over it." He hit a fist slowly against his chin, thinking. "But there is another problem we're working."

He had all of our attention. McCall asked quietly, "What sort of problem?"

"Please understand. It hasn't been verified. We'd need field testing to be sure. Cars aren't secured the way we have covered the airplanes. There's no requirement."

McCall was clearly struggling to be patient. "What's the issue, Eric?"

Zygler took a deep breath. "These cars have our new drive-by-wire system. The engine and safety systems are all run by a central computer. We, well, we identified a way to hack into the system via Wi-Fi, through the tire pressure sensors." That was a new one on me.

He looked back at our simultaneous blank stares, and frowned. "The car uses the cruise control and brake systems to slow it down if a tire goes flat. The tire pressure monitor uses a radio link from inside the tire to report to a receiver under the hood. The radio link is uncovered and...um, you can make the car...well, go out of control. Sort of. We found a way to hack in using Wi-Fi. Cell phones might work, too. Not sure."

McCall was incredulous. "Do you mean to tell me that a hacker can break into a car while it's on the road through the tires? And wreck it?"

"Well, yes."

McCall shook his head. "Jesus. What the hell kind of world are we building?"

"One where there doors don't have locks," Sally said.

Zygler held his hands out, as if pleading. "We're working on a patch to fix it."

McCall answered quietly. "Good idea."

"Who'd do such a thing?" He sounded wistful, and disappointed. "But I think we should admit that it has to be some sort of sabotage. Maybe hacking, or maybe something else. Planes and cars both. The plane has been tested and reviewed a million times. We know that system inside and out, and the French checked it all independently." If it had been anyone else McCall or I would have cautioned about reserving judgment. There was silence for a few seconds.

"And hacking the cars wouldn't be hard?" McCall said.

"Not once you know it's possible," Zygler said. "There are a lot people on the site that could have done it. Hell, if you gave me enough time I could probably do it myself."

McCall waited for a moment. "But we need a motive. Why would anybody want to kill... What was his name again?"

"Corso," Zygler said quietly. "J. Wesley Corso. Wes. He was a friend of mine." After a pause, Zygler began to explain about the financial doings at ZYCO. He described Tom Sutton's role in the period before the initial public offering of ZYCO's stock.

McCall listened for a while. "I guess that much money could make anybody crazy."

Zygler held his arms out in front of himself and stared absently into space. "One FBI agent questioned Tom yesterday, and was planning several more hours today. There is another agent coming from Denver to help. Tom didn't have a lawyer, so I got him one."

I sagged against the bed and McCall looked at me. "Mike, I think you've had enough for one day. I fly east first thing tomorrow, so I'll see you when the docs let you come home." He pulled an airline itinerary printout from his coat pocket and put on his little half-frame reading glasses and studied his departure time. "I am having a hard time getting a replacement out here for you. With Lew down too, I'm short of people."

I spoke, louder than I meant to. "Hey, I don't need a replacement. I'll be OK."

The exertion of speaking loudly had used up all my available oxygen, and the room began to turn colors again.

McCall looked at me askance over his glasses. "That's probably the concussion talking. We'll discuss it later."

Zygler looked up from his depression. "I'd hate to lose Mike right now, Mr. Chairman. His insights are really central to the work. I need him to get my company's reputation back. I'll make sure he's all right."

McCall considered it for a moment. "Eric, you and I will need to work something out."

At that point the floor nurse walked in and ordered everybody out. Everyone stood and filed out of the room.

I was asleep before they were gone.

McCall returned the next morning to say goodbye. He related Steve Penney's condition to me--improving but still dopey--and said Steve did not have any memory about the accident. He was awake for an hour or so but couldn't say much.

"He wanted to warn you about something," McCall said, "but he can't remember about what. I've worked a deal with Zygler. He's going to make sure you don't work too hard for a few days, and keep you close by for consulting. Sally, Wang and that FBI fella can finish with the wreckage. And we're following up on your metallurgy idea. It may pay off."

He smiled wolfishly. "I'll have to drop you on your head more often." With a huge F. Brooks McCall flourish, he swept out of the room.

By later that day, I was getting distinctly tired of hospital life. The swelling on my knees was going down fast after treatment with ice and drugs, and the amazing colors of my legs had begun to change from angry blacks and the occasional fleck of red to more benign greens and purples. My eyes were slowly returning to a normal color, and a glance in the mirror revealed that the bruises on my face had begun to fade ever so slightly. I had even gotten to the point of being able to stay awake for more than an hour at a time.

In the afternoon the doctor said I should get some exercise, so I ambled into the hall and walked down to where I remembered Steve Penney's room was. I knocked on the door and stuck my head in. Steve was asleep, and his wife sat by the bed, reading a magazine. We exchanged pleasantries, and she said that he was out of danger and that the hospital was treating him well enough, but that he was still sleeping almost constantly. After a few minutes, I walked back to my room. I noticed as I went that there was a state police officer standing watch halfway between Steve's room and mine. He nodded as I passed.

The hospital nutritionists had a "comfort food" menu, and I had time to down a peanut butter and jelly sandwich before another doctor visited to examine my progress. He declared that unless I suffered some form of problem overnight, the next day would mean freedom. Not a second too soon. Checkout time was at 9:00 a.m.

That evening I had another reason to think twice about Eric Zygler and the ZYCO leviathan that he had created. Yet another bright young man, who could have been Clinton Harding's illegitimate brother, appeared at the door of my room just after eight with a bag in his hand. He quietly and earnestly wished me a good evening and disappeared before I could thank him or ask what the bag held.

When I opened it, I found a comfortable-looking knit shirt in my size, fashionably baggy pants that would fit over my swollen knees, socks, underwear and a pair of Gucci boat shoes whose leather was so soft and buttery smooth that I wanted to sleep with my face on them. I hadn't thought of the fact that the clothes I had been wearing during the accident had been cut off me in the ER, but someone obviously had.

After checking the sizes of everything, I tried on the shoes, and they fit like I had worn them for years. Standing there in my hospital robe and comfy Italian footwear, it hit me: How in hell did they know my sizes? Was this a sign of efficiency and concern, or invasive obsession?

I didn't sleep much.

Sally called the next morning and said she would meet me at the front entrance. The tradition of leaving the hospital in a wheel chair was alive and well, and I was rolled to the door with my gimpy legs propped up on the chair's stirrups, after signing insurance and release paperwork for fifteen minutes. I thanked the nurse's aide and relaxed on a bench, enjoying the sun and a warm breeze under a portico for a few minutes, hoping that this was the front entrance. I had arrived via the helipad on the roof. Just as I was beginning to get really worried that I was in the wrong place, a big silver Mercedes executive car with heavily tinted windows pulled up and stopped in front of me.

An earnest young man jumped out of the driver's door--ZYCO apparently didn't hire anyone who slouched--and raced around to the passenger side as the sunroof slid open. He stood waiting expectantly.

Sally popped her head and shoulders out of the

open sunroof like a dancer from a cake at the kind of parties I never got invited to.

"Hiya, sailor" she said with an expansive smile. "Want a ride?"

I looked the limo over from bow to stern for a second. "Well, OK," I said with a shrug as I walked to the now open door. "Were they out of Chevys or something?"

"It was all they had," she said with a little laugh.

She dropped back inside while I got in, and the sunroof slid closed as I crawled painfully into the huge rear seat.

I looked at my surroundings. "I hope the Inspector General isn't watching," I muttered.

The car purred smoothly out of the hospital parking lot and into traffic. Sally was dressed in soft white silk pants, high heels and a tan cashmere sweater just tight enough to make my day complete. I wanted the driver to hit the road and keep going. She really was the prettiest woman I had ever known, and the softness of her sweater seemed to accentuate the smoothness of her skin and lush curl of her dark shoulder-length hair.

I wanted to tell her that she could just have me, bruises and all, to keep around as a spare guy to use when she didn't feel like going out. Little sister. Big brother. Supervisor. Appearance issues. Sexual harassment rules. Shit. Again. I stared out the passenger window.

She sat on the aft-facing couch, and she tilted her head to one side. "Hmmm? Too rich for you?"

I was shaken from my trance. "A little. ZYCO?"

"Eric," she said. "The chairman said we all looked burned out, and ordered everybody to take the weekend off while you rest up."

"Is this a weekend?" I looked at my watch, but it was broken, the crystal shattered and the face covered with dirt.

"It's Saturday. Welcome back to the world."

I sagged against the leather seat back and laid my newly minted medical records on the floor. "It was nice of you to come up and ride with me."

She smiled again, less for show and more personably. "Well, you gave me quite a scare. I've never had a boss as nice as you before, and I also have quite a bit to bring you up to date on." She hesitated and began to look devilish. "And I've never ridden in a limo like this before. Have you?" She raised her eyebrows.

I looked around at the burled walnut and leather, and the TV, and the bar. "Not one this color."

We both paused and then laughed together.

She pulled a pad from her purse and flipped through it. "Let's see. We got the wreckage all moved from the site to the ZYCO hangar, and it's under control now. George and Lee pulled the elevator hinges, and we shipped them off to the Washington lab for the check you wanted, although Dr. Schmidt says he doesn't think he'll find anything."

"I was under the influence of prescription pain medication when I thought of it. We'll see."

She went on. "Eric says he'll have the simulations you wanted ready by Monday morning. You have an appointment at nine Monday morning in a lab at ZYCO headquarters."

"Aren't you coming?"

She looked up from her notes. "Well, I thought you would want to handle the important things."

I shook my head and cut her off. "No, I want you in on everything from here on. You're an expert on this business."

She tilted her head and looked sheepish. "Not really."

"Yes, really. You've had a lot of good ideas so far, and I need you around to call them on anything that you don't like, OK? Learn to be an obnoxious government puke. Your judgment has been right on."

She closed her note pad and smiled widely. "Thank you."

I looked around the car again. "So what are your plans for the weekend? Do you ski or anything?"

"You and I are going to Eric's. You're going to rest, and use his Jacuzzi, and we're going to hang out with a lot of very rich people. Are you ready?"

She stuck her pad back in her purse, and sat with her hands clasped in her lap.

I frowned. "I'm not sure we should be doing this. There are all kinds of ethics rules."

She seemed both annoyed and amused. "You have issues about authority. Do you always obey the rules?"

"Pretty much."

"Well, relax. We checked it all out with Legal, and they said it's OK under the circumstances. Eric's lawyers talked to the board's attorney directly yesterday. ZYCO isn't selling us anything, so most of the rules don't apply. In fact, we're already on record as saying that their software is a possible cause, and they've agreed. And we can get a little work done over the weekend this way. Besides, Eric made the offer."

The car spun through a couple of turns. "I still don't like how it looks," I said. "And I need to get into the office. I have a lot of things to catch up on tomorrow."

Sally stopped me. "Mike, don't be a jerk. You were in a car accident. Your car went off the road at a hundred miles an hour. We're lucky you're alive. And you have a concussion."

I held a hand up, feeling tired suddenly. "Just a small one."

"The doctor said you have to rest and that's what you're going to do. Eric really wants to help. He was very happy you could come to stay." She paused. "He seems kind of lonely."

"Yeah. Isolated. Not only is he stinking rich, but he's also a genius, so he's had it coming and going." I stretched in the seat and squirmed to a more comfortable position. "It's not easy to feel sorry for a guy like that."

We rode south toward Colorado Springs, and there were more rotations, but the spin rate was getting lower. Gravity increased and pulled me down in the seat. I slept.

chapter
11

I woke up as Sally was putting down the handset of the driver's intercom. We were pulling up to a large gate in a high white stone wall that seemed to stretch from horizon to horizon. There was no address number on the wall and no sign of a mailbox.

"We're here," she said.

I sat up, rubbing my eyes, and instantly regretted it. They still had that gritty abused feeling from high decelerations and hemorrhages. I blinked hard and looked around. My neck and shoulders protested the movement. The weather was sunny and mild, and the harsh sun brought a hint of tears to my eyes. I blinked again.

We were high in the western foothills overlooking Colorado Springs. The driver had his window open, and he leaned out to speak into an intercom embedded in the stone pillar holding one side of the wrought iron gate. I could hear him through the window that separated the rear cabin from the front. "It's Andy, with Mr. O'Hara and Ms. Montez."

There was an unintelligible buzz from the speaker, and he pulled his head back into the car. The gate silently swung open, and we rolled through as it closed behind us.

As the limo picked up speed, Sally looked around intently. "I can't wait to see this," she said, her eyes bright with excitement. "It's supposed to be the world's most comfortable place."

How do the absurdly rich live? Absurdly well.

We rolled into Eric Zygler's private world, and Sally and I rode with our noses against the windows, marveling at the scale of the property. We drove slowly along a two-lane drive, over low hills and past hundreds of acres of golf course-like lawn. At one point, the Mercedes cruised quietly past a grounds keeper on a small tractor, mowing the grass to a carpet-like texture. He mowed in a pattern that left the grass looking like a huge green checkerboard, the way I'd seen it done in sports stadiums.

I also spotted what appeared to be surveillance

cameras at frequent but irregular intervals. The Rockies made a fabulous background, and forest took over from the manicured lawn in the distance.

I timed our drive to estimate how big the place was. After seven minutes at thirty miles per hour, or three and a half miles, we topped a small rise and headed down into an arroyo, losing sight of the city behind us. Ahead, a low ranch-style house spread out across the end of the private road, with a circular driveway curving in front of a portico for arrivals. There was a heliport a hundred yards away from the house. The helicopter parked on it was a new model I hadn't seen except in Aviation Week.

The house was a Spanish style hacienda, complete with a red tile roof, stucco walls and arched entryways. As we pulled up I tried to gauge its size, but the floor plan appeared to consist of wings set at irregular angles and spacing. I had seen military installations like this. They were typically designed to disguise the true floor area of buildings from prying eyes, either adversarial or congressional. Whatever the intention, the overall effect of the architecture was large but not overbearing.

The Mercedes glided to a halt in front of two enormous mahogany doors. I creaked and moaned as I struggled my way out of the back seat.

By the time my feet hit the driveway, Andy had raced around from his side and slipped a hand unobtrusively under my elbow.

I stood in the Colorado sunlight, muscles screaming and joints popping audibly, while I tried to stretch out the kinks that had formed on the drive.

One of the huge doors opened, and Eric Zygler walked briskly out to greet us. Sally came around the car to stand with me, while Andy pulled our bags from the Merc's trunk and hurried inside. Zygler wore a knit shirt like mine, sweat pants and leather sandals that made flop-flop noises as he walked.

He pushed his glasses up on his nose and held his hand out, smiling broadly as he greeted us. "Mike, Sally, welcome to Casa Nerd," he said over handshakes. "I'm glad you're here."

We both laughed before I thanked him, and Sally gushed a little.

He looked me over. "Man, you look a hell of a lot better than the last time I saw you."

As we walked toward the entry, I said, "Thanks. I'm feeling much better since they released me. There's something about being in a hospital that must make you feel sick." I let the last syllable trail off as we entered the house. This was the second time that a space owned by Eric Zygler had taken my breath away.

The foyer opened out into a huge room, sunken several steps, faced on the opposite wall with two-story plate glass windows framing the Rockies. The main room was at least fifty feet square, and the ceilings were easily twenty feet high. The floors were terra-cotta tile, with gigantic expanses of thick grey wool carpets covering most of the floor area. The color scheme was intended to accentuate the presence of an eclectic collection of art and other objects spaced casually around the periphery. I'm not an expert on art, but I did recognize Pablo Picasso's signature on a painting near the door and the work looked original.

There was an eight-foot-high metal sculpture resembling a suit of armor opposite the Picasso with somebody's light jacket tossed casually over the mace that it held in one hand. The armored figure had an artistically-rendered weapon in the other hand that was more than ten feet high from the floor to near the ceiling. The weapon was dull brown metal, except where it was honed to a dangerously sharpened two-foot edge, suitable for shaving a giant or chopping heads off bad code writers. It was whimsically threatening, dangerous, charming, funny, weird and scary, all at once. I was starting to think that might be a good description of its owner, too.

Sun poured into the room through several skylights, and the sunken space was dotted with comfortable-looking couches and chairs, arranged to encourage conversation. The entire room was dominated by a two-story-high cut-stone fireplace.

The house was magnificent, richly designed and

decorated, while still feeling as if it were intended for human habitation. It was perfect for parties with the President or lying around doing crossword puzzles on a Saturday afternoon.

"Eric, this is so beautiful." Sally's voice was a stage whisper.

"Oh, thanks," he said casually, as if a little surprised at the reaction. "I had a lot of help putting it together. We're really happy here." He waved a hand around and smiled proudly.

He spoke again, apologetically this time. "I'm afraid I have to leave you and do a bit of business, just for a few minutes. I have a chat going online with one of our teams in South America."

The driver entered, walking toward us from a hallway on our left, and Zygler beckoned to him. "I think Charlene is out by the pool. Andy will show you.

"Oh, and by the way," he said, while poking me in the stomach with a finger, "I talked to your doctor. No liquor, and we have a bunch of prescriptions for you. And you're supposed to take a nap this afternoon. I have an EMT to check up on you. Got it?"

I held up my hands, laughing. "I surrender."

He grinned expansively. "Good. I'll be with you in a few minutes and we can grab a quick lunch."

He turned and walked away briskly, disappearing into another side hallway as Andy led us across the great room and out onto a broad, sunlit patio. Beautiful.

He showed us to a table and chairs protected from the sun by a large umbrella next to a Olympic sized swimming pool. The table was set for lunch and a uniformed woman hovered unobtrusively near the edge of the patio, twenty yards away, preparing food.

As we arrived, another figure appeared from around a row of cabanas on the far side of the pool, a striking woman, tall and blonde. She was wearing a frilly white cover-up over a colorful bikini that showed as the frills moved, high-heeled cork sandals and a large sun hat. The cover-up was tied at the waist, and even from this distance her figure looked past Hollywood voluptuous and into the Las Vegas outrageous range. She waved and walked vigorously around the pool to greet us. The effect was very friendly and vaguely pornographic.

"Wow," I muttered under my breath.

Sally glanced at me and spoke quietly out of one side of her mouth. "We seem to have beamed down to the knocker planet."

I answered her even more quietly, smiling. "Yeah, well don't beam me up."

"You should put your tongue back in your mouth before you trip over it." She frowned at me, her eyes slits.

"What?" I said with an innocent smile.

Sally rumbled as the woman approached, her hand out.

"Hiya," she said in a perfect Gone With The Wind drawl. "Ah'm Charlene Zygler. You must be Sally." The two exchanged limp all-girl handshakes and Sally mustered a smile. Mrs. Zygler turned to me with a bright smile, the patio scene reflecting in her sunglasses. "You have to be Mike. Eric has told me all about you. He just practically hasn't talked about anyone else for days." She had a laugh built into her speech, and every sentence seemed to end in an exclamation mark. "Let's have some lunch. Eric's working again, but he'll be along in a minute."

We sat around the table, her wrap falling partly open to reveal national park-scale cleavage and a glimpse of breasts that would have made a good stage for Shakespeare. She took off her hat and shook out her long full blonde hair.

"Well, I'm just so glad you two are here," she said happily. "I don't get a chance to entertain very much. Eric's worried about security. And he stays so busy." She turned to me. "Mike how are you feeling? I heard about your terrible wreck." She tilted her head in concern.

"I'm doing much better, thanks," I said. "I just have some bruises and things."

"I'm supposed to make sure you rest this weekend. Doctor's orders." She waved a hand, and the uniformed woman came to the table. "Consuela, honey, let's start lunch. Mr. Zygler's gonna be late, as usual."

Consuela brought iced tea and salads. We made more small talk, and I noticed that Charlene and Sally began to hit it off, the two laughing more as the time went on. Charlene was a charming woman, not terribly bright but not stupid either, and she seemed very outgoing and genuinely happy to have visitors.

At the end of our salads, Zygler appeared, rushing in with apologies for his lateness. He stopped to kiss his wife on the cheek. "The Sao Paulo project has hit a little snag," he said breathlessly as he set a digital assistant down by his table setting. "The simulations they're doing now are showing problems with rush hour traffic and gridlock, that sort of thing. My team is putting together an algorithm for the Sao Paulo transit authority to factor-in surge loads on the rapid transit system, and dynamically reset traffic light timing to optimize traffic flow. The place turns into a parking lot every morning and afternoon, and we're trying to make that go away without laying down any new roads." He shook his head at the enormity of the task.

I frowned. "I suppose you'll have to vary the timing of trains and buses, too."

He looked back at me, his face blank but serious. "I hadn't thought of the train schedule. We'd always assumed that was a constant. That's a terrific idea, Mike." He typed a note on his pad. "I'll pass it on to the group. I don't know how much freedom they have with the trains, but I'll make sure they take the time to look into it."

He slouched back in his seat and crossed his hands contentedly in his lap. "It looks like my shy bride has come out of her cocoon long enough to keep you entertained." He smiled, and we all laughed. "I hope you don't mind, but we're going to have a few people over tonight. Harry Randall, and the mayor of Colorado Springs. It was already hard scheduled or we'd have cancelled it."

"Fine. I'm not sure how much fun I'll be."

Zygler cut me off with a smile. "It's strictly on a non-interference basis with you resting. The minute you get tired, just wander off. Everyone knows about your accident. Er, is that what you call it?"

"It was a crash," I answered. "At least that's what it sounded like."

He nodded seriously and leaned forward, putting his elbows on the table. "I'm getting the simulations together that you wanted. McCall gave me full information from the data recorder, and I've been on the phone to Paris, to get some other information we need to do the sims." His voice lowered slightly. "I also have a professor of aeronautical engineering from Princeton backing up what the French are doing, just to make sure they're being entirely straight with us."

He leaned back again as Consuela appeared with sandwiches and more tea. "I'll have the gang work through the weekend and have it all ready on Monday morning."

We made more polite talk about the weather, and Colorado, and other things while we ate. Zygler still seemed distracted by work and also by his friend's death, which was understandable. He also dominated the conversation, Charlene becoming oddly silent in the presence of her husband.

The rest of lunch was lobster salad sandwiches that made my mouth want to vacation in Maine, a good-looking Australian wine that I had to skip, and a flaming dish of caramelized bananas over ice cream that Consuela prepared expertly beside the table. I protested the calories, but Charlene insisted that I needed to build my strength up.

After lunch, Charlene invited Sally on a tour of the house, and Zygler and I stood as the ladies left. We sat back down as coffee appeared, and Zygler's gaze followed the two women as they departed.

"Isn't she beautiful?" he said absently. I wasn't sure which female he was talking about, or if I was expected to answer.

I mumbled, "Yes, lovely." Zygler didn't respond until they were out of sight. He continued to stare across the room, and I heard him sigh a little. Out of the corner of my eye I saw him shake his head a little.

We talked on, while the ladies toured. I got him

talking about the Mustang and he went on for several minutes without pausing. I told him a story from my education about how the Mustang nearly didn't happen. The military didn't want it for budget reasons, and President Roosevelt had to direct the Air Force to buy it.

"Blatant political interference trumped good management." I said as he laughed. "And it's a damned good thing it did."

Zygler threw his head back and roared with laughter. He nodded and became serious. "If the President hadn't had his way and overruled the bureaucrats, we might have lost the war. Wow."

Zygler stirred sugar into his coffee and eyed me. "Mike," he said quietly, "I have something personal I want to talk to you about. Strictly top level, and I don't want you to respond right now." He lowered his head and smiled a little. "If McCall knew I was talking to you about this he'd be mad as hell. I hope you don't mind."

My interest was piqued, and I sat forward in the patio chair. "Sure, Eric. About what?"

He sat back and balanced his coffee cup on his not-flat stomach. "I have been having some trouble lately, keeping track of the technical content of some of the company's products. We are very heavy into transportation issues right now, and I see that trend continuing. My staff--they're super guys, don't get me wrong--but they're very business oriented. They see everything as a management problem. Finance. Return on invested capital. The stock price." He shook his head. "And I have the opposite problem with the technical types. Nobody looks at everything."

He set his cup on the table, and took his glasses off, checking them for smudges. "I need leadership in product development. Somebody that's been there and done that."

"Don't your customers keep you focused?" I said. "If I hired ZYCO, I'd want to keep communications open during development."

"Sure," he nodded vigorously. "And we do that. But I really want to get a good real-world look before anything goes out the door. I need someone with lots of real world experience, someone who's really been around."

I smiled and sipped from my cup. "I can think of a thousand guys who'd apply for that job, Eric."

He drank and nodded. "So can I. I've interviewed most of them. I've used our flight department to help with some of the aircraft control projects, of course, but they don't have the education or a broad enough background to help the way I have in mind."

He put his cup back on the table and sat with his fingers in a pyramid across his chest. "I've read several of your reports, Mike, and I talked to McCall about you on the ride up to Denver the other day. He's very high on your capabilities. Now that I've met you, I think I'm more impressed than he is." He paused, and looked at me over his glasses. "This is really personal, but I have a bad habit of diving into things like this. How much do you make at the NTSB?"

What was this? He wanted to hire me? I cleared my throat. "Well, I'm a GS-14 step five and I get extra pay for working in the DC area. You can check it on the internet." I didn't think much about money. I always seemed to have enough to pay my bills, and I put a little aside every month for retirement. I thought for a second, and named a figure that I thought was accurate.

He chuckled. "The people you would have under you make three times that much, Mike. The position I have in mind would report direct to me. No billing or marketing, just a sharp eye on safety and practicality. Are we doing our best? What can we do better? Where do we go next? I'd make it worth your while to jump to the private sector."

I was stunned. Could I even talk to him about employment? What would the Inspector General think about this?

"Um, Eric, I don't feel real comfortable talking about working for you, and I am happy where I am." I said. "The job sounds great, of course, but I'm sure you could find somebody better. I'm just a low level government bureaucrat."

He shook his head vigorously. "No, Mike. You're one of a dozen or so real experts in the world on transportation system safety. I can't believe the government only pays you as much as it does. Your insights would be invaluable to me."

I rolled it around in my head. I was weakening fast. "I'm not a business guy," I said finally. "I'm a government Joe. I couldn't care less about your corporate earnings before interest payments or your internal rate of return. I'm an engineer, not an MBA."

Zygler snorted. "Man, I am up to my armpits in MBAs. They all went to Harvard Business School or Wharton, took all the same courses, have all the same answers. They measure everything in dollars, like I said. It's all any of them give a shit about."

He paused, and when he started talking again he sounded bitter. "Money grubbing whores. I built this operation from zero, with no help from the MBAs. I've made them billions, but they still aren't happy. And none of them understand how to actually do what we do. They don't understand what it takes. Wouldn't know a good system design if one bit 'em on the ass." There was a lot of anger in his voice, even a tinge of hatred.

He took a deep breath and looked out his massive windows at the fabulous view. He seemed to curse under his breath before he went on. "My name starts with a Z."

I stared at him, not understanding. "I don't get

what you mean. What's wrong with 'Z'?" I asked.

"Ever since I was a little kid, I was always last in every line they put me in. The whole fucking world works like that." He seemed to grind his teeth. "The teachers all have a book they follow. Business is like that, too. The first step always says line up everybody in alphabetical order, so little Eric always goes last, you know? Well, I'm first in line now. I own every line." He smiled broadly. "It's pretty cool. You should try it." More smiles. "I need you really bad here."

"But, I mean, how can you know that much about me? Why are you so sure?" I knew I was frowning.

Zygler looked out the window and gathered arguments. He might not be used to having anybody say no, I guessed.

"I'll tell you what convinced me about you. Three words. I almost missed them. Summa cum laude. In engineering physics, man. You're scary smart. But you never mentioned it--not in your resume, or applications or anything. Your astronaut paperwork had your transcript from grad school in it and I saw it there."

I shrugged dismissively. "It was a government school."

He laughed out loud and smiled broadly. "Bullshit, man. See, I know who you are. You keep yourself a secret. You have to keep your brains close-hold so people won't treat you like a freak. I know, man.

Believe me. You and I are practically the same guy."

I didn't like the conversation as much as I would have thought. It was creeping me out a little, like the clothes bag in the hospital. "Come on, Eric. I mean, you just met me. All you've seen me do so far is wreck a car."

He answered immediately, laughing a little. "You're doing it again. Look, I've known Brooks McCall forever. When I asked about you I couldn't shut him up. He went off for a half hour about how you understand the physics of everything, like nobody else he has. You really understand how everything works. The thing he said that impressed me the most was that you're a guy he can really count on. He said once you sign on for something you put everything into it. He said you never plot or scheme.

"I've had enough of that shit around here. Once a guy gets in charge of something really big, everybody wants stick their knives in him. But not you. You just go straight at every problem and won't let go until you have a solution. McCall said that."

He clapped a hand on my shoulder, his face smiling but serious. "I know where you're coming from, and that's all I need."

He leaned toward me. "Listen, hiring leadership is like buying a Ferrari. I bought my first one used. They won't sell you a new one unless you have a used one already." He chuckled more. "I lost a couple because I didn't move fast enough when I saw the right one. You've left quite a trail behind you. I've been looking around for a while. I had my VP of human resources make a roster of candidates last year, and you were on the list then. There were five others but none of them were the right man. I know who you are. I've figured out what you can do. Your skills are what we're missing. And I can promise that this position wouldn't be the end point for you. Just the start."

He looked off at the mountains. "Help me keep the barbarians outside the gates."

When he spoke again he was more relaxed, talking to a friend. "Anyway, what you said is exactly what my ethics attorney said you should say. I understand about you not wanting to talk about a job until your investigation is done, of course. Your hesitation speaks very well for you. You're exactly the guy I need." He leaned toward me, his voice dropping to a confidential whisper. "I'll get back to you after this business is cleared up."

He looked around and caught the eye of Consuela as she tended her station across the patio. She walked quickly to his side. "Consuela, this was just wonderful," he said, sweeping an arm across the table. "You really outdid yourself again. The ladies were very impressed, too. Thanks very much." He smiled personably, and she beamed as I added my praise.

Zygler didn't have to make this much effort to keep his people happy, but he seemed to take joy in making everyone who worked for him feel needed and important.

Zygler ordered me to bed and led me to my room, leaving me at the door after a long walk down a carpeted hallway. "Dinner's early around here. Drinks at six or so. I'll send somebody around at five if we haven't heard from you. I took the liberty of checking you out of your hotel. There's a Jacuzzi on the terrace outside your room, if you feel like it. Make yourself at home."

He waved as he left, and I closed the door behind me.

The room was actually a suite, with a sitting room complete with well stocked bar, sans alcohol, per doctor's orders, and refrigerator. The bedroom had a king-size bed with enough pillows for a party, and a huge HD TV. I found the clothes that his people had removed from my hotel room in a walk-in closet that was bigger and nicer than my apartment in Virginia. The clothes were cleaned and perfectly pressed in a way that they never were in my closet at home. Socks and skivvies were in a bureau drawer, also freshly cleaned and neatly stowed, along with swimming trunks that turned out to be my size.

In the bathroom, I found my travel kit, with my disposable razor replaced by a new one of a better brand. There were three pill bottles on the counter, a painkiller--

I was beginning to need those and I took one--a muscle relaxer that I would be due to take about bedtime, and sleeping pills if needed. Not much chance of that.

There was a knock at the door and a young man came in. He had the usual ZYCO shirt on, but looked more mature than the other company guys. He carried a small bag that proved to hold medical equipment, and he invited me to sit down. He checked my blood pressure, eye responses and a few other things that were handy, and made sympathetic noises about my knees. I looked at the tattoos on his well-muscled forearms and guessed ex-Army, probably Special Forces, more probably a combat medic. He left me with his phone number and said he would be down the hall if I needed anything.

By the time I had washed my face and used the john, I was out on my feet. I stumbled to the bed and fell instantly asleep. I dreamed about being rich, and living in Colorado with Sally.

Sleep let go of me just before four. I sat up, stretched, and decided to try the Jacuzzi to knock out the kinks before dinner. A peek through a glass door showed that the tub was waiting just outside. It was large, big enough for a rifle squad or two if they were all close friends, and already steaming.

The swim trunks fit and I checked myself out in the mirror. My legs had reached a beautiful shade of green as the bruises started to fade. My knees, while better, were still larger than as built, and I was sure they would throb in the hot water. But there were ice bags thoughtfully left in an ice bucket on the bar so I could use them before dressing.

I grabbed a towel--luxuriously thick Egyptian cotton--and went outside, slipping slowly into the almost too-hot water. The bubbles swirled and I relaxed, the heat and motion magically draining pain from my beat-up body. My knees protested briefly, but even they began to feel good after a few minutes.

A swirl of motion made it through my half-closed eyelids and I looked up to see Sally standing next to the hot tub.

She had her hair pinned up and was wrapped in a white cotton robe. "Like some company?"

"Absolutely. Jump in." I moved out of the center of the tub. I found myself holding my stomach in, even though it was under water.

She slipped out of the robe to reveal a strapless yellow one-piece suit that shimmered in the late afternoon sun. It fit her like a coat of paint and her figure was breathtaking, tiny and pixie-like in certain places, a tad over the top in a few others, and pretty much perfect everywhere. I also noticed she was a little cold. Mercy.

She lowered herself gingerly into the water at the far end, gasping at the heat. "Oooh, this is just hot enough," she said with a smile that I returned.

"Did you get a good night's rest?"

"Oh, yeah." I lowered myself until my chin was at the water's level. "I'm getting a little better, but right now I just seem to zonk out every four hours or so."

"Good." She sighed and looked around. "This place is incredible. I just love it. You should see all the art. And I love the way they've decorated. Not stuffy or formal at all."

"Is this the only Jacuzzi?"

"No, I saw five." She pointed to a door next to mine. "That's my room, right next to yours. There's an adjoining door in the sitting rooms, by the way." She grinned. "I don't think they're quite sure what our relationship is."

I wasn't either, but I let it pass. "So, did you have a good visit with Charlene?"

She leaned back. "Yes. She's very nice. A little crazy, but really sweet." She looked at me with her eyes shifty and half closed, as if hiding a great secret. "They're fake."

"What are fake?" I said, in total innocence.

"You know." She slipped her hands under her breasts and lifted them slightly.

We both laughed, and I was glad for a few minutes that the water was as deep as it was and all bubbly.

"Nope," she said, relaxing with her eyes closed.

"She is not an entirely carbon-based life form. There's definitely some silicon in there. Those items are not natural phenomena."

"I'm a technology guy. Sometimes nature is overrated." I smiled happily across the foaming water.

"She recommended her cosmetic surgeon."

"You don't need one."

"Maybe not yet." We rested in silence for a few more minutes. "She's really funny." Sally dropped into a perfect imitation of our hostess. "Ah didn't marry for money, honey. Ah just hung around with rich guys 'til ah fell in love with one."

We both chuckled and then fell silent for a few seconds.

"She told me about her pre-nup. Recommended her lawyer, too. If they split up she can buy Canada. She said he was really sweet about the whole thing. Wants her taken care of no matter what. He sounds nice. Maybe a little strange, but I think he really loves her." She enjoyed the swirling water for a few seconds. "She seems kind of bored here."

"What makes you say that?"

She splashed a little. "I don't know. Her tone of voice, I guess. She seems so happy to have us here, like she never sees anybody but Eric's business people, or politicians. And she was always talking about Eric doing this or that, and never anything that she does."

I shook my head, with my eyes closed, which had no ill effects for once. "Poor little rich girl?"

Sally sank lower in the water. "She also thinks you're really cute."

I tried not to guffaw. "How the hell did that subject come up?"

"Girl talk," she said, as if that explained everything. "She saw you didn't have a ring on and asked about you, and it went on a while. And that bruises-and-contusions thing you have going on is apparently really working."

I rolled my eyes. "You had to be able to come up with something better to talk about."

She glanced across the bubbles and smirked. "No." She laughed quietly. "I told her about your little speech. About all the rules and things, and I told her about how serious you are about everything."

"That makes me sound like a dork."

"Yes. But you are sort of cute, in an engineer-ish way."

I must have blushed, even allowing for the hot water. I wanted to figure out how to change the subject but I was pretty sure she wasn't into car racing or beer, and I didn't want to talk shop. I must have frowned.

"I'm sorry," she said seriously. "I'm embarrassing you, aren't I?"

I didn't say anything.

"She said Eric is a really good judge of people, and he thinks you're great." She channeled Charlene again. "'And he's nevah wrong.' She said a good guy should never be wasted, and that if I didn't like your rules I should figure out how to get the game changed."

The conversation melted down in the steam, and I was left wondering how Sally liked the rules.

Drinks were at six, with Harry Randall, the mayor and their wives. Sally and I met them in the great room, and Zygler and Charlene appeared a few minutes later. Sally was back in her slacks and sweater, with some simple jewelry added. She looked fabulous, an effortless knockout.

The two wives were pleasantly upper-middle class, upper-middle-aged ladies, and the conversation was light and trivial. Sally and I had to explain at length about our jobs, and both of the women were fascinated that Sally should be in so technical a vocation. They seemed to be the last two non-working women in North America, and spoke mostly about their families.

Charlene entered wearing a low-cut, spectacularly cantilevered little black cocktail dress, and the overall effect rendered the three male guests unable to string long sentences together for several minutes. Zygler seemed to enjoy the effect.

The wives were annoyed, but Sally was amused and Charlene herself seemed not to notice. Probably used to it, I thought.

Zygler spent some of the time before dinner on the phone and thumbing text messages.

Randall caught me alone at the bar for a few seconds. "I'm awfully glad you weren't hurt badly in your adventure, Mike." His Ivy-League accent was thicker than I had heard before. He poured himself a gin and tonic as I thanked him for his concern. "How are you getting along with the big ZYCO machine?" He pronounced it "psycho".

"Fine. Eric's been great, and I think we'll be making some real progress." I poured a ginger ale.

Randall leaned near. "Eric is pretty high on you. I've been researching your background. I made a couple of discreet recommendations. Hope you don't mind. There may be an offer, old man. He likes to hire friends, and the company'll take damned good care of you." He took me by the elbow and spoke more quietly now, almost whispering. "Strictly between you and me, there may be some openings in upper-level leadership in the near future, too. Don't worry about taking advantage. He wants you to, and I do, too. It's not always easy or pleasant, but there are rewards. He's a good man, but he tends to be a bit, well, removed from reality. Do yourself a favor. Believe me, no matter what develops, we'll need your help and a good deal of it. Think it over."

I wondered what Randall's version of reality was, and what he thought was developing. "I don't think it's proper for me to discuss anything like that while the investigation is underway," I said quietly.

"Of course," Randall said with a broad smile. "I understand. Just keep an open mind. Life can be good if you let it."

As we finished the conversation the mayor, an elderly political warhorse, walked up to the bar and reached for a bottle of twenty-five-year-old scotch.

"Damn, Eric keeps a good bar. This stuff is like drinking gold. I bet it's actually been to Scotland, too." He splashed an inch of the precious liquid over ice and looked up at me. He leaned against the bar and took my elbow in one hand.

"Son," he said, and the fumes from his drink made me crave alcohol, "I hope you're taking good care of ZYCO. Mighty important to this city, and to the entire nation I think. Why, you know how much ZYCO brings into the economy in foreign trade, don't you?"

"I certainly do, Mister Mayor."

He clapped me on the shoulder, and I winced but he didn't notice. "Call me Joe, son. Everybody calls me Joe."

"Well, Joe, Eric has put every asset he has at the board's disposal to find this problem. He's made it very clear to me that he thinks it would be best for the company to find the problem and fix it. I wish we got that kind of cooperation from everyone."

"Great, son, that's great," the mayor said with a cheery smile. He leaned close and uttered quietly, "I know the President will appreciate your good work. Eric's been a strong supporter, you know." The mayor's voice rose cheerfully. "Of course I have, too, but then I don't have the kind of clout young Mister Bits here does."

Zygler looked across the room and smiled at the mayor's jibe. He walked across and clapped the old pol on an arm. "Taking my name in vain, Joe?"

"Sure am. I was telling Mike here about your pull with the President." He took a long drink. "I knew him when he was a college professor in Wyoming. In fact, I was on a committee that picked him for his first nomination."

The mayor talked on for several minutes about campaigns past and future, and the stories were surprisingly interesting. The three men talked seriously about the upcoming round of elections and of the merits of public election financing. I found myself standing back from the group, listening and tiring.

I was leaning against the bar, checking my watch when a soft hand slipped around my arm. I turned to find Charlene Zygler, pulling my arm to her, and standing close by. She leaned closer to whisper in my ear, slipping my elbow between her breasts. Interesting and awkward.

"Mike, how are y'all feeling?" she breathed, her voice sultry and seductive. I could smell alcohol on her breath. "I wouldn't want you to get too tired, now." She smiled, and raised an eyebrow.

"Oh, fine. I'm fine," I said lightly, staring down at the luscious view like a Japanese tourist at the Grand Canyon. "I'm just listening."

"To those tired old men." She laughed, tossed her hair back with a flip of her head, and licked her lips. Oh, golly. Under other circumstances I would have given a year's vacation time for this, but just then I was trying to figure out a smooth escape route.

Sally came to my rescue, walking up to take Charlene's other arm. "Charlene, Consuela has dinner about ready. How do we tear these guys away from the bar?"

"Let's eat, then," Charlene said without moving her eyes from mine. She gave one last flick of a smile, and then released me just as Zygler walked past the bar. She moved past me to Eric, the semi-precious jewels on the front of her dress scratching my arm.

Sally remained beside me. "Thanks," I said.

"Don't mention it," she said as we followed the others into the dining room. "She drinks like a fish. I think she had four martinis while we were talking."

"Martinis? Jesus, gin makes me barf," I said in her

ear quietly. It was a nice ear, especially up close.

"Me, too," she whispered as we entered and looked for our seats.

I shook my head and whispered. "I guess it depends on what you're thirsty for."

chapter

12

The weather had turned colder and rainy on Sunday. We shared a late breakfast and conversation in a small dining room off the kitchen. Charlene wore loose satin pajamas, which allowed me to relax a little.

Zygler and I turned out to share a love of old science fiction movies, "The kind with bug-eyed monsters and flying saucers," we agreed. He announced at the end of the meal that he was taking the day off. He closed his pad and shut it down with a grand gesture.

We adjourned to a large media room filled with

extravagantly sized and extravagantly comfortable furniture. There was indirect lighting, lots of movie posters and a popcorn machine that we quickly put to work. One wall of the room was covered completely with another huge television and audio gear, and Zygler operated it all expertly from a remote next to the central couch. We decided on Howard Hawks' classic "The Thing From Another World," starring James Arness as the Thing itself. Zygler had obtained a rare uncut version of the movie, and I was treated to several scenes I hadn't known existed.

Zygler and I annoyed the ladies by shouting fractured dialogue at the screen, and laughing in all the wrong places. Charlene and Sally left us to a double feature, preferring conversation and quiet to the giant ants of an un-colorized version of "Them!" with James Whitmore in what we decided was his best role ever.

After the formicidi gigantae were safely incinerated in the sewers of Los Angeles, Eric and I walked out into the gray daylight, stretching and blinking. Zygler went to the huge windows in the great room, and stood next to the gigantic fireplace, admiring the mountains that were swathed in patches of clouds.

He shoved his hands in his pockets, and sighed. "I was thinking about taking the Mustang out this afternoon but it looks like the cloud cover's too low to have much fun."

I stood beside him and shrugged. "It's getting a little late, too. It'll probably be clear tomorrow."

He continued to stare at the mountains. "It's hard for me to get away. Everybody wants my time, you know? I thought they'd want my money, and I can spare that. Time's the thing I don't have enough of." He paused again for a moment, and looked down at the floor. "Wes and I used to goof off like this once in a while."

He stopped and grabbed my arm, suddenly smiling. "Let's make an appointment. We'll fly the Mustang tomorrow afternoon. I'll have Grimsby meet us at the hangar, and we'll take turns, OK?"

I could blow a couple of hours of vacation time. "Great. Just don't tell my boss I'm goofing off."

"Deal," he said. He leaned against the fireplace, staring at the floor, still smiling. "I really am glad you're here, Mike. I'm sorry you got hurt, but I haven't had this much fun in a long time."

"I could get used to this. I hate to think about going back to work tomorrow."

"Yeah." He stared at the Rockies again for a few seconds. "When do you want the simulations?"

I didn't want to think about the job. "I'll need a couple of hours to get caught up. I'll plan on a staff meeting at ten or so. Could you have them ready by then?"

"Sure. I can run my progress meeting tonight and

have it all set up by seven, if you want it bright and early."

I held up my hands. "Whoa, ten is fine. Noon would be OK if you need the time."

He nodded his head again, sheepishly this time. "Sorry. I'm not very good at relaxing."

As he spoke, shrieks of laughter came rolling out of the kitchen, echoing across the great room.

"I think I know where the girls are," I said.

"And they are having entirely too much fun, from the sound of things."

We walked into the kitchen in time to find Sally, Charlene and Consuela laughing uproariously around a flour-covered work-island. They looked up and hushed each other into silence, staring at us like deer. The silence lasted for a few seconds, and then the three dissolved into giggles, Consuela adding the shrieks we had heard before.

"So, I guess you found something to amuse yourselves," Zygler said.

They shushed themselves again.

Sally covered her mouth for a second, and then said in an unsteady voice, "Charlene was teaching us how to make pecan pie."

Charlene smirked. "Pecan pah is a very important part of Southern culture, as you know."

The three women were subdued for a few seconds, and then Charlene said, "We were just talking about what a couple of nerds you two are."

Sally whooped. "Two peas out of the same nerd pod."

They all laughed again, and then Charlene walked to her husband, wrapping an arm around his waist and pressing herself to him. She ran her fingers through his hair, and said, "You're a real nice kind of nerd, honey." He reddened visibly, and she turned to us with a broad smile. "See y'all in a while." She led her husband from the kitchen by the hand, and they didn't return until just before dinner.

After a night's sleep and another check by Eric's medic I felt ready for Monday morning, still creaking at every joint, but serviceable.

Two plain, full-sized sedans pulled up to the house at 7:30 a.m. George Tidings jumped out of the front car as a ZYCO aide loaded our bags into the trunk.

The FBI agent ushered Sally and me into the back seat as Zygler and Charlene waved goodbye. "Let's go," Tidings said to the young female agent at the wheel, and the two cars swung around in the circular drive and rolled back out the private road, toward the real world.

"George, what the hell is this?" I shared a puzzled looked with Sally.

Tidings half-turned, putting an arm over the seat back, revealing the pistol under his jacket. "What this is, is a full FBI security detail. You go nowhere without it until you go back to Washington."

"What the hell for?"

"It seems your boss had occasion to talk to the President last night, and told him about the circumstances surrounding your accident, and Penney's. The President called the Attorney General, who called the Director, who called me." He paused. "At two o'clock this morning. I received the assistance of the Denver office, as you can see." He waved a hand toward the driver, and she sent a quick smile over her shoulder.

I looked across at Sally, who shrugged. "Well, this is probably unnecessary," I said. "Sorry for the trouble."

"No big deal. I don't get a chance to act like a no-shit special agent very often. This will look good on my next performance review." He dropped into official-speak, dictating to the dashboard. "'Commanded a special protection detail at the direction of the President.' Yeah, that sounds nice."

I looked at the car following us. Two unusually large young men rode in the front seats, and I spotted a rack behind them that appeared to hold several heavy automatic weapons. Who were they expecting, Al Qaida?

I pointed to the other car. "Two cars?"

"Escort-pursuit team. Get used to it," Tidings said.

After my car wreck and the luxurious weekend at Castle Zygler, I was not ready to face the job that morning.

In addition to a barrage of texts from the Washington office, six screens of email and the now-massive 6120 file, there were four phone messages waiting in the voicemail queue. I had been called Friday by Dr. Anders at NSA and had received calls that morning from Dr. Schmidt at the NTSB lab, Chairman McCall, and Liz Fowler, the Rocky Mountain Times reporter I had managed to piss off at the post mortem briefing. She had called just a few minutes before, and said she would try again.

I scanned through the messages quickly while Tidings made coffee and Sally sorted new entries that had stacked up for the 6120. Wang was at the ZYCO hangar, working on a few final details in the wreckage. The paperwork was mostly licensing and certification paper for the airplane, and file reports on the ZYCO flight department that I had been promised by a researcher in Washington. I passed it all to Sally for sorting.

I dialed Anders at NSA first.

"Ah, Mike, it's good to hear from you." He sounded a little distracted. "I have had time to get a look at the hardware Ms. Montez sent me. There's some good news and some bad news."

I pulled a note pad and pencil to the ready.

"Anything you have is progress, Doctor. Shoot."

"The bad news is that I haven't been able to read what was left on the blank sections of the chips you sent yet. They have been pretty thoroughly written over, and finding anything in there is a going to be a real long shot."

I wrote notes furiously. "Hold on a second, doctor, I'm going to put you on the speaker phone with Sally Montez." I clicked on the speaker and motioned Sally over. "Now, you said you hadn't read anything yet. Do you think there's a chance you can get any information off the hardware at all?" Sally sat across the table from me and stared at the phone, listening intently. Tidings sat at the end of the table and put his feet up on a corner.

Anders went on. "Possibly, but not easily. The format used was a common commercial scheme, and that helps. I am willing to keep at it, but even with my facilities, it may be several weeks."

I rolled my eyes, and Sally nodded in resignation. "OK, you said you had good news, too. Have you got anything to cheer me up?"

"Ah, yes." His voice sounded bright. "I have been able to break down what an overall structure of the code probably was from the shape of the hole it left behind. There were several command-type structures, followed by an object that contained only one large command." He spoke Martian for a few more seconds, describing general patterns in the code. Sally nodded a lot.

I hit the mute button. "I think I've seen that sort of thing before. I worked on flight software standardization at Airbus with the FAA and their certification guys. French industry does common commands that way. They teach it at the Ecole Polytechnic, the big French university outside Paris. It's the French version of MIT. I think the design is supposed to save processing time."

Sally half closed her eyes. "You studied flight controls in France?"

I nodded suavely. "Oui."

Sally leaned forward on her elbows and turned the mute off. "Hi, Doctor Anders, this is Sally Montez. Do you have a guess about what language the missing stuff was?"

"It appears to be a highly structured, high-order language, like Ada or C++. The rest of the code is in Ada, and I assume what was missing is, too."

Sally nodded again to herself, staring at the phone as she spoke. "No sign of bindings or anything?"

Bindings? I got a picture of her in a Victorian corset in my mind for a moment, but suppressed it quickly enough to hear the answer.

"No," Anders said without hesitation. "I would expect some sort of artifact to be present if there were any interface between languages, and I didn't see anything like that."

Sally nodded again, appearing satisfied with the information.

He promised a quick-look report that day. I thanked him, and gave the number for the office. I punched off the phone, and got up to get a cup of coffee. Sally sat back in her chair, and I tried not to think about bindings again.

"Ada?" I said. "What's Ada?" I motioned an offer of coffee while I talked.

She shook her head. "A kind of specialized computer language that the Department of Defense developed for aircraft flight controls and missile guidance, that sort of thing. ZYCO specializes in it. It's a very odd language, old, hard to work in and not known by very many programmers."

"Why would anybody use it if it's so hard to work in?"

"It's useful sometimes." She sighed, as if pondering one of the Great Questions of the Universe. "Um, it's kind of esoteric."

Tidings snickered, and I laughed. "So you think it's over my head, huh? You're probably right."

I dialed Doctor Schmidt's number at the Board's offices in Washington, and punched on the speaker again. An assistant answered this time and I drummed my pencil on the table while I waited for him to come on the line.

"Mike, hello!" Doctor Schmidt spoke into the phone. "How are you feeling? Was your accident bad?"

"Never had a good one." I answered as cheerfully as I could. I outlined the crash and Zygler's admission about the hacking vulnerability. "There may have been some tampering, maybe by a hacker, maybe something messed with on the car. If I sent you chips out of the engine control processor, and maybe the brakes and cruise control, could you check them out? Steve Penney's car, too. Could you render an opinion for me?"

"Sure, Mike. Just ship them back here, and I'll get back to you." He gave me his mail stop at headquarters.

I slouched back in my chair and stretched my legs out to straighten my knees. "You called me. Did you have something?"

"Oh, yes, the hinges you sent." I could hear him typing in the background. "We took a look at them. The metal around the hinges themselves appears to have been heavily overloaded, which is consistent with a hard impact into the ground." He ruffled more paper. "The question you asked about the position of the control surfaces, though? I'm afraid I couldn't make a call on that. There was nothing conclusive."

Sally didn't appear to have any more questions, and neither did I. "OK, then. Well, I'll get the chips to you as fast as possible.

"Give me a buzz if you find anything."

Sally talked with Tidings over a mound of paperwork while I dialed the chairman's number. His receptionist, the formidable Ann, answered immediately. She announced that the boss was in a conference with the Secretary of Transportation and could I please call back? I left a message that we were going to check out Eric's progress on simulations, and that I would try again later.

I hung up and sat at the table, oblivious to the others working around me. My knees were beginning to throb, as if to highlight the fact that the two most promising technical inquiries I had going had just bombed out. The weekend in the lap of luxury had been just enough to break my flow of reasoning. I sat for a moment, wondering where the hell I would go next if the simulations didn't show anything revealing.

Damn Lew Hills and his stinking arteries, I thought. How was I supposed to finish the investigation? Could I cite evidence of criminal sabotage? How would the FBI react if there weren't enough proof to convict anybody? I would have killed for something obvious like a blown engine or a tree line with an airplane-shaped hole in it.

My phone vibrated with a new text. It was Grimsby, the chief pilot. The simulations were ready, and Tidings called the three agents waiting outside to form up the great FBI convoy for another trip.

On the drive around the field to the ZYCO facilities, I sat quietly, staring out the window. Halfway around, Sally nudged me. "You feeling OK, sailor? We can do this without you, you know."

I shook my head and leaned against the door. "I'm fine. Just a little sore." I sat for another second, and then said, "George, you talked to Sutton on Friday, didn't you?"

Tidings turned in the front seat and looked back. "Yeah, but his lawyer wouldn't let him say much. He denies everything. The lawyer rehearsed him real well. The guys from the Denver office are looking into a couple of statements he made, to check out alibis and so forth. We're going to talk to him again tomorrow."

I rubbed my right knee. "Do you think you're going to be able to prove anything?"

He frowned. "Not likely. The access to the flight control systems on both the planes was just too damned easy. Hell, we'll probably end up questioning the guy who went to Australia, for all the good it'll do. We'll never be able to get a grand jury to indict." He pointed a finger at me over the seat back. "But Sutton's the guy. He's got motive, access and ability. I can spot 'em mile away. I guarantee you he did it."

We pulled into the parking lot outside the ZYCO hangar and found a parking place reserved for me next to the door. Eric Zygler's Mercedes was in the next space again. We walked into the reception area, the three agents of the protection detail remaining behind to lurk in the bushes and ambush bad guys. Grimsby met us as we entered, and we were ushered directly into the conference room where I had interviewed the chief pilot days before.

Zygler was waiting for us in the conference room, and he greeted Sally and me with a broad smile and warm handshakes. He motioned us to sit in front of two large computer screens set up in the far end of the room.

We sat with Zygler at a workstation near the screens. He stretched his fingers and began to work over the keyboard, looking like a church organist playing hymns on Sunday.

He fingered a key, and the lights went down slowly, until the light from the large screens dominated the room. The ZYCO logo splashed across on both.

"The first display will be a simple depiction of the data recorder's information." He spoke in a hushed tone as a bright figure of a GlobalMax appeared on the left screen. The airplane had the smooth look of a computer-generated image, and the view was from above and to the right front. The right screen suddenly contained two pictures, one of a map-like downward shot of the airfield's runway with a small GMax outline parked at one end, and another below it that looked like a side view of the same picture. The runway was a straight yellow line against the blue background.

"This is in real time. I'll start the run from the time they went forward to takeoff power on the engines," Zygler said, alternately watching the screens and his smaller display of the workstation in front of him. He suddenly seemed oblivious to our presence, fascinated by the flow of the story being played out at his command.

The large aircraft on the left stayed in the middle of the screen as the runway began to stream past it, lights flashing past at increasing speed. The two small shapes in the right displays crawled imperceptibly across the screens.

At the bottom of the left screen, numbers began to scroll across the view: speed, changing quickly, with altitude and pitch and roll angles staying temporarily static. "Fifty knots," Zygler said. "One hundred knots. Watch the pitch angles, now. They start changing quickly."

The nose of the GMax rose off the runway, slowly at first, as it should have. As the wheels broke free of the surface, the rate of pitching suddenly increased. The two small displays on the right screen followed the action, the small plane-shapes leaving a trail of dotted lines behind them as they crawled across the blue background.

"The speed continues to build to about here," Zygler said dispassionately. I watched as the speed scrolled up, stopped at one hundred eighty-three, and then began to fall. "They reach maximum altitude about here," he said with a slight pause, "and you can see a little rolling motion from where he tries to turn. Um, Mike, you called that a vertical recovery maneuver, I think. Anyway, it didn't work. It looks like a stall happens...here."

The plane in the left screen suddenly gave a shudder, wavered for a second, and slowly rolled to the right. The roll continued as the nose fell to the horizon. As the plane rolled all the way over back to an upright attitude, runway lights signifying the ground suddenly reappeared in the bottom of the display.

"Impact," Zygler said. The plane struck the ground with a lurch, and began a stylized slide across the computer generated ground, leaving a trail of brown behind it against the blue of the background. A small orange and white block appeared in the edge of the screen and slid quickly across, intersecting the aircraft's nose. The picture froze. That was it.

I sat silently, fascinated by the sanitized view of the deaths of three men.

Tidings muttered "Jesus" behind me.

Sally sighed.

Zygler sat up straighter, and fingered more keys. "We analyzed the pitching. The right display will show the elevator displacement necessary to produce the motions you saw. Here it is." A plan view of the aircraft's tail appeared. The horizontal control surfaces moved slowly, and then flapped full up and stayed there. "Both the French and the Princeton professor I mentioned concurred that this was the way the elevator had to move."

Zygler drummed the keys again, talking over his hands. "Mike, you asked about the failure of the plane that crashed in Canada. I have a study we did of that, too."

The right display was filled with another view of the tail of a GMax, this time in stick figure form. I recognized the pattern as a finite element analysis grid, a tool commonly used by engineers to study the strength of structures.

"This is what happens when the elevator deflects all the way up at takeoff speed, like happened here," Zygler said as his fingers flew over the keys.

The control surface flipped up, and the main fixed surface it was attached to flexed downward, slightly but obviously. "There's some bending there, about what you'd expect. The loads were high, but well within the levels the structure was designed to handle. Now," as he keyed the computer again, "I'll run it assuming a typical mid-mission cruise speed and air density at forty-thousand feet."

The aircraft figure reappeared and the elevator flipped up as before. But this time, the fixed structure it was attached to flexed downward alarmingly, rebounded slightly, and then flexed still further. The grids broke apart suddenly at the inboard ends of both horizontal stabilizers, and the displays froze.

"As you can see," Zygler lectured, "the horizontal stabilizer failed vertically downward." He turned to Sally. "You called it right. My Princeton advisor felt that the damage to the vertical fin must have been from the broken structure hitting it."

He moved his fingers over the keys again, and a full shape of the GMax appeared in the same grid pattern. "The last run we did was a full airframe response model. I'll run it at the same conditions that the tail failed under. I'll run it at one-tenth speed. Things happen pretty quickly."

I watched as the tail control surface flipped up again. The nose of the skeleton plane-figure bobbed up twenty degrees, and the wings flexed alarmingly, but did not break under the load. A few seconds later, or less than a second in real time, the tail failed as we had seen before.

"And here you see that the tail would fail before the wings, as we actually saw from the Canadian wreckage. With no horizontal tail, and in the balance condition you'd expect them to have at that point in the flight, the plane would go into a vertical dive, with no recovery possible. It probably tumbled end-over-end."

Zygler pushed himself back from the keyboard and turned the lights back up. "I ran a few tries with the elevator up a half and three-quarters of its full throw. At cruise speeds, the airframe still failed, but the wings went first instead of the tail."

I blinked for a moment in the light, and then wrote a few notes quickly. "Eric, did anybody you consulted suggest any other possible causes for the failures that might fit what we've seen?"

Zygler got up and moved to the table, sitting across from me with his hands folded as if in prayer. "I asked, and both said that nothing else would fit what we've got."

He paused, and studied his clasped hands, sighing heavily before going on. "I think it's pretty clear now that we have a flight control software problem. I said that before, and I'm absolutely sure, now. I appreciate the way you've been trying to keep an open mind, Mike, but it's clear to me that there isn't any other answer. ZYCO software, my software, killed seven men. I may have a murderer working for me, maybe an old friend of mine, and I think he might have tried to kill you and your assistant, too."

He looked across at Tidings, and the agent nodded.

Sally cleared her throat. "If there was something wrong with the software in one of the computers, wouldn't the other two computers just overrule the messed-up one, and continue the flight normally?"

Zygler put his elbows on the table and interlaced

his fingers, studying his nails. "Of course it should work that way." He launched a discussion on the state of control systems in industry, the superiority of ZYCO's approach, and his plans for dominating the global market.

Sally fired questions at him several times, and her eyes showed how much she was enjoying the talk. They spoke in tongues for a couple minutes and I recognized several words. Artificial intelligence. Triple-redundancy. Steered failover. Chaos theory. Multiple independent variables.

I held up a hand. "Just to make it clear, if we assume something evil has been injected into the code here, could you make the single computer overrule the other two and cause a crash?"

Sally added to the question with her arched eyebrows.

Zygler looked at the table in front of him, as if he didn't want eye contact. "Yes." He inhaled, and spoke in a rush. "It wouldn't be simple, but if you put the right bogus code into a machine, you could disable all the safety features and make it happen." He stopped speaking and didn't look up. "But it wouldn't be simple. Our process is called steered failover. If one computer has any kind of problem, the others vote on it and flip control to one of the good ones that's left. It's pretty complicated. One of the things they watch for is bad code. If somebody tried to screw with the software, it should have been caught by the system unless they got it exactly right. I'll send a briefing on it to Sally."

"Are those safety methods only used by ZYCO?" Sally said quietly.

Zygler smiled weakly. "They'd better be. We hold the patents."

His face darkened. "And Tom Sutton. We share credit with inventors. He invented the techniques."

13

"Well, shit," McCall said quietly over the speakerphone. "You feel sure, now? You don't have any other explanations?"

We were back in the office, and I had called the chairman to bring him up to date. "No plausible ones at this point, sir. I'm pretty well convinced. Montez, too. I'm just trying to figure out how to write it up. The FBI doesn't think there will be enough evidence to convict anybody. They have a strong suspect, but they're afraid they'll end up like the OJ Simpson trial. They think the case is too complicated to get a conviction from a typical jury. I don't know. They may be right." I waited.

McCall swore under his breath. "How long a rubber hose would you need to beat a confession out of one of those computers?"

Sally set a cup of coffee in front of me and sat down across the table with hers, leaning on her elbows.

"I think we're about ready to wrap things up out here, sir," I said. "We'll ship everything off and head back there ASAP."

"I know you two did a great job getting the puzzle put together so far, but it isn't the final answer. I want some hard data." He was silent for a few seconds. "What's Eric Zygler's number? Gotta couple of things to talk over with him."

I read the number from my notebook, and gave him the name of Zygler's secretary.

"OK," he said briskly. "Y'all go on with your plans to finish things up out there. I'm going to pass an idea or two by Zygler, and I'll get back to you."

"Yes sir. I'll give him a ring and let him know you'll be calling."

McCall clicked off before I could say goodbye, the way he always did when he was thinking about a problem. I had learned not to be offended by the boss's abrupt habits.

Sally looked across at me. "I wonder what he's planning." Her voice echoed the annoyance that showed in her face. A small line appeared between her eyebrows.

I half-smiled. "It isn't that he doesn't trust us. He's just been in the DC arena long enough to know he has to be pretty conservative sometimes."

"He's probably being pressured by somebody in Washington."

"I doubt it. He'd just pressure 'em back."

I dialed Zygler's number and got a receptionist. When I gave my name, she put me straight through to Zygler, although it sounded like he was in a conference.

"What have you got, Mike?"

"I just wanted to give you a heads up that the chairman is going to be calling you in a few minutes. He said he had a few ideas to suggest to you."

"What kind of things? Do you know?"

"No, he didn't tell me. I told him that we're about done out here, and that I'll be wrapping up and heading home by the end of the week. Maybe tomorrow."

Zygler sounded disappointed. "Sorry to see you go. Don't forget about our, er, appointment this afternoon. What time can you make it?"

Appointment? Ah, I remembered. The P-51 ride. "About five, I think." I tried to keep the excitement out of my voice. We said cheery goodbyes. Sally had gone back to her paperwork, and as I hung up I noticed that the message light was glowing red. After ten keystrokes, the message crackled out of the speaker.

"This is for Mr. O'Hara of the NTSB," it began. It was a woman's voice, and a murmur of activity rumbled in the background. "This is Liz Fowler of the Rocky Mountain Times. We met at the medical examiner's office. I know you're busy, but I'd really appreciate a call back. I have just a few quick questions for you. Please give me a call. I'll be in my office until late." She quoted her number, too fast for me to copy, and hung up.

She was away from her desk, and her voicemail beeped into action. I dictated a message to the effect that I was terribly sorry to miss her--a lie--and hung up, glad to have evaded actual contact.

Sally, Tidings, Wang and I worked through the afternoon on the accident files, getting everything in order for work in Washington, and catching up on a mountain of filing that we had been putting off until the last minute, which it now was.

The chairman called me back just after three. "Mike, I talked things over with Eric Zygler and the head of Aries just now. I think we want to do a series of flight tests to verify that the system works all right as designed. Aries is all in favor. I think they want it as a confidence building kind of thing. Zygler volunteered his other GMax for the testing, and the French are putting together a test plan for us."

I pulled up a pad and began to write notes. "Here?

Or do we go over there?" Paris with Sally came to mind.

"I'm looking for a sea-level site to run the tests out of. Gotta call in to the CO at Pax River. He's an old friend of mine."

The Patuxent River Naval Air Station was the Navy's version of Edwards Air Force Base, located on the shore of Chesapeake Bay southeast of Washington. "We're just talking about a couple of days of tests. You can simulate the flying conditions for the accident pretty well there and still have a mile of air under you."

"Sounds good to me," I said.

"Y'all handle it, of course. It's your case, Mike. See me when you get back, and we'll talk it over."

Just after four, the most beautiful mechanical sound I had ever heard, a combination of V-12 exhaust noise, propeller howl and aerodynamic urge, roared in through the building's windows. I raced over and pressed my nose against the glass in time to see a small, brightly painted single engine plane flash down the nearby runway at fifty feet altitude and roar into a near-vertical climb to the west of the field, rolling inverted and upright again as it ascended.

The distinctive wail of the Mustang's Rolls-Royce engine shook the windows, as if to announce to a timid and work-obsessed world that Eric Zygler was playing. The Mustang's outline shrank into a dot and disappeared against the sunlit cloudy background.

"Wow," I said hoarsely.

Tidings came to my side, his nose compressed against the glass. "What was that?"

"Zygler's Mustang."

He nodded, understanding.

"He offered me a ride in it this afternoon."

"It should be safe. There's no flight control software in it." He snickered at his own joke.

I looked at my watch, and at the now-orderly pile of paperwork on the table. McCall would be gone from the office by now, the two-hour time difference working in my favor. What the hell? "It's a day, people. George, I need a ride to the ZYCO hangar."

There was a sage-green flight suit in my size hanging on a peg in the pilot's locker room. On the left breast was a leather name tag with the words "O'Hara NTSB" beneath the golden twin crossed anchors of a Naval Flight Officer's wings. I shook my head again at the amazing mixture of consideration and intrusiveness shown by Eric Zygler. He had caught from my resume that I was a naval flight officer rather than an aviator and gotten the dual-anchor insignia right.

I put the flight suit on and walked to the flight line as the P-51 rumbled to halt in front of me. Zygler rode in front and was clearly handling the controls. He had cranked back the Plexiglas canopy, and Grimsby sat in the rear seat with his hands behind his head.

Zygler manipulated controls below the canopy rails: a scoop on the belly opened to draw more air through the under-slung radiator, and the engine RPM rose, holding steady near a thousand RPM. After ten seconds to circulate coolant through the engine, the power cut smoothly, and the huge propeller swung quietly to a stop. Two guys pulled up in a gas truck and went to work to get it ready for more work like a NASCAR pit crew.

Zygler pulled off his headset and jumped down onto the wing and then to the ground. He beckoned me to the plane, and met me with an exuberant handshake.

"Hey buddy," he nearly shouted. "She's all yours. The parachute's on the seat. Don't let Grimsby fly the damned thing. He doesn't deserve that much fun!" His eyes were bright with excitement.

Grimsby smiled down from the rear seat, his Ray Bans hiding his eyes but not his enjoyment.

Zygler grabbed my arm as I started to mount the wing. "I talked to your boss. I'm going to handle the flight tests personally. You and I can run 'em together. I'll see you at Pax River in a couple of weeks. Gotta run." Before I could thank him he turned with a wave and walked into the hangar.

Fifteen minutes later I was soaring over eastern Colorado, searching the skies for Messerschmitts and Zeros. Grimsby coached me through rolls and loops, the power of the ship numbing my mind, the deep bass engine roar building a physical pressure in my ears and the G-forces pulling at my muscles. I hadn't used my pilot's license for anything other than government ID for months, and this was the absolute best brush possible to knock off the rust. How many civil servants flew Mustangs? I grinned so hard my face hurt.

As we flew through the tops of the clouds at three hundred miles an hour, a feeling of awe came over me. This was how the rich lived. This was what a man did when he got what he wanted. And Zygler wanted me to be a part of it. And why the hell not, I thought? If this was a drug, I wanted more.

Landing and leaving the Mustang behind was hard. I left my personalized flight suit on a peg in the locker room, and vowed to fly the Mustang again.

I made a pass by the office before heading to the hotel to re-register. Liz Fowler from the local paper had called again.

I ran a web search to see who I was dealing with before I called her back. The search brought back hundred-plus items. She was listed as a technology and policy reporter for the local paper. She had a string of articles on ZYCO over the last year, none that sounded complimentary, and had been nominated for a Pulitzer prize for a series on political influence and public safety, but didn't get it. Probably angry about losing, I thought.

Once you get a good look at that kind of target it is hard to forget. There would be fireworks, I was sure.

I punched in her number, hoping to miss her and leave a message. She answered on the first ring.

I apologized for not getting back to her sooner and we exchanged artificial pleasantries for two seconds. As I spelled my name for her, I could hear the clacking of a computer keyboard in the background. I knew my responses were going straight into her story.

"Have you come to any conclusions yet about the crash?" she said.

"We've eliminated several possible causes, and I'm about finished with the inquiry here. We'll be finishing the field phase of the investigation this week and heading back to Washington to go over the findings and draw conclusions." Perfect, I thought. It was vintage Boardspeak, and it didn't mean squat.

"Um-hm." She typed for a few seconds. "Can you give me some of the things you've eliminated?"

I hesitated, but her question was legitimate enough. "The engines were working properly, the airplane was loaded within acceptable limits, that sort of thing. Crew training looked OK. The investigation is focusing now on the flight control system and the software that went in it."

"The stuff ZYCO wrote?"

"Yes."

She typed some more. "Mr. O'Hara, are you working with ZYCO in your inquiry?"

"Yes. I've gotten excellent cooperation from ZYCO throughout the investigation."

"Do you think the software that ZYCO has done for Boeing and other airliner manufacturers might have the same defect?"

I was beginning to understand where her angle was coming from. "I have no reason to think that, Ms. Fowler. Nothing that I have seen points to that."

"Has the NTSB grounded the GlobalMax since the crash in Canada?" The clack-clack sounds continued.

"The NTSB doesn't ground airplanes. The Federal Aviation Administration is responsible for the certification of aircraft, and they rule on matters like groundings. They would have to consult with the French authorities, too. We would make recommendations about groundings."

"Have you?" she interrupted.

I put a statement together in my brain before speaking. "The Aries Company and ZYCO together have decided to voluntarily ground the aircraft until the matter is straightened out. There are a relatively small number of aircraft in service, so they can do that without any major disruptions, and I think it's very responsible of them."

Clack-clack-clack. "Is it possible that someone may have tampered with the ZYCO software?"

Where was she getting this information?

"It's possible. We're looking into it."

"Do you have a suspect?" she asked quickly.

"That's a matter for the FBI to look into, and you'd have to ask them."

"Do you think it is unusual for the FBI to be on this case?"

"No." I didn't feel a need to explain.

Clack-clack. She paused. "Do you resent the FBI taking part in your investigation?"

What the hell? Resent? "No."

Clack-clack-clack.

I was getting tired of the conversation rapidly. My post-flight buzz had been replaced with a high-gravity feeling, as if the room had suddenly been moved to Jupiter. I bounced a pencil on the table in front of me in annoyance.

She was silent a moment before asking her next question. "Did you and your female assistant have a good time at Eric Zygler's ranch this weekend?"

Holy shit. Where did that come from?

Even if the boss had cleared the weekend at Eric's, what would the press make of it? I was afraid I was about to find out. The rules that went with being a federal employee could make simple human kindness into a federal case. Literally.

I made up as truthful and innocuous a statement

as I could. "I had a very quiet and restful two days. I was in a car accident last week, and Mr. Zygler was kind enough to invite me over to recuperate. I slept a lot. My assistant had a restful, quiet weekend, too. That's it." My head was throbbing, suddenly.

I heard Liz Fowler typing madly away on the other end of the line, and I wished I could reach through the phone and strangle her. "If you don't have any more questions..."

"Are you going back to Eric Zygler's place tonight?" she said quickly.

Anger began to build higher in me. "I might, Ms. Fowler," I said sarcastically. "If I'm invited. I am an American citizen. I get to go where I want. At least, I think I still do." My voice was beginning to rise in volume, probably exactly the response she wanted. I cut myself off. "If you don't have any more questions, I have to go. Goodbye."

As I slammed the phone down, her voice buzzed out of the handset, but I didn't stop to find out what else she wanted.

The throbbing in my temples continued, despite my orders for it to stop, and my knees suddenly hurt like hell. One goddamn weekend in a nice place with some friends, and now I had a reporter after me, complete with an axe to grind. Shit.

The FBI platoon dropped me off at the same

hotel that I had stayed in the week before, and I growled at the desk manager as she handed me my key. The FBI agent in charge of the cars left another agent on watch in the parking lot. I wasn't sure what he was supposed to watch for, but he was there. The head agent agreed to pick us up at seven-thirty the next morning, leaving me alone to trudge to my room. After hanging my clothes in the suddenly crummy closet, I flopped on the tiny, too-soft bed and fumed.

The phone rang, shocking me out of my lethargy long enough the stretch an arm over the thin hotel pillows to answer.

"Hi, sailor, it's me." Sally sounded chipper. "Have a nice plane ride?"

"Yeah, fine. It was pretty incredible." I tried to sound enthused, but failed.

"Um," she hesitated, as if she hadn't gotten the response she expected. "Are you feeling OK? Do you want to have dinner, or anything?"

I sighed theatrically. "I guess I'm hungry. I don't have a car. Where do you want to go?"

Sally was in the mood for a decent dinner, although anything would have been a come-down after two nights and days Chez Eric. She convinced the agent in the parking lot to give us a lift to a nearby steak house. We ordered dinner and drinks--wine for her and a ginger ale for me--and we settled in to wait for our meals.

After the excitement and annoyance of the afternoon, I was voraciously hungry, and I used most of my will power to resist slamming down an entire basket of bread the waitress dropped in front of us. Sally's eating habits confirmed what her figure had telegraphed: She used bread, butter and most other forms of food as sort of theatrical props, and didn't seem to eat much at all.

She leaned on her arms over the table, her hair spilling down over her shoulders. "So, tell me about the Mustang ride."

I smiled back a little, and worked on enthusiasm again. "Unbelievable. Tremendous. It was everything a little boy could possibly want."

She laughed, and her eyes flashed like runway approach lights in the darkened room.

"It was fast, and loud, and smoky, and fast and loud. It was worth every cent of Eric's money."

She smiled again, and asked for details.

I went on at length about the climb rate, and control forces, and everything else I could remember.

She took a drink of wine. "I took flying lessons for a while in the Air Force, at the base aero club. I want a ride too. I bet I could fly it. Do you think Eric would let me?"

A frown crossed my face as I remembered Liz Fowler's call. "We'd better cool it with Eric. I took a call from that reporter from the local paper that I pissed off.

Somebody told her about us spending the weekend at Eric's place."

Sally shrugged and crooked an eyebrow. "So what? McCall said it was all right."

The waitress brought our meals. After she left, I said, "Yeah, technically, we're OK, but we're Federal employees. Everything we do is the public's business. And remember, the public and every damned politician in the country thinks that civil servants are the root of all evil. We're easy targets. Catching a fed doing something that looks comfortable or fun is always a juicy story, no matter how innocent it may be. Then the inspector general comes in and does a report that says you're a jerk, and you never get promoted."

"That's stupid," she said quietly. "We're still citizens."

"That's what I said. I got a little hot. I have to learn to work with the press. McCall is really good at it."

"What did she ask?"

I went over the questions Fowler had put to me, and my answers. She listened calmly, until I got to the one about female assistant.

Sally listened impassively. She stared down at her dinner, clasping her knife and fork so hard her knuckles were white, and when she looked up, her face was an angry mask. "It's starting again," she whispered.

"What do you mean? What's starting again?"

She sighed deeply, twice, fighting off the anger, or sadness.

"Why can't I just have a job, like normal people? I just want to go to work, and earn a salary, and have people leave me alone." She sniffed a little. She took another deep breath, and swallowed a couple of times, calming back down.

"When I was in the Air Force," she went on, still nearly whispering, "I had a base commander who harassed me. Sexually harassed. He was married, with about eight kids. He wanted to sleep with me, and when I refused him, well, life got very strange. He acted like we were doing it anyway. He treated me like some kind of trophy in front of everybody."

I felt disgusted. "Did you report it?"

"I was a second lieutenant, twenty-three years old, and he was a big-stick fighter pilot hero. Nobody would have believed me." She sighed again, and pushed her plate away. "I asked for a transfer, and after nearly a year, they finally moved me to the wing staff."

"Did things get better?"

She clasped her hands together on the edge of the table. "For a while. I worked for the commanding general. He was a great guy, and I explained everything to him. It was a great job, and he and the vice commander thought I did OK. But the rumors started up about me again. People thought the general and I were having an affair.

He didn't get promoted, and he retired earlier than he should have. His wife left him. I think it was because of all the rumors." She pursed her lips, and then took a huge gulp of wine, setting her glass down with a flourish. "People are such assholes."

I shook my head in sympathy. "Well, you don't need to worry about this business. Everybody at the board knows me. Nobody would believe I could get that lucky."

She looked at me a little more seriously than I would have liked. "You don't think about me that way, do you?"

Danger signals went off in my mind. Flares. Skyrockets. Warning! How did I answer that?

Truthfully? Yes, every second of the day since the instant I met her. Guys do this. She was lovely, charming and sexy as hell. A pretty good engineer, too. Could I fall in love with a woman in a week? Probably not, not even one like her, but the thermonuclear lust point was definitely in range.

"Uh-umm." I hesitated for as long as I could.

She looked back at me expectantly.

"Look, Sally, be fair to me, OK? I'm single, I'm straight and I'm not dead. You're the most attractive woman I've ever been in the same time zone with. But I don't have a great record in this department, and you've made it pretty clear that you want to have a strictly professional relationship. You deserve the respect. If that's what you want, that's what you'll get from me. OK?" Was that good enough? Was I safe? Shit.

"Thanks. You're already the best boss I've ever had."

"Better than the general? The second one, I mean," I said.

"A tie. So far. But watch it." She shook her head, as if to flush the whole business out of her mind. She sat up straight and waved the waitress over. "I feel like having dessert."

A river of hot fudge and ice cream followed, topped with enough whipped cream and chopped nuts to derail a freight train. That was just hers.

The sugar in the slice of latex-cream pie I had while watching her would normally have knocked me cold for the night, but I was still staring at the ceiling at 2:00 a.m. My brain was in high gear trying to fold the facts of the case together and come up with a clear answer. It wasn't happening.

What the hell happened to N215ES? There should have been a straightforward answer, a simple technical cause for this wreck so we could call out a certain, direct cause and specify a fix for it.

There wasn't one.

In fact, it wasn't just that we didn't have evidence of system failures, we had hard evidence of no problems in the major technical areas. And yet there were two fatal crashes in a week. Coincidence? Not a chance.

The FBI was convinced that there was some criminal act, probably sabotage, which caused the accidents. They would think that. When all you have is a hammer, every screw looks like a nail. And that sweaty sap, Tom Sutton, practically had "Convict Me" tattooed on his forehead. There were others, even Eric, who could have caused whatever the problem was. Sutton's main problem was that he just looked really, really guilty to the Bureau. He had the ability and opportunity, and motivation. I wasn't sure why I didn't buy it.

Then there was ZYCO. The business environment between the executives, investors and their French friends was like the wardroom on a Klingon battle cruiser. Poisoned whiskey, marked cards and knives in everybody's back. Stock manipulation was in the mix. A billion dollars or so might stress people out enough to do anything. Zygler was determined to hold it together, but he had a lot of blades sticking out of him.

It would have been easier to relax and let the FBI take over, but what if I hadn't found some critical fact or piece of data? What if there was some critical flaw in control design or some other damned thing? There was stuff in the GMax that was used all over the aerospace industry. Other executive jets, airliners, military and more to come. I didn't have enough hard data to close the arguments that I knew were coming, to get conclusions through the board's review or to get the FBI a conviction. I had to come up with some critical bit of data or a breakthrough idea that would drive toward closure, but nothing came.

And of course, there was a better than even chance that somebody had tried to kill me. Would whoever it was that tried it take another shot?

What would Lew Hills do with this pile of shit?

The whole set-up crawled.

Eventually, it got light outside.

Morning was clear and cool. I grabbed a cup of coffee in the hotel lobby and pulled a morning paper off the complementary stack on the front desk. I stretched in the early sunlight, working out the last of the kinks from the accident while I waited for Tidings and Sally to meet me by the FBI cars.

I traded greetings with the special agent who was driving the first sedan. I was early, and after a couple of minutes I decided to sit in the back seat and read the paper.

The front page had a headline about an upcoming election. The stock market was down a hundred points in heavy trading, presumably because the head of the Federal Reserve Board had emphasized the wrong syllable in an important word during statements to Congress. The

Colorado Rockies had lost the previous evening's game to the San Diego Padres, but were still in the pennant race.

I flipped the folded paper over to check the weather report near the bottom of the page, and a headline caught my eye: FEDERAL INVESTIGATORS "COOPERATE" WITH ERIC ZYGLER IN LATEST GLOBALMAX CRASHES.

"Oh, shit," I said, loud enough to attract the notice of the agent in the front seat.

He turned with a quizzical expression, his eyebrows arching over the sunglasses perched on his nose.

"Uh, there's a story." I held the paper up, and he nodded, turning back to the wheel.

The story was four inches deep and two columns wide, under Liz Fowler's byline.

Colorado Springs (AP)--Federal investigators assigned here to sift through the remains of a fatal airplane crash took a weekend off to party with the aircraft's owner, reliable sources said. A highly placed source inside the giant ZYCO corporation confirmed that National Transportation Safety Board investigation team leader Michael F. O'Hara and an unidentified female assistant spent last weekend together at computer software magnate Eric Zygler's palatial ranch, located in the foothills above Colorado Springs. O'Hara had earlier been involved in a suspicious one-car road accident. Although alcohol has apparently been ruled out in the wreck, the crash was the second traffic accident involving a member of O'Hara's team in a week.

"Jesus H. Christ," I said out loud. The agent turned again, and I mumbled apologies. The article went on to depict me as a bumbling, bureaucratic yo-yo from Washington, on the town and looking for action like Shriner at a convention, and only incidentally investigating a plane crash.

The real target of the article was Eric. Although Fowler made no direct accusations, the story hinted strongly that Zygler was trying to cover up a major flaw in his company's products, one that called into question the operating safety of a large portion of the world's newest airline fleets as well. For proof, the story cited the crash of the other GlobalMax in Canada. She made several errors about the technical aspects of the crashes, but the article would persuade a lot of readers.

Fowler quoted two former ZYCO employees, including one who described Zygler as a megalomaniac with an obsession about control. He described frequent screaming and verbal abuse incidents, and several employees who had settled wrongful termination suits. The other wasn't named but was identified as a former Chief Operating Officer. The ex-COO spoke at length about Eric's campaign contributions and frequent political visitors, including the Western governor who would become President. The story didn't imply any significant illegalities but ended with a discussion of the flap with the Board of Directors over the P-51. One member had apparently resigned in protest. But Zygler was too popular with shareholders to be pressured out then, despite several tries. There had been a string of fired vice-presidents, but Fowler said things were more stable now that Zygler had a team of lickspittle lackeys he could control.

The NTSB and I were left looking merely stupid and corrupt, as opposed to overtly evil, as ZYCO was shown to be. Stupidity and corruption were the natural province of the federal government, after all, while true low-down gutter crawling deviltry was reserved for the corporate sector.

I sat in the back seat, feeling light-headed and slightly nauseous, as Tidings and Sally arrived and climbed into the car. I held the paper up for Sally. "Did you see this?"

She looked grim as she nodded. "Have you read the editorial?"

I did a full-zoot, Three Stooges double-take. "There's an editorial, too?"

She closed her eyes and nodded again. "In back of the first section."

I flipped back to the right page of the paper, finding the editor's comments splashed across the top of what passed for an Op-Ed page in El Paso County. The headline was "ZYCO Dupes the Feds." It went downhill from there. The general gist was that Eric Zygler had corrupted a lowly public servant, and in doing so was threatening the lives of every member of the traveling public. Pretty heavy stuff. I was named, as was the mayor and Chairman McCall. Sally was referred to as my "comely female assistant."

"Well, this is going to go over big at headquarters," I said, after catching my breath.

"How could anybody write a thing like that, Mike?" Sally sounded wounded.

I grinned across at her, weakly, as she leaned her head on the seat back. "Hey, I'm the one that's a dirty government bastard grubbing at the pig trough of corruption. You're just female and comely, and we knew that already."

She didn't think I was very funny, and looked pissed off. I motioned for the driver to go, and Tidings rode in silence.

At the office, George and Sally worked on a few last packing chores while I called the chairman's number. He wasn't in and I didn't want to leave a detailed message about the story on his voicemail so I hung up, scanned the story and emailed it, marked personal for McCall. Next, I wrote an email explaining the background behind the story, and detailing my contact with Fowler. I sent the message to the chairman with a copy to the vice chairman and the head of the public affairs office in Washington.

As soon as that was done the phone began to buzz. I clicked on the speaker and answered gruffly.

"Mike, it's Eric." Zygler sounded his usual self.

"Uh, hi Eric. Did you see the paper?"

"The story in the daily rag?" he interrupted cheerfully, his voice booming throughout the room. "Yeah, I saw it. They run one like that about me almost every week. They slow down if the skiing's good or the Broncos are winning. I keep a scrapbook."

"Well, it was pretty rough. The things she said about you..." I tried to collect my thoughts as I talked, but he interrupted again.

"Hey Mike. Relax. I have two outstanding libel suits going against the Rocky Mountain Fish Wrap now, and another one won't hurt. It won't affect me, buddy."

It would me. I picked up the handset and spoke quietly. "Eric, I could get fired over this. I'll probably have an investigator from the inspector general's office waiting for me when I get back."

"Am I off the speaker?" he asked.

I went on the hand set and held it to me ear. "Yeah, now."

"Look, Mike, don't worry about that civil-servant bullshit. You don't understand what you have to offer industry. I'll take care of you. Just keep me informed of how they're treating you. You're important to me."

I was silent for a few seconds. "Thanks," I mumbled.

"Hey, I was just calling to see if you were coming with George to question Tom Sutton again."

I covered the phone with a hand and looked up at the FBI agent. "When are you going to question Sutton?"

"Nine-thirty." He looked at his watch. "I'd better get going."

"Mind if I come?"

He shrugged.

I pulled my hand off the handset. "Sure, Eric, I'll be there. I'm headed back today, and I wanted to talk to you one last time."

"Good. I can count on them being fair to Tom when you're there. Thanks, man."

We said goodbye and hung up.

I gave Sally instructions to ship the files and other results of the investigation back to Washington, close up shop, and then check our reservations for our travel back. Tidings would be staying behind to finish work on the case against Sutton, and Sally and I arranged to meet at the gate in the Denver airport terminal for our fight back to Dulles.

I took one last look around the office and walked out the door, following Tidings to the car.

chapter

14

Sutton looked even worse than he had the day I met him. We were in a conference room attached to Eric's office, a bright, cheery place with thick, pale-purple carpets. Floor-to-ceiling windows looked across the impossibly clean ZYCO parking lot out to the city below.

Tidings had been reinforced by two special agents from the FBI's Denver office. They were both older and tougher looking than the sharp young Millennials of our protection detail. One, a tall thin man with a face like a hatchet blade, who introduced himself as Special Agent Cardin, set up a small digital recorder on the table that filled the center of the room. The other special agent was shorter and thicker, but still every inch an FBI man. From the team's demeanor, he was obviously senior to the other agents. He sat next to Tidings, the three lined up along one side of the table.

Sutton sat across from the agents with his lawyer, Mr. Ailes. Sutton's skin tone had faded from sallow to cadaverous, and huge blue bags had appeared under his eyes. He had wound his hair around his balding head in a swirl again, but the strands were bathed in sweat and lacked the adhesion to stay in place to cover the bare areas of his naked scalp. Several clumps of greasy black hair hung limply over his ears and down to his collar. He seemed not to notice. His head was as pale as the rest of him, except where the sun had raised blisters at one time. Those spots were a bright pink, and they seemed to accentuate his pallor.

Ailes, in his late forties, was smooth and polished, with a perfect dark gray suit. His graying hair was slicked down in the latest fashionable rich-guy look. He wore cuff links the size of boat anchors, gold with little jewels, which would have looked prissy on a less intimidating figure. He was exactly what I thought of when I closed my eyes and imagined a lawyer.

Eric Zygler stood at the far end of the room when we entered, and he gave me a wave of recognition. I walked to him and we shook hands as I took in the room.

"Mike, thanks for coming," he nearly whispered, sounding like a bereaved family member at a funeral. "I appreciate you being here. This is hard for us."

"Not a problem, Eric," I said, in the same hushed tone. "I wanted to check with you before we left about the follow-on testing."

He stared at Sutton as he spoke, his face blank. "Good. I'll be there, with Grimsby and a copilot. We'll fly the other GMax out to Pax River." A small smile crossed his features briefly. "They wanted me to fly in a separate airplane, but I said to hell with that. I've got to show faith in our products. If the plane flies, so do I."

I'd started to answer, when there was a stirring behind us. The senior FBI man cleared his throat. "Can we get started, gentlemen?"

Zygler and I took seats at one end of the table, and he poured us both cups of coffee from a carafe.

Cardin turned on the recorder, the senior agent spoke, and Tidings listened. They all took hand-written notes, as did Ailes.

"Mr. Sutton, thank you for assisting us with our inquiry again today. We have several more questions for you, mostly to follow up on the information you gave us in our previous session." The agent's voice was clear and loud for the benefit of the recorder. His voice hardened slightly. "I want to remind you and your counsel that the Bureau believes that a crime or crimes may have been committed, which may have caused the crash of the Aries GlobalMax with registration number--" He looked at his pad quickly. "--N215ES. Also, we are cooperating with French and Canadian authorities on an investigation into a crash of another GlobalMax aircraft in Canada."

He looked up from his notes and stared directly at Sutton, who drew back in his chair, and went on brusquely. "If a crime has been committed, you would be one of several suspects. You should understand that before we begin."

Sutton sat quietly, sweating, and didn't respond.

Ailes leaned forward, and cleared his throat. "My client has and will continue to cooperate fully with you in your investigation." His voice was low and smooth, and loud enough for the recorder, too. "Mr. Sutton has not been a party to any crime, nor has he any direct knowledge of any criminal activity that you may be looking for."

The agent wrote a note, and went on. "That's about where we left off the other day," he said quietly. "I'd like to go back to your access to the net over which software updates could be sent to the aircraft."

"I told you I had access. I had plenty of access, goddammit," Sutton said, loudly. His voice squeaked. He was dripping sweat, now. He had removed his jacket--the only one in the room to do so--and his shirt was soaked under the arms. The white fabric stuck to him as completely as the veiled accusations from the FBI agent did. "I could get in any time I wanted." He began to shout. "So could everybody else in the goddamn world! There must be twenty people in this place that could have done the kind of thing you're talking about. "

Ailes put a hand on Sutton's arm, to calm and quiet him. "Gentlemen," he said in a scolding tone, "I believe we established that Mr. Sutton had access to the aircraft's software in our last session. We also established that there was no reason to assign any suspicion to Mr. Sutton, nor is there any reason to expect that my client would have any exculpatory knowledge regarding others' access."

The questioning went on at length, with the FBI asking leading questions, Sutton denying knowledge, and Ailes chastising the agents for even dreaming that Sutton might have had the least interest in harming a single transplanted hair on Wesley Corso's head. Ailes was good. The agents made thrusts, Ailes parried, Sutton sweated.

I had zoned out when Ailes said the word "exculpatory."

I looked at my watch during a particularly heated exchange. It was nearly eleven, and I began to think about starting to move toward the airport in Denver.

Zygler leaned across and touched my arm. He flicked his eyes toward the door, as if to say "Let's get out of here." I gathered my notes and stood.

We excused ourselves and moved toward the exit as unobtrusively as possible.

As I walked behind the seated agents, Sutton stared at me. He looked like a trapped animal, desperate, lost, and pissing-scared. But something was missing. For a few seconds I tried to imagine him murdering someone, whether it was with bogus software code or a cheap handgun. It didn't come. Had this crazy computer loon really tried to kill me, personally?

But as we stared at each other, another expression appeared on Sutton's face. Resignation? I couldn't tell. I pulled my eyes away from Sutton's face, not wanting to see the throes of a dying animal.

I leaned down and spoke in Tidings' ear, as quietly as I could. "Gotta go. Can you get a ride?"

He turned his head. "Sure. See you in DC next week," he whispered.

I followed Zygler out into the hall where he waited, leaning against the wall. He grinned and greeted a mixed knot of male and female software weenies as they passed him, but when he looked back to me, his face was grim. "Tom's not doing very well in there."

"They're grilling him pretty hard, considering he's not charged with anything." I tilted my head back toward the room. "I think they know they can never prove anything and they're annoyed. I've seen my brothers from the Justice Department attack folks like this before."

"Sharks," Zygler Eric looked at the floor. "I just don't believe he'd do a thing like that, Mike," he said, his voice serious and resigned. "Jesus, I know we've had some conflict here, but damn."

"Eric, brilliant people seem to generate their own stress. Maybe he just flipped out," I said. "If it hadn't been over the money, it would have been something else."

He stared at me. "You think he did it?"

"Not my call. I'm not sure we'll ever know for sure. All you can do is put some safeguards in place to keep it from happening again."

He looked back at the floor. "We're doing that. I've done what I could for him. I'm paying for the lawyer. Ailes is very good. A real human torpedo. And if Tom needs mental help, it's all covered under our corporate insurance program." He began to ramble, but then caught himself. "You're leaving now?"

"Yeah," I said, trying to sound a happier note. "I have to head back to DC and write the damned report. Sally and I'll be up to our ears in paper for the next few weeks. Then we have to sell our findings to the internal review group and then a full meeting of the board before it goes anywhere. With an open-ended thing like this, it could be a year before the final report comes out." I gave him a sardonic grin. "Besides, I have to go duke it out with the Inspector General about fraternizing with the enemy."

He looked disgusted. "I couldn't work like that. I can't believe your patience, Mike."

I smiled broadly, and held out my hand. "I can't believe lots of stuff about you, Eric. It's been a real pleasure to meet you, and thanks for everything."

He shook my hand strongly and held the grip as he spoke. "I meant all those things I said at the house. We'll keep in touch, and when you're ready to jump, I'll be there with a net. I'll see you in a couple of weeks at Pax River."

We parted with a friendly wave, he returning to the questioning, and I heading for the elevator. I flagged down the waiting FBI sedan, and told the driver to depart for Denver. The second car fell in behind us, and as we rolled north I daydreamed for a while about living in a grand house, doing fun work and being rich.

After a half hour, the two-car caravan drove up the freeway past the site of my accident. As we went under the overpass just south of where I had gone off the road, I spotted scars on the concrete abutments on the left, two hard scratches about door-high. They were marks from my rental car's outside mirror and door handle. A few seconds farther on, faint skid marks curved gently off the pavement to the right, leading to the beginnings of two ruts. My ruts.

I hadn't expected to be affected by the sight, but the accident scene filled me with dread and fear. Sweat broke out on my face and arms, and I tried not to hyperventilate as we rolled past. I'd been warned. It went with the concussion.

The two agents in front didn't seem to notice anything.

I slumped back in the seat and contemplated again the idea that Tom Sutton had tried to kill me, and nearly succeeded. The sweating, fearful little man in the conference room hadn't looked like a murderer, but seven people were dead. Another was injured, two if you counted my banged-up knees, which I did.

Sutton, the balding, terrified rat of a human being, had struck out against a man who had kept him from being something else, and killed him with the only weapon he understood: computer software. He had struck again and again as the net tightened around him. The irony of it all was that he would probably get away with the crimes, the rules of evidence being what they were.

I spent the rest of the trip thinking about my situation. Investigators at NTSB usually didn't last long. The stress of delving into so many cases of human and mechanical destruction kept the burnout rate high. Lew was an exception I thought, but then reconsidered. Maybe he wasn't. Maybe his fun-loving, cigar-smoking, hard-drinking, late-night ways were a reaction to all the body parts he had recovered, and all the blood mixed with hydraulic fluid and other hydrocarbons he'd seen and smelled in the twenty-five years he'd spent with the board.

I watched the outskirts of Denver cruise by at seventy-five mph as I made up my mind. There was more to life than the next wreck, or the next crash file. I'd done my share, and seen enough agony. To hell with it, I thought. Some other asshole could take over. There were always plenty of applicants when we put out an announcement.

When this case was over, so was my federal career. I would wait as long as the ethics lawyers demanded, and then I would take Eric Zygler up on his offer. Get a real job, making real money, and have a real life outside of Washington. Who knew, I might even find somebody to marry. An Earth woman? For Iron Mike? Was it possible?

Yes, even for me.

Maybe Charlene Zygler had a sister.

Maybe Sally... I stopped myself. Eric Zygler had opened the door into a different world for me, but it wouldn't do any good to get too deep into the next phase of my life until I had tied up the ends of this one. Finish the case, I thought, and then make a move.

The weird, tent-like terminal of Denver International Airport loomed suddenly, jolting me out of my thoughts. We swept around the freeway ramps and into the loading zones in front of the airline ticketing desks and luggage carts, stopping next to the curb.

I said thanks to the two agents for the security and

the ride, and lugged my suitcase out of the trunk, heading for the end of the shortest looking line. The federal office that rules on such things had determined that no free upgrades were allowed while flying on government business, but my million-plus frequent flier miles qualified me to use a special check-in line. I had my bag checked and was sailing through the cool-guys line at the security check minutes later.

Sally had gotten us booked us on a Boeing 777 nonstop to Dulles, which was where I had left my car in my rushed departure. With nearly a half-hour to spare, I stopped for a magazine. I was headed for the cashier's desk when a familiar face caught my eye.

Eric Zygler stared out at me from the cover of Business Week, and another story headlined on the cover of Time. On the top line of the Time cover was a blurb that asked, "Can Eric Save ZYCO?" I picked up the magazine, thumbing my way back to the cover story. ZYCO's problems were outlined in excruciating detail, complete with an arty full-face portrait of Eric. The gist of the article was that, with the sale of the company to the public, Zygler the genius had lost control of his process and products, having to spend too much time managing his new-found financial empire. The story's bottom line was now that Zygler was getting back in the hunt, up to his elbows in software, the technical excellence of the company was sure to rebound. There was some puff at the end on his philanthropy--he gave away tens of millions every year--and parties at his palatial home with Charlene.

The cover story in Business Week featured a full-figure shot of Zygler in a military flight suit. He had a crash helmet under this arm and there was a jet fighter parked in the background, matched to an article titled 'Top Geek'. The article talked about challenges to him at ZYCO and how he was handling them. There were activist investors who wanted his head, angry that he spent so much on engineering when other companies spent less, built lower-quality products and returned more money to stock holders. There were rumors of a secret hostile takeover attempt that he had managed to crush through adept work with US investment banks and wealthy individuals.

The article also talked about gripes by Wall Street analysts about lavish spending. A picture of the P-51 was in there. I read a discussion of operating margins--not too good--and internal rate of return--worse. Earnings Before Interest and Taxes--EBIT: I had to look that up--were tracking slightly lower over time. His best weapons were the force of his personality, his astounding technical ability and his love for the company. They had that part right, I decided. The question they left open was whether it would be enough to hold off the takeover artists forever.

On the last page, a graph held a picture of

ZYCO's stock price since the company had gone public. The growth after the IPO was almost vertical for few months. A slow upward slant after that was interrupted in June by a sharp vertical spike downward, reflecting the stock manipulation by the asset manager that Randall had told me about. From a start upward at just over twenty dollars, the price had stabilized near fifty dollars a share in July, dropping to less than forty after the crash. The magazine had been on the racks for less than two days.

I purchased the two magazines and headed for the gate, taking the underground tram to the midfield terminal. The gate agent was just calling for early boarders when I arrived. I hung back looking for Sally.

She waved across the crowd, from near a window.

I walked to her side and we stared out at our airplane. The huge twin engines of the 777 hung nearly to the ground, while the tail far off in the distance towered over sixty feet above the ramp.

"Nice-looking plane," Sally said. "My favorite airliner." She grinned sheepishly, and turned toward me. "I always like to look the plane over before I get on it."

I chuckled. "Me, too. It's a professional hazard, I think. I'm amazed that people will just jump on an airplane without even knowing what it is." I held up the magazines. "Did you see these?"

She glanced at Eric's face on the covers and shook her head. "He's everywhere. I want to read that story."

"I'll bring it to you when I'm done." We compared seat assignments, her in the middle of the cabin and me near the front.

Sally's row number was called as we spoke, and she picked up her bag, slinging the strap over her shoulder. Before she headed for the end of the line, she said, "Do you mind if I ask you something?"

"No, shoot."

"Um... Are you going to be with the board for a long time?"

I shrugged again, slowly this time. "I guess so. Nothing's permanent anymore. I don't have any plans. Why?"

She adjusted her shoulder strap, and pushed her hair out of her face. "Eric asked about you a lot, while you were sleeping. And he talked to McCall. He seemed really impressed, and I thought..." She regarded me for a second without saying anything. "I'm having a great time working for you, and I'd hate to have you leave right away. That's all."

I could feel my face redden. "You're nice. But you've only known me for a couple of weeks, and I was knocked out half that time. Give me a month in the office and I promise I'll get on your nerves. You'll probably want to steal my desk."

She laughed, and the sound of her laughter made me feel warm, and very, very good.

"Seriously, Eric mentioned some things, but the lawyers wouldn't let me go with ZYCO until this job is done, anyway." It wasn't a lie. I would just be cool until the time was right.

She smiled again as she walked away, calling over her shoulder, "Bye, bro."

I watched her leave, lust in me roaring like a big, furry lion. "See ya, sis," I whispered to her back.

I was desperate to get my mind on something else, and I plugged into the Business Week for the three-hour flight. I read the ZYCO article for details. Business articles always seemed like a shortened, redacted version of the actual activity to me, like a CliffsNotes rendition of reality. Whenever I saw the business media's take on technical subjects, it always seemed like a comic book about the real world.

One section caught my interest. There was some actual numerical analysis of how to take over a business, using ZYCO as an example. The problem with a takeover was that ZYCO had expanded too fast and too far, based on Eric's reputation and several high-profile wins. Zygler had backed it up with some amazing technical innovations that put him at the forefront of the industry.

But things had topped out over the last year. None of the big investment houses would agree to foot a bill big enough for a takeover based on the expected return. Aries was circling over the huge target like a vulture hoping for a break. Somebody had tried to make the stock price fall, but they didn't manipulate it far enough down to make the Harvard Business School alumni association open their wallets. Zygler and the Board of Directors were in a coffin corner--they couldn't slow down or speed up, or even climb or dive, or it would all fall apart. It would take some major development, either the good kind or bad kind, to break the logjam. In the meantime ZYCO's stock languished and produced returns just good enough to prevent a major sell-off. The embedded computer code bloom was off the digital rose.

I dropped the copy of Business Week off with Sally halfway across the continent, stopping to chat for a few minutes. But the seat belt light came on before we could say much, and I rode the rest of the flight with my attention out the window and my mind elsewhere.

On the ground, we shuffled off the plane into the center field terminal. I carried her heavy carry-on bag for her as far as the baggage claim and the terminal exit. We didn't talk on the trip across the field, but I made up my mind to offer her a ride home, and to ask her out for a cup of coffee. Strictly as a courtesy, of course. Professional courtesy.

I carefully rehearsed a casual sounding invitation, and began to speak the words as we rode down an escalator between the baggage carousels on the lower level.

Before my lips could form the first syllable, she

began waving to somebody in the crowd ahead. A compact, handsome man in a tight polo shirt and pressed khakis waved back to her and walked forcefully toward her, parting the throng like a destroyer pushing through a heavy sea.

He threw his arms around her and kissed her, and she kissed his cheek in return.

I looked him up and down. He seemed bigger up close, muscular and slim. He was roughly V-shaped from lots of gym time. I guessed he was the type who looked at himself in the mirror while lifting weights. He had dark hair that hung fashionably over his ears, expertly styled just so. It probably took hours to make it look that casual. His walk and the look in his eye suggested the type of aggressive, hard charging non-government executive type that DC was filled with.

Sally turned back to me, and he draped a hand casually around her waist, pulling her close, his Rolex sliding down on his tanned wrist. "Mike," she said, "this is David. David, this is my boss, Mike O'Hara."

He reached across the gulf between us with a friendly hand. Bastard. His hand was dry, and his grasp was strong and manly. Son of a bitch.

"Mr. O'Hara." His voice boomed powerfully. "How are you? Sally's told me all about you. I'll take that." He reached for her bag after dropping my hand. As I mumbled a response, he shifted his attention back to her. "C'mon, baby, let's go." The two of them walked away, up the ramp and into the night. She stopped to wave goodnight before they headed out the door.

She didn't seem like a "baby" to me, and certainly not his.

I stood by the baggage carousel, hands in pockets, staring at the floor. The crowd swelled around me, jostling, sliding huge overstuffed bags away, chatting cheerfully with reunited loved ones. Gradually the bustling ebbed, and eventually I realized that the belt had stopped. My bag had gone by several times and ended up fifty feet from where I stood. I was alone in the claim area except for a janitor who swept the floors and whistled tunelessly.

I grabbed the bag and headed out to find my car.

My apartment smelled musty, and the armload of mail that had filled the mailbox covered the kitchen table. I poured the now-sour carton of milk down the drain, and shuffled through the pile of letters and colorful paper: marketing mailers; catalogues from companies I never had and never would do business with; bills, some late, most not; a letter from my brother in Seattle. Four credit card offers. I sorted, discarded and read for a few minutes. Three magazines, including an Aviation Week and an Aerospace Engineering Digest, completed the pile.

I wrote a check for the rent, placing it on the counter to remind me to deliver it before leaving for the office the next day, and sorted the bills into a pile to be paid the following evening.

The message light on the answering machine glowed red, and I pulled a note pad and pencil out before hitting the play back button.

The robot voice--they could do better, I knew, but people liked the science fiction touch--announced gravely that I had twenty-two messages. I pulled up a chair.

Eleven recordings were hang-ups, three were calls from marketing agencies, four were calls from my mother, wondering where I was--I resolved to call her--and two were from friends.

None were remarkable enough to save, and I erased each as it was finished.

The last, time stamped just an hour before my arrival, started out as a long silence, with labored breathing, even sobs, in the static-filled background.

The caller began speaking, his voice low, tortured, like the wail of a wounded animal. It was Sutton. "Mr. O'Hara. You have to believe me. I didn't do it. They...he..." He stopped, and sobbed again. "I didn't do it. I don't understand why they're doing this to me." His voice increased in volume. "I didn't do it. I swear."

The phone clicked, and there was a beep,

announcing the end of the recording. I put down the pencil I was holding, and sat in silence, considering Sutton's message.

Why the hell had he called me? What was I supposed to do? Was I a goddamned defense lawyer? The jerk. Wasn't it enough that I was going to spend another goddamned night alone in this shitty little apartment while good old Dave had a long night of really great, athletic sex with the woman of my dreams?

At that moment, I would have cheerfully thrown poor Mr. Sutton and his bald spot and sweat stains off the top of the Washington Monument, with good old Dave chained to his ankles. Innocent? My ass. Put him in the electric chair and I'd flip the switch.

I showered, and flopped into the musty, empty bed.

I popped some pills and slept better than usual, waking about 4:00 a.m. I stared at the ceiling of my bedroom as long as I could, before finally rolling out about five. Another long, hot shower woke me well enough to go to work, and I headed for the Metro station. I was at my desk before six forty-five, and had to turn on the lights in the large open bay when I arrived. I put on a pot of coffee in the common office kitchen and went to work.

A total of five weeks had passed since I had seen my desk, and the sight wasn't pretty. My in-box was stacked a foot high with paperwork, most of it marked "urgent," and a pile of memo slips from the front office receptionist covered the blotter. I flipped on my computer and logged into email, finding over two hundred messages. These were just the ones I had left for action after a smart phone triage.

It all sorted into urgent, do-later and overcome-by-events. The urgent group had messages from Dr. Anders at NSA, Lee Wang in the Denver office, and George Tidings, who had left a phone number in Denver for me to call. I stuck notes to my calendar blotter and waded into the in-box.

One unopened letter, actual stamped-and-posted paper from the state of Alaska, caught my eye. It was in an official envelope from the state government. I was expecting a receipt from the state for the report I had written on the condition of their school bus fleet. The letter was date-stamped the previous week, and I tossed it to the top of my desk for reading later. I started answering emails.

By seven-thirty the office was beginning to fill with bureaucrats and engineers, and by the time I got around to getting a cup of coffee, the pot I'd brewed was gone. I put another on, swearing under my breath about the one-way toads I worked with as it brewed, and returned to my desk with a hot, sweet cup of caffeine.

Sally sat at the formerly unoccupied desk next to

mine, brushing her hair. It was already perfectly glossy.

She wore a short black skirt and dark hose with glossy black high heels, plus a pale blue blouse just sheer enough for me to note that she gave a lot of thought to her lingerie. She looked luscious, outrageously pretty, in a different league from the faceless female feds and policy wonkettes in running shoes that I normally met in DC.

I tried not to ogle.

She looked up as I approached. "Good morning," she said brightly.

"Hi," I answered. "Coffee?" I motioned toward the pot, but she turned up her nose.

"Never touch it. I'll get some tea later. Did you have a good night?"

I flopped down in my chair, producing the usual squeak. "I haven't been home in so long, it seemed weird to sleep there. You?"

"Oh, I just went straight to bed," she answered cheerfully. I gritted my teeth, trying not to imagine too much. "I hope it's all right with you that I took this desk. Lew said it was available." I smiled vacantly, still dealing with the bed idea, and tried to concentrate on work.

I continued through the email stack as Sally made her tea and prepared for the day. When the sorting was finished there were really only five messages of interest, one from Dr. Schmidt in the lab downstairs, three from the chairman, plus a note with a file attached from

Clinton Harding at ZYCO. I put the rest aside.

I looked at Harding's message first. He had attached answers for all the items Tidings had requested. I looked at the file. Most of it was personal information on Corso, his contacts, itinerary, etc. He was scheduled to meet with the Aries CEO and CFO after arrival, in a meeting with a subject listed as "Stock Price." Randall had said that was the plan.

After that there was a working dinner with the CFO and someone named Jalbert from a company called Capital Dynamique. The subject was listed as "Liquidity Event." That sounded like a cocktail party. Jalbert's name was familiar but I couldn't remember where I'd heard it.

Corso must have been a really tough guy to take two meetings in a row after a transatlantic flight. I'd have been totally flaked out, especially after all the wine the French liked with meals. Out of curiosity I did a web search for Capital Dynamique. It turned out to be a Paris investment house that spent a lot of other people's money on technology companies. Jalbert was le President, and there were links to news stories about activist investors. There were at least two activist investor operations involved that wanted to fire Eric, dismember ZYCO and turn it into a financial holding company that didn't make software or anything else except money. I skipped the rest and forwarded the message on to Tidings, including a--I hoped--funny line about Corso's schedule and open bars.

Schmidt's message was dated the evening before. He had examined the electronic devices out of both crashed rental cars. They didn't appear to have been physically tampered with. All were of the proper type, and the FBI said there were no usable fingerprints on any of them. He apologized for not solving the whole case and asked what I wanted him to try next.

I sent him a reply suggesting he call ZYCO to discuss the vulnerability and anything a hacker might leave recognizable behind--nothing, most likely--and went on to the three messages from McCall.

The first was ten days old.

Mike: The governor of Alaska just called to thank me for the assistance with their school buses. He was so enthusiastic about your help I was kind of embarrassed. What the hell have you been doing to those people? Expect a personal letter from the gov. Nice job. McCall.

I smiled. That explained the letter.

The next was from the previous Thursday.

Mike: Got things all set for your flight tests at Pax River next week. You haven't done any flying work for a while, but don't hesitate to stick your oar in the water if you see something you don't like. Use your judgment. See me before you go.

He listed phone numbers, times and places, and I wrote them in my calendar for future reference.

The third was from the previous day.

Mike: An investigator from the Inspector General's office will be by tomorrow at ten AM to question you about ZYCO and your investigation. Stop by my office and bring your notes from the field in C. Springs. See me before ten. McCall.

I had been expecting the Spanish Inquisition to show up, but not so soon. I swore loud enough to draw stares from Sally and the other inmates in the cube farm.

chapter

15

McCall was waiting for me in his office at nine-forty-five.

The vice-chairman, Les Minton, was there, too. I didn't normally see much of Minton. He was a lawyer, formerly a corporate guy with a big aerospace concern, and was mainly responsible for day-to-day operations of the board. He didn't really mix in with the rest of the board members. Short and gray, he looked like he would be more at home in an office on Wall Street than in an airplane's cockpit or the control cab of a train engine.

I said good morning as I entered and they

returned my greeting without rising, or really even moving. They weren't being impolite. I was junior and getting investigated so pleasantries weren't required. McCall did give me a smile of welcome.

The office was in a corner, with large windows on two sides. The day was dark and cloudy, and only weak daylight made it in through the glass. McCall sat in his leather guy-in-charge chair, behind his large, messy desk. He was slouched back in his usual comfortable pose, feet perched on one corner of the desk beside a pile of budget projections for the following fiscal year. Minton sat in a government-issue office chair at one end of the chairman's desk, a stack of reports in his lap. McCall motioned for me to sit in one of two remaining seats in front of the desk.

"Mike," McCall said as I sat down, "I got you in here early specifically not to tell you what to say to this Inspector General guy. Have you even been in an IG investigation before?"

"I've got over ten years of government service, civilian and military, and I've never had the pleasure."

McCall waved a hand in dismissal. "Hey, don't sweat it. This guy's just another government bureaucrat. He's a GS-14, just like you. He's got a checklist to follow and a report to write. He'll ask you some questions, and you answer 'em, and that's it." He winked at me over his glasses. "Of course, he could shoot us all down in flames if he felt like it. That's how they make GS-15 in that shop."

I tensed up, and he laughed out loud. "If you tell 'em only the truth, it's easier to remember what you said." He looked across at his deputy. "Les, anything to add?"

Minton shook his head and adjusted the pile of papers in his lap. "Don't be scared. They can tell. And don't get mad." He half-smiled when McCall chuckled again. "Answer the questions, and don't volunteer anything. If they ask you if you know what time it is, tell them yes. They will follow up with more questions if they need to. Understand?"

I swallowed and tried to nod confidently, but it turned into a spasm.

McCall crossed his arms on his desk. He was actively regulating the level of his Texas accent up or down as required, and he spoke at his folksiest now. "Look, Mike, they aren't after you. Everybody in the press and in the other party in Congress is trying to get at the President. They all seem to think they can get at him through Zygler or me. It's just the usual game they play here. Nothing unusual, nothing personal. You want a friend in Washington, buy a dog. The IG is responding to congressional questions. That's all. In fact, if you look at it just right, they're actually on our side."

I wasn't sure I had a side, but if they were trying to help me relax, it certainly wasn't working.

McCall handed me a slim file across the paper-strewn desk. "This is the flight test plan from the Frenchies for the tests at Pax River. Look it over and recommend anything you want added or removed. And check with Zygler's guys to see if they have any changes they want made."

I took the folder and looked inside. It contained a few pages of Aries letterhead, with a cover letter and five pages of checks and demonstrations. Each checkpoint was covered in a short paragraph, specifying altitude and airspeed, control inputs and expected results. The basic plan was to climb to the approximate altitude of the runway at Colorado Springs, slow to near stall speed, and duplicate the takeoff conditions as precisely as possible. There was a page in the back that specified a simple recording set-up, and some suggested documentation to be produced after the tests. McCall had initialed the top page.

I closed the file and nodded to McCall. "I'll look it over and get back to you."

McCall looked at his computer. "Oh, and I just got a call from Transport Canada. They found the black boxes in the Canadian crash. They have 'em on the surface and they're on their way to Ottawa for reading. They said it would probably be tomorrow."

"Any word on how they looked?" I said.

"The data recorder is pretty much destroyed but

it's possible the voice recorder may be readable."

I grimaced. "Better than nothing."

Before McCall could respond, there was a knock at the door. McCall shouted to enter.

The door swung open and a tall thin man in a cheap-looking suit walked in. He had a hawkish hooked nose and dark blank eyes that reminded me of the IRS agent who had audited me two years before, or the shark I had stared down at an aquarium ten years earlier.

We introduced ourselves. His last name was Mr. Odett, and he didn't give a first name. Fine. I was Mr. O'Hara, thank you. After a few minutes of unpleasant pleasantries, Odett and I adjourned to a small conference room next to McCall' office.

We sat down on opposite sides of the table, and I put a pad and pencil in front of myself. I didn't expect to take any notes, but I always liked to have a prop to fiddle with when I talked.

Odett opened his notebook and smiled a smile that I thought might put his entire face out of service, but when he spoke everything still seemed to work.

"Mr. O'Hara, thank you for taking your time to talk to me today." Like I had a choice. "I'm looking into the conduct of an investigation of the crash of a business jet in Colorado, that I believe you are in charge of."

"OK." I tried to slouch casually, but I felt like a beached whale in the unfamiliar, uncomfortable chair.

He put on a pair of little reading glasses that perched dangerously near the end of his nose and looked at me over the half-lenses. "I have already taken a statement from Chairman McCall, and I visited Mr. Hills in his hospital room." Bastard. "Do you have anything to say before we start?"

I folded my hands on the table in front of me. "Nope. Fire away."

He launched into a series of questions about the overall conduct of the investigation, and I filled him in on the background of the crashes, describing the history of the GMax, and of the unusual aspects of the flight control system. He took copious notes, filling several pages of yellow legal paper in the first few minutes.

After a half-hour of general information about the case and about my background, we spent several minutes covering what I thought to be normal procedure for investigating a plane crash. After additional notes, he began to ask more detailed questions about my actions.

When did I first meet Mr. Zygler? Was there a social relationship prior to my car accident? Did I think the two accidents were related? Did I seriously think that someone had tried to kill me? Why had I not formally reported the murder attempt to the local police? Had Mr. Zygler or any other agents of the ZYCO company appeared to be trying to influence the investigation? Was there any sign of a cover-up by ZYCO, or Aries? Had anyone from ZYCO tried to allay suspicions about their products? Had I been pressured by anyone else? From inside the board? From above, perhaps?

I answered each question the way I thought McCall wanted: directly, succinctly and accurately. I finally stopped Odett. "Look," I said, "I have been in charge of this investigation from the start. Nobody's tried to influence me. ZYCO has been totally cooperative from the word go. Zygler assumed that his software was at fault before we did. He was actually tried to convince me the ZYCO code was the problem."

He looked at his notes for a moment, and then peered at me over the half-lenses again. "Do you feel that the weekend at Mr. Zygler's ranch might have been an attempt to influence your pursuit of the investigation?"

I held back the irritation that was growing. It was like the silly sack of shit hadn't been listening to anything I had said.

"No, Mr. Odett, I don't." I sounded disgusted, and he looked me in the eye as I spoke. "I think it was a very nice invitation to a guy who had been in a car accident from a lonesome man who had just lost a good friend in a plane crash. I slept. I used his Jacuzzi. He had some friends over. We watched some old movies. That's it."

He wrote a note, and asked his next question without looking up. "Did Mr. Zygler discuss employment with you at any time?" This was his bombshell.

Where had he come up with that? Despite the advice from McCall, I found myself searching my memory for the exact wording of the regulation that governed post-government service employment, to make sure I didn't say anything incriminating. Had I stuck to the letter of the law? I thought so.

"Yes," I said. "He did."

Odett peered back at me over his nose-beak, with a look in his eyes that said "Gotcha!"

"And what did he say about employment, Mr. O'Hara?" he said with an oily smile, his eyes half-closed.

I took a deep breath, and spoke louder than I intended to. "He said that I was underpaid. He said that he would like to have me in his company some day because his computer nerds had a hard time coming up with safe real-world solutions, and that he thought I might be able to help. He did not make me an offer, but he led me to believe that the salary he had in mind would be substantially higher than I now receive."

Odett continued to smile. "And you responded?"

I spoke louder still. "I responded by saying that I thought it was inappropriate to discuss that matter while an investigation was in progress, believe it or not. I didn't give him a resume. He didn't make an offer. I told him I was happy in my current position, which is true. That was it. OK?" I looked at the ceiling. "And, oh by the way, did

I mention that he gave me a ride in his private World War II fighter plane? It lasted about an hour. It was possibly about the high point of my life. Is fun against the federal regulations, now, too?" I was almost shouting.

Odett didn't respond to my threatening tone, except by writing more notes. Finally, he answered quietly, "I wouldn't know about that, Mr. O'Hara."

Odett ruffled through another small notebook. I was hoping he was running out of questions, but he had one more shot for me.

"Have you felt pressure from any source to keep the FBI from taking over the investigation?"

This was from deep left field. "No."

"None at all?" He stared at me.

I stared back. "None."

More silence.

"Special agent Tidings has been a good addition to my team. At the current stage of the investigation our work is very technical, and I think you will find he is not an engineer or scientifically trained, nor is he a pilot." I didn't add that he didn't seem to be the sharpest chisel in the toolbox, either. "His help has been very welcome, but I think it would have been inappropriate to shift leadership of the investigation to the Bureau earlier. Situations change as an investigation develops."

We sparred back and forth for another fifteen minutes, until he declared that he had all he needed for the time being. "Will you be in the area for the next few weeks? I may have follow-on questions."

"That depends on what falls out of the sky," I said as we rose from the table. "Aircraft accidents don't follow a schedule. Sorry." We walked out of the room and shook hands stiffly. I escorted him to the lobby, took his visitor's badge and watched him as he waited for the elevator to make sure he got on. When I ducked my head into the McCall's office, he looked up from a thick report with a questioning grin.

"You got mad, didn't you?" he said.

"Yes, I did."

He relaxed, leaning back with his hands clasped behind his head. "I heard you through the wall. Better to be pissed off than pissed on, I guess."

"What happens now?"

He leaned forward again, elbows on the desk. "What happens is, he goes back to his little office and writes a report that says what a crappy job you're doin' in your little office, and it goes up the chain, and everybody whines for a while, and that's about it. Unless you did something wildly illegal, of course. In which case, get yourself a lawyer. Did you?"

"Do something wildly illegal?" I shrugged. "I don't think so."

He sighed heavily, and took his glasses off. "Got a minute? C'mon in. Have a seat." He motioned to the near end of a long leather sofa next to the south-facing window. As I walked across the room and sat down, he came out from behind the desk and sat at the opposite end. He put his feet up on the coffee table, wrinkling the covers of several back issues of Aviation Week and Government Executive magazine with his shoes.

"Haven't seen you in a while. Not vertical, anyway. Feeling OK? Knees better? Head good?" He stared out the window at a plane departing from Reagan National Airport in the distance.

"Fine. Much better." I tried to relax, but I was still keyed up from the interview.

"Good, Mike, good. How did you like running your own investigation?"

I scratched my chin, noticing a place I had missed while shaving that morning. "I liked it, once I got used to Lew not being there. I just wish I could have found a smoking gun."

He shook his head, still gazing out the window. "Don't always find 'em. Montez still working out OK?"

"Yes sir. Great. We work really well together, and she's added a new technical dimension to the team we didn't have. I'm very impressed. She writes well, too. I'm going to have her do the initial draft of the accident report."

McCall looked across the sofa at me, his face serious. "How are you going to word the findings?"

I thought for a moment before answering. "I don't think we can call out a definite cause, even with all the evidence the FBI is bringing in. If they don't indict, I'm not sure we can justify calling the bad control-system code the proximate cause. So I guess I'll say a probable cause is errors in the flight control computer software, possibly inserted by, um..." I searched for the words.

"Person or persons unknown, I think is how they say it," McCall said.

"Yeah."

"You think this guy Sutton did it?"

I shrugged. "Hell, I don't know. I'm not Sherlock Holmes. The FBI types sure seem to think so. He had a reason, and hardly anybody else had both a motive and access. And I do think he's nuts, personally. He called me last night, before I got in."

McCall looked across at me, surprised.

"He left a message on my machine. Said he didn't do it. Sounded pretty crazy."

"But?" McCall fixed me with one of those stares he used to make you stretch your head out.

"I don't have any hard data. But he looks like-- I don't know. I was there when they questioned him. When I looked in his eyes, he didn't look like a predator to me. Not a murderer. He looked like a scared rabbit. I don't usually do gut feelings, but that's all I have."

"That's not hard data. But it'd probably work in

Texas." He checked out the same spot on the floor I was studying. "What did he say in the message?"

"He said he was innocent."

"Keep your eyes open." He sat silently for a moment. "Minton's pissed. Says I let you get too close to Zygler. The legal types aren't happy with me at all." He made a sound like an angry German Shepard. No para break "Shit on 'em." He seemed to have something else to say, but he didn't, and then he stood up. "Check out that flight test plan. Keep me informed of how things are going. Careful how you write the report. Keep it factual. Boring, if you can." He walked back to his desk, the audience over.

I thanked him and headed for the door.

Lee Wang was away from his desk when I returned his call, but he had left a message that the work at the ZYCO hangar was wrapped up. I dialed the number that Tidings had left, but he was not available. I left a message for him to call me back and phoned Anders at NSA.

He answered with the usual extension number and didn't identify himself until I had said my name first.

"Ah, Mr. O'Hara, I'm glad you called," Anders said. "I've been working around the clock on your hardware, but I'm afraid that we're just out of tricks."

I harrumphed. "Doesn't look like you'll be able to read any of it after all?"

"I'm afraid not." He sounded genuinely chagrined. "The code's just been overwritten too many times. What should I do with the hardware?"

I sighed. "It's ZYCO's property. Send it back to them, I guess." I gave him the address on Grimsby's card, and thanked him for the effort. He was still apologizing when I hung up.

I asked Sally if she wanted to have lunch, but she had a date. I got a plastic-wrapped microwave nightmare from a nearby sidewalk kiosk and spent the noon hour at my desk, munching and doing admin, answering emails and reading the must-do paperwork that I had saved.

The test plan that Aries had sent in made good reading, and I added some specific information I would need to the products page. Otherwise, it looked good. I set it on Sally's desk with a note for her to check it out and comment. I also dropped her an email to watch for reports on the Canadian voice recorder and send it to the lab right away if she heard anything.

A nasty note from the travel office came in just before one, reminding me that no travel claim had been submitted for my trip to Alaska. Since the government owed me big money for my expenses on the three-week trip, I got to work on the claim.

I rooted around in my briefcase and found a pile

of receipts, scanned them all into a file after taping them to paper so they wouldn't jam in the scanner, emailed them to myself, downloaded and filled out claim forms, emailed the entire mess to the travel office, and dropped copies of everything, plus all the originals, in my file drawer. On an admin roll, I found receipts from the Colorado job and did them, too. I had to call for help from the travel specialists to make sure I was claiming everything right and wouldn't accidentally draw per diem for the days I spent at Eric's. I wrote a note explaining about the wrecked rental car and attached a copy of the accident report that Officer Maxwell sent me. Attach electronic signature, print, hit send. Neither Alaska nor Colorado is cheap, and the two claims totaled over ten thousand dollars. I crossed my fingers that the payments got to me before the bills were due, but it wasn't likely. I had over three feet of paper files like this in my drawer. Such is the glamor of government service.

Sally rolled back into the office just after two, looking embarrassed. "I'm sorry to be so late," she said quietly to me, looking around to see if anyone else saw her late arrival.

"Have a nice lunch?"

She shrugged, and hung her purse on her chair as she sat down. "It was OK." She named a trendy place on Capitol Hill. "Have you eaten there?"

I looked at the greasy sandwich wrapper in my

wastebasket. "No. I've heard of it. Was the food good?"

"Fine. I saw the Speaker of the House. He's not as fat as he looks on television. All the bigwigs eat there." She was clearly still impressed with being in Washington.

"How's Donald?" I said, while opening my email window.

She was confused for a second. "Oh, you mean David. I didn't see him. He's a VP at a big defense firm on the hill. He's always busy. Kind of cute, but, you know..."

I didn't.

"Anyway, today's guy was a staffer for a senator from Maine. I met him while I was looking for a job, and he called me for lunch over the weekend."

I tried not to get depressed listening to her recital. "Nice guy?" I didn't look up from my computer screen.

"I guess." She sighed. "His phone kept going off. He could have put it on silent, but it buzzed the whole time. He was trying to impress me."

I looked across at her. "That's really DC. Sounds like he did impress you, but not like he wanted to."

"I'm sorry for being late. It won't happen again."

"Don't worry about it. We have such long hours in the field I'm not going to follow you around with a stopwatch. If it's a problem, I'll let you know."

She thanked me, and we went to work.

The shipment from Colorado Springs was

delivered just after three, and we unloaded files until five, unpacking and arranging things so that we could refer to specific parts of the file easily as we drafted the report.

We spent the rest of the week writing. Your typical engineer can't write a snappy sentence or cogent paragraph if his or her life depends on it. The products of the NTSB are usually interesting enough in their contents to get by, but over the years a style has grown up around the board's reports that is at once distinctive yet banal. I showed Sally the standard format, and gave her a couple of old reports to read in order to convey to her the proper mixture of public spirited concern and passive voice pomposity that the wise ones who would review and critique our work would expect.

Her typing was fast but inaccurate, and we found the most efficient sharing of duties was for her to compose the draft, while I revised and copy-edited. As she needed specific information I would find it in the dozens of files we had generated. The arrangement also helped me review the field work the others had done in my absence. I also sent our notes on the test plan to Grimsby at ZYCO, and he returned thanks me and sent a revised, final copy back. There were initials on the scanned cover from himself, the head of the GMax engineering group and Zygler.

By Friday afternoon we were half done, moving at a record pace toward completion. We only needed the results of the flight tests and a few more days to finish the draft.

Just after four, we were shutting down for the weekend when my phone rang. It was Tidings, and I put him on my speakerphone for Sally to hear.

"We're all done questioning Sutton." His voice was scratchy on the speaker.

"Did you come up with anything new?" I said, hopefully.

"Nothing." He sounded tired. "His lawyer is good, and he kept Sutton calmed down. We were hoping he'd break and he seemed close to going off the deep end a couple of times, but every time we had him going, Perry Mason would call a timeout and we didn't get anything solid."

I slouched in my chair, disappointed. "So, no indictment?"

"Doesn't look like it," he said. "I briefed the U.S. attorney last night. She doesn't think there's enough to convict yet, and we're short of resources right now. I can't get agents assigned. She wants a confession. They always want a confession. I need more to convince her, so I can get more agents to work the case. Kind of a big legal pretzel."

"Can you get help from the state police or the locals?" There was a long pause. "This is a federal case. The Bureau works it."

I rolled my eyes in frustration, and tried not to sound pissed off. "Come on, George. Bureaucracy?"

"Yes, bureaucracy. Federal bureaucracy, the very best kind. Deal with it." He left it hanging.

Finally, I took a deep breath and moved on. "Sutton called me the other night. Left a message on my machine."

"No shit?" Tidings seemed surprised. "What'd he say?"

"He just said that he was innocent, and that he didn't understand why they were doing this to him."

"I wonder who his version of 'they' is?" It sounded like a rhetorical question. "He's crazy as a loon, for sure. Even if we took him to court, that lawyer of his would get him off on an insanity plea. He's got all the right twitches."

I nodded into the phone. "He does."

"Are you still doing the flight tests next week?"

"Yep. The ZYCO guys are flying in Monday night." I described the test plan to him. "We have two days set aside, but I think we can do the whole plan in one."

"Any room for an observer?"

I looked at Sally, and she shrugged. "Sure," I said. "I'll check up on that and get back to you Monday by noon. You'll be in your office?" I rolled my eyes at Sally.

He said he would be, and we clicked off after

going through desulatory, regulation polite goodbyes.

I pushed the off-button and looked across at Sally. "If you don't want him around, I'll call him back Monday and tell him to buzz off. I'll make something up."

"I can always carry a whip and a chair."

"He'd probably just like that," I answered, and was rewarded with a smile. "I don't mind. We don't owe him anything."

"It's OK. Really." She smiled for me again, and brushed her hair away from her face. I liked that more than I should have.

At five, I still had a ton of paper to look over, but I told Sally to go home for the weekend. She thanked me and headed out immediately. I imagined she was going on yet another date. Probably with Mr. Right this time, I thought ruefully.

By half-past-six, I was getting tired, and my knees were giving out one more set of accident-induced throbs. I was the last one out of the office for the twentieth time and the lights were out everywhere but in my bay. After tossing two reports from other investigations into my case, I started to reach for my desk light, when the letter from Alaska caught my eye, lying unopened in my in-box. I picked it up and slit the envelope open, thinking that if a reply were needed, I could draft one Saturday after I'd made final changes to the test set-up. I sighed heavily.

I wondered for a minute what Sally would be

doing Saturday night. Dancing? I could imagine her dancing, but not with me. Wild, steamy sex? That, too. I thought briefly about what her hair would look like on her pillow.

The letter.

The governor's note was two pages. It was a personal letter, addressed to McCall with copies to the US Secretaries of Transportation and Education and a courtesy copy to me. It was dated three days after I had left Alaska. It read:

> *Dear Mr. Chairman:*
>
> *Over the past few weeks, Mr. Michael F. O'Hara of your organization has conducted an inspection of a large portion of the school bus fleet used in Alaska, at the request of the State Superintendent of Education. Our buses have been involved in an alarming number of minor accidents, and the NTSB's expertise was invaluable in tracking down the causes for those accidents.*
>
> *Mr. O'Hara worked with our maintenance personnel over three arduous weeks, working in Alaska's cold rain and summer mud, many times more than eighteen hours a day.*
>
> *All who worked with Mr. O'Hara, from the*

garage mechanics to the Superintendent herself, remarked on his technical acumen, hard work and selfless dedication to duty.

Mr. O'Hara recommended a series of detailed inspections of all our school buses, to look for excessive wear caused by the difficult operating conditions in this state.

Despite our tight budget, I ordered the inspections to be carried out over a weekend on an emergency basis, largely due to Mr. O'Hara's persuasive report and presentation.

I want to inform you that these inspections turned up potentially catastrophic problems with four buses and heavy wear on many others. Those problems are being corrected on a warranty basis free to the state by the buses' manufacturer, again largely due to the excellence of Mr. O'Hara's effort.

Mr. O'Hara's dedication and superb work have certainly prevented the injury or even death of many Alaskan school children. I wanted to take this opportunity to thank you for the support that you and your organization have provided to the people of Alaska, and to personally commend the dedicated public servant to whom this state owes so much.

It was signed by the governor himself, no autopen.

I looked at the letter for a long time. It was nice, I thought, but so what? Most of the public thought that all civil servants crawled on our bellies like snakes. All of the federal government's problems were traceable to me personally, or so it seemed from the way political candidates spoke. And I couldn't take a weekend off without some administrative angel of revenge landing on my shoulder and shitting down my back.

Where would I ever go inside the government? I had no great management skills that I could transfer to other agencies or departments. The FAA was a hidebound bureaucracy, and NASA was too. The Department of Transportation was laying off, not hiring. If I worked forever, I might make GS-15 with the Board, or even be an exalted member of the Senior Executive Service. With enough long hours and the right connections, I might be able to make as much as a good real estate agent. I would never be the head of anything, never get past counting my vacation days and writing draft reports that some political appointee would chop the heart out of just because he could.

And besides, there were always plenty of

applicants for jobs on the board, weren't there? If I walked out, ten guys would apply behind me. I had done enough. I was still young enough to make a new start, even if Zygler didn't or couldn't use me. I had done my share, seen enough dead bodies, and worked enough late nights.

I tossed the letter back into my in-box. Flipping off the office light, I headed down to the now-deserted Metro station alone.

c h a p t e r

16

The weekend went by slowly, the way most of them did. Laundry, oil change for the car, workout. I tried to shut the casework off in my brain for the day, to think about anything else for a few hours. It didn't work. Sutton's face kept appearing in my mind. Scared prey instead of hungry predator, being chased by a bloodthirsty pack of FBI wolves. I tried to force myself to concentrate on hard data, technical information, things I knew for sure. But the things I was sure about were the problem. The data were letting me down. The inputs didn't match the outputs.

I thought about going out to a bar or something

on Saturday night, but any place I might have gone would have been filled with people who already knew each other, having fun together. I would have ended up alone in a corner, drinking warm beer and thinking about work, or guessing what kind of fun Sally was having. I could do that at home just as well. So I called in a pizza, got brews from the fridge, watched TV, and reviewed reports and my pile of mail with my feet up.

The latest Aviation Week Online had stories on the GMax crashes and an obituary of Marcel Covert of Aries, dead in the crash off Canada. He had apparently been a lead control software engineer at Airbus before being stolen away by Aries, with lots of French hard feelings and offense taken. A lawsuit apparently got settled somewhere along the line. He would be succeeded at Aries by Stefan Darlan, an ex-professor of computer systems engineering at Ecole Polytechnique. I followed a link to Covert's biography and found his life summarized in three lines--family, education, career. The two pilots got one line apiece.

I wondered how many lines I would get, if any.

There was a link on Stephan Darlan. I followed it out of curiosity, far enough to see his career-arc from academia to industry and back. He had several papers published. They appeared to be in French. With my small French vocabulary I could just make out a few titles that looked like a mix of technology and corporate management. But there was one title in English, a paper titled "The Economics of Innovation in Technology". It had been published six years before, in the Harvard Business Review, and there were a couple of co-authors. One was an H. Randall. Harry Randall. Small world, I thought.

I wrote notes and comments on the two reports until late Saturday, and then went to sleep. Slumber was punctuated by dreams, mostly about Sally and about not being a civil servant anymore. I would be rich, at least a little. I would marry Sally, and trade in my Ford on a supercharged Jaguar. What did those two dreams have in common? Something Freudian?

I didn't know, but while I was awake I tried to imagine what it would be like to be rich and respected. What would I do with more money? I didn't know. Take a vacation? One that didn't include visits to relatives, maybe with some debauchery in Vegas or some place like it. I'd never taken an actual vacation, not a real one.

My mother called on Sunday, during the last quarter of the Redskins game. How was I feeling? Fine. Any dates? No. Was I going to be in town for a while? Hard to tell, Mom, but probably, yes. Dinner next weekend, with the Millers? Sure, Mom, and yes, I'd met their daughter Susan. She was nice, if you got past the annoying laugh and the mustache. She sold computers in Rockville and I was pretty sure she did recreational drugs.

I hadn't told Mom about my car adventure, or the hospital time, or Eric Zygler, or that I was thinking about leaving the board. And I damned sure hadn't talked to her about Sally. She would castigate me for not being engaged already.

Sunday night, while I was putting fresh groceries away after a trip to the nearby megamart, the phone rang. I was expecting Mom again, but it was listed as an unknown wireless number on Caller ID.

"Mike? It's Eric." Zygler sounded relaxed and excited at the same time. There was a lot of side tone noise on the call. "Hey buddy, how are you? Have a good weekend?"

I grinned to myself. "I've been catching up on stuff around home. Trying to get things put away, you know."

"Do you like to skin-dive?" he said.

I said yes, although I hadn't used a mask or fins since I was in the Navy.

"Listen, I found the place. I'm in the air right now. Just left Aruba. Charlene and I found a guide who took us out to this private island. It was outrageous, man. There's this sunken ship, and reefs, and it was a blast. I may buy the goddamn place, just to keep it to myself." He was like a really rich little kid.

"That sounds great, Eric." It really did, too.

"Listen, Mike, are you free in a couple of weeks?

I'm thinking about flying down there again, and we could swing by Washington and pick you up, no problem." The excitement grew in his voice as he talked.

It was too much. There was no way. Not now, not yet. The IG would crawl up my ass with a power tool. "Eric, I can't."

"Sure you can. You get away early Friday. Maybe Sally can come, too." God, that bathing suit, or maybe a bikini this time.

The phone crackled.

"Eric, I'm sorry." I had to speak up to distract him. "I've got the Inspector General down on me now, just for that weekend at your place."

There was a long silence on the line, and the static of the airborne satellite link rose and fell. Finally, Zygler said, "Shit, Mike. Can they do that? Keep you from doing stuff on your own time? You're an American citizen. They can't do it."

I sighed. "Yes they can, Eric. There are rules I have to follow. They think you're trying to influence me."

"Who thinks that?" he shouted, indignant. "I wouldn't do that, and even if I tried it, I know you wouldn't stand for it. This is such bullshit." He sounded on the verge of tears.

"Eric, we'll get this investigation done, and then I'll talk to you again, OK? We can do stuff later, when the paperwork is finished." Having an out-of-control multibillionaire making rude gestures at the Jesuits down at the IG's office wouldn't help my case any.

He was quieter when he spoke again. "Are we still on for the testing on Tuesday? Will the bastards at least let us work together?"

"Yes, sure. I'll meet your plane down there. I've got a little coordinating to do tomorrow, and then I'll head down Tuesday morning. I think we can get all the testing done in one day if we push it."

When he talked again, he was all business. "I looked the test plan over personally. I'm prepared to support the testing any way you want. I'll bring Grimsby and a copilot from Aries, plus all the recording gear you needed. When do you want us there?"

I thought the timing over. It was a three-hour drive to Pax River from my place if I stopped at the office on the way. "I'll meet you at the transient aircraft ramp at nine, and I'll have a brief of the local operating area ready for your pilots."

"OK. Good." He paused, as if he was taking notes. When he spoke again, he sounded more cheerful. "I'll bring a bottle of good scotch and when we're done we can uncork it. OK?"

I laughed and agreed.

"OK, man. See you there." He clicked off.

I stared at the phone for a moment before hanging it up, wanting to laugh out loud. How had all this happened? The call might as well have been from Mars, I decided as I looked around at my apartment. Sure, ace, let's go skin diving in Aruba. Why the hell not? Buy the island if you feel like it.

Monday was hectic. I worked with Sally on the draft, while at the same time checking out details for the testing at PAX. Tie the plane down overnight? Yes. How about renting cars? That was harder, but Hertz would deliver one to the front gate. Could they buy fuel at the base? Yes, and the Navy would take major credit cards. Most of the planning I was doing would never be used, but if we needed them the services would be there.

Cell coverage might be spotty on the flight line so I arranged for a phone line to be run to the airplane on the ramp. We would oversee a complete reload of the software into the GMax's fly-by-wire system, taking about an hour, and then fly the checks called for in the test plan.

My load of paperwork had helped time go by, but near the end of the day I found myself thinking about the entire case again, looking for closure. The relationship of the two crashes seemed obvious, but it didn't close out any of my problems. It should have, I thought, and it annoyed the hell out of me that it didn't. I stared out the office window, desperate for inspiration, or at least motivation.

A Delta Airlines 737 climbed steeply out of Reagan National's main runway and rolled left to follow the Potomac River as it flew out of town. It maintained a precise pitch attitude for the climb-out under the expert control to two professionals on the flight deck.

Sally worked at her desk, hunched over the report draft. I didn't want to disturb her as she wrote, but she seemed relieved when I spoke to her.

"You know, I'm still having a hard time making a couple of pieces fit together."

She looked back at me with a pleasant "so what" expression. "What pieces?"

"The two crashes are so similar."

She glanced back at the screen briefly. "Um, that seems like good news."

"It is. But how does it fit into the whole case?"

She frowned at me, probably peeved at me for starting a new train of thought on a Monday. "It proves there was the same sabotage on both crashes."

"Does it? I think it proves the sabotage was different."

She frowned again, thoughtfully this time. "Keep going."

"Look at it from the angle of some hypothetical whoever that's doing all this. If you were going to kill somebody with bogus fly-by-wire software, would you crash the plane on takeoff? No. If you did that, you'd lay the whole thing out for a crash investigation to find, spread out all over the airport. I'd crash it in the ocean someplace."

"Like the second plane."

"Right. The only reason we have the information we do from Canada is that they had had a radar track and found an oil slick."

She looked at the ceiling. "I see what you're saying. How was it triggered? The Colorado crash happened at the beginning of the flight. Canada was hours after takeoff. If it was just working all the time they would have triggered it earlier in the flight, or caught it during pre-flight checks."

I nodded and ground my teeth a little. "Whoever is did this isn't stupid. It took skill and experience, and a lot of special know-how. But even Einstein made mistakes. There has to be something."

She shook her head. "It had to have been triggered by a timer in the software, or maybe by some event. I don't think you could make a change like that in flight. The special phone connection is gone and the computer modes are wrong in flight conditions. So..." She pointed an accusatory finger. "The bogus software wasn't exactly the same in both planes. The triggers were different."

"Right," I said, louder than I meant to. "So, say the first crash didn't go how our killer wanted. Say it happened too soon. So he made a change and got it uploaded before the second flight took off." I stopped for a second to formulate the right question. "If you had the original bad code in front of you, how long would it take you to make that change?"

Sally considered. "An hour. Maybe less."

"You could do that on pretty short notice, then. How long would it take to transmit and load the change into the plane if it is was hooked up for maintenance?"

She pulled down the calculator on her phone and punched in numbers, mumbling to herself. "About twenty megabytes. Divide by sixty." She looked up from the phone. "About a minute and a half. Say two minutes to allow for loading protocols and everything."

"So we should look for calls going to the French plane or hangar or whatever about two minutes long before the second plane got prepared for its last trip. Maybe the FBI can do something with that."

"Maybe. I hope so. But Mike, I looked at the stuff Eric sent me on the control system. Remember, that special logic he called 'steered failover'? It would have to have been completely disabled, without showing a sign of it ahead of time. I studied it, and it's really complicated. It's beautiful work. But it's really intricate."

"Baroque software?"

She pondered for a second. "Like that. The failover logic is woven into everything, like a special thread in a fabric. You know what I mean?"

"You don't think the FBI can handle it? They're actually pretty good."

"I know. But whoever did this isn't some teenage propeller-head working out of his mother's spare bedroom. It would be as hard to mess with as it was to design in the first place. Maybe harder. We're not looking at stab wounds from a knife fight. This is open heart surgery." She paused and arched an eyebrow. "It's like something out of Sherlock Holmes."

"Sam Spade, sister," I said.

I tried to call George Tidings, but he was away from his desk for the afternoon. No answer on his cell, so I left a message saying we had news for the Bureau, and suggesting he meet me at the base ops building at Pax River the next morning. I wrote his number in my book and shot him an IM to back up. He answered back with a "thanks" and sent an email that came in a couple of minutes later, thanking me for the information from ZYCO. He explained that the liquidity event reference on Corso's schedule was probably about a stock sale, public offering or some other capital project to raise liquid financial assets--as in money--and had nothing to do with beer.

My phone rang at just after four. I answered without looking at the caller ID. To my surprise it was Liz Fowler from the Colorado Springs newspaper, the reporter who had written the hatchet-job article and the editorial about the investigation and me. It was Friday night, I had spent too much of the last week with the IG, and I didn't have the time or urge to discuss anything more with her. She started to talk but I cut her off.

"Ms. Fowler, if you have any more questions about the investigation, you should call the board's public affairs officer. I have her number for you if you need it." I listened to the background and didn't hear her typing. Hand written notes now, I thought.

She spoke quietly, not the truth-machine word warrior she had been the last time we talked. "I don't blame you for being mad. I am sorry to disturb you, but I want to apologize."

This was an interesting tactic that I hadn't heard from the press before. I stayed silent, shields up, waiting for more.

She went on slowly and carefully, like she'd rehearsed her lines.

"I want you to know that the article that was published was changed extensively by my editor, and I had nothing to do with the headlines or the editorial. That work did not meet my personal standards as a journalist."

Personal standards as a journalist? Big deal.

I snapped a little. "So, do I have to file a claim or something to get my seventy-five cents back?" Sarcasm worked for me. It felt good. I waited for her response.

"I hope it didn't cause you any problems personally."

"As a matter of fact, it did," I answered, sounding a little hotter than I should have. "Unless you can invent a story that will suck all that crap back out of the heads of everybody who read it, I'll be dealing with it for a while. I'm very interested in hearing what you plan to do along those lines."

Enough. She was probably recording all this for a television special or something. I shut up.

"Mr. O'Hara, I resigned from the paper."

I was silent for a few seconds, caught on the wrong foot by her news. If it was a tactic, if was working. I did a mental double-take. "I, uh, well, I'm sorry it came to that."

"Yes. I am, too." She started talking now, like she needed somebody to dump it all out on. "I think you've been manipulated by Zygler, and all the money and things he has. But I realize now that I've been manipulated, too. Everybody involved seems to be screwing with somebody else. I've been searching for good guys here, and I'm not sure there are any now. But I don't think that makes you a bad guy. I looked over my notes again, and I may have been overzealous about going after you. And then the editor made it worse. I don't know how I am going to get it right, but I am going to somehow." Sure you are, I thought. Sure.

I heard her take a deep breath. "You should be careful. This has all been pretty hard for me to understand, but as I said, it's more complicated than it looks."

All this was interesting but not useful. I wished her well, thanked her for her interest in transportation safety and hung up on her. I slammed the phone down harder than I should have with government equipment. That felt good, too.

I offered to meet Sally at the office and drive her down to the base. She agreed quickly, and I arranged to meet her at 5:00 a.m. I looked forward to the drive alone with her, even if I could only listen to her voice and hear her laugh. And maybe if we talked about the whole case it would start to make sense to me.

At the end of the day, I preloaded all the paperwork and gear that we would need for the tests in a large canvas bag. I parked the bag next to my desk and, 5:00 p.m. having arrived, announced that we were done for the day. Sally cleared off her desk, and we headed for the elevator together.

While we waited for the doors to open, I tried to summon up the optimum words to ask her to dinner. Nothing fancy, just friends. Two professionals, sharing a quick bite. Maybe we could talk about her impressions of the office.

The elevator arrived before I could say anything. We got on, elbowed our way into the crowded car and rode down in silence, exchanging muted goodbyes as I got off to head for the Metro station.

I caught the Orange line Metro train as usual, riding out to Virginia in a car loaded with tired-looking women from the Department of Education and men in cheap suits trying to sleep standing up. I pretended to read the paper, surreptitiously eyeing my fellow riders. Could they guess I would be running flight tests of a multi-million-dollar business jet tomorrow? Or that I would be out of the Washington grind forever in another six months?

Probably not.

I walked the two blocks to my apartment from the station with a spring in my step, flipping my brief case around dangerously, swinging it by the handles, and garnering stares from my fellow commuters. Check this out! Spin! Catch! I smiled to myself. Let 'em guess what I was thinking about. They'd be torqued if they knew, I thought with warm detachment.

I grabbed the bills and fliers in my mailbox and took the steps two at a time up to my apartment. It felt like gravity had suddenly been cut by half, as though the funding for all gravitational activities had been cut for the current fiscal year. Maybe there was more oxygen in the air than usual.

The message light was glowing on the phone, announcing that it had received two calls while I was out. I tossed the mail on the kitchen table and considered ordering a yet another pizza as I pushed the retrieve button.

The first call was a botched marketing attempt, with the clicking of an auto-dialer filling a few seconds before announcing a call time of 10:48 a.m.

The next call was from Tom Sutton.

His voice sounded sad, tired, miserable, like he had no friends left in the world. Tidings had hinted that the FBI was going to let him off the hook, and if so I would have expected him to at least sound relieved. But he was even more morose than he had been in the previous call.

"This is for Michael O'Hara." He stopped to sob quietly. His speech was slurred, as though he had been drinking. "I'm giving them what they want. I don't understand why they're doing this to me, but it's all over. I can't take it. I'm totally innocent. You've got to believe me. Nobody else does. Even my lawyer thinks I did it. My family..."

He cried again, longer this time. "I can't take any more of this. I just hope they don't do the same thing to you that they're doing to me. Tell them they have all they want. I have no reason to lie about this. I am going to do the one thing I can do to make you believe me. I am innocent of whatever the hell it is they think I did. And I have no reason to lie. Not now." I heard him take a deep breath. "Goodbye."

There was a thunk, the sound of the telephone being set down on a desk or table. There were mechanical clicks in the background noise. I shook my head as the message ran on, wondering why he had called right then and what the hell he wanted from me.

A crack rang out from the recorder, loud enough to startle me out of my thoughts. I stared at the machine now. What the hell was that? A gunshot?

Almost immediately after the crack, a thud came out of the speaker. It sounded like a sack of gravel hitting the floor. I listened in horror for a few more seconds. I sat down heavily in a chair next to the kitchen table.

I could hear the sound of a door opening, and then a woman began to scream. "Mr. Sutton! Oh, my God!" The scream came again, longer and louder as the screamer neared the phone.

More clunks came from the speaker as the screamer picked up the handset. "Hello!" she shouted. "Who is this? Get off the line! I have to call 911!" There was a click as the line went dead.

The machine went through its normal sequence, as though the suicide of a pitiful, tortured, insane man had not just been captured in its memory. "Monday, 3:51 p.m." There was a beep. "End of messages."

I stared into space. Time passed and I sat there trying to grasp what had happened.

Jesus.

I looked at my watch. The call had come in just over two hours before. What the hell do you do when somebody two time zones away commits suicide on your answering machine?

I picked up the phone and started to dial 911, then stopped. What good would that do? What was I going to report?

I thought for a minute. Who needed to know?

I dialed Eric Zygler, punching the numbers from memory. The phone rang several times before a distressed sounding woman answered.

"Mr. Zygler's office." Her voice was clipped, stressed out.

"Hi, this is Mike O'Hara at NTSB. Is Mr. Zygler available?"

She hesitated. "No, I'm sorry, Mr. Zygler isn't taking calls. We've had a problem here in the office."

"Yes," I said. "I know. How about Mr. Randall? It's very important."

She agreed to check, and a few minutes later a tired sounding Harrison Randall came on the line. "Randall," he said.

"Harry, this is Mike O'Hara."

"Oh, Mike, my god, have you heard? Poor Tom Sutton's killed himself."

I nodded into the phone as I spoke. "Yes, I know. He left me a suicide note on my answering machine. I heard the whole thing."

"Oh, God. How awful for you. I'm so sorry. His secretary said the phone was off the hook when she walked in."

"He was calling me." I inhaled deeply. I was starting to feel ill, from stress and shock and, weirdly, hunger. "Is there anything I can do?"

"No, I don't think so." He sighed. "They've taken the body away already. I suppose the police might want a copy of the message. Where can they call you?"

I gave him my phone number. "Will Eric want to reschedule the testing, Harry?" I asked. "I can move things a few days if he does."

"No, no, I've already asked him, but he's adamant. Eric and I are heading for Paris right after the tests. We're leaving for the airport in just a few minutes. We'll meet you as scheduled."

"Does the press know about Sutton yet?"

Randall sighed again, theatrically. "I'm writing a press release now. The jackals will be circling in a few hours."

"That's probably why he wants to leave town. He

wants to work and avoid the shit that they'll throw at him." I couldn't think of anything else to say. I felt powerless and frustrated. "Look, tell him if there is anything I can do to help, just call. I guess I'll see you both there." We commiserated for a few more minutes and hung up.

I called the chairman at home but his wife said he was out of town, which I knew but had forgotten. He carried his phone all the time but was hard to get to answer. After leaving a message to call me at home later that night or at the Pax River Operations Office the next day, I called his voicemail at the office and left the same message there, too.

What else? I called Tidings, who was having dinner in a room full of noisy children, and told him about Sutton's suicide. His response was typical FBI. "OK, we kind of expected that. He was guilty as hell."

"I thought the Bureau was going to let him go."

"For now. I was going to tell him tomorrow. But it was just temporary. Zygler's guy has been giving us plenty. We were going to keep watching Sutton to see if he did anything incriminating. I guess this is pretty incriminating. It was probably the best thing for him to do when you think about it. See you tomorrow."

I hung up, thinking about Tidings' words. Best thing to do? And who was Zygler's guy?

I called Sally but she wasn't home. I decided not

call her cell or leave a message. I shook my head.

Alone and out of ideas, I walked to the kitchen sink and splashed water on my face.

I stood and stared at the answering machine again for several minutes, wondering what to do. Finally, I punched up Sutton's message and listened to it again. A little morbid, I thought, but it was my message.

I heard the sad, insane voice of Tom Sutton one more time, listening to his voice, parsing his words. I wondered what my last words would be.

As he spoke, something caught my attention. What the hell had he said?

"I can't take any more of this. I just hope they don't do the same thing to you that they're doing to me. Tell them they have all they want. I have no reason to lie about this. This is the one thing I can do to make you believe me. I am totally innocent of whatever the hell it is they think I did. I have no reason to lie now."

And then he said goodbye.

His last sentence stopped me.

"I have no reason to lie now." He knew his next move was going to be to blow his brains out. It was the last statement of a dying man. A deathbed declaration. Like a deathbed confession in reverse.

I was numb. I felt that the weight of all the stars and all the planets had fallen and landed on my head. I couldn't breathe. This couldn't be right.

Tom Sutton had wanted me to believe that he was innocent, and now I did.

"I have no reason to lie now."

Sutton had said seven words and the pieces started to fall together.

The evening passed surreally, like I was on some mind-altering drug.

I drank all the beers left in my refrigerator.

Sleep was impossible. I stared at the ceiling.

I could hear Lew Hills laughing at me. "Once you eliminate all the bullshit, you have to fit what's left together. That will give you an answer, even if it looks wrong. The hard part is eliminating the bullshit. You have to answer all the questions in your mind, not just the easy ones."

It was as if I had been sleepwalking since the case started. The evidence had been in front of me all along, but I had chosen to ignore the inconvenient parts. I had no technical or legal case, just enough innuendo and circumstantial evidence to be absolutely sure.

There were probably a hundred people in the world who could have committed these crimes, but the investigation had fingered two other men besides Tom Sutton who had ability and opportunity to wreck N215ES. Marcel Covert from Aries was one. He was dead in a crash, and Sutton was now, too. Leaving one.

Eric Zygler.

It had to be him. Ability, motive, opportunity. It had to be. Didn't it?

The killer had murdered seven people, eight now if you counted Sutton. And if I couldn't come up with proof or a confession, I would be helping him get away with it.

Eric Zygler.

I didn't want it to be true. I couldn't make it work in my mind. But he had manipulated me like a computer. He had waved money and the promise of an easy life in front of me, and I wanted it to be true so much I checked my brains at the door and bought off on it. His friendship and concern and promises must have been as fake as his wife's tits. What a jerk I'd been.

More hours staring at the ceiling. I worked harder at making the pieces fit together in my head. The facts would provide an answer. They had no reason to lie, either.

At three I got up and drove my car to the office. The building was deserted and dark, and my footsteps echoed across the lobby and down the halls as I walked. I had to use my security pass in a special slot to make the elevator move, and again to open my office door. I flipped on my desk light and sat there in the little cone of illumination. I felt more alone than usual.

The hard questions gnawed at me. Did he really kill all those people? Did he really try to kill me?

Why would he do it? They were trying to steal the company from him, true. But he was unbelievably rich and powerful. He could just start a new company and hire all the ZYCO guys who weren't traitorous bastards away. With his money, surely he could keep it private and run things the way he wanted to. Or just sit on his billions and play. Whatever.

And how did Covert get involved? I had assumed Zygler needed help to do the bogus software. But he could probably do the job in his sleep. Why get some outsider involved that could chicken out and turn him in?

Maybe my new best friend Eric Zygler was just an insane, murderous nut job. People committed arson to see the Fire Department come running. Maybe he got off on crashing planes and watching the NTSB. He didn't seem like a homicidal maniac to me, but then I'd never actually met a maniac, homicidal or otherwise. He wasn't a loner and didn't keep to himself or anything. I wouldn't know a serial murderer if one crawled up behind me and bit me on the butt. What did they look like?

But it had to be Eric Zygler. Who else could it be? He'd manipulated me, used his money and friendship and offers to share in his fortune to influence me, to the point of obsessive creepiness. That couldn't have been real. Every pat on the back and appreciative word must have been carefully calculated to draw me off and protect him. And I'd fallen for everything.

What to do? If I went forward with what I had now, nobody would believe me. I wasn't sure I did. It would be the word of a world-class technical talent and billionaire entrepreneur against a petty federal bureaucrat. I'd get sliced into small pieces.

Why hadn't those clowns from the FBI cracked this case? Why was it falling to me?

It didn't all add up. All the pieces weren't there. But it was time to bring it together.

I would have to extract a confession. They always wanted a confession.

I sat, not moving until just before five. Then, after turning off my desk light and picking up the flight test bag, I walked numbly to the elevators and rode down to my car.

Sally was waiting for me with a bright smile that evaporated when she saw me. "Mike, what's wrong?" she said as we got into the car.

I didn't answer, and tossed my bag roughly into the back seat.

I drove the car hard, faster than I should have, secure in the knowledge that the district police were usually too scared to come out in the dark. Sally finally grabbed my arm and sternly told me to slow down.

As I dropped to a legal speed, she asked me what was wrong again.

"Sutton killed himself," I said in a harsh tone.

"Oh, no. He must have felt so guilty."

"He's not guilty. He's just dead. That makes eight."

She looked across at me, her eyes wide. "What do you mean? Didn't the FBI--"

"Tidings doesn't know shit." I muttered this time, and forced myself to calm down. Sally must have felt like she had fallen in with a mad man.

Finally, when I'd turned onto the Washington Beltway and was heading east into the brightening sky, I was calm enough to speak. "Sally, I'm afraid I've screwed this investigation up pretty badly. I think I'm going to resign."

"I think there's been an attempt to influence me, to keep me from seeing the truth, and up until now it's been working really well."

We rode the rest of the way to Pax River in silence. By the time another twenty miles of rural Maryland passed by, I knew the hardest question I had to answer. I just didn't know how I would do it.

17

The Patuxent River Naval Air Station is the home of the Navy's flight test center. The field is located in southeastern Maryland on the shore of the Chesapeake Bay on a large peninsula called Cedar Point. I had taken a training class there during my Navy time and had badly wanted to return for the excellent and hard-to-get flight test engineer course. But I had left the Navy before the selection board reported out.

I had looked forward to this trip back to the old base, but the station and the day both looked bleak to me despite the warm breezes, clear skies and the lovely woman who rode with me. The job I had to do that day would be harder than any I had ever tackled, and the cost of failure higher. I had to get it exactly right the first time.

I showed my Navy reserve ID to the gate guard and he waved me through to the security office where we checked in and drew passes. I followed the main drag to the turn-off for base ops, and drove down the road past the old bachelor officer's quarters, which were still as scuzzy as I remembered.

I pulled my car into the parking lot adjacent to the wide expanse of sun-bleached concrete that marked the transient aircraft parking area and left Sally in the car while I went into the front office for an airspace brief. She was happy to wait outside, probably to avoid being around me in my surly mood.

I hadn't felt able to explain myself. I am an engineer. My entire being demanded a clear answer from hard data, and I didn't have one. But at least my task was clear and that gave me a kind of inner peace. I had one path to follow: Identify the murderer and then announce it to the world, or at least to the FBI. Success could mean the downfall of a new and brilliant friend who held a key to a future I couldn't have dreamed about before I'd met him. Failure would almost certainly cause the end of my career and life as I knew it. I couldn't possibly win either way, but there it was.

McCall had greased the skids thoroughly. A full

commander met me and gave a fast but complete brief in the military fashion on everything I needed to know. There were no extra words or niceties, just blast the facts to me and let's go. I filled a page of my notebook, found the two hundred feet of telephone cord stacked inside the door onto the flight line as promised, and checked out the crew briefing room I had arranged. The fuel truck would meet the airplane on arrival, to bring its weight up to the desired level, and sandbags were available to adjust the aircraft's center of gravity, if needed.

McCall hadn't called as I'd requested, but I was almost glad. I didn't want to have to explain things.

All set.

When I returned to the car it was nearly nine, and Tidings pulled up as I walked out. I waved him over and greeted him as cheerfully as I could.

"Morning, George," I said with an artificial smile. My face felt wooden.

"Morning," he answered gruffly. "They here yet?"

"Due in any time. We're all ready." I gave him another artificial smile. "So, do you have your gun with you today?"

He looked at me like I had grown another eye. "Of course. I never go anywhere without it."

I raised my eyebrows. "Handcuffs?" I made the question a joke.

He became even more perplexed. "Got something

kinky planned?" This guy never failed to annoy me.

"You can never tell."

"So Sutton offed himself, huh?"

I answered through clenched teeth. "Yeah. Bummer."

I told him about our idea on what to look for to find last-minute download for the bogus code. He was interested enough to make a quick call to get his team searching phone records again. Even if the effort produced usable evidence, there was no way it would happen soon enough to be in time.

We turned at the sound of high-bypass fanjets approaching. Sally got out of my car and joined us by the parking area fence. The Aries GlobalMax, number N216ES, resplendent in its high-gloss paint and flashy ZYCO logo on the tail, was taxiing across the ramp from the active runway precisely on time.

A sharp young sailor in blue utilities directed the gleaming jet into a parking place between a new Navy F-35 fighter and an elderly, soot-stained Orion patrol bomber. I could see Grimsby in the pilot seat, his head moving as he shut down engines and set brakes. The air stair door at the front of the passenger cabin swung down, steps folding neatly into place, and Zygler bounded down and onto the ramp with a wave and a broad smile. Harry Randall was a few steps behind him, looking tired, and also relieved to be out of the airplane.

We walked the fifty yards to where Zygler greeted me at the foot of the stairs, face smiling but serious, pumping my hand. He was telegraphing just the right mixture of sorrow over Sutton's death and happiness at seeing me. "Hey, buddy, great to see you," he said with quiet warmth.

He turned to Sally, and the two exchanged friendly hugs and a peck on the cheek, like old friends. That must be how he did it, I decided at that moment. He manipulated people with his smiles, his unexpected friendship, the money-amplified personal charm of a mega-billionaire.

Sally smiled her most beautiful smile for him and I seethed, wanting to grab his neck and choke the life from him, killing him like he had killed the others.

"Shall we get this show on the road?" I said above the roar of an F-18 taxiing past. I forced another smile.

"Let's do it!" he shouted over the din. His expression was serious, but he slapped me on the back, sharing guy vibes like a football player after a touchdown.

Grimsby asked the young sailor to summon a fuel truck and gave him details about fueling the beautiful ship. The petty officer looked the new plane over with wide eyes and ran off to arrange the work.

Sally, Tidings and the copilot, a handsome young man in Ray-Bans with a perfect tan, went to work stringing the telephone cable to the airplane's aft equipment bay, to begin the process of downloading the flight software from ZYCO headquarters in Colorado. The complete transfer of computer code for the entire system would take more than a half-hour.

I led Zygler and Grimsby to the operations room for a pre-flight brief.

The briefing room was windowless and the walls were plain white. The florescent lighting flickered slightly as we spread a chart of the local area out over the conference table that filled the center of the room. I passed out copies of the test plan to Zygler and Grimsby. Grimsby copied numbers and words onto a clipboard as I recited radio frequencies and call signs.

I put my copy of the plan down in the middle of the chart. "The basic idea is that we are going to duplicate the conditions existing just before the crash as carefully as possible. We'll have the loading as close as we can get."

Grimsby nodded his agreement.

"We'll climb to sixty-one hundred feet, about the altitude of the field at Colorado Springs. You'll slow the airplane to minimum speed in the takeoff configuration, then go to takeoff power and climb out normally. We'll run through the test sequence several times, and Sally will record data as we go. Any comments?"

Grimsby flipped to the second page of the test plan. "I've got one thing. I've been in the simulator, working on a better way to reproduce takeoff conditions.

I'd recommend we start six hundred feet above the test altitude. I'll put the ship into a wheels-down, power-off stall, or as close to one as the flight control system will let me, then push the nose over and let the plane drift down to sixty-one hundred feet at minimum speed. About fifty feet above the right altitude, I'll go in with full power, and fly through the acceleration to takeoff speed in a level attitude." He looked across the table with a smile. "Make sure your seat belts are tight. It's a little acrobatic, but the simulation's much better."

Zygler was enthusiastic. "Harry hates stuff like this. Twenty bucks says he throws up." There was a chuckle around the table.

"OK, that's the plan, then." I pointed on the chart to a small island across the bay from the base. It was surrounded by a large box, and the words "Military Operating Area," with fine print explaining the penalties for unauthorized penetration. "This is the bombing range at Bloodsworth Island. They normally test bombs and missiles there, but nobody has anything scheduled today. We'll use the operating area around the range for our tests."

Grimsby studied the chart, copying coordinates to be punched into the plane's navigation system. "I'll start at the north end, and we can do two or three cycles before I'll need to turn around. Is there a special controller for the range?"

I quoted another radio frequency and a special radar transponder code. "Call Echo Control when you enter or leave the range. Otherwise, the area's ours."

We all agreed on the test plan and spent another ten minutes discussing details.

I relaxed enough to respond to Zygler's comments, but as the flight drew nearer, I was filled with raw tension made my head pound and skin feel cold. I recognized the sensation from flying in the Navy. It was a peculiar sort of fear: A fear of failure.

Sally entered the room a few minutes later and announced that the download and refueling were complete. We gathered up our gear and walked out onto the ramp together, blinking in the fall sun.

Grimsby and Sally climbed the air stairs into the GlobalMax's cabin, but Zygler hung back, and caught my elbow before I could board. "Are you OK, buddy?" A look of deep concern showed in his eyes as they peered out through his thick glasses.

I didn't answer, avoided eye contact, and tilted my head toward the open door. "Let's go."

He hung back for a moment searching my face, and I looked away again. "Sure, man, let's do it."

I climbed the stairs and Zygler followed close behind, pulling the door up after him. He secured the heavy door handle for flight with a practiced flip of the wrist, arming the cabin door seal so that it would inflate and hold the door in place when the cabin pressurization kicked in after takeoff.

Sally and Tidings were already seated in a pair of forward facing seats in the middle of the cabin. Sally was in the seat where Wes Corso had ridden during the accident flight. Randall was by himself in the next row on a side-facing couch. He looked nervous and clutched at his seat belt.

Zygler and I slid into the two opposite aft-facing seats and fastened our seat belts as the engines started. Their whine built in volume as they lit off and spun up to idle speed.

As I looked around the cabin, the word "opulent" crept into my mind. I had never seen the interior of a GMax that wasn't burned out and splashed with blood. The seats were creamy leather, indescribably soft but comfortable enough to spend hours in without discomfort. The cabin was furnished in soft wools and polished hardwoods. The fixtures on the bar at the rear of the cabin were coated in gold, and the door that separated the flight deck from the main cabin had a large ZYCO logo etched in.

Sally had unfolded a small table from the cabin wall next to her seat and placed her laptop computer on it, securing it incongruously with large rubber bands. On the floor below her seat was a small digital recorder to save sounds and voices during the tests. A microphone was taped to the ceiling in the middle of the cabin. She activated the recorder, leaving the computer off in accordance with FAA directives about running electronic equipment during takeoff, but she checked a cable that was plugged into a port in the computer's rear panel. The cable ran aft to a connection into the main flight control system bus outside the rear equipment bay.

Zygler picked up the telephone intercom. "Ready whenever you are, Dave."

Almost immediately the brakes released and I felt the plane taxi smoothly away from its parking place. Grimsby had left the door to the cockpit open, and over the low whine of the plane's massive engines I could hear him discussing taxi instructions with the Pax River ground controller. We rolled between rows of military airplanes, past several aircraft of various types that the test pilot school employed, and past a large white four-engine jet with odd bulges on its wing tips. I recognized it as a nuclear command aircraft, a relic of the cold war, waiting for the call to launch into the relative safety of the sky in the event of a nuclear attack: a TACAMO--it stood for Take Charge And Move Out.

That was what I had to do. The thought of a nuclear war reminded me of the reception I was going to get if I failed in my plan that day.

At the end of the active runway we waited while a small trainer took off, and then we rolled out onto the mile-and-a-half-long concrete strip. Grimsby, audible on the cabin speakers, made another deal with the controllers, and the GlobalMax began to accelerate.

Despite being heavily loaded with fuel and sandbags to simulate the conditions of a Colorado-to-Paris flight, the plane drove hard down the runway and lifted smoothly. The nose pitched up to a fifteen-degree angle as the wheels broke free of the ground. The jet surged upward without hesitation, climbing quickly through the low-altitude turbulence that was common in Maryland skies. I felt myself pressed into the seat bottom, while being thrown aft out of the backward-facing seat, and I held onto the seat's arms to brace myself. Randall was bracing himself on the couch. He had assumed the scared-of-flying position, hands on his seatbelt, eyes closed, head down. He twitched every time we hit a bump.

I glanced across at Zygler. He was smiling at Sally, who was grinning back. "Isn't this great? It'll out-climb my P-51. I love this ship." He continued to smile while the naval air station rapidly disappeared below and behind us.

I tried to imagine how Corso, Fleet and Berry had felt as the now-dead GMax had stalled in the clouds on that dark night. How had the terror of knowing of their impending deaths felt? Like a sagging loss of lift and an uncontrollable roll? Like hanging upside-down from your seat belt while a jet airplane fell to earth? Or maybe it was more like a stab in the back.

It took less than three minutes to reach test altitude. Grimsby pushed over to level flight more quickly than he would have had he been on a routine mission to deliver techno-nerds to some distant customer. The maneuver left us all light in our seats for a few seconds. Randall was in agony briefly. Tidings grabbed his seat belt momentarily, and then grinned sheepishly. A little hot-dogging by the pilots was acceptable on a test flight.

We turned back over the field and I stared out the window pensively, still avoiding Eric Zygler's eyes. I was afraid he would know what I was about to do and try to talk me out of it, or maybe strike me dead somehow.

The good weather on the Chesapeake had brought the crabbers out in huge numbers. A strong, steady wind blew out of the south, whipping up white caps, and the boats and the red and green buoys marking the shipping channel bounced visibly in the waves. I watched as the boats slid into view in the forward end of the window, cruised past and were lost from sight astern under the GMax's broad wing. I tried to count them all to keep my brain busy but there were too many.

After only ten minutes, Grimsby turned on the overhead intercom speakers. "Mr. Zygler, we're in the test area now. I need to burn off about two hundred pounds of fuel, so I'll be doing a few turns here for a couple of minutes." It was time to get down to business.

Zygler picked up the handset. "Fine, Dave, let us know when you're in position and ready to start." Grimsby clicked his mic button twice to answer and one wing dipped, the plane swinging around in the first of several steep turns.

As we turned the sun shone in through the windows, round shafts of harsh light sweeping the cabin, illuminating first Sally, then Tidings and then Zygler, and me in turn.

Grimsby's voice came over the intercom again. "I'll be set up shortly, Mr. Zygler."

Zygler thanked him and turned to Sally. "All ready?"

She nodded, her expression business-like, and opened the computer, booting up and clicking her way into the data-collection program she had assembled. "All set."

Grimsby called again, giving a thirty-second standby. Zygler gave me the handset. "You're in charge, Mike. Ready whenever you are."

I took the intercom and spoke to Grimsby. "I'll give you a time mark at minus thirty seconds, and you can push over and start the first test when you're ready. Switch to the center computer, with the flight control system in normal mode now."

"OK, normal mode confirmed, and FCS

computers are now in 'B' lead." I nodded to Eric.

The engines slowed noticeably and Grimsby raised the plane's nose. "I'm setting up the takeoff configuration now." There was a rumbling from the floor as the wheels lowered. As I watched, the wing flaps moved to their takeoff setting, sliding back a couple of feet and deflecting down ten degrees. "Ready," Grimsby said finally.

I looked at Sally and she nodded to indicate that the data recording program was running. "OK, mark. Thirty seconds and counting," I said with a look at my watch. "Go ahead and push when you're ready."

"Roger," Grimsby said, his voice rasping over the cabin speakers. "Twenty-five seconds to push."

My heart was beating so fast and hard now that I could hear the blood pounding in my head, even over the engines. If I didn't make my move now, there would never be another chance. It was time.

Smiling my best, I cleared my throat. Suddenly, my fear was gone. I leaned forward and spoke up for the benefit of the recorder and everybody in the cabin. "By the way, Eric, did I tell you about the breakthrough the NSA had?"

Randall relaxed his death grip on his seatbelt, and gave me his attention. So did Tidings.

Zygler looked at me. "No, what did they find?"

"They finally got the code off that erased section

of the computer memory I sent them. It took a while, but they got a good copy." I was a little disturbed by how well I lied.

"Twenty seconds," Grimsby said from the cockpit.

Zygler showed some surprise, but he nodded. "A good copy? Do they know what it is?"

I said cheerfully, "Oh, yeah, turns out it's the driver for the elevators. They aren't sure, because they didn't have another one to compare it to, but they said it looked pretty normal. Can't tell why it was erased."

Zygler was hard to read. He was deep in thought, considering the news.

"I'm glad we got it in time to test," I said. "I got it out to your people in Colorado Springs this morning by wire, and we downloaded it into the 'B' computer. Great work, don't you think?"

Zygler spoke calmly, his voice clear. There was no conflict in his face or his speech now. "Good. I have complete confidence in the code and the system. Let's test the hell out of it."

That was another piece of the puzzle, and it had clicked into place. But this piece changed the picture instantly. Zygler's face was filled with confidence and pride. He didn't look like a predator, either.

I had a feeling that I had experienced once before, on my first parachute jump, right when the chute cracked opened. Eric Zygler hadn't tried to kill me. He didn't crash those planes or kill those people.

I looked across at Randall. He had a death grip on the cushions of the couch, and his face was stretched tight with fear now.

"You mean it's loaded now?" Randall nearly cried, his voice a squeaking shout. He knew that software was a proven killer. It had worked like a charm, twice. It would do its job again, no problem.

I nodded slowly. "Yep. We're flying with the code from the crashed plane driving the flight controls."

"Ten seconds," the pilot said.

Tidings was staring at all three of us, not understanding what we were talking about. A confused stare crossed his face, like he was a spaniel listening to an opera.

What was left of Randall's Ivy League cool had dissolved. His skin was white and dripping sweat. "You can't." He shook his head, the first tinges of panic starting to show.

My plan was working.

"Don't do it!" His voice rose still higher. He leaned over toward me, reaching for the handset. "Stop! It'll crash! It'll go down! We'll crash!"

I held the microphone out of reach. "Why, Harry? What's wrong with the code?" I spoke loudly, trying to keep the venom from my voice, and not succeeding.

"Five seconds."

He was quaking in terror, and his face was pale and shiny with sweat, the way I had seen Tom Sutton while he quaked under questioning by the FBI. His eyes opened wider than I thought possible, grotesquely contorted by abject, gut-wrenching fear. He was sure the bogus code would kill him.

"Stop the goddamned test!" he screamed at the top of his lungs, gobbets of spit flying from his lips. He grabbed at his seat belt, trying to run forward to scream at the pilots, but I put a hand across the aisle between us and held him in his seat.

That was it, the last piece of the puzzle. I felt vindicated, relieved, even exultant. It didn't last.

"Why, Harry?" I shouted back. "Is the flight control software sabotaged?"

Randall was contorted as if by electric shock. He twitched and clawed at his shirt and gasped like he was asphyxiating. "They have to stop!" he screamed. "STOP THE TEST!"

Zygler shouted, "You did all this. You're the one who talked the Frogs into screwing with the flight software, aren't you?"

Randall cried, "It wasn't supposed to work like this. I didn't think it would come out this way."

Zygler roared like an angry animal. "What the fuck did you expect, you ignorant asshole? You killed

Wes, goddammit." He looked ready to kill Randall.

"Mark time," Grimsby said. "Pushing over."

The long graceful nose of the GlobalMax pushed down under the precise command of David Grimsby. The beautiful ship plunged at nearly zero-gravity toward the start altitude for the first test.

Sally gave a little yelp, and grabbed at her computer as it started to bounce under its restraining rubber bands. Tidings held onto his seat bottom, his eyes wide, watching as the scene played out in front of him.

Randall screamed and unbuckled his seat belt, flailing up out of his seat, bouncing off the ceiling in the reduced gravity and flopping back down into his seat at a strange angle. He drifted back up toward the ceiling, trying to swim forward to the pilots' cabin. "Stop them!"

"Test initiated," Grimsby called out.

The engines surged, making full takeoff power now. We were suddenly at the bottom of the elevator shaft, the reduced gravity of the previous second replaced by heavy loading as the plane rounded out of its dive and leveled off, accelerating toward the planned liftoff speed.

Randall fell abruptly from his place on the overhead, landing hard on the floor between the seats. He knew in his heart that he was about to die, murdered by his own hacked computer software. Panic had replaced all his normally formidable intellect with pure animal survival instinct. He screamed a feral, wild scream, clawing at the lush carpet, trying to crawl in the heavy gravity to the front of the cabin.

I knew I had him. "Why did you do it, Harry? Why did you kill all those people?"

The GMax's nose tilted upward, simulating takeoff.

Gravity returned to normal. After a few seconds of climb, the engines slowed audibly.

Grimsby's voice came over the intercom again. "OK, Mr. O'Hara, the first test is complete. Do you want to me to keep climbing, or level here?"

Randall looked up at me, suddenly calm, his face a picture of confusion.

I returned his look, disgusted, angry, feeling triumphant now. "I lied."

That was the last part of the puzzle. I had won. "Just hold it for a minute, Dave," I said into the handset. "Orbit here while we get a look at the data."

"Roger," Grimsby answered, oblivious to the drama playing out in the cabin behind him.

I stared at Randall as he cowered on the floor. "You tried to have me killed." I was keeping my voice in control, not shouting.

He started to cry, holding his head in his hands.

Zygler's face was on fire now, his eyes blazing like lasers, face shaking with anger, chest heaving with the pulsations of hyperventilation.

When he spoke, it was a hoarse, unworldly rasp. "You son of a bitch! You were stealing my company!"

Randall pulled back into himself, face pale and chin trembling.

"This has got to be the weirdest murder weapon ever," I said. "There was software built and installed that would make the elevators go full up and lock in place so the pilots couldn't control the planes. With the computers in control in the fly-by-wire system they couldn't overrule it or fly the plane manually. It was all set up so the code erased itself after it worked.

"The NSA guys told us a lot about the code, even though it was erased. Sally says the structure looked like a French engineer wrote it. The way they teach it at the French school, Ecole Polytechnique. Marcel Covert from Aries went to all the right schools. He was head of flight control software for Airbus before he moved to Aries. He was supposed to be coming here to help us, but I bet he had a sudden case of remorse and was going to rat the deal out to the FBI. Or maybe he was just going to try blackmail. Whatever. Anyway, he's dead, too."

I looked across at Tidings. I couldn't tell if he was following or not. "George, Eric did some simulations that proved that the same trick, locking the elevators full up, but at cruising speed instead of way slower after takeoff would tear off the horizontal tail. That's what they found on the plane that crashed in the water off Canada."

The FBI agent nodded slowly. Was the light coming on?

Zygler was twitching, and his face was red with anger. He looked me in the eye, and his voice was clear. "Mike, I had nothing to do with any of it. I swear to God, you have to believe me. I would never do something like this. I would never let it happen."

I looked back at him and nodded slowly. "I know, Eric. I believe you." I turned and spoke to Tidings. "In order to get this takeover thing to work, they needed an insider to supply them information to set up the deal. They didn't want Eric. His numbers weren't good enough, and they figured they could hire technical genius. The whole damned thing was about money, that's all. What they needed was a financial type, somebody on the inside who could give them the company's confidential money numbers to let them set the minimum possible price. You have to screw every cent out of a deal like this."

I looked across the cabin at Randall. His eyes were those of a cornered animal. A predator. "Isn't that right, Harry?"

He didn't move or respond for several seconds. Finally he said, "You can't prove any of this."

"Actually, I think we can," I said. "For one thing, you did a full-zoot terror-freak out just now, when you thought that the hacked software was loaded into the flight controls. And there's plenty of hard evidence we can put together and we're going to nail you to the wall."

I turned to Tidings. "George, all these code transfers probably went out over the phone. The last one ought to be about two minutes long. You can subpoena phone records and confiscate computers to figure out how it was all downloaded. It's the thing I told you about."

Tidings considered this. "We're working on it. Might be tough. Internet protocols and all that stuff, too. But we can do it."

I changed course. "I had assumed that Marcel Covert was in on all this, but then you had him killed, too. You had to get the same thing done to the second plane that crashed, off Canada. That couldn't have been Covert, at least not by himself. So there had to have been an accomplice somewhere who could do the hacking to bring the second plane down. There is a French professor of engineering from Ecole Polytechnique who is going to replace Covert at Aries. His name is Stephan Darlan. He and Harry here published a paper together a while ago. I think if you subpoenaed his phone records you would find some interesting things."

Tidings smiled wolfishly. "A known associate. It's a good place to start. The French police are pissed. They'll help."

At the mention of Darlan, Randall looked around the cabin as if he wanted to find a way out, to run away, anywhere. Finally, he looked back at me, but his eyes weren't focused. He looked like the broken man he was.

"The thing I don't understand," I continued, "is why Corso was murdered. Was he backing out?"

Randall seemed to deflate. "It wasn't supposed to crash. Darlan said it wouldn't crash. It was just supposed to look bad, to scare them."

"I believe that, too. I didn't think you'd really want to kill Corso. You might need him for something later. Was it supposed to switch off after it scared the shit out of the pilots?"

"Two point one seconds. That was what he said it would take. It was just supposed to scare them!" he shouted. That actually made some sense, if you were a psychopath.

Eric exploded again. "You aren't just a murderer, you're a total asshole. You don't know jack about anything but money. You're a fucking whore."

I said, "George, you said Zygler's guy was giving you plenty of information on Tom Sutton. I guess that was Randall. He maneuvered you into going after Tom Sutton, too."

George nodded.

Randall didn't respond, staring at his hands. He was somewhere else, disconnected from the scene.

Rage overflowed from my mind and into the space between us. "Harry, once you started killing people, was it easy to keep going?"

Randall didn't answer, which made me madder still. "After you crossed that threshold, I bet it was just another profit and loss problem to you."

My voice rose further until my throat ached. "Just out of curiosity, you piece of shit, what made you decide to kill me? What the hell did I do to you besides showing up for work?"

Randall stared across the cabin at me, appearing more surprised than angry or defensive. When he spoke quietly again, to himself, he seemed bewildered. "You know, to tell the truth, after Wes died I don't think I ever considered not killing you. I was afraid you'd figure it out."

Tidings lean forward, his expression hard. "Mike, I can put twenty agents on the case now. Data searches, interviews, the whole thing. We didn't have it put together like this."

I tried to sound sympathetic. "I know. It's been there in front of us whole time, but I just didn't believe any of it. I couldn't believe it." I gathered my thoughts and tried to line it all up. "I got a message from Sutton, just before he committed suicide. He said he was innocent, and that he had no reason to lie. And then he offed himself on my phone. That made me believe him."

Tidings stared down at the quivering mass of Harry Randall. I went on, wanting to drive the point into the FBI agent's brain. Never an easy task, I knew.

"When Harry heard that the French were coming, he figured Covert had lost his nerve, was going to rat him out to the FBI. I think you'll find that Professor Darlan sent bogus code to the Aries test team and they loaded it without thinking about it. And we know they can hack into the cars." Zygler looked away, embarrassed. "They probably hit both Penney and me on the spur of the moment."

Tidings considered it all and spoke, quietly at first. "We've got motive and opportunity. I'll have to get some subpoenas for phone records and a bunch of other things to build the case. When I'm done we we'll have plenty."

Zygler was contemptuous, disgusted. "You convinced them you could make more profits. Make more money in the out years, or some other business school bullshit." His voice rose in an angry crescendo. "You can't build systems. You couldn't piss your name in the snow. Neither could your French friends."

I saw movement out the corner of my eye. Tidings had loosened his seatbelt and was pulling a pair of handcuffs out of a pocket.

The FBI agent spoke gently, quietly, like he was talking to a dog he was going to put down. "Mr. Randall, I am placing you under arrest for attempted murder. There'll be other charges after that. You have the right to remain silent, and I recommend you do."

"You have the right to an attorney, and if you can't afford one, uh--" He stopped talking while he fumbled with the cuffs, momentarily distracted.

When Randall moved, it was like a snake striking.

We all reacted as if in slow motion, surprised and not understanding until it was too late.

Randall jumped up from the floor, launched himself toward Tidings, slamming the agent's face with a clenched fist.

Tidings recoiled and twisted away for a second while the two wrestled.

Zygler moved into the fight and tried to wrestle with Randall, surely propelled by anger and a lust for revenge against the money guy.

But Randall was fighting for survival. He hit Zygler in his chest with a shoulder.

Zygler went down, striking his head on a table as he fell. He landed limp and unconscious as I reached over him to restrain Randall.

When Tidings and Randall separated an instant later, the agent's pistol was in Randall's hand.

Randall spun in mid-air with the grace of a gymnast, pointed the gun at my heart and pulled the trigger.

18

There was a click from the pistol, but no bang.

Randall swore loudly, cursing me and the gun, and pulled the trigger again and again.

I curled up in a ball, winding myself around my seat belt buckle, trying to make as small a target as possible, imagining the effects of bullets entering flesh, tumbling, ripping, deforming against bone. It actually occurred to me to be embarrassed by this ridiculous display until I saw Sally doing the same thing.

Tidings recovered from Randall's blow and jumped from his seat. He hit Randall like an NFL lineman, and the two rolled up the aisle, fighting for the gun, arms and legs intertwined, cursing and spitting.

I finally began to move in lethargic slow-motion, stepping over Zygler and up the aisle toward the two struggling men.

Amazingly, Randall continued to fight, even with two hundred pounds of enraged FBI agent beating him senseless. Tidings had already smashed Randall's nose. Blood poured onto the expensive earth-tone carpet. Seeing the blood, Randall pulled back for a few seconds, apparently frightened by the sight.

Tidings, finding an opening, charged him again, diving with both arms out toward the gun that Randall still held in his hand. He roared in anger and smashed into Randall again with an audible crunch.

The pistol fired twice. The first round went through a cabin window, which cracked open and dumped the cabin pressurization, filling the cabin with fog for a few seconds. Air whistled and howled around the broken window.

The second round hit Tidings in the leg.

In the movies, a man shot in an extremity will shrug off the wound and continue to fight, or make a dramatic speech or whatever. George Tidings, hit by a 9-millimeter hollow-point round in the lower leg, fell to the floor like a gut-shot deer, writhing in pain and crying out.

In the movies, an evil-doer who has shot a pursuer

will be energized by the victory, redoubling his efforts to fight.

Randall screamed louder than George did and dropped the gun on the cabin floor, pushing and sliding on his butt away from him, as if horrified by the realization of what he'd just done.

The scene would have seemed funny to me if I hadn't been scared shitless.

Over the cabin speakers, I could hear Grimsby on the radio, his words tumbling out in a rush. "Mayday, mayday, mayday. November two-one-six echo sierra, declaring an emergency. Echo control, six echo sierra needs a straight-in to NAS Pax River right fucking now!"

I felt the floor dip under me as Grimsby hauled the jet around in a wings-vertical turn and dove toward the base.

The controller answered the emergency call immediately. "Six echo sierra is cleared to land any runway. State the nature of your problem, and, ah, souls on board, over."

Grimsby fumbled for words as he swung the GMax to the west. "Uh, Echo control, I have, ah, seven people on board, and ah, I've got shots fired in the aircraft."

As the incredulous controller made the pilot repeat his bizarre report, Randall continued to crawl, unarmed now, backwards up the aisle toward the etched glass divider that hid the galley and the exit door. The g-forces from the sharp turn slowed him.

I dropped into a crouch and picked up the still-warm pistol.

I pointed the gun at the shuddering, sobbing executive.

He looked back at me, at Tidings, and then back at me again.

I saw Sally in my peripheral vision as she moved to help Tidings, pressing a bare hand over the pulsing wound in his right calf muscle.

Randall and I stayed like that for several seconds, staring at each other, silent.

Sally found a medical kit in the john at the aft end of the cabin and tended to George's wound. Finally, more g-forces and a reduction in engine noise told me we were nearing the base.

A quick glance out a window confirmed that we were at low altitude--less than two thousand feet--and that Grimsby was slowing the GMax for landing.

When I looked back, Randall had moved around the divider, and stood with his hand on the cabin door release lever.

"Get away from the door," I shouted over the din, but he didn't seem to hear. I tried waving the gun menacingly, but it had no effect.

"I'm sorry, but I'm afraid I can't stay," Harry

answered formally. His eyes were unfocused, and his voice slurred. Tears and blood rolled down his face. He sobbed.

Zygler stirred and raised himself up on an elbow, looking at the scene in astonishment.

I sensed Sally move close behind me.

"Harry, you don't have to do this," I said. "You're rich, man. Hire a bunch of ass-rip lawyers and plead insanity. I'm telling you, this will work. You'll walk, I swear it."

"I'm sorry about all this, Eric," he shouted over the scream of the wind whistling around the window. "It was nothing personal. It was just business."

He gripped the door lever and pulled it hard. The door was not built to open in flight and normally cabin pressure would have held it closed. But with cabin air blowing out through the broken window he was able to pull it inward, swinging it up and then out.

The wind blast, still over one hundred fifty knots, snatched the door from his hands. The door flopped down against its hinges, bounced once, and then broke away.

I saw the door fly aft and upward, past the cabin windows toward the tail. There was a lurch and we all fell. Heavy g-forces smashed me into the floor, followed by reduced gravity as Grimsby struggled to regain control of the hurtling jet. I thought momentarily that the door must have hit the tail or an engine as it flew past, and wondered what damage had been caused. Would the pilot be able to bring the crippled ship to a safe landing, or would we become a flaming smear on the turbulent surface of Chesapeake Bay?

At that instant, with a cry of agony, Harry Randall pushed himself out the door.

Without thinking, I dropped the gun and lunged toward the door, reaching out to save him.

My hands found a wrist and I grabbed hard. The weight of his body dragged me toward the door and I fell with him outside the cabin, me inside on the floor. My chest slammed into the doorframe. The aluminum alloy beam smashed at my ribs, knocking my wind out. Waves of pain filled my senses and I saw stars.

The full force of the airstream hit my face and shoulders like a cold hammer, head and arms out the door, hands still clamped around Harry Randall's wrist.

I felt someone grab at my legs from behind, holding me in, preventing me from falling. Sally.

Harry swung below me, the wind blast forcing his mouth open and distorting his features grotesquely. His eyelids flapped in the wind, and drops of blood from his smashed nose flew into the slipstream.

We hung there like that for a long time.

I saw crab boats floating by below, and buoys and waves. The water of the bay was a pleasing blue-green. Disorganized gaggles of seagulls wandered about in the boats' wakes. The wind was cleansing, healing. In its cold wash, I suddenly understood it all. Everything was clear to me.

I looked down at him. He'd tried to kill me. Twice. Murdered seven other men. Left John Penney crippled in a hospital. Destroyed the life of Tom Sutton. His basic drive was greed, and every move he made was to serve that. He'd been educated and rewarded and promoted to squeeze more and more money out of other people's efforts, and business school had never placed any limits on it. Maybe he slept through that class at Harvard.

The wind was strong. Randall was heavy.

I think my hands slipped.

I don't think I dropped him on purpose.

I'm pretty sure.

When falling from a great height, the human race divides itself into two general groups. First, there are those who fall to their deaths tucked in a fetal position, paralyzed by terror. The second group goes down flailing their arms and legs wildly, as if trying to fly like a bird.

Harry Randall was a flailer.

His body receded in my vision quickly at first, and then more slowly, finally seeming to hang in mid-air for a few seconds, a pinpoint hovering in the distance, as if his wealth allowed him to defy gravity.

There was a pitifully small splash when he hit the white caps. The wind washed it away as I watched.

I didn't see his body after the impact. Seagulls and boats began to gather even before we flew away.

Aviation Week published pictures of the GMax showing the damage that the departing door had caused.

The door had hit the top of the port engine nacelle, smashing the top of the jet intake and causing a compressor stall in the engine. Grimsby had been forced to shut that engine down and continue the landing on the other one. As the door continued along the side of the aircraft, it had hit the top of the vertical fin, and finally smashed squarely into the port horizontal stabilizer, ripping it and the port elevator cleanly off.

The fly-by-wire flight control system, sensing a change in available control surface configuration, had autonomously reprogrammed itself, enabling the pilot to land safely, under control, without further damage. The software had performed perfectly, saving all on board. The self-reprogramming feature had been developed for military aircraft under a contract from the Air Force as a counter to the effects of combat damage. ZYCO had included it in the civilian system as a safety-oriented sales feature.

Eric Zygler hired a new CFO from a bank in New York. He didn't know squat about software or any sort of technology. I am pretty sure that was a hard requirement from Eric. The Harvard Business Review published an editorial talking about what a genius Harry Randall was, and how the pressure of growing ZYCO had driven him to kill himself. A group of Harry's very rich friends endowed a chair at Harvard in his memory, ensuring a continuing supply of MBAs with minors in finance for the benefit of society, in perpetuity. It made me feel all warm and moist.

ZYCO stock fell to twenty-eight and three-eighths on news of Randall's death but rebounded within three days, closing at sixty-one and a half on the following Friday. Aries decided not to proceed with the buyout.

Zygler figured out a way to take ZYCO private again. He doesn't have to report his financial results like when the company was public, but it seems like he is still doing well. All these complicated business matters are pretty hard for me to follow. I'm only an engineer.

George Tidings got a decoration for valor from the FBI for getting his gun taken away by a money whore with poor upper body strength.

I went to Tidings' award ceremony at the J. Edgar Hoover building on Pennsylvania Avenue, and I didn't laugh once. The FBI building's exterior is astonishingly ugly, built in the 1970's in what is now called the "Brutalist" style--all hard angles and cast concrete. Inhuman yet cheap. The interior is worse--long echoing halls with unbroken walls and poor lighting. The ceremony was held in a conference room off the Assistant Director's office that was bare and ugly despite the panoramic view of DC out the windows.

I waited a few minutes at the end of the ceremony to shake George's hand and congratulate him. We both smiled politely and he thanked me for coming. He leaned in to speak privately as we shared a manly handshake.

"So, how is that Inspector General thing going?" he said in a conspiratorial tone.

"Pretty much done," I began, but then stopped. I looked him in the eye. "Funny thing, George. I don't remember telling you about an IG investigation. Where'd you hear about that?"

His hand stopped moving and his face went pale.

Bingo. I had been given one more piece of the puzzle.

"So you're the one that called the IG down on me, right? I bet you called that reporter and set her on my ass, too." His face got even paler. "Man, I hope the Director of the Bureau doesn't find out you've been leaking to the press without authorization. He's got no sense of humor at all, from what I've heard."

By his expression it was apparent that George was now thinking about a reassignment to the FBI field office in Minot, North Dakota.

I looked down at the new decoration his lapel and smiled. "Nice little medal, George. See you around." I turned on my heel and walked out, strolling down the barren hall with a grim smile on my face.

On the day we completed work on the 6120 for the ZYCO accident, the chairman called me into his office. McCall sat in his leather power seat, behind his desk with his feet up, wrinkling important papers with his shoes.

In a chair opposite the desk sat a barely recognizable figure. It was a man, old but muscular, gray headed. It was a different Lew Hills than I had ever seen, leaner, stronger. He was well-tanned, which in late January is a neat trick.

"Damn, Lew, look at you!" I said. "You look like you're ready to join the Marines."

He rose, and we shook hands, his grip sure and strong. "Watch yourself, young fella," he said with a smile. "I could kick your ass any time I felt like it."

McCall motioned me into another chair, and I sat across from Lew, relieved to see him. "I heard you were recovering, but you look better than I've ever seen you."

"Lost forty pounds. Cut out the cigars. Getting some exercise. Fiber. Vitamins. All that stuff. I feel good."

"That's great," I said, and meant it.

Lew's voice rose into the old happy-warrior tones, joshing me heavily. "I read about the wreck I sent you out on. What the hell were you thinking about?" He laughed, and so did McCall.

I shook my head in mock agony. Finally, I said, "So, are you coming back pretty soon?"

McCall cleared his throat. "Mike, that's one of the things we wanted to talk to you about."

Lew interrupted. "What makes you think I'd want to come back to this sweat shop? I bought golf clubs, pal. Learning to use 'em, too."

McCall grinned. "Lew's taking retirement, Mike."

"I coulda gone three years ago, but things just kept crashing. So, you know, I decided to go while I had the chance. Came in to sign the papers today. I'm outa here." Lew smiled broadly, but when he spoke again his tone was serious. It the first time I had ever heard him like that. "You're doing OK at this. I feel like I can leave now."

I looked across the messy desk at McCall, who nodded a confirmation. "Mike, you know the budget is going down again this year, and we're having to make some adjustments in staffing." He hesitated. "I'm looking for somebody to run the aviation accident investigation team who's dumb enough to take the job without a pay raise, and I think you're the guy. I may be able to swing a promotion in a year or two, but no promises."

I thought it over.

What a great deal. More responsibility without

the added pay to go along with it. So Civil Service. Swell.

I thought about that letter from Alaska, and the pile of paperwork on my desk, and my good buddies at the Inspector General's office. And my crappy little government paycheck. Zygler had said the offer would stay open.

I started to answer, but before I could finish a sentence, Sally stuck her head in the door.

"Hi Lew," she exclaimed brightly. "It's good to see you again. You look great."

Lew stood and hugged her. He smiled widely, like a large, old cherub. They exchanged happiness for a while.

McCall caught my eye while they talked. "Mike, you need to think about what changes you'll make in personnel. You rate a deputy."

I tilted my head toward Sally. "Got one."

McCall made a little tent out of his fingers, his feet still on his desk.

We spent another hour telling old war stories, and ended the afternoon by taking Lew for a late lunch in an impromptu retirement ceremony. It turned out to be a good day.

The FBI went after the case full blast, despite the deaths of all their prime suspects. Their investigation of phone and computer records revealed a definite pattern of information transfers, although it was not possible to trace all the calls and internet traffic moving code. Randall was guilty as hell.

The French police arrested Professor Stephan Darlan, who promptly started spilling his guts. Covert had been guilty as hell, too. Professor Darlan also implicated two other French engineers, who were arrested for aiding and abetting. They are investigating the hacking of my car and Penney's. By helping the authorities, Darlan avoided charges of manslaughter and attempted murder. He is serving a twelve-year sentence for lesser crimes. I understand that French jails really suck.

Good news.

The car companies wanted to sue ZYCO over the hacking into the vehicle drive-by-wire systems, but they decided not to in order to avoid publicity about the whole thing. There was a series of recalls to get the change installed that Eric's people developed, and there haven't been any instances of the problem coming up again.

Steve Penney didn't recover all of his memory of the last days before his wreck, or all of his faculties. He retired on a medical disability a little while later. Darlan and his hacker friends had succeeded in keeping him from telling me his information, but I have pretty good idea what it was, so in the end they didn't win that round.

From talking to the French authorities, it was clear that the Aries chief engineer was in on the plot from the beginning. I am betting that Harry Randall was telling the truth about the first crash not being planned, and if so maybe Covert was overcome by regret. Whatever. If the French know they're not talking. Might hurt France's foreign trade numbers, I guess.

Steve was probably aware that Randall and Covert--or maybe Darlan--were listening to our cellular phone calls, which isn't that hard to do. Too bad he didn't just tell me, though.

In the end, there were two accident reports: The one that I wrote, and the one that we released.

The one we released said the probable cause was a fatal error in the flight system software, and the effects of the problem were probably exacerbated by the special test hardware configuration of the computers used in the two aircraft that crashed. The software drivers for the aircraft's elevators were probably disabled or defective, rendering the aircraft uncontrollable and leading to the crash. We noted the possibility that malicious software installed by persons with uncontrolled access to aircraft flight control systems would have contributed to the conditions leading to the crash. We offered cooperation to the French and Canadians, but left it to them to investigate the other crash.

My original draft of the accident report also

talked about how we had become obsessed by money as our only measure of success, and were losing our ability and desire to build brilliant things. The reward that an engineer feels when he or she drives for perfection would be lost, but we would have plenty of money. Maybe we could buy some creative satisfaction instead, like a drug.

The FAA has ratcheted down on flight control test configuration management and increased measures to stop tampering throughout the industry. ZYCO put improved security measures in place, and there were no issues with other aircraft in service. The public was safe. With staffing as tight as it was at the board, I was out on another job before I could do much else.

I kept a copy of the version I wrote on my personal computer, which is strictly forbidden, but I figured screw it.

The IG report called me an incompetent moron, as IG reports usually do, but McCall refused to accept it. He said that I handled the case properly and well, that he wasn't going to let anyone mess with his field people, and what did the IG think he was going to do about it? There was a brief pissing contest far above my pay grade, and the matter petered out.

Liz Fowler wrote a series of freelance articles about how good management practices and Wall Street's drive to maximize shareholder value at any cost were killing excellence in American industry, and could even compromise the safety of the traveling public. The suicide of Harry Randall was prominent at the start of the story. She was a laughingstock in business circles at first, but her articles were published as a series by the New York Times.

I followed the resulting food fight between the Times and the Wall Street Journal for a couple of weeks. She also wrote a best-selling book on the subject. Others picked up the theme, and there were a couple of congressional hearings. More regulations on business operations were piled up that didn't seem to have much impact. The last I heard Fowler was a professor of journalism at an Ivy League J-school. She finally got her Pulitzer Prize the next year.

I tacked the letter from the governor of Alaska up on the wall over my desk where I could see it all the time, to remind myself of what the job was about. There were no major accidents involving school buses in Alaska for three years after my work there.

Somewhere along the line I decided to stay with the board a little longer. Zygler still called me once in a while, and Charlene asked Sally and me out to their place whenever either of us was in Colorado. Zygler and Charlene wanted take us to the Superbowl in one of their planes the next year, but we were both out on a job and couldn't go. He still needled me occasionally to come over to ZYCO, but there were a lot of cases open. As soon as I got caught up I'd go. I made GS-15 a couple of years later. It was underwhelming signal of progress.

Sally saw Donald, or David or whatever the hell his name was a few more times, but we settled into a pattern of work that precluded her having much of a social life. We both worked late at the office a lot. She didn't go out on lunch dates any more. She said she wanted to avoid the calories.

After a couple of months we started meeting most days for breakfast at the coffee shop in the office building. She said we could plan out the day that way. Efficient, good management, et cetera. And I got to see that smile every day. She smiled a lot, and laughed sometimes, too. It always sounded good to me.

One day, we sat across from each other at 7:00 a.m., talking over coffee and bagels. It was gray and rainy in DC that day and commuters hustled through the gloom outside the shop's windows. There was a lull in the conversation for a couple of seconds, but we were comfortable with silence by then.

She cleared her throat and looked at me, her face serious. She was nervous for some reason.

"Um, I need to tell you something," she said. Her voice was low and I sat forward over my cup to hear her. She hesitated, which wasn't like her. "I had a talk with Doctor Schmidt at the tech office yesterday. He, um... He has as an idea to improve our interface with the lab. He has a position open for a computer engineer, and he wants me to fill it on his organization chart. My resume fits the position description perfectly. I know it does because I wrote the description for him."

I could feel my face go as cold and gray as the day. "You want to leave?"

I must have sounded really bad. She shook her head. "No, no, I won't be leaving. He just wants to have a liaison in place full time. I would still be on your team. I would just work for him officially and we'll have a direct line to the lab that way. You wouldn't have to write my evaluations and all that administrative garbage. And anyway, it would open up another position in the office that you could hire somebody for. I just wouldn't be your direct subordinate that way." The last part came out in a rush.

"I thought you liked how things were going. You seem pretty happy." I sat there for a second with my hands on the table in front of me, not knowing what to do with them.

I heard her sigh, somehow managing to sound amused and exasperated at the same time, all in one breath. She reached across the table and brushed the back of my hand with her finger.

This was new. It felt dangerous, and good. Electric. "Honestly. You are such an engineer. So proper. You're so slavish about rules and regulations."

I looked back at her and fiddled with my flatware.

"I wanted you to be comfortable in the office."

"Yes, and I appreciate it." She went on, quieter, in a conspiratorial whisper. "Look, I really like you, OK?"

My face felt warm like the sun was on it, and the coffee shop rotated slowly in a pleasant, intoxicating way. "Thank you. I like you, too. More than that, maybe."

She smiled again, more broadly this time. "This way, you wouldn't be my supervisor. If I'm not in your direct chain of command, all those rules you care about so much don't apply. The ones about us having a relationship, I mean. I talked to the board's ethics lawyer. It's all good."

I pondered this. "Oh." More pondering. "Oh." I started to smile then, too. I felt the weight of duty and responsibility begin to evaporate, and this time I didn't try to stop the possibilities in my head from running off to play.

She grinned broadly over her breakfast.

I fixed her in what I hoped was a stern glare. "So you have this all arranged. Were you going check with me first?"

More grinning. "No. When I find something I really want, I just go after it. I didn't like the rules so I got the game changed."

Things got much, much better after that.

ABOUT THE AUTHOR

Al Haggerty served in the Navy for 27 years as a ship driver and rocket scientist. He has been a factory worker, a ditch digger, a skydiver, a pilot, a ship navigator, a radar engineer, and a contestant on the Jeopardy! game show. He served as United States Deputy Undersecretary of Defense at the Pentagon, where he worked in technology security and counterintelligence. Mr. Haggerty holds degrees in oceanography/atmospheric science and in engineering. He is currently a consultant on defense technology and clean energy, and lives with his wife in Richland, Washington.

Uncial Press brings you extraordinary fiction, non-fiction and poetry. Put a world of reading in your pocket.

www.uncialpress.com